One Domingo Morning

One Domingo Morning

The Story of Alamo Joe

Ned Anthony Huthmacher

VANTAGE PRESS
New York

This is a work of fiction. Any similarity between the names, characters, and places in this book and any persons, living or dead, is purely coincidental.

Cover design by Joseph Musso.

FIRST EDITION

All rights reserved, including the right of reproduction in whole or in part in any form.

Copyright © 2004 by Ned Anthony Huthmacher

Published by Vantage Press, Inc.
419 Park Ave. South, New York, NY 10016

Manufactured in the United States of America
ISBN: 0-533-14862-6

Library of Congress Catalog Card No.: 2004091372

0 9 8 7 6 5 4 3 2 1

For Joe

Contents

Preface ix

One	A Few Advance Scouts . . . Do Not an Army Make	1
Two	Burnt Tea and Cannonade	18
Three	Arson for Breakfast	25
Four	Reminiscing and the Louisiana Dockman	30
Five	Shoring Up Daze	40
Six	Silvie and San Felipe	43
Seven	A Joining Journey	51
Eight	San Antone—Set a Spell, Why Doncha?	59
Nine	Moonlight Fandango	65
Ten	Parting Promise	73
Eleven	A Decidedly Different Tune	79
Twelve	A Choice in the Matter	84
Thirteen	One Domingo Morning	104
Fourteen	Shaking Off the Dust	134
Fifteen	Red Vengeance—Yellow Accord	142
Sixteen	Can't Be Too Careful These-A-Days	148
Seventeen	Inferno Revisited	156
Eighteen	Nettlenuts and Cornbread	163
Nineteen	The Handy Way to Houston	170
Twenty	Retreat to Lilliput	178
Twenty-one	Over the Walls Like Sheep	183
Twenty-two	The Great Skedaddle	191
Twenty-three	Hot As Hades and Twiced As Damnable	194
Twenty-four	A Dip in the Brazos	202
Twenty-five	A Hard-Enough Decision	207
Twenty-six	Sisters in Sorrow	214

Twenty-seven	How a Town Dissolves	220
Twenty-eight	On the Wings of the Wind	225
Twenty-nine	Eastward with the Wayward Geese	231
Thirty	Rivers of Return	239
Thirty-one	That Which Must Be Done	242
Thirty-two	The Passage of Hope	247
Thirty-three	As Far from This Place As Possible	251
Thirty-four	Freedom by Water	257
Thirty-five	From the Reaches of the Cow and King	262

Afterword   273

Preface

There is a well-worn old maxim that holds how "truth is often stranger than fiction." Yet a stirring piece of fiction, if well woven, can sometimes be even more compelling than a stark truth. The Alamo certainly has had its share of beloved myth: Travis, challenging his men to fight to the death by crossing over a line that he drew with his sword, is one, while the 1824 flag, shown flying in numerous representations of the battle, is yet another. That the line may never have been drawn, or the 1824 flag flown, does not seem to bother the keepers of the tale. To paraphrase a line from an old movie, when the myth becomes more palatable than the history, run with the myth.

Joe's story is comprised of the stuff that a historical fiction writer might only dream of. For as the slave of the Alamo's co-commander, Lt. Colonel William Barrett Travis, not only was Joe in the Alamo battle, he survived it and left his own documented account. Notwithstanding, he was not lauded to the skies for his deeds, as was Travis, or folk heroes Jim Bowie and Davy Crockett. Joe's reward for his role in the Alamo saga was to be returned to the bonds of slavery for some time after the smoke of battle had cleared.

While few historians may dispute the fact that Bowie, Crockett, and Travis all perished bravely in the Alamo, that Joe, an Alamo battle survivor, ended up being treated very shabbily thereafter by the young Republic of Texas is a fact that few seem desirous of addressing.

My initial dilemma when approaching Joe's tale was the hard fact that, aside from several second-hand newspaper accounts of Joe's statements and a few jottings in Travis' law diary, so very little is known of Joe's history. That being the case, I felt compelled to enhance Joe's bare-bones biography by bumping corroborated elements of it against accepted accounts of the Texian Revolt and then hammering out all of the chronological possibilities of Joe's movements. While historians may never be able to discover, or agree upon exactly, what transpired within the walls of the Alamo in the chilling pre-dawn hours of March 6, 1836, that Joe emerged from it a true Texas hero cannot be denied and should not be forgotten. Reams of myth and a plethora of prose have all been penned on the glories of Texas' illustrious forebears. Now it's Joe's turn.

One Domingo Morning

One

A Few Advance Scouts...Do Not an Army Make

"Get out! Run for your life and head for the hills," screamed the warning. "Santa Anna is coming! The merciless dictator of all Mexico is on the march for San Antonio de Bejar, heading an army of thousands. Death and destruction await anything and everything in his path. Hasten packing and pack light: take flight, take flight!"

As rumors go, it was a pretty spectacular one, chuck full of caution and elements of ill-foreboding. But to the Anglo-American inhabitants of this predominately Hispanic, Southwest Texas town, two months of repeated telling had only served to blunt the rumor's impact. Newcomers as they were to the region, these Anglos could only shake their heads in wonderment at the town's curious Mexican culture, customs, and very way of life.

Compared to some of the other small villages and shantytowns that dotted the vast prairie, the San Antonio de Bejar of 1836 was a sprawling metropolis—and *old*. "Bejar"—as it was more commonly called by its local inhabitants—had been established over a hundred years previous along the banks of the meandering San Antonio River. As was common of most Mexican towns of the period, Bejar had been built around a series of plazas. The plaza was a place where townsfolk could meet to socialize, do some shopping, and conduct the business of the day. In Bejar, the "mercado," or marketplace, was conveniently located on Military Plaza, as was the massive church of San Fernando. Only in Bejar, some townsfolk bragged, could a visitor gather nourishment for both body *and* soul, all in the same place.

For atmosphere, Bejar boasted the ruins of five secularized missions spaced an hour's walk from each other, the furthest one out being a good four-hour stretch of the legs from Main Plaza. To reach the nearest and oldest one, however, the pedestrian only needed to stride a mere eight hundred yards or so, for this particular mission had once been the very heart of the town. Originally christened San Antonio de Valero by its Franciscan founders, the compound had served as a station for troops as far back as 1792. But when a homesick garrison of Spanish soldiers from a place called Alamo del Parras set up quarters there, they decided to dub the "fort" after their hometown. The name stuck and from then on, everyone continued to refer to the place as simply "The Alamo."

From a humble mission settlement, to a flourishing, if fortified, town, Bejar had seen it all. Its low, flat-roofed limestone and adobe buildings had witnessed battles and displayed the scars of a succession of revolutions. Ashes and debris wrought from the most recent conflict between Burleson and Cos, scarcely three months back, yet screamed in unharmonious, mute contrast to the hum and chatter of the town's everyday life. Yes, Bejar had all of the flavor, levity and romance of a typical Mexican town.

In the doorway of an inn on Bejar's Main Plaza, a youth stood watching. He was handsome, about twenty-three years old, of medium build and of swarthy complexion. His jet-black hair was parted down the center and combed back in tight waves from his broad forehead. Features such as these would not have been considered uncommon for a citizen of Bejar, but a citizen Joe was not. He was black, he was a slave, and he was awaiting his master's return.

Joe gazed across the plaza to where his master, Lt. Colonel William Barret Travis, stood questioning members of a caravan of departing citizenry. Over the past few days, Joe had seen folks leaving town in twos and threes with their carts and wagons laden with what must have been all of their worldly possessions. But those sporadic departures were nothing compared to this. These people were scared. Even from the distance, Joe could read it in their hurried step and desperate stride.

Lt. Colonel William Barret Travis, a twenty-seven-year old lawyer from South Carolina and now the Alamo garrison's co-commander, had scoffed at reports from the friendly locals that a large army was advancing on Bejar. "A few advanced scouts poking their way around the broad outskirts of town do not an army make," Travis had assured Joe.

All the same, in the waning morning of this February 23rd, the Colonel had ordered a lookout posted in the tower of the San Fernando church. The tower had a commanding view of the surrounding prairie and Travis had reasoned that if the lookout *did* see anything, a mere clang of the bell would give the garrison ample time to react.

As it turned out, their wait was not a long one. For in the quiet of the morning, with only the drone of oxcarts rolling out of town to break the silence, the deep reverberations of the church bell rent the air. One glance over at the sentry in the church tower frantically tugging at the bell rope was enough to convince Joe to get busy. Elsewhere around the plaza, it was the appearance of all hell breaking loose, as the disorganized handful of half-awake Texian citizen-soldiers began a frantic scavenge for provisions.

Joe needed no orders. With the mad scramble ensuing all around him, the young slave stuffed all of Colonel Travis' personal effects into an old canvas sack and then slung the makeshift saddlebag across the waiting horse's pommel. He was still fumbling with the sack when Travis jogged up.

"This is it, Joe," the Colonel announced excitedly, practically leaping into the saddle as he spoke. "Gather as many provisions as you can and meet me in the Alamo. Maizy is in the Alsburys' wagon; she's all right. Hurry along smartly yourself."

Then, just as suddenly as he had arrived, off down the Portrero Street footbridge Travis galloped, shouting off orders and encouragement to the jumbled surge of humanity that was making its way toward the Alamo mission, just across the bend of the river.

With his master galloping off toward the Alamo, Joe took a momentary pause to think about his *own* best course of action. Should he stay put in town, follow Travis into the fort, or leave Bejar altogether? If he chose to stay in town to await the arrival of Mexican President Antonio Lopez de Santa Anna and his army, Joe reckoned that he would be well treated by them. After all, hadn't El Presidente made it a point of preaching about his magnanimity toward blacks? El Presidente might even be inclined to give Joe his freedom! There was always a chance in that. Then again, if Joe didn't exactly buy *that* sentiment, he still had more than enough time to gather his pick of provisions from the abandoned dwellings and shops and then strike off unmolested down the Gonzales road, toward the east of town. Toward the east lay San Felipe, Mill Creek, and Joe's sweetheart, Silvie. Joe could be miles away down the road and on his way back to her loving arms, before he was even missed. Silvie would doubtless be overjoyed to see Joe and Joe Silvie, and yet . . .

It wasn't enough for Joe to merely "follow his heart," without the promise of some clear and concrete end in sight. For Joe bore the infectious need of belonging somewhere. He didn't belong in town with Santa Anna's army; that was a certainty. Merely being treated well by the Mexicans wasn't basis enough for staying put. Why, as far as that went, even Travis treated Joe well. Joe and his master were on friendly terms and shared a camaraderie that came with their closeness in age. But for all of Travis' kindness, he was still the master and Joe was still the slave. So kindness and friendship were not it, either. And finally, how could Joe justify slinking back to the safety of San Felipe like a whipped pup, when the reason he'd sent Silvie back there in the first place was to provide her a place of refuge?

No, Joe's immediate destiny lay somewhere else, just ahead of him. It was out there. He could almost smell it and taste it and it tasted of freedom—freedom for him and then freedom for Silvie and Maizy too. Somehow . . . some day . . .

But for now, that "some day" would just have to be postponed, for something Joe felt was calling to him from across the river.

Joe gazed across the rippling surface of the water toward the Alamo mission where Travis and the others were preparing to hole up in a fight for freedom. A handful against an army! To willingly shut himself up with those few souls in their ramshackle limestone and adobe fort with its few ditches seemed an unlikely course for Joe to pursue. But somehow, there was just no turning back. Freedom, the restless slave concluded, would begin right here. So, after taking a deep breath, Joe gathered up his solitary spare shirt and knotted his extra pair of shoes together by their laces. Then he struck off for the mission compound with a determined stride.

Falling into step with some Texians who were hoofing it over a footbridge near the bend of the river, Joe noticed some of the local women standing along the wayside, much like the women of Jerusalem must've stood on the way of the cross. Some of the ladies, with handkerchiefs buried deep in their faces, were clearly crying. "Pobrecitos," they choked through deep-throated sobs. "Pobrecitos, you will all be killed."

Casting away any misgivings, Joe arrived at the compound's southernmost profile where shirttailed men with picks and shovels were laboring over a low, yet heavily fortified earth and cedar palisade. The barrier was being constructed to close off a large gap of open space between the ruined church and the main plaza wall. Joe headed toward an arched gateway at the center of that wall and as he did, he nearly stumbled over a barrier of strewn sandbags and junk lumber that were apparently being utilized to set up a gun position. Once completed, the battery would guard this access into the fort's large, open plaza.

Gingerly picking his way through the shadows below the double-walled gate, Joe stepped through the passageway into the main plaza and a tumult of confusion. Men were everywhere, scrambling for provisions in and out of the low huts that lined the plaza's inner walls. Some of the cooler headed ones, Joe saw, were passing out arms and ammunition, while yet others seemed feverishly intent at rolling artillery into place. Then there were the inquisitive ones; gangly volunteers, who scurried up rickety ladders and onto the flat roofs of the buildings to gawk at the troops who were pouring into the center of town, scarcely eight hundred yards away.

Joe made for a room in the west wall of the compound that Colonel Travis had predetermined as his headquarters and found the Colonel's lathered horse tethered outside. Inside, the cell proved low, dark, musty and cramped for space. A low cot and a table with chair were all the accommodations that the quarters had to offer. So Joe unloaded his master's saddlebags in neat order upon the cot.

No sooner had Joe finished setting up shop, than the door burst inward with a sudden clunk, ushering in a clump of men, with Travis bringing up the rear. There was buckskin-garbed Davy Crockett, the bear hunter and ex-congressman from Tennessee, and John W. Smith, the old Indian scout. Between these two figures sagged Dr. John Sutherland, wincing with pain. It was Sutherland and Smith who, earlier that morning, had responded to the church tower sentry's tolling by riding out to investigate the alarm. On the return gallop, Sutherland's horse had folded on him, badly wrenching the doctor's leg.

Travis seated himself at his "desk" and began scribbling off a note in the margin of an old copybook. Once done, he scattered a handful of coarse sand over the finished document to blot up the excess ink. He was just about to hand the paper to Smith with voiced instructions, when Sutherland interjected.

"I can't be of much use here," the doctor began, "but I can still set a horse. Let me ride this dispatch and Smith here," he gestured with a nod, "can be free to cover additional territory."

"Very well, Doc," Travis acquiesced. "Get this to Gonzales with all speed. Let them know that we have only 150 determined men against a large force. Stress that we need both men and provisions, if we're to hold out. Smith, you can see him to the Post Road. You'll know what to do from there."

Nodding his reply, the scout turned to his mount, while Crockett helped the limping Sutherland into the saddle of his. Soon, the two messengers were galloping eastward and kicking up a shower of muddy divots in their wake.

Then it was Crockett who spoke. A man with an undeniable gift of the gab, Davy's spellbinding Tennessee backwoods drawl was usually enough to guarantee his getting a crowd's rapt attention—if not always their *admiration.* "Well, here I am, Colonel," Crockett announced, almost casually. "Assign me an' my Tennessee boys a stretch o' ground an' we'll hold 'er all right."

Travis knew just the place. Eyeing the glaringly low earth and cedar palisade that closed off the yard in front of the church, he said with a gesture of his hand, "Does that pile of ground by the church suit you, Davy? It's the soft spot in this suffering excuse of a fortress. But then again, where isn't there a soft spot?"

"Soft spot's in our haids, Travis," Crockett replied askance. "Cours'n I bin called worser things than teched afore, so thets no shucks! Indians hold sort of uh high respeck fer a feller that e-fects signs uh lunacy. Steer right clear of him, like he was holy, or sacred, don't you know?"

"Marvelous!" Travis chuckled with a hint of irony. "I've a garrison of saints defending a broken-down church! How can we fail to conquer?"

"How, indeed," Crockett replied with a wink of his eye. Then he was off to see to the billeting of his men.

Travis was no idler himself. "Things are going to be happening fast now, Joe," he said, when the two of them were alone at last. "Stick close to me. I may need you at a moment's notice. Meanwhile, hand me my spyglass and we'll have a look for ourselves."

"But do we really want to see?" Joe returned in half humor, as both master and slave tramped up a sloped earthen embankment at the plaza's southwest corner. The embankment led them to a heavily timbered gun platform that upheld the Alamo's largest artillery piece, an eighteen-pounder. The gun, Joe noted, was aimed directly at the town.

Travis aimed his spyglass in the same direction and, after a moment's observation, creased his brow. "See for yourself, Joe," Travis offered, handing over the spyglass.

It was a sobering sight, indeed. Lancers, Joe saw, in a column that appeared almost endless, were clattering into Main Plaza, greeted by the blare of a military band and a throng of cheering townsfolk. The early afternoon sun, catching the gleam of the brightly decked lances, made Joe blink and look away. What Joe saw when he screwed the spyglass to his eye for an even closer look, prompted him to observe aloud: "Several lancers breaking away from the main body, Colonel Travis. One of them's tooting on a bugle for dear life."

"I can hear the bugle, Joe," Travis returned with a smile.

But then the Colonel's mood seemed to change and he became deathly serious. With a wire prick that he'd picked up nearby the eighteen-pounder Travis pricked the cannon's vent hole, piercing its bagged powder charge. Then, after ladling in a small quantity of priming powder, Travis re-approached the vent with a slow match.

"Stand well clear, Joe," Travis cautioned, as he touched off the gun's readied prime. The cannon seemed to hesitate at first, but when it exploded at last, its fiery roar shook the building to its very foundations.

"So much for your parlay, gentlemen," Travis offered almost blandly, as a hot round shot bounded over the heads of the approaching lancers. Though startled at first by the cannon's report, the horsemen nevertheless reined up, then held their ground by the footbridge at the bend of the river. When, moments later, one of the riders unfurled a somewhat belated flag of truce, a Texian emissary from the fort galloped off to meet them, issuing forth through a small break in Crockett's palisade.

Travis was incredulous. "Who is that man?" he bristled. "Who ordered him out? I gave no such order!"

"Looks to be Benito Jemison," Joe replied, peering through the spyglass. "Colonel Bowie's order, I guess."

"Bowie! Damn him," Travis seethed, abruptly curtailing the emotion in the same breath. "Well, we'll just have to see about that! What's Jemison doing now, Joe?"

"Having words with the Mexicans. Now they're handing him some kind of paper and, why, now here he comes at a gallop."

Jemison came, clattering back into the Alamo, dismounted, and then, without a word, headed for Jim Bowie's quarters in the Low Barrack, near the main gate.

"Come with me, Joe," said Travis sternly, descending the rampway of the eighteen-pounder in a clear huff. Joe knew, without asking, that they were heading for Jim Bowie's room.

"Go easy on him, Colonel," Joe interceded. "You know Mr. Bowie's been ailing lately. He's not altogether hisself."

"Sick or well, Bowie is a man to be reckoned with," Travis countered. "But then again, so am I!"

There were few souls in the Alamo who hadn't heard of the exploits of the steel-eyed giant, Colonel James Bowie, late of Louisiana. Inventor of the wicked-looking fighting knife that bore his name, Bowie had once been a planter, land speculator, and adventurer. He'd married Ursula de Verimendi, the daughter of the vice-governor of the province of Tejas y Coahuila, sired two infant sons by her and held title to, some said, over a million acres of Texas land, all prime. Fortune seemed to smile upon Jim Bowie. But then disaster struck, when the cholera epidemic of 1833 swept away Bowie's wife, children, and parents-in-law. Sick and sorrowing, all Bowie had left to keep him going was a love of the land. An old lung wound he'd received from the thrust of a sword cane in the famous Vidalia sandbar duel recurrently tore at him and Bowie, in turn, fought it off with that old frontier cure-all, whiskey. Travis made much of Bowie's drinking.

"That drunkard's overstepped his authority this time!" Travis growled, as he and Joe arrived outside Jim Bowie's door at last. "We're supposed to be making joint decisions, Bowie," Travis continued, pushing his way into the low, dimly lit room without so much as a knock. A standing figure, Jemison, holding a rolled piece of parchment, turned to regard both Travis and Joe. Bowie, meanwhile, was seated upon a cot with his head between his legs, giving way to a fit of violent coughing. And there was Maizy with him, steadying the sick man with her arm about his neck and shoulders.

"Hold steady, Colonel Bowie," she comforted. "And hold steady yourself, Colonel Travis, sir," she added. "No need to be getting all fiery red like your very own thatch of hair. Listen to Colonel Jim, if you please!"

Maizy was amazing. She was a tiny, wiry woman who, save for a few strands of gray in her otherwise jet-black hair, appeared almost childlike. But there was a wisdom in her, far beyond her years. Like Joe, she was one of Travis' slaves, but as a woman of ripe middle-age, she was also old enough to have been Travis' mother and let him know it on more than one occasion. Maizy had a calming effect on people and situations that was almost magical. Small wonder then that both Joe and Silvie had come to love her so.

"My apologies, Maizy," Travis clicked, bowing stiffly as he did. Then, "What's contained in that paper, Jemison? There should be no secrets between co-commanders."

Jemison was about to reply, but Bowie stopped him with a gesture of his upraised hand. "No secrets, Travis," Bowie began, pausing to clear the phlegm from his throat. "Merely buying us some time, however fleeting. You were rather hasty with that cannon shot, but, to make a long story short, your reaction was right on the mark. Santa Anna will settle for nothing less than unconditional surrender. Otherwise it's the red flag of no quarter and the Deguello—El Presidente's melodic call to slit our throats. I cannot be of much use to you now, Travis, else I would be up on those parapets ramming a little hell down the dictator's throat myself. The game's yours, now. I hereby relinquish full command to you. God help you."

Travis seemed momentarily stunned by the very weight of Bowie's remarks. Then, with the eyes of all in the little room upon him, the young colonel waxed quite solemn, indeed. "Sorry for my hastiness and for questioning the nature of your motive, Colonel Bowie. Lord grant you a swift recovery. Maizy, stay with him for as long as he needs you. Come on, Joe," Travis concluded, with a nod of a salute to Jemison that saw the both of them out the door.

Back along the west wall once more upon an earthen firing step, Joe and Travis observed Mexican cannon crews in the distance going through the ritual of unlimbering their guns. Soon the besiegers few small cannon were barking and spitting both shot and shell over the Alamo's defense works. But the effects were minimal, to say the least—almost comical, in fact. For as a frowning Travis stood by in silent disapproval, shouting, cheering, and hat-waving Texians danced upon the exposed rooftops of the Alamo in a show of utter contempt of Mexican artillerymanship. At least the garrison's morale was apparently high, but for Travis to see his men taunting the enemy to shoot them down was apparently too much for the fledgling Lt. Colonel.

"I'll be in my quarters until further notice, Joe," Travis said. "You may take the freedom of the yard, for now, but mind again, stick close by." Then, Travis was off.

"As if he didn't have enough weighing upon his mind," a voice from behind Joe sounded, that turned out to be Jemison's. "Much as Travis has railed against Bowie, it's for certain sure, he needs him now."

"We all need Colonel Bowie," Joe replied. "I expect we'll all be in need of each other before this is through, Mr. Jemison. But now, if you'll excuse me, I'd best be getting to where I'm most needed. By your leave, sir," Joe concluded with a respectful nod. Then he too was off to take "the freedom of the yard."

Joe had been in the Alamo on several occasions in the past, but he had never really given it much consideration, save for one moonlit evening when he had wandered its shadowy grounds with Silvie. On that occasion, its weathered walls and dark crevices had served as a romantic backdrop—an almost dream scene where things, surroundings, and sounds were wont to take on surreal qualities that would, upon reflection, seem almost downright foolish and quizzical to someone not in the throes of unbridled love. But now, Joe had to look at the place as a safe haven—a bastion against come what may and how much—as a fort.

From his vantage point near the southwest corner of the mission plaza, the old fort—comprised of over three and a half acres of ground space—spread out before Joe like a self-contained little town. The larger of the open areas, the plaza itself, ran north and south. An oblong court, it was surrounded on all sides by huts set right into the walls themselves. The walls, which for the most part stood from eight to twelve feet high and two and three quarters feet thick, were constructed primarily of baked adobe brick. Ruined portions of an arbor-capped limestone arcade fronted the buildings around the compound and the Texians had filled in the few arches that yet remained with earth stuffed cowhides and sandbags as a defensive measure.

The eye-catching building filling the gap on the eastern side of the plaza, however, was the exception to the rule. For not only was it of limestone, but a full two-stories high, to boot. Formerly the living quarters and offices of the mission's Franciscan founders, it now served as the Long Barrack and hospital of the fortress.

Set off from the plaza, and only joined to it by a single, high wall running east off of the Long Barrack, stood the old stone church. Tumbled down and cavernous as it was, the church proved the stoutest structure in the entire compound. Its roof had long since collapsed, but a few of its flat-roofed side rooms were more or less intact. The building's walls rose up to an impressive height of twenty-one and a half feet, while its ornate façade provided the only real sense of dignity that the Alamo possessed. There it stood in solemn silence, brooding over the scattered compound like a watchful mother hen.

Taking it all in, Joe could only shake his head in disquiet wonder. The fort was just too damned big; the walls too thinly manned. If Travis didn't get his reinforcements and soon, an all out attack could carry the place without much effort. Maybe, Joe mused in retrospect, he should have just left the Alamo back when he'd still had the chance.

Joe was still ruminating over that delicate thought when the sound of music, issuing from the small courtyard in front of the church, caught his attention. Joe went to investigate.

Crossing over the uneven ground of the plaza, it wasn't long before Joe found himself near the palisade defense work where Davy Crockett and his Tennessee boys sat sprawled in a casual circle, eating. They laughed while they ate and they laughed with good reason, for Davy himself was entertaining them in high style. Crockett's repertoire of antics was vast. Sometimes he'd leap atop the palisade barrier to shake his hands and war whoop at the distant enemy. Other times, he'd break into a war dance—actually more of a jig—and then taunt the enemy to come into his parlor for a mite of fire and brimstone. But the thing that got everyone roaring most every time was Crockett's peculiar attempts at fiddle playing. "Attempts" was a decidedly kind understatement, for the discordant screeching Davy was producing on the borrowed fiddle reminded Joe of two tomcats going at it in earnest.

Caught up in the merriment of Crockett's performance, Joe didn't even notice Maizy coming out of Colonel Bowie's room. It was the sound of her voice that made Joe turn with a start.

"That Colonel Davy's a wonder, I do declare," Maizy said with a smile. "Why, you'd hardly imagine that there was a war going on at all, from the way his men are carrying on! But then," she considered, "I guess that that's Colonel Davy's intent, God bless him! Are you . . . " she digressed with a reflective pause. "Are you sorry that you sent Silvie away to San Felipe, Joe? Believe me, it was the best thing that you could've done. It's hard enough making decisions about how your life's going to turn without worrying over Silvie's welfare. Lord knows that I miss that little girl myself, but then I also know that it's an altogether different ache that you're feeling for her now. This Texas is a big place and a wonderful country. It's a place where a man and a woman can start a fresh life—if they're free. Now Master Travis has gone and thrown his whole efforts into fighting to make Texas a free land where people can make their own choices, instead of bowing down to the likes of a slave master like Santa Anna. But then he continues to keep us bound as slaves. It doesn't ring true, Joe, it just doesn't! The way I see it, it's freedom for one and all, or else it's just not the kind of freedom that's worth the laying down of your life for. Go to Colonel Travis and tell him that. He's a good man and I'm sure that where it counts, his heart is in the right place. Ask him straight out about your freedom and Silvie's. In the end, I'm sure that he'll do the right thing by you. But you've got to step up and let your feelings be known. Lord knows, I'd do it myself, if I thought it would help, but then it's not my place to be overseeing your life. Go to him, Joe," Maizy implored tenderly. "Think of Silvie and go."

As Joe started to reply, he was surprised by a tightness catching him in the throat. "You've no idea how often the thought's crossed my mind, Maizy. But it's just not the right time. Sure, Travis is fighting for freedom and such a fight it looks to be! But then that's a man's place, to fight for hisself and his loved ones. I can't rightly see myself going crawling to the master—begging him to let me go. No sir! I've got to prove worthy of my own salt, first. Try and understand that. It's just not the time. Not yet."

"All right, Joe," Maizy sighed in resignation, though shaking her head in disapproval all the same. "It's your decision. Just don't wait until the walls start a'tumbling down on us before you make it. But then," she said, pausing a beat to change her tack, "I guess I've said too much already. Are you hungry? I've got this loaf of real bread. Gathered it from Nat Lewis' store," Maizy added in an air of embarrassment that Joe found charming. "He would've just left it anyhow," she repaired. "Storekeeper Lewis could only carry away so much goods before the Mexican army swooped down upon us. There was no sense in leaving them all to Santa Anna as spoils of war. Here," she offered, tearing off a hunk of crust, then handing Joe the greater portion of the loaf. Then the two of them sat down upon the low wall there by the church and partook of their meager supper while Davy Crockett kicked up a wild high-step nearby.

Evening's shadows drew on at last, and with them came a curiously relaxed atmosphere. No one—not the besieging army, the defending force, nor apparently, even the Bejar citizenry—seemed to take the idea of a siege in progress to heart. So merchants, vendors, and the curious all passed between the thinly drawn battle lines at their will. Bejarians who only that morning, had taken up refuge in the fortress, now had friends and relatives from town paying them a leisurely call. And the vendors, eager to fill their purses at anyone's expense, hawked their goods to both defender and oppressor alike. It was all the same to them.

It was an intoxicating air of excitement and it sagged over the Alamo like a heavy vapor. Few indeed would be the numbers of souls possessed of the inclination to bed down early on such a night. Why the very coals of the cook fires themselves even seemed to dance and leap to the tune of sizzling, brazen beef, and cauldrons of amazing stews. There were fresh, steaming tortillas and plump tamales to be had, tangy chili peppers for spice, refried beans topped by a crust of gooey, melted cheese for bounty and pan dulce for afters. For a brief passage, eating, drinking, and merrymaking supplanted all thoughts of sleep, war, or even tomorrow.

When one of the local women doled Joe out a big bowl of

boiled beef, laced with chili peppers, he attacked the foreign-tasting dish with a fervor and without thinking. But this, Joe quickly learned, was a big mistake. For with watery eyes, steaming ears, and a nose that ran with a fury that would not abate, Joe planted himself face down into an irrigation ditch and practically drank it dry.

So caught up was the garrison in its reverie, that even the occasional sounding of a Mexican howitzer, greeting the night with a hollow bang, could not disturb it. Indeed, the effect that this momentary reminder of battle had upon the revelers was fleeting. For the succeeding high-pitched scream of a shell arcing its way high above the plaza floor only provided the Texians with an additional cause for mirth. With no timing fuse, these shells would usually explode too soon in a brilliant spray of light that went fanning out in all directions. In due response, the awestruck Texians would holler and even cheer, as though they were but spectators at a fireworks show on the Fourth of July.

Joe searched for Maizy in the wavering splash of revelers, but she was nowhere to be found. When she finally did appear at the fire, it was with a pair of shears and a bolt of Nat Lewis' blue gingham material from which she then proceeded to cut long, narrow strips. She alone seemed to sense the seriousness of the impending conflict and these were bandages.

Joe brought Maizy some steaming tortillas and stringed beef, along with a tin of fresh drawn water to wash it all down. "Rest a spell," Joe advised her. "There'll be time enough for such as that," he concluded, pointing at the rising swathes of cloth at Maizy's feet.

"Time, Joe," was all that Maizy had to say in reply and she looked deep into Joe's eyes as she said it. The smile faded rapidly from Joe's face; the taste went out of his food.

As the night waned into early morning, even the most diehard of revelers started calling it quits in favor of bedding down for a few welcome winks. Joe spread out his own pallet beneath the arbor-capped remnant of an arch that overshadowed the headquarters room. As he lay there, looking up at the stars, the weight of Maizy's words burned deep into Joe's mind and he could not shake them. He thought of Silvie in San Felipe and of his promise to return to her there, once things in Bejar had settled down. Settled down! Things were just beginning to happen and, in spite of the past evening's frivolities, they didn't look at all good. What if he should never get back to Silvie? What if he should never get back, period? Joe brooded over the unthinkable thought as a lantern-toting Colonel Travis came tromping by on his nightly rounds of the compound. But when the glow of Travis' lantern was no longer visible, Joe shook his head to clear his muddled thoughts and then tried to sleep.

Two

Burnt Tea and Cannonade

Kabam! The Mexican batteries let loose, sending rumblings through the earth. Shaken, Joe leapt up from his pallet with a start, just as the first streaks of vibrant orange sunlight came streaking in through the trestlework of the arbor roof overhead. It was February the 24th and the Alamo garrison was awakened. Oh unhappy reveille! All around the compound, a mumble of protest was raised, as the men groggily arose in little clumps to scratch their legs, break wind, and then set off for breakfast.

Joe wasn't feeling especially hungry himself, but a little coffee would've made for a nice wake-me-up. But, as coffee was a commodity that the Alamo sorely lacked, the garrison had to make do with a sort of burnt corn and molasses concoction that somebody was trying to pass off as tea. Oh well, it was warm, anyway. Warm and welcome in the suddenness of the morning chill.

Eighteen-year-old Sue Dickerson, wife of one of the artillerymen, brought a bucketful of the steaming stuff by Travis' quarters and ladled out two tins for both Travis and Joe. "See to it that he drinks this, Joe," she mothered. Then Sue was off to the other battle positions with her bucket, trailing wisps of vapor.

Balancing both tins in one fist, Joe knocked upon Travis' door with his free hand, but found, upon entering, that Travis was not in. Then Adjutant Baugh stepped up from out of nowhere. "I believe I saw Colonel Travis heading for Bowie's room, Joe," Baugh offered. "Might still be there."

"Thanks, Mr. Baugh," Joe said, making his way for Bowie's

room in the South, or 'Low Barrack' across a bowing plank of wood that somebody had thrown across the mucky irrigation ditch as a sort of makeshift bridge.

But just as Joe was about to step inside Jim Bowie's room with the tea, a sudden commotion from overhead caused Joe to look up. There upon the Low Barrack roof stood Davy Crockett and a few of his men, laughing and having a high time of it. All of a sudden, one of the caterwauling Tennesseans stopped in mid-guffaw to point at something just beyond the wall. Noticing this, the rest of the group followed suit, their eyes riveted in the same direction.

Now there were times in Joe's life when his curiosity would get the better of him and this was one of those times. So, laying his tins aside, up the rickety ladder Joe clambered to see what Crockett's boys were gawking at. And there it was. There in the distance by the footbridge at the bend of the river stood the solitary figure of a Mexican soldier. The fellow seemed to be surveying the Alamo's defense works for weak spots, for after each peek through a spyglass, the soldier would casually jot down a few notes in a memorandum book, or something of the sort. Apparently the surveyor assumed that he was out of the range of even the Texian's deadly rifles.

The men upon the roof of the Low Barrack roared their approval of the solitary soldier's assumption, for this was an opportunity not to be missed—a shooting exhibition extraordinaire!

A respectful hush fell over the rooftop as Crockett moved to the fore. Leveling his "Old Betsey" long rifle with precision between an embrasure of piled sandbags, Crockett drew a breath, drew a bead, and then squeezed the trigger. After the puff of smoke, followed by the rifle's slight report, all eyes focused upon the solitary uniformed figure by the footbridge at the bend of the river as he crumpled to the ground to rise no more. Crockett's men raised up a huzzah upon the sight. They backslapped each other and pretended to fight. Joe, however, an onlooker and nothing more, kept a prudent distance between himself and their shenanigans until the whole bunch finally tumbled back down the wobbly ladder at last to get a bit of something to eat. Joe forgot all about his teacups.

The siege intensified. Mexican batteries, light and distant as they might be, were finding their range and occasionally a shellburst would occur in the plaza itself, scattering dust and debris everywhere. In turn, the jumpy defenders would scatter in a mad dash for cover, as accompanying round shot, bounding off the walls, kept adobe and limestone chips a-whiz like angry bees. Under the heat of bombardment, the festive mood over the Alamo was beginning to evaporate.

Though Joe would have been content to linger beneath the minimal shelter offered by the headquarters room arch, he did not remain there long, as both Travis and the bombardment kept him on the run. So it was bang, whoosh and scatter, throughout the never-ending morning. "Fetch this, Joe," "Do that, Joe," "Mind the shell fragments, Joe."

Come noontime, some of the more skittish souls had no stomach for eating. Those who did eat merely gnawed upon a cold fare of day-old tortillas and leathery tough beef, gulping and choking under the serenade of the Mexican batteries and the frightened lowing of the livestock in the quartel and cattle pen.

Then, just as suddenly as the bombardment had commenced, it ended. In the ear-ringing silence that prevailed, Travis emerged from his quarters for a look. "Let's go check the damage, Joe," he said.

As they trod their way through the dissipating dust, Joe and Travis observed Lt. Dickerson and Benito Jemison trying to run the eighteen-pounder back onto its platform. As both powder and shot for the big gun was scarce, Travis had had the gun crew roll the piece down from atop the wall to make it less of a target to the Mexicans' own artillery. As it was, the Colonel only allowed the eighteen-pounder to be fired three times a day—morning, noon, and night—as a sign to the outside world that the Alamo was still holding out. Travis smiled in approval of the two cannon wranglers, for both were professional amateurs of sorts. While Jemison maintained the highest aspirations for the Alamo as a fort, Dickerson's prowess as a blacksmith made the young lieutenant feel at home with most any piece of ironmongery.

As to the condition of the rest of the compound, there was surprisingly little to report. No one had been killed and the walls had sustained only minimal damage. True, some of the men had inhaled gobs of adobe dust; still others, hit by limestone fragments, had scrapes that needed some binding up, but that was about it.

Satisfied with the general condition of things, Travis, accompanied by Joe, returned to the headquarters room to write a letter. Within the dimly lit cell, Travis sat at his table with quill in hand, while Joe stood by, holding a greasy candle aloft. Then, when he'd finished the dispatch at last and was waving it dry, Travis said, "This letter is a request for reinforcements, Joe. It also explains our situation here and what we're all about. As it concerns you as well, I'd like for you to hear its contents."

Travis read: "Fellow Citizens and Compatriots, I am besieged by a thousand or more of the Mexicans under Santa Anna. I have sustained a continual bombardment and cannonade for twenty-four hours and have not lost a man. The enemy has demanded a surrender at discretion; otherwise the garrison is to be put to the sword if the fort is taken. I have answered the demand with a cannon shot and our flag still waves proudly from these walls. I shall never surrender, or retreat. Then I call upon you in the name of Liberty of Patriotism and everything that is dear to the American character to come to our aid with all dispatch. The enemy is receiving reinforcements daily, and should no doubt increase to three or four thousand in four or five days. If this call is neglected, I am determined to sustain myself as long as possible and die like a soldier who never forgets what is due his own honor and that of his country. Victory or Death!"

When he'd finished his recitation of the dispatch, Travis looked to Joe for some sign of approval. But Joe surprised him.

"May I speak freely, sir?" Joe asked.

"You've always had the opportunity to do so in the past, Joe," Travis replied with some puzzlement. "You know that. Pray, proceed."

"Well, sir," Joe began, "those are noble, fine words you've written there, with all such talk about liberty and honor, and all. But you said that they concern me too. How so, sir? The liberty of Texas is a grand dream, but where in this dream do I fit in? The way I see it, whether we win this fight, or lose it, I'll still be nothing but somebody's slave. So tell me how I fit in, sir. I would like to know. I need to know."

Travis' jaw dropped and the rest of his face waxed over with such a look of embarrassment that for a few short moments, he said nothing. Finally, Travis spoke. "I scarcely imagined I'd be hearing words of that sort pass your lips, Joe. How long have you had such feelings? I daresay you don't mean to imply that I've been somehow mistreating you, do you, Joe? I've always endeavored to be fair with you in the past."

"Nothing like that," Joe replied. "And it's nothing new, as far as that feeling goes. As a slave, it's always with you and you can't shake it. You wake up with it, walk with it, eat with it, and you sleep with it. Maybe, just maybe, you don't die with it, but then I'm not looking that far ahead. I can wait until my time for passing over arrives of its own accord to see if that's so. You talk of freedom, Colonel, but then you've never been a slave like me. Still, in all, you must know at least a little bit how the hankering for just treatment cries out in you. A hankering that won't be silenced, except maybe by the pile of dirt they throw over your grave."

When he'd digested the gist of Joe's statement a great sadness seemed to come over Travis. His eyes filled with empathy, but it was his voice that formed the words. "You are right, Joe. I do have only an inkling of what your desire for freedom must mean to you. As to me, I'd die for it, plain and simple. But with all talk of dying just a wee bit premature, it's a thing that's worth the living for, too! I have Rebecca and my little son Charles to live for," Travis noted softly with a faraway look in his eyes. "And you, Joe, have Silvie," he added. "And I imagine that your wishes for you and yours are the same as my wishes for me and mine. My preoccupation with the war effort may have caused me to temporarily forsake those in the narrow sphere of my everyday activity, but I would never forget you, or Silvie, altogether. I'll keep in mind what you've said, Joe, that's a promise. And the promise of William Barrett Travis is a very good one. Meanwhile," he exhaled, "to business. Tell Al Martin that I need to see him, muy pronto. Will you do that for me, Joe?"

"Yes, sir," Joe beamed with a new respect for Travis that showed in his bearing. Armored in a aura of fresh confidence that seemed to exude from the core of his very being, Joe felt, for the first time in all of his twenty-three years, that there was actually hope for the future—his future—and Silvie's. Life could be good—would be good—from that moment on. So off he went.

Moments later, when Joe returned with Captain Martin as bidden, Travis wasted no time with wordy formalities. "Get this to Gonzales, Al, and let them know that our situation here is untenable without help. Have the good people there send out riders to the far regions with the word that there is still time for the colonies to strike a decisive blow against Santa Anna. The dream of Texas—our Texas—rests inside these walls... but our time is slipping away. Go with godspeed, Al, and wake 'em up."

"I'll kick 'em awake if I have to, Colonel Travis," Martin replied, easing out the door past Joe, dispatch in tow. In the fading twilight, it was all that Captain Martin could do to read the hastily scrawled salutation that was plainly imprinted on the documents' outer surface. So he held the parchment close to his face and breathed the words just as swiftly as his adjusting eyes could discern them. "To the People of Texas and all Americans in the World," it began. Then the captain passed from earshot.

Three

Arson for Breakfast

Joe could hear it in his dreams. Though the rest of the garrison dozed through the peaceful, starry night like drugged men, Joe became roused every now and then into a semi-conscious state from where he would almost swear he could hear the sounds of clinking and thudding. It was the distinct, dull clinking, such as a shovel might make when digging into the hardened ground, followed by the thudding of freshly turned clods of earth. Joe tried to shrug off the constant, monotonous sounds as but elements of a bad dream. He'd shoveled enough dirt in his day to recognize the unwelcome noise when he heard it, and it was not something on which he would now willingly choose to dwell, let alone dream upon.

Morning arrived all too early to find Joe standing watch alongside of Colonel Travis and Adjutant Baugh atop the eighteen-pounder platform. Maizy had brought each of them a tin of the spurious tea and as Travis stood sipping at his, he made a mental picture of the enemy's progress of the previous night. The Mexican corps of engineers had apparently been busy. For there, looming in plain sight of the theretofore-abandoned huts that stood clustered near the mission's outer walls, was a newly constructed earthwork, teeming with unseen activity. The occasional bobbing up and down of the tops of their tall, plumed shakos was the only way to discern enemy soldiers moving about in the work. It made for an impressive sight—too impressive.

"We've got to raze those huts on our side of the river, Baugh," Travis briefed his adjutant. "If they should manage to plant a battery there, right under our noses, there'll be hell for breakfast and no mistake. I want volunteers for an immediate sortie. Use your own judgment in the choosing."

"Very well, Colonel," Baugh concurred, "but we'd better create some sort of diversion. It's not going to be any Sunday social out there and the enemy most likely anticipate our every move."

Adjutant Baugh was right. For even as he and Colonel Travis were yet speaking, skirmishers already occupying the huts on the Alamo side of the river began laying down a brisk fusillade upon the mission defense works. Then the Mexican batteries, silent up to now, started firing grape and canister to cover another body of troops that was swarming over the footbridge toward some huts that stood in the very shadow of the fortress. In mere moments, the charging troops would be in possession of strategic, valuable cover.

Suddenly, the hut-bound troops staggered to an abrupt halt, as a sheet of musket, rifle, and cannon fire slammed into the foremost of the column, decimating it. Incredibly, the pause was only momentary, for the determined remnant of soldiers swiftly dressed down, then came on all the same, pushing through the dense fog of sulphurous smoke in search of cover—any cover.

Travis sensed that the moment was right. "That smoke will serve as ample cover for the sortie party, Baugh," he said. "Send them forth to their duty."

The south gate swung open and a party of torch-brandishing Texians, stripped to their shirts, started running toward the nearest huts. They encountered little resistance along the way. It was as though the besiegers were content with merely hunkering down and waiting it out. It did not prove to be much of a wait, though, for as soon as the sure-footed Texians arrived at their goal, they sent their torches sailing in through opened windows and upon the dry thatched roofs of the huts. Then, just as suddenly as the Texians had arrived, they were gone.

The stricken buildings seemed to shudder at first, before exploding at last into walls of leaping flame. In no time at all, the spindly framework of the consumed huts was belching skyward upon the fanning winds in a swirl of hot ash and soot, while accompanying unquenched cinders rained down upon the surrounding prairie, creating mini-conflagrations of their own.

"Give them cover, boys!" Travis bellowed, pointing toward the now-visible volunteer arsonists that were making their way back to the fortress at a dead run. Then something happened that was to change Joe's life forever.

"Here, soldier," Travis offered, handing Joe a loaded musket to bear. "Lend a hand." Clearly, there was a knowing smile upon Travis' face as his eyes met Joe's. Joe returned the look, but kept the musket. *Travis understands the way it is*, Joe thought to himself. *He really does.*

Joe handled the musket with love. He felt the weight of it at first and then the balance. He was the musket. The musket was he. There would be no more bowing down or scraping to any man, for now he was a man to be contended with. Joe pressed the stock into his shoulder and then pulled the trigger. He felt a jolt, as the flash of priming powder ignited the weapon's charge and sent a ball whizzing through the distant wall of smoke. And though he would never really know if he'd hit so much as a barn door, Joe nonetheless got his first taste of what it was like to be an actual, contributing member of the garrison. But more importantly, Travis had acknowledged him as a man, something that no other white being had ever done in the weary course of his shackled life. There could be no turning back now.

At last, the sooty sortie party stumbled back into the mission through a break in the palisade defense work by the chapel, while the Mexicans, in acknowledgment that enough was enough, stumbled back over the footbridge with their casualties, while a thin skirmish line provided them with token cover.

With the threat over and the Texians claiming all the laurels, the field and the day, it seemed only natural that they should celebrate. But, as they stood upon the ramparts, whooping and hollering on the sight of the retiring Mexican troops, Joe had a sudden inspiration.

"If you please, Colonel," Joe began, capturing Travis' attention, "we're going to be needing some more firewood before too long, and lumber for building platforms. There's still a few huts standing out there that are just plain too close to our walls for comfort—in my mind, anyway. We could go out again and pull them down, get our wood, and also keep the enemy from using them for cover. They'd never expect us to be making two raids in a row. If we move now, I believe we can do it before they even suspect anything's up."

Travis looked at Joe in wonder; his eyes lit up on the idea. "It's a good plan, Joe," he voiced in admiration. "We'll do just that. Are you up for a little excursion outside these walls?"

"You can count on me, sir," Joe beamed with pride, drawing himself up to full stature. Travis set the plan in motion. "I want volunteers for another sortie," he shouted above the huzzahing din. "We need lumber and the Mexicans need those huts. I say let's take'em, before they do! Who'll be the first? Quick!"

Half a dozen eager youths sprang to the task, but Joe sprang faster. Out the main gate he sprinted, bearing a crowbar and a good coil of rope, while the rest of the foraging party followed, trailing close behind. A welcome wall of silence greeted them a quarter of the way to their goal. At the halfway point their luck still held. But at the three-quarter mark, the Mexican batteries awakened at last to greet the sortie party with a raking hail of grape and canister. Making themselves small against this horizontal storm of lead and iron, the Texians careened their way along the last agonizing steps. Amazingly, they reached their goal unscathed and set about a systematic ritual of dismantling. They worked fast and none worked faster than Joe. In a rattle and clatter of but a few moments, the wall he was working on was reduced to a sizable pile of lumber at his feet.

As there would be no opportunity for a return trip, Joe tied up as much of the wood as he could into a tight bundle and then slung it across his back. He was just turning to dash for the main gate of the Alamo when he got a rude surprise; a hand reached out of the hut's window and made a snatch at his shirt. Joe tensed and then started running, straining against the equal and opposite reaction. First the material of his shirt, and finally, the grip upon its tail, gave way. Free at last and covering ground faster than even he would've believed, Joe sprinted for all he was worth. And though the sound of bullets whizzed by him and a jumble of shouts, all in Spanish, rang in his ears, Joe never looked back.

Once inside the Alamo, Joe collapsed upon the ground, along with his bundle of wood. By and by, all the foragers made it back into the fort. Ever vigilant, Maizy stood at the ready with dippersful of water for every thirsty soul and Joe drank his own dipperful almost greedily. When he'd recovered enough to speak, Joe stammered out: "They're still on our side of the river, Colonel Travis! One of 'em nearly grabbed me as I was going by! They're still there," he repeated, before sinking, fatigued, to the earth once more.

"Get yourself something to eat, Joe," Travis said, patting him on the back. "The rest of you men, as well. It was a splendid effort. My thanks to you all."

Though no one else said a word, the overwhelming crush of silence screamed volumes. The sortie, begun in confidence, had ended in failure, leaving the brief boost of morale, like the cinders of the burned huts, to disperse in wispy clouds upon the flagging winds. Suddenly, some of the defenders began to notice that their eyes were watering; others started getting the feeling of being trapped again. Both the atmosphere and the siege ring around the mission were indeed thickening.

Four

Reminiscing and the Louisiana Dockman

Shannon was a beauty. A pleasure to behold. Her lines, her bearing, the way she held her head; all these things and more made Joe love her so. And how dearly he loved to watch her run. Just the sight of Shannon gliding through the tall grass with the early morning sun glaring off her long, bared limbs was enough to hold Joe madly, hopelessly spellbound. But Shannon, free spirit that she was, did not belong to Joe. True, she would, at times, allow Joe within close proximity of her and she seemed to appreciate his gentle caresses and the way he would massage her legs and run his fingers through her cascades of hair, while whispering sweet nothings into her ears. But still, in all Shannon was a wild child and not one to be altogether tamed. That Colonel Travis had not sold her off long ago stood as testament to his wonder at Joe's winning ways with her. Was there ever such a bay horse as Shannon?

Back when, in the days when Travis and company had first arrived in San Antonio and Shannon had an entire stable in the Alamo to herself, Joe would come to visit and groom her there on a daily basis. Now, Shannon was crowded out of her shed and had to coexist amongst the lesser siring of horseflesh in the all but open quartel. *It wasn't fair,* Joe thought, *this shabby treatment of Shannon.* But then again, were the human folk faring any better? Joe would do his best by Shannon and continue to visit, feed, and groom her, though the world around them all seemed on the brink of falling apart.

It was to the quartel that Joe was coming to give Shannon her evening feed. It was through a low door in the rising wall that jutted off the church that Joe walked to get to the area behind the Long Barrack where both the cattle and horses were kept. The air he encountered within the small, enclosed area reeked of both manure and death, as pools of warm blood from a freshly slaughtered steer gathered in the steaming waste product of those yet living. Some men, Joe saw, were carving off thick steaks from the dressed and hanging carcass, while squadrons of anxious blowflies circled in for their taste in between swattings. It was plain to see that more was up than supper, when a sentry stationed upon a low platform that faced the outer wall began shouting and pointing.

"Riders coming in, all in a lather! They're under fire," the sentry added, as though no one present could hear the distinct report of half a dozen or so muskets. Suddenly Travis appeared, as though from out of nowhere. "Give them some cover, boys," Travis ordered, "and get that gate open!"

In swift response, Joe and another Texian unbarred and then swung open the narrow gate, while a dozen or so other marksmen tumbled up onto the platform to lay down some cover fire.

Soon the clattering thud of approaching shod horse's hooves heralded the entrance of two mounted men hunched low in the saddle that reined up abruptly and dismounted. The forced ride had clearly taken its toll on both the men and their beasts. One of the fatigued riders, Joe noticed, was black, like himself.

"DeSaque, Jean," Travis hailed in welcome. "I hardly expected to be seeing the two of you back so soon! What word do you bring us from the outside world?"

DeSaque, a small dark-eyed, dark-haired, mustachioed youth, accepted a dipperful of water from Joe, then gargled and spat before replying.

"Mon Dieu, Colonel, what do you have here? There's an army out there, you know, and by the looks of the way they are digging, I believe that they plan on staying awhile. As to the outside world, they know less than nothing, which is about half as much as I. In

Gonzales, there is talk, talk, talk, but no action. Jean and I passed Al Martin along the way here. We hurried on as fast as we could."

"Well, thank Providence that you're both safe," Travis said. "I was just about to send out another courier to San Felipe. Why don't you two rest up and get yourselves something to eat?"

But DeSaque would have none of that. "Put me upon a fresh horse with a little water and some jerked beef and I will gladly go," he said. "At least I myself know the way out through the enemy lines. Jean," he beckoned his slave, "you remain here and take especial care of my beloved Antoinette." Antoinette was his horse. "Give her plenty of fresh hay and water and brush her down. Adieu!"

And so, after tendering his beloved Antoinette into the capable hands of Jean, DeSaque was off riding dispatch once more upon a fresh mount. With particular skill, he got beyond the startled besiegers, before they could even offer up a shot in reply.

As for Jean, although seemingly abandoned by his master and still smarting from the long ride in, he nevertheless set fast to grooming DeSaque's mount with an old horse blanket, while his own lathered horse stood shuddering nearby.

Joe was quick to respond to the situation. "Here," he offered, grabbing another blanket from the gnarled fence post. "Let me help you with your horse."

Jean's face broke into a broad grin. "Merci, my friend," he said, "it is more than kind of you." Then he turned and continued at his toil.

Jean was a big, burly, barrel-chested fellow with a congenial face that seemed half-hidden behind a droopy mustache. And he had a silver earring! Yet Joe was more taken aback by Jean's peculiar style of speech, than by his appearance, for Jean spoke in an incredible composite of mangled French and English.

"The name's Jean," he offered. "DeSaque, if you'll have it. It is as good a name as any. Came from New Orleans, mostly. Born in Natchez-Under-The-Bluff. Dock worker. DeSaque's Pappy. Speak

French plenty good—English, not so good. Dock work not so bad. Better than these stinking livestock, no? No offense to you, Antoinette, mon cheri," he added, as though the horse actually understood him. "Young Francois DeSaque, he get plenty sick, dock life, and he came to these Texas. Not so much choice, me. We wander around plenty much, but DeSaque, no can he settle down. We end up in Sant Antoine and take to riding dispatch for Colonel Neill. Then, back we come... same time as Santanna! Now, DeSaque sees opportunity to wander off plenty quick enough once more, you see? And so now, here I am, swabbing these stinking livestock. Quele barbe! But again, not you, dear Antoinette," he added when the horse seemed to whinny in rebuttal.

Joe considered this "Louisiana Dockman's" brief history with a hint of both envy and awe. New Orleans! The Mississippi River. Natchez-Under-The-Bluff! These were exotic places that Joe, in his years of confinement, had only heard in passing and yet here was a man who had seen them all. *Some people just plain had all the luck*, Joe concluded.

"And you, my friend," the Dockman said, breaking Joe's spell, "what you doing this place and where you from, eh? Monsieur Colonel Travis is going not from here, so you plenty stuck like me, yes?"

"Plenty stuck here and how," Joe inwardly sighed. Always plenty stuck somewhere. Why, his earliest recollections were of being stuck in the "big house" on Lewis Bosley's plantation. The place had been Joe's home for as far back as he could remember, although he'd been told that he hadn't been born there. The fact that he had been born, Joe more or less took for granted. He had seen babies birthed before and considered himself no less of a man that he should have entered the world in any more lowly of a fashion than that of being good and properly born.

Old Jerob, the houseman at Bosley's, and his wife, Essie, had been good foster parents to Joe; better ones, in fact, than most slave children could've hoped or dreamt for. For while the other children learned at an early age what it was like to toil all day in the sweltering, shadeless fields, Joe became acquainted with the lighter duties of the big house.

The Missus Bosley herself, a woman of strict Presbyterian upbringing, had christened him "Joe" in a ceremony witnessed by the entire complement of house help. Joe could count amongst his blessings the fact of how very soon after the event his young mind had succeeded in effectively blocking out all the particulars of the terrifying ordeal during the course of his waking hours. But it was in the darkness of the night that the haunting was to revisit him, time and again. Even to this day, as a young adult, the horrific episode often recurred in monotonous detail to further plague the depths of his restless sleep.

The dream would begin with a diffusion of bright light, as though someone was shining a lantern through a sheer veil of gauze. This would be accompanied by the muffled sounds of voices, chanting in jubilant intonations. The haziness would gradually dissolve to reveal a halo of faces, all peering down upon Joe, as though he were looking up from the depths of a well. Next would come the water, like the contents of a well. Plenty of water—gallons of it—raining down upon his young brow like a burst dam. But the terror was not in the splashing water, no. It would come, rather in the most frightening part of the vision imaginable: total body immersion!

For it was at this point of the dream when Joe would see the hands—overpowering hands that would thrust and then hold him beneath the surface of the water. And though he would be able to see the surface, the surface was never his. There, beneath the silent depths, gazing up at the wavering light of the moving waters above, all Joe could manage to do in response would be to flail his arms in the futility of his stark terror. It was usually at this point in the dream when Joe would awaken, trembling, soaked in sweat and grasping at thin air.

The sad irony of Joe's premature awakening lay in the fact that the dream's outcome—if he allowed it to get there—was a positive one. If only he could remain asleep long enough to realize that it was but a replay of his baptism and, in spite of appearances, would not succeed in killing him, after all. As it was, Joe remained saddled with a dread phobia of water that would take him to task, time and again.

It was a delicate matter, this fear of water and not one to be shared with a stranger. So Joe gave the Louisiana Dockman a brief, expurgated, waterless account of how he'd come to be in the Alamo.

"Name's Joe," he began, "Joe Travis, for now," he added pensively. "Don't rightly know where I was born. Ma and Pa was sold off when I was just a wee baby, so I was told. Lived most of my own days on the Bosley place, near Gainsborough, Tennessee. I was a deal more fortunate than most black folks on the plantation, I expect. Reared a house man by a kindly couple that took me under their wing like they were my own kinfolks. Nothing much, but it was a sweet deal better than working in the field all day. Master Bosley was kind enough, I reckon, but he gone loco after the Missus died suddenly one day. Took to drink, ran up debts and then sold us slaves off, one by one. I was bought by Master Mansfield on his way to Texas. Bought off himself by Master Travis, back in '34. The Colonel was a lawyer back then, you know. Court business and such. I ran errands and went messages for him mostly, at first."

Joe recounted to the Louisiana Dockman how he'd come to bunk behind the pot-bellied stove in Travis' cramped and indecorous law offices in the booming community of San Felipe de Austin. Back in those early days, the young attorney's bustling practice had usually kept him away from the office for the better part of the day. But on the evenings that followed, when Travis would stop by to pay his respects to his sweetheart, Rebecca Cummings, and her brother, John, at their residence on Mill Creek, Joe usually found himself bedding down upon a mattress of coarse straw in the livery, near the Cummings Mill. On the plus side, the livery had also housed Travis' newly acquired horse, the bay mare, Shannon. An avid gambler, Travis had won the horse in a game of cards, only to find out later and much to his chagrin, that the mare was unbroken. But Joe and Shannon had clicked from the moment that they'd first set eyes upon each other. So evident was the bond, in fact, that Travis had not hesitated in allowing Joe to undertake the taming of the beast. It had been a labor of love; one that had paid off Joe in more ways than he could ever hope to explain.

When Joe had filled the listening Jean's ears with so much of Shannon's numerous, shining attributes, the Dockman felt compelled to respond, in like manner. "So," Jean countered cheerfully, throwing down the gauntlet, "swift as the wind, is she? Well, just give me the time and the place and my Antoinette will give your Shannon the run of her life! What say you to that?"

Joe was all composure; his response reflected the reality of the moment. "Well, I reckon that the time and the place for that will just have to wait until this war is over. I was there when it commenced—I can wait until it's done."

Joe went on to relate how Travis had come to join the War Hawks party. Joe could still remember all those meetings of angry colonists spouting off with their big talk and fiery resolutions about state's rights and the man who they claimed was threatening to take them all away: Santa Anna.

It had been a risky business in those early days, when not every soul in Texas was as eager to assert their rights as Travis and his co-conspirator. So the War Hawks went underground, masking themselves for night raids upon Mexican symbols of authority.

Joe had harbored mixed feelings about military life from the get-go. While he didn't exactly relish shivering out under the stars with nothing between himself and the frozen ground but a threadbare horse blanket, he did like the idea of getting to ride Shannon all over the countryside. And his change in status from manservant to orderly was something else Joe could only see as a plus.

There had been no uniforms, but, perhaps to keep his own men from shooting each other by mistake, Travis had provided each of them with a shiny, patent-leather cap; that alone seemed to have given them some sort of sense of uniformity. Joe wore his own trophy cap thereafter, rarely removing it except when indoors. He was still wearing it, here in the Alamo.

Joe had been present at one of the most famous of Travis' prerevolution raids and he let the Dockman know it.

"You may hear talk of Austin and Milam and Burleson, but I tell you the solemn truth that Colonel Travis practically went and started this whole revolt thing on his own! It was back in the late June of '35 that Travis and twenty-seven picked men—me included—sailed the sloop *Ohio* right up the channel before the port city of Anahuac. The town had Captain Antonio Tenario and forty troopers guarding its Customs House, but Travis marches right up and after a few shots, forces them to surrender, kit and caboodle. Twenty-seven against forty! And did they surrender? You bet they did! I was standing right next to Master Travis when Tenario handed over his sword. Yes sir, I've seen some action, for a fact!"

The Louisiana Dockman listened to Joe's account of the capture of Anahuac in a polite display of interest, nodding every now and then whenever Joe would attempt to drive a point home. At length, Jean spoke.

"So," he chided, "you are the veteran of this war business, yes? Well, it you can have. Me? The river, anytime!"

Bruised by the Dockman's remark, Joe snapped back at his newfound friend in a tone that even Joe found uncharacteristic of himself: "Not so much a veteran yet. But I am learning! I figure a man's got to fight for his own rights sometime. Leastwise, nobody's going to do it for him! I fired a gun today and it felt good. And for just a few minutes, maybe just one, I was my own master. And that seems like something that's worth fighting for—maybe even dying for, I suppose."

"Vraiment! Of course it do seem so," the Dockman returned gravely. "It seems that way to me sometimes, as well. I say to myself, 'Jean, you have the rare opportunity to run away from young Master DeSaque. Many times he is drunk too much and he is only one man, as you. But then, I think not so much without brains. If to run, I am, I stand the chance of getting captured by a man not so amiable as DeSaque. Then, it's plantation work, like you Joseph, for me. Mon Dieu, but thank you, no."

The Louisiana Dockman paused a moment in his oratory to air the soily horse blanket over an uneven fence post; then he rested himself against the railing and continued.

"Much freedom have I with DeSaque. Not so much work do I do that Desaque does not do himself. We get drunk some, but I, not so much as he. We travel around these Texas, plenty good fun! And now, he is gone. Likely, I never see him no more again. So, now, free am I of DeSaque, but what of it—and where? This broken down monastery is freedom? So if I run from this place, what? Mexicanos think I am but Americain and I am plenty shot like fun. If, on the other hand, I stay this place, Texians think I am but a slave and treat me like so much dirt, swabbing these stinking livestock. So, where is my freedom, eh? At least you have you Travis to facilitate your decision. He say 'do this' and 'do that' and no time, have you to think. Me I have plenty time thinking, but little choice in acting. So do not, my friend, ask for something that you are not certain you want, or can handle. Get it, you just might."

The power of the Dockman's words had little effect on Joe's tenacity and he dismissed them. "I don't figure that I'm asking for too much," he began, swelling up in even greater determination. "Just the freedom to make my own choices, good, or bad, my own choices! Right now, the way I see it, there are only two times in a slave man's life when he's truly free. The minute he's born and the minute he dies. 'Cause we were all born the same. A suckling babe don't judge the color of the tit that feeds it. It's a difference that's got to be taught—pounded into his young head. It's the color of our skin brands us all slaves in the eyes of some white men. If only the whole world was color blind, then it would be looking at what's inside of a man—his honesty, his courage, and the goodness of his heart—not the tone of his hide. But that ain't happening and, until it does, people of color got only two choices in the matter: to keep on running toward freedom, or to stay put and die, never knowing. Well, this Joe is not about to stay put! He's rearing up on his haunches and fools just better keep out of his way! But, if it's written that that don't play out and I'm to die in this fort, then so be it. Leastwise, one way or the other, I'll be going my own man. Now, I gotta go tend to Shannon, Jean, or she'll be no match for your Auntie Net when this is all over. Goodnight to you, then."

"Good night to you, Joseph," the Dockman responded with empathy and a weary smile. "I hope that someday you get your chance."

Storm clouds overhead had been threatening business all evening, when a roaring thunderclap rent the early night sky. "Easy, girl," Joe whispered to soothe the jittery Shannon, even as the contrary skies let loose with rain. Then Joe belatedly stretched a tarp over some tall, upright polls into a sort of shelter for the horse. "Sorry, Shan, but that's the best I can do," he said. "I'll be back to check in on you a little later." But the horse only whinnied in anxiety. It apparently did not like the rain any more than Joe did.

Joe headed back for the headquarters room through a passageway in the Long Barrack. The last image that he had of Jean was of him standing in the same spot by the cattle pen fence with upraised arms and face tilted skyward. *That Louisiana Dockman seems to enjoy water in any form*, Joe thought.

Five

Shoring Up Daze

The siege dragged on without any notable occurrence to break the monotony—inside the Alamo, anyway. Outside, the entrenchments around the fort continued to snake in ever closer; for a change, it was now the Mexicans who were the more active. And they were also the ones who were being reinforced. Joe could see fresh troops tromping into town almost anytime he took the opportunity to peer over the wall. This in itself was getting to be monotonous, to a fault. Joe was angry—almost indignant. *So where were their reinforcements?* It had been days since Travis' messengers had gone out for help. Not a one had returned. *Were the people of Texas actually going to leave their defenders of freedom hanging out on a cracking limb?*

Time told. It was in the early morning of March the 1st when a chill in the air icily persuaded Joe to arise in the darkness to get the cook stove going, along with a pot of the spurious tea. Drawn to the cook fire by its promising warmth, the already risen Jean stepped under the arbor from out of the shadows. Joe was surprised to see a musket cradled in the crook of the Dockman's arm.

"So, how you like this soldiering now, my friend," Jean hailed. "Not so much excitement now, yes?" he chided. "Me? I find this worthless piece of junk of a musket in the armory. Not so much gun, she, but I fix her up and try this soldiering myself. Better you get yourself a weapon of your own, Joseph. Santa Anna's soldiers pay us a visit plenty soon enough, I think. They no say 'howdy do,' or ask questions. They just stick and shoot and shoot and stick.

How you like that, soldier?"

"S'that all you're good for is bad news?" retorted Joe, sullenly. "We've got enough of that, without you adding to it!"

"Mais non, Joseph," the Dockman returned, frowning. "I make the try for humor, that is all. Don't worry so much, you. Things shall happen all the same, no matter. Now, let us sample some of that hot tea, or whatever it be, yes?"

But the tea would have to wait. For from somewhere down by the north wall, the blam of a musket exploded into the night. Soon, there were voices and the sound of pounding feet, followed very swiftly thereafter by the thudding of gun butts against stubborn wood. The aroused garrison sprang into action as both Joe and Jean, along with a passel of other curious defenders, dashed across the open space that lay between themselves and the postern, a sort of glorified little door near the northwest corner of the plaza. Could this be the attack that they had all been dreading?

"Sunzabitches! We's 'mericans!" a voice sang from beyond the wall. "Stop yer goddam shooting and let us in!"

There was no mistaking the shouter's tone, or the vernacular. They were Americans, all right, and Americans none too keen on the prospect of lingering long in such a precarious position—a position that one of their own comrades-in-arms upon the walls had occasioned by the firing of his musket in haste.

The northern postern creaked open and, as the wary defenders thrust freshly lit torches into the passage, the reinforcements came in—all thirty-two of them.

"Too few," the Dockman commented, shaking his head in disappointment, as the last of the reinforcements crowded through. "Merely a few more cherries for Sant Ana to bite off." But even that dreary sentiment did not prevent some of the grateful defenders from breaking into a hearty cheer.

Joe recognized John W. Smith amongst the newcomers. The old Indian scout had ridden out for help on the first day of the siege. How long ago that now seemed! Along with Smith traipsed

Al Martin, a friend of Captain Dickerson's and Travis' "To The People of Texas and All Americans in the World" courier. Martin allowed how this small contingent represented the bulk and total fighting force of the town of Gonzales. They had heard of no others.

Travis formally greeted the men of Gonzales; he applauded their courage, lauded them for their fortitude, and then asked them to pitch in with getting the Alamo into fighting shape.

The mission's old walls had taken such a terrific pounding from the Mexican's light artillery pieces over the past few days that it was all the defenders could do to bolster up the shuddering stone and adobe. So, to his credit, and alongside the brave men of Gonzales, Joe dove into the very thick of it with grim determination. Shoring up was back-breaking, sweat-pouring, throat-rasping, bone-chilling, nerve-wracking, never-ending, thankless work. For no sooner would the Texians shovel up a pile of wall than the enemy would bring it all down again in a cloud of dust splinters and grit. Then it was back to square one for the work parties.

Joe found himself shoveling dirt with a zombie-like frenzy. Zombie-like, because his muscles, indeed his entire being, had passed beyond the threshold of bearable pain. And so, as he toiled on in a daze, Joe's memory drifted back to happier times and another place. To Silvie and San Felipe . . .

Six

Silvie and San Felipe

Although most of its buildings were of clapboard construction, San Felipe de Austin was the oldest Anglo-Texian founded settlement in all of Cohuila y Texas. Its symmetrical, if rutted, streets ran down a gradual embankment that emptied out onto a riverbank-hugging boardwalk along the Rio Guadalupe. The town, named in honor of the late colonial leader, Moses Austin, even boasted a post office, a courthouse, and a church. For the southeast Texas of 1835, this was civilization to the hilt.

William Barrett Travis struck gold when he decided to set up his law practice there. True, his thriving business was not one that would make him rich, dollars and cents wise—he'd once accepted a yoke of oxen in payment of service rendered—but it was, nevertheless, an exciting one. Too, it afforded him the opportunity to spend his free hours with his girlfriend, Rebecca Cummings, at the inn that she co-owned with her brother, John, on Mill Creek, just a few miles out of town.

Judging from the number of Travis' late night visits to the Cummings, Joe suspected that the young lawyer was clearly, hopelessly, bitten by the love bug. Joe, after all, was not a complete stranger to the feeling. On those occasions when Travis would linger at his nocturnal carousals, Joe, in the solitude of the livery, had ample time to dwell upon the yearnings of his own heart. The night was a time when a man alone either had thoughts of being with his sweetheart, if he had one, or of finding her. It was the still depths of the night that held promise, Joe told his yearning heart.

But wasn't it just like fate to step in and prove a fellow wrong? For it was during the gleaming glow of morning hours when the dew yet lay upon the ground, on what had begun as but a drab, ordinary, office day, that Joe met Silvie. He and Travis were in the office early that day to take care of some backlog when a sudden rap upon the door heralded the entrance of Uriah Sanders, a colleague at law of Travis. The two lawyers fell into immediate conversation. But because Joe was in the rear of the office, stooping to gather some papers that Travis had unintentionally scattered all over the place, he didn't hear but the tail end of the exchange.

"In all sincerity, I have no use for any servants," Travis insisted. "My manservant, Joe here, takes care of all my needs quite adequately."

Hearing his name mentioned heightened Joe's interest; he listened tight.

"I wish that you would reconsider," Sanders plead on. "Maizy and Silvie are not only good workers, they're practically family. Maizy's been with the household for years—why, she's raised me from a sprout! And she's also been a good mother figure for Silvie. I'd hate for the two of them to be separated, but if I'm forced to sell them off, who knows what the future may hold for them? Now I know that I owe you a good deal of money, Buck, but to be quite frank, I'm flat busted. That's the reason I'm leaving San Felipe and Texas for good, folding my practice, cutting my losses, and packing it in for Louisiana. Here is my dilemma. I cannot afford to pay you back and I cannot afford to keep on two servants. If they're with you, however, I know for a certainty that they will be well-treated. Give us all a break, if you will, Buck."

Reading the earnestness in the eyes of his colleague, Travis softened. "Well, maybe I can work something out. The Cummings' have been complaining that they need more help at their inn on Mill Creek. Maizy and Silvie can both work and board there. If there are any additional expenses, I will cover them personally. Done and done," he concluded, shaking hands with the much relieved Sanders. Then the two lawyers stepped off to draw up the legal paperwork.

Two females, Joe considered, when he was alone with his thoughts. It was a kind enough thing for Travis to be taking them under his wing and no mistake. But how would their addition to the Travis household affect Joe himself? He wouldn't have to cook or clean anymore, that was for sure. Horse grooming and a little more time to spend with the bay mare, Shannon, he mused; perhaps a little errand running and office upkeep—Joe could live with that. Anyhow, with two womenfolk around, he wouldn't have to be feeling so godawful lonesome all the time. Company was company, and welcome, even if that company was only a bent old woman and a noisy little sprout of a girl.

"Joe," Travis said, stepping back into the room, "come and meet your new associates, Maizy and Silvie. We're all going to have to get to know each other better and now's as good of a time as any to start."

Joe walked into the antechamber of the office where Uriah Sanders stood speaking with his servant women. Joe's eyes lit up on the sight of them. Maizy was no bent-over matron after all, and Silvie was, well, pretty. Not only pretty, but also of an age enough to stir Joe's interests. Though only in her late teens, the girl appeared to be about twenty or so. *Must've ripened early*, Joe noted to himself, giving Silvie the once over from head to foot. Silvie was something to behold. She had large, lustrous eyes and a mouth that, Joe imagined, begged to be kissed. Her tresses of shining hair were pulled up tightly upon the crown of her head and the resulting ponytail dipped down along side of her delicate cheek oh so provocatively. But it was the look in the eyes of both Maizy and Silvie that Joe froze upon. For it was a look of fear, desperation, and gnawing apprehension.

"You can rest easy, ladies," Sanders was saying. "The good Mr. Travis has concluded to keep the both of you together. You'll be well looked after, I promise. Why, he's even got some new situations lined up for you, working at an inn! Travis is a man of his word, else I would never even have considered the venture as sound. So rest easy."

Maizy and Silvie went wide-eyed over the news that they would be staying together. With shouts of both joy and relief, they hugged and cried, then hugged some more.

Embarrassed, Travis broke into a somewhat exaggerated smile. "The situations that you promised are not a sure thing, Uriah," he whispered aside to Sanders, but within Joe's earshot. "But then I am sure that both Becky and Jack Cummings will trust my judgment. Meanwhile, I'll have to see that the women get put up properly. Joe," Travis continued aloud, stooping over a side table to jot off a note with the old stub of a pencil, "escort these ladies to Gay's with my note." Gay's was the only boarding house in town. "See that they are well kept," he added.

Wearing a smile of his own, Joe took the note and ambled over to where Maizy and Silvie stood waiting. "Hello, ladies," he saluted, half bowing. "The name is Joe. If you'll come with me, I'll help you to get situated and bedded down. Let me help you with your baggage there," he offered cheerfully, reaching for both Maizy's and Silvie's canvas bags. But Maizy's only response was to jerk her arm away and then place herself between Silvie and the oh-so-helpful Joe.

"We can handle our own personals," she said curtly, with a look of suspicion in her eye that cut Joe like a dagger. "Lead on, Mr. Joe."

Joe led. Out the door, down the rutted street, and finally unto the rear entrance of a rustic, if comfortable-looking, one story clapboard structure with a sign that said simply, GAY'S-ROOMS painted along its side. Joe knocked and was answered by a tired-looking, middle-aged woman with a tassel of uncombed hair. After eyeing Travis' note, the woman peered out upon Maizy and Silvie.

"Come in, you two," she welcomed. "I'll have some pallets laid out for you near the scullery hearth. You'll be warm and cozy enough, I'll wager. Rabbit stew's for dinner."

Silvie and Maizy entered their new, temporary home, leaving Joe alone upon the stepstone. "If there's anything else I can do," he said suavely, smiling at Silvie and getting, he thought, a hint of response from the girl. "If there's anything I can do," Joe repeated, as Maizy banged the door shut in his face.

I'll have to earn the heart of both of them, Joe mused, walking back toward Travis' offices on a cloud. "Something to work on," he said to himself, smiling. "Something to work on."

As it worked out, or as fortune would have it for Joe, Maizy and Silvie did get situations at the Cummings Inn on Mill Creek. And while Travis and Joe did come a'calling rather frequently, it was only upon Joe's third visit to the Cummings that the ice truly began to break. As Travis sat inside the parlor sipping tea and making points with his sweetheart, Rebecca, Joe tested his own luck by dawdling near the water's edge in the hopes of chancing a moment alone with Silvie. But the moment he shared instead was with Maizy, as down to the water's edge she came, laden with two cumbersome buckets. There was no escape.

"Afternoon, Miss Maizy," Joe stammered, jumping to his feet. "Let me lighten your load a bit there," he offered, relieving Maizy of one of the buckets before she could voice an objection.

"I'm fully capable of handling—" she shot, but Joe cut her off just as swiftly.

"I'm sure you are, Ma'm, but it's just a gentleman's place to help out a lady whenever he can. A gentleman cannot help hisself, Ma'm. It just comes naturally."

Maizy gave Joe a half-hearted sidelong glance of suspicion, but that dissolved into a welcome smile. "I suppose a gentleman cannot at that, Joe," she said. "And a lady recognizes that. I'm sorry for my hastiness in judging you and in seeming so cold. It's just that I think the world of my little Silvie and take her safety and welfare—and feelings—rather seriously. I've been around long enough to know what's on the minds of some men. I've had my own share of heartaches and just figured to shield Silvie from living through too many of her own. But then I can't pretend to guide the wheels of her heart, once they are firm set to turning. I suppose that I shouldn't rightly be saying this to you just yet, but she speaks of you often. Why, she keeps remarking over and over about the day we all met like it was some kind of holiday, or something. What I'm trying to say," Maizy concluded, with as much maternal tone in her voice as she could muster, "is that if you want to come a'calling on Silvie like a gentleman, I have no objections to the notion."

"Miss Maizy!" Joe shouted in irrepressible joy, dropping the bucket to give the startled woman a big bear hug that practically lifted her off her feet.

"Now Joe, Joe," she protested in feigned irritation, "does a gentleman do that?"

"A happy one does, Miss Maizy, a happy one!"

Then Joe and Maizy drew their buckets full at the creek and headed back to the scullery door of the inn. Silvie was inside setting two supper plates on the sideboard; one for herself and one for Maizy, when the two water fetchers walked in. "Set out another plate, my Sil," Maizy enlightened her. "We got a guest to table this evening."

Silvie, dressed in a blue gingham smock with a white ruffled apron, turned with a look of surprise, but her face lit up when she realized who the guest for supper would be. Quickly, Silvie dabbed away a fleck of cooking flour from her nose that Maizy subtly brought to her attention by motioning in pantomime.

"Evening, Miss Silvie," Joe said, a little nervous.

"Evening to you, Joe," Silvie replied in like manner, brushing back a wisp of stray hair with her hand. Then, they both just stood there for a few awkward moments, shooting glances at Maizy and then at each other.

Maizy cleared both her throat and the tense atmosphere. "My, but doesn't that stew smell good! And the bread! Do you know, Joe, that Silvie baked that loaf fresh this evening? Baked it especially for you, when she heard you might be coming to the inn."

"Mama!" Silvie protested with panic, clearly embarrassed.

But Joe's, "I'm sure that it's good if you made it, Silvie," had an immediate calming effect upon the girl. And, oh how she beamed.

Then the three new friends sat and ate and conversed with one another, and as they did, the opaque barrier of doubt and mistrust melted away. Three souls enmeshed that day. Three little souls, cast together, as though by destiny. But oh, if they could only know where that destiny would eventually lead them . . .

Supper ended. "We haven't been seeing much of you, or Mr. Travis, of late, Joe," Maizy said, pouring out three tall glasses of buttermilk from an earthen pitcher. "I know that there's more than one young lady in this household who's been pining over her fellow's whereabouts. Miss Becky and . . . " she paused for dramatic effect, " . . . somebody else!" But, instead of blushing, Silvie only smiled bewitchingly at Joe, signifying to Joe that he had at least gotten his feet into the doorway of her heart.

"I've been minding shop, down at the law office," Joe offered in explanation, while slurping down a big draught of buttermilk. "Taking and going messages and such. I miss my visits here, too, as does Shan, my horse. She's always one for a canter. But Travis is gone quite a bit now, what with all the talk brewing of a fight with Mexico. Travis says how Santa Anna's gone and stomped on all the freedoms set up by the honorable Mexican constitution of 1824. Made hisself a dictator. That's like an overseer of slave folk who tells you to 'do this,' or 'do that,' or else be punished. Only Santa Anna fancies hisself an overseer of all Mexico, Texas included! A lot of the colonists, Master Travis included, won't hear of such and are planning to fight. Talk is how Travis and twelve riders raided a cabbalada—that's a place where they raise horses—in the fierce wilderness, near Laredo. Ran off with three hundred saddle-broke Mexican mounts and got back safely, all in ten days! If I hadn't've been stuck in the law office, I'd've see it myself," Joe added, with a tinge of regret. "Anyhow, the master got a commission in the cavalry for that from Governor Smith, on the recommendation of Stephen Austin hisself! He's a full-fledged Lieutenant Colonel now, though some say that Santa Anna's put a price on his head."

"I don't like to hear such talk of war," Silvie frowned. "People get killed in wars. They lose their lives, their homes, and each other. Then what are the womenfolk to do without their men? And the children?"

Joe remonstrated. "Travis say's that if the people of Texas don't stop Santa Anna now, then there won't be any future worth the living for anyone. I've been on raids with the Colonel before and I'll most likely be on 'em again sometime in the future. I'm sorry, Miss Silvie, but that's just the way that life turns sometimes."

Hearing this, Silvie pressed her lips together in silent dissent and anguish, laid down her half finished glass of buttermilk, and then folded her hands in her lap, while her eyes welled with tears.

"Now, now," Maizy declared. "There's no sense in ruining a perfectly good supper over such things, while it's still light outside. I'll clear up here and you two can take a turn down by the creek. The air is especially mild. Run along now," she bid them, dismissing both Joe and Silvie as though they were but mere children and in the way.

Joe and Silvie took their turn down by the water's edge, while the mill wheel creaked, the water gurgled, and their hands and hearts joined fast for the very first time.

Seven

A Joining Journey

The series of events which hurtled Joe, Silvie, and Maizy toward the presidio of San Antonio de Bejar were both varied and exciting. Talk of war led to the genuine article itself, when a detachment of General Cos' cavalry from Bejar were driven off by a band of armed citizens from the town of Gonzales in a scuffle over a small cannon. The almost useless, small-caliber gun had originally been given to the citizens of that town by the Mexican authorities to ward off marauding Indians. But when Cos and his 1,500 men landed in Texas at Copano, under orders from Cos' brother-in-law, Santa Anna, Cos occupied Bejar, declared martial law, and then set off to confiscate all firearms from the colonists. The men of Gonzales responded by taunting the cavalry to "Come And Take It." The Gonzales cannon banged off a wild shot, the troopers withdrew, and the war was officially on. Texian militia quickly responded, subduing the Mexican garrison at Goliad, while Jim Bowie and his volunteers defeated a force four times their number at the mission Concepcion, near Bejar. Soon, the push was on for Bejar itself. After a short siege, Cos surrendered the town and the Alamo up to Texian commanders Austin and Burleson, whereupon Cos and his men were paroled back to Mexico under terms that they should nevermore take up arms against Texas. Santa Anna, however, would later break this pledge of honor for Cos himself.

During the course of this short-lived conflict, Travis and his cavalry had been busily engaged in burning forage grass and bridges as a means of harassing the enemy. But such action had only served to make the young Lt. Colonel feel cheated. He wanted real action, such as befit his rank; not the petty grass burning duties of a junior officer.

Well, Travis got his wish soon enough. It was after he'd returned to San Felipe from the region of Bejar that he received the order; received it from the newly appointed Texian commander-in-chief, Sam Houston himself! It happened on a day in mid-January. Travis was pouring over some paperwork of his long-neglected practice when, without warning, Houston's large frame filled the doorway of the law office. Six-foot-six, some soldiers bragged the general was, and to the five-foot-nine Joe, he seemed even taller. Houston was broad-shouldered, square-jawed, and barrel-chested—*such as every general should be,* Joe mused. Although apparently only in his early forties, Houston's auburn-tinged full beard was shot with gray. His steel-gray eyes demanded attention and usually got it.

"General," Travis saluted, rising from his chair. "Do come in and have a seat. Something to drink?"

"No need, Joe," Houston waved off, as Joe was about to uncork a decanter of port wine. "Houston prefers to stand . . . and he carries his own," he added, patting his coat to indicate a hidden flask. "But to the business at hand. Travis, I need you to recruit a force of cavalry to reinforce Colonel Neil's position at Bejar. The Mexicans have the finest cavalry on the North American continent at their disposal, while the Texas army has but a few farmer boys on plow horses. Neill himself has scarcely a hundred men in Bejar and they're all volunteer infantry. Neill allows that the Alamo defenses are all in a shambles and adds that should a malevolent cavalry force swoop down upon the place, the garrison would be left with no avenue for withdrawal. In effect, they'd be trapped and at the mercy of skillful lancers. That's why Houston forcefully stresses to you the importance of rallying and training a decent cavalry force. A hundred well-equipped riders in Bejar might be a godsend. I dispatched Jim Bowie thither to better apprise me of the true situation, but Bowie only has thirty or so men under his command. If he decides that Bejar should be maintained, then that piddling force will not suffice. I cannot further stress the urgency or the necessity of your task, save to remind you that the salvation of Texas is at risk. So rally as many men as you can possibly influence."

"What about my expenses?" Travis inquired hopefully.

"As to funds, I myself have only fifty Yankee dollars and my blessings to aid you in your recruiting efforts. The provisional government of Texas has visions of grandeur, but a decidedly barren treasury. Just do the best you can. The focus of my own immediate attention is upon the Cherokee. Rumors abound that Santa Anna may seek to influence that tribe against the Texian cause. But, as an adopted son of Cherokee chief, John Jolly, Houston may still exert a little influence of his own. So off to John Jolly goes Houston. May our joined efforts meet with success, Lieutenant Colonel Travis."

Travis immediately set up a recruiting station there in his law office and, along with Houston's fifty dollars, kicked in fifty of his own to set about provisioning his pending cavalry unit. Joe, meanwhile, helped to pack the goods necessary toward keeping a mounted unit in the saddle for an extended period of time. These included flour, tinware, coffee, sugar, corn, and warm woolen blankets. Travis also kicked in the added incentive of seventeen dollars in advance to any volunteer who would agree to sign on for the duration of winter. But, in spite of these spirited efforts and Travis' gift of the gab, all Travis could muster by January 22, 1836, were thirty-nine men.

"Thirty-nine!" Travis spat in disgust, trotting alongside of Joe on their way toward Mill Creek and the bosom of their sweethearts. But this particular visit was more than a mere social call; it was the eve of Travis, Joe and Company's departure for Bejar and this was a time of farewell.

"Thirty-nine!" Travis repeated in exasperation. "Hardly the hundred I'd anticipated rallying!"

"Well," Joe considered in a futile effort to cheer up the Colonel, "at least we won't have to worry about running out of provisions for a while."

"Provisions be hanged!" Travis shot back, none the cheerier. "Leading thirty-nine men to Bejar is as useful as leading none. When Santa Anna arrives there in mid-March—and it's a certainty he will—his thousands will chew up and spit out thirty-nine like hors d'ouvres! All we can hope for is to perhaps pick up a few more volunteers along the way. Meanwhile," Travis paused, shifting thought, "it going to be difficult to break the news of our departure to Becky. She's all against my going to Bejar and, if I were in my right mind, I'd agree with her and post off a request to Governor Smith to relieve me of command of so few men! At least you won't have to be saying your good-byes to Silvie and Maizy, Joe—they'll both be accompanying us on our journey. No offense intended, but Maizy's cornbread and beans are a deal more palatable than yours. And anyway, she and Silvie can act in the capacity of nurse, should the need arise."

Silvie, on her way to a possible battle! Joe cringed on the thought. He didn't like it—didn't like it one bit. But he kept his silence, all the same and rode on, hoping for the best.

"It's a good thing that we travel light, anyway," Maizy remarked, as Joe was loading up a pack mule with the ladies' canvas bags. "There's not that much room on a mule's rump for a lady to light upon." But, be that as it might, when Joe offered Silvie the comforts of riding double with him astride the bay, Shannon, Maizy curtailed the notion. "Wouldn't be proper for a single young lady to be getting so familiar. And in front of all those men! Wouldn't be proper!"

It was time to go. So, after bidding his Rebecca and her brother John a tearful farewell, Travis and Joe headed back for San Felipe on horseback, while Maizy and Silvie trailed along upon a rather laden mule.

The volunteers Travis had recruited were waiting near the law office when the foursome arrived back in town. A quick roll call, a check of provisions later, and the small parcel of riders—the Texas Cavalry—was off for Bejar at last.

There would be at least one detour along the way, however, for Travis fully intended to see his little son, Charles, a towheaded youngster of six, whom Travis had been keeping at a boarding school near Washington-on-the-Brazos. When the troop arrived at the school, the little boy received his father with delight and a request.

"Please, Father, I need four bits in the worst way."

"My son," Travis replied warmly, "what do you need with four bits?"

"To buy some molasses from Missus Scott to make candy with," came the reply.

"But four bits, Charlie! Why such an enormous sum for a dime bottle of molasses?"

"Why, to make enough for my entire class, Father!"

He got his four bits. And the very last image that Travis and Joe ever had of Charles was of a beaming young boy proudly holding a steaming cookie sheet of fresh-made candy.

As the troop trotted onward, ever onward, across the barren landscape for San Antonio, icy blue-northers cut through even the most heavy of the troopers' coats. It was well for the riders that Travis had had the foresight of providing each of them with a warm, woolen blanket. Some of the men, Joe noted, had cut neck holes in the blankets for wearing in the saddle, serape-style.

Then it rained. Not misty drizzle, or a warm summer's shower, but a good, old-fashioned, seek out all the dry places, winter's downpour. No one and nothing was spared. Hunching down as best they could did no good; the ranging procession of riders was soon soaked to the skin and chilled to the bone. It was as though the powerful elements of wind and water had joined together in a common fury to drive both men and beasts into submission.

When Travis finally called a halt at Burham's crossing on the Colorado River, the storm had, for the most part, spent itself. But the winds continued. Playing across the surface of the water, they whipped up a swirl of fine mist, straight into the faces of the suffering troop. Travis ordered bonfires ignited. Soon, steaming pyres of wetted wood were hissing in protest and casting up billows of white smoke. Around these the soggy soldiers crowded, trying to dry off and ease the chill out of their bones. Coffee was brewed up and when Silvie brought Joe a big, billowy tin of it out to where he was standing watch over the hobbled horses and pack mules, he felt all the warmer still.

"Didn't figure to be bringing you into a situation like this, Silvie," Joe said, hugging his welcome tin of coffee for its warmth. "At least the Cummings Inn was warm and clean—and safe."

"Don't you go fretting on my account, Joe," Silvie replied in a half-scolding tone. "I heard some of the men talking around the campfire. They say that it's not too much further to San Antonio de Bejar and San Antonio's supposed to be an even bigger town than San Felipe—and more comfortable. But anyhow, comfort's not everything. I'm usually one to dread packing up and moving on to face the unknown, but just knowing that you'll be there too makes it seem that much easier—and more welcome. I'm," she hesitated for a heartbeat, "I'm glad we're together, Joe."

Joe dropped his half-empty cup and tenderly took Silvie's hand. "I feel exactly the same as you do, Silvie," he said softly. "And from this minute on, I'm going to try and prove myself worthy of your attention—and trust."

In that moment, both Joe's and Silvie's pulses quickened, for they had revealed the secrets of their hearts at last and had not come up wanting. But as they stood oblivious, staring into the depths of each other's eyes, other less-than-caring eyes stared at them.

"I say knock 'em both over the head and grab the stock," spoke the owner of one pair of observing eyes. "Can't wait all blamed night!"

"Madre de Dios!' replied the impatient observer's companion. "You cannot strike a helpless senorita, companero. Paciencio—have patience, por favor."

"Cut the Mex lingo and talk American!" the impatient one snapped back. "Patience, my bum!"

"Silencia!" the companion cautioned, "someone comes."

"Sorry to be interrupting you two," Maizy half-apologized, breaking Joe and Silvie's reverie, "but it's getting late. Silvie and I'll be early risers tomorrow, getting the breakfast going for everyone. We'd best be getting back to the fire, Silvie," Maizy concluded with finality. "See you in the morning, Joe," she said speaking for both herself and the still glowing girl.

Poor Joe: off his guard and still on a cloud, he made an easy target for the two horse snatchers. Stealthy footsteps, a pistol-butt across the back of the head, it was over very quickly. Joe was unconscious before he even hit the ground.

The next thing Joe remembered it was daylight and he was staring up into the faces of Silvie, Maizy, and Travis. In spite of the cool poultice that Silvie was applying to it, his head throbbed something awful. "Holy jeez," he moaned, trying to rise and then thinking the better of it when his head sank back down of its own volition. "Holy jeez, what happened?"

"Take a care, Joe," Travis cautioned. "You've got quite the knot on your noggin. I'm afraid that a dozen or so deserters absconded last evening with all of our supplies and pack mules. Must've been just after midnight. Don't worry," he added, sensing Joe's rising alarm, "Shannon's safe."

"Thank the Lord for that," Joe exhaled in relief. "But deserters, Colonel? All the supplies?"

"It wasn't your fault, Joe," Travis reassured him. "The important thing now is that you are all right."

"Amen to that," Silvie interjected warmly.

"Meanwhile," Travis continued, "if you think that you can ride in your present condition, then I believe we'd best be getting on our way. The sooner we arrive in San Antonio, the better."

So the depleted party rode on and, in the absence of the mule, Joe and Silvie rode double, as did Maizy and a scrawny, sixteen-year-old volunteer, whose plowhorse proved more than accommodating. And although Joe's head ached and his stomach growled, the feel of Silvie's arms around his waist and the sweetness of her hot breath upon his collar more than balanced out the sting of those personal inequities. For all Joe cared, San Antonio could be a million miles away.

Eight

San Antone—Set a Spell, Why Doncha?

"So that's San Antonio," Silvie observed admiringly, peeking over Joe's shoulder from where she sat on horseback. "It's green! And how the water from the river sparkles. And the buildings—why they're plastered over milk white, not like those bare boarded houses in San Felipe."

"Bejar's an old town, Silvie," Travis briefed her, as with a wave of his hand, he reined up his trail weary procession of riders below a small ford that waded a branch of the Alamo acequia. This was trail's end of the old San Antonio road, Travis went on to explain. Any traveler with sudden eastward inclinations could follow the glorified trace clear back to the Sabine River and the U. S. of A. But that homesick pilgrim would first have to bypass this muddied lot of thirsty riders, for eastward was anything but their destination. Wherever San Antonio de Bejar was, they were there.

The avenue leading toward the town was flanked on both sides by rows of stately, if gnarled, pecan trees that guided the approaching cavalry troop up the principal thoroughfare of Bejar in a most royal fashion. But this "Royal Road" of bygone days now went by the less than glorious name of Portrero Street.

How the horses neighed in acknowledgment of the cool water playing upon their hot hooves, as Travis' command splashed across the little ditch, then drew up before a rude plank footbridge. To their immediate right, just north of Bejar, stood a collection of meager huts surrounded by a low, crumbling rust colored wall and overshadowed by a more imposing stone ruin. "This was Fort Alamo," Travis said. Once a Spanish mission, the place had served as a station for troops guarding the town since 1793. Judging from its present appearance though, the Alamo seemed far from military-like, for aside from a lone figure that strolled upon the roof of one of its adobe buildings, the Alamo appeared all but deserted.

Travis pointed off toward the ruin. "We'll head for the fort, gentlemen," he commanded, to the collective sigh of his parched-throated men. "The cantinas of Bejar will just have to keep."

As Travis' cavalry drew up before the long stretch of weathered wall, it was met with initial disinterest by a shoddy lot of militiamen who lay sprawled beneath the shade of a covered arbor. Just the sight of them was more than Travis could bear. In indignant fury, he announced himself, then demanded to see Colonel Neill.

One of the loafers, all in tatters and clawing at the anatomy beneath them, responded at length. "Culnal Neill's in town to his own business," the fellow yawned in a slow, wearisome drawl. "We's on guard duty. Set a spell, why doncha?"

To his credit, Travis said nothing. With a look of exasperation, he turned his horsemen back toward the footbridge and then headed for Bejar proper. As they clattered over the footbridge and into Portrero Street, the town of Bejar spread out before the riders in a clutter of disarray and careless abandon. While Portrero itself seemed to expand and narrow with amazing facility, four or five other streets fanned off from it in no particular direction and toward who knew where or much cared. "Fella who laid out these streets must've been drunk," Joe said in a quizzical tone that caused Travis to chuckle.

"You're not too far from the mark at that Joe. Some say that the Indian name for San Antonio is 'Drunken Man Going Home At Night,' or words to that effect."

At last, relief from the tiresome maze was gained when Portrero Street emptied the riders out onto the Main Plaza before the large domed San Fernando Church. It was early afternoon and so the mercado or marketplace was a bustle of activity, with vendors hawking their assorted wares in open-air stands and oxcarts. One clever tamale entrepreneur had his table set up in front of the shop of Nat Lewis in the hopes of catching some of the North American merchantman's clientele, both coming and going.

"The best place to get news in your average town is either the barber's shop or the local tavern," Travis clued Joe. "But it's a good bet that the men we are seeking are not being barbered at the moment. We'll inquire within there," Travis said, gesturing toward a nearby building that had the word CANTINA emblazoned in bold, broad letters across its façade. "We'll light here, ladies," Travis told Maizy and Silvie. "Boys!" he shouted at the men, "Dismount and stretch your legs a bit. Joe, you come with me."

Travis and Joe entered the cantina through a brace of creaky swinging doors and then panned the room for familiar faces. They found one, no, two. For tucked away in a shadowy corner of the dimly-lit room sat none other than Jim Bowie himself, semi-engaged in a conversation with Colonel Neill. Travis approached the seated officers and made himself known.

"Neill," Travis began, extending his hand solely as a formality, "what the deuce is going on here? My cavalry's been assigned to help bolster the garrison here in Bejar and yet it would appear that the better part of that garrison is either drunk, or hard intent at becoming so. Drunk or sober, their functionality as soldiers remains decidedly suspect. The Alamo," he continued tersely, "is in no better shape than when captured from Cos, back in December—nor, I perceive, are its commandants. Colonel Bowie," Travis saluted haughtily, "your servant, sir! Pray, do not get up on my account. Most likely, you are incapable of the feat. Neill," he continued, "how many men do you have here, drunk or sober?"

The seated colonel considered Travis thoughtfully, before responding. And while the effects of the alcohol played upon his reasoning faculties, his fat fingers played upon the ends of his droopy moustache. "Hunneret an' four," Neill slurred. "Mos'ly drunk. Try it yourself. Does wonders toward one's presentiments that he can actually hold this sprawling metropolis against God knows how many thousands trained troops Santanna's got up his sleeve. Welcome to the Alamo and Be'ar, Buck," Neill concluded, extending his hand at long last to meet Travis' grip.

"I've twenty-seven men and horses to quarter," Travis said, returning Neill's handshake. "They'll be housed in the Alamo, of course. May I be so bold as to suggest that playtime is over? This garrison is in sore need of a more pressing pastime. We've got to band together as brothers and whip that mission into shape and soon, or else it is Santa Anna who will so engage in the whipping of our collective buttocks, clear to the Sabine! My men shall be granted the remainder of the day off to refresh themselves and get billeted. I suggest we commence with work parties on the morrow, over at the Alamo. Is it agreed?"

Jim Bowie looked up. Though his eyes were a-glaze with fever, he focused them upon this young pup of an officer who seemed so intent on single-handedly challenging the might of all Mexico. "You can count on the officers to work, Travis," Bowie began, "but the men are all volunteers and so have to be paid for their services, or it's no go. There hasn't been a single Yankee dollar in Bejar for over a month. Those men yet hanging on here are only doing so because they lack the funds to leave. The more adventuresome of the foolhardy, as you know, traipsed off with Grant and Johnson on their 'Matamoros expedition,' a scheme that they hoped would carry the war to Santanna himself! They stripped Bejar of all her stores and then marched off with the wild notion of pillaging Matamoros and thereafter, rallying the disgruntled local Mexicans to their cause, to boot. Most probable, we shan't see them again. Two hundred men, expended for naught. Fortifying and holding the Alamo," Bowie continued, "is not an idea new to us. Both Neill and myself have expressed and stressed the point to Houston, who'd advised us to dismantle the place and withdraw the garrison, if we thought it prudent. But that would be cowed submission before the fact, and we are not so hangdog yet that we should consider such a course, or line of thou . . . "

Bowie was cut short in his delivery by a fit of wheezy coughing that tore at his chest, causing him to grip the table's edge with white knuckles. When the fit released its grip on him at last, Bowie rallied for another effort.

"We'll gather what men we can and meet you in the mission at first light . . . maybe second light," he reconsidered.

Though Travis' men were lodged in the Alamo, Travis himself took up quarters at an inn on Main Plaza as a sort of temporary base of operations from where he could get the lowdown of happenings in town. And while he saw to it that Maizy and Silvie had a room to themselves, Joe bunked on a pallet on Travis' floor. As there was no livery located near the inn, Joe concluded to house the bay mare, Shannon, in a covered stable in the Alamo. It was only a few hundred yards or so from the inn and, anyway, Joe did not mind the walk.

It was the morning of a glorious, sunshiny day when the town was just beginning to stir. In the porte-cochere of the inn, Maizy stood, shaking and airing out both her and Silvie's "personals" with a look of mild distaste.

"Wrinkles and horsy scent," she observed, wrinkling her nose, at the same moment Joe walked out of Travis' room. "Reckon I'll have to wash the whole kit and caboodle. Morning, Joe," she hailed. "Trust you slept well. What, may I ask you, did you learn in the cantina yesterday? Master Travis' dander really seemed up when he came a'stomping out of that place."

"Slept fine, Maizy," Joe returned. "Well, it seems that Colonels Neill, Bowie, and Travis are of a mind of staying in Bejar to get ready for Santa Anna. Master Travis says how it's a certainty that Santa'll be coming with a large army. We got barely a hundred and thirty men here, counting both sick and wounded. Didn't set well with Travis, not at all."

"Hard news," Maizy said with a frown, "not very hopeful. I'm afraid for Texas, but mainly, I fear for both you and Silvie, Joe. Why don't you and Silvie go and draw some fresh water from that ditch I saw running by the church? I'll be needing it to launder all of these clothes. With things happening so fast and uncertain now, perhaps it's a good thing for you to be spending as much time with Silvie as you can. Don't mean to push and don't mean to pry, but that little girl loves you and I know that you love her too."

"Miss Maizy!" Joe interjected in surprise, but Maizy merely shushed him.

"No, let me finish, Joe. You both love each other and deserve a fine courtship, but in times like these, perhaps that propriety just needs to get set aside. You got to start considering your future and when I say 'you,' I mean you and Silvie as a couple. Think on that, Joe. Think hard. Now, here's Silvie," she trailed off abruptly as the girl herself appeared at the door. "Get me that water, Joe," she continued, not even greeting Silvie. "There's a big earthen jar in our room—Silvie can show you. Remember what I said. Now, go on."

"What was that all about?" Silvie asked, as she and Joe were strolling across the plaza to draw their water from the San Pedro ditch, near the San Fernando Church.

Joe thought for a moment about the all things that Maizy had said to him—and their implications. Then he responded. "The signs of the times, Silvie," he said mysteriously, "the signs of the times."

Nine

Moonlight Fandango

Thanks to Maizy, Joe and Silvie saw a good deal more of each other over the next few days. For, while Travis' focus was upon strengthening the mission defenses across the river, Maizy's was upon keeping Joe and Silvie together. Her tenacious efforts to wrangle over Travis' indulgence finally paid off one morning.

"I need Joe's help in town," Maizy pleaded in an earnestness that did her proud. "There's so much to be done and so little time, sir!"

"Do you need Joe's assistance to work, or are you working on Joe?" Travis countered facetiously, a twinkle in his eye.

"Why, I daresay I don't know what you mean, Colonel Travis," Maizy replied, putting her hand up along side of her cheek in feigned shock and humility.

"All right Maizy," Travis laughed, "but cease and desist these constant implorations. I've still a bit of the romantic in me, you know."

Joe and Silvie got their time. Time for sunlit strolls along the lazy river. Time for searches through the marketplace to marvel over and to sample the many fresh foodstuffs there. Time to pay a visit with Sue Dickerson and her infant daughter, Angie, at the Musquoz's dwelling adjacent to the inn. Time to just sit together for a quiet moment beneath the shade of a bougainvillea-laden trellis to watch delicate blossoms floating gracefully to the floor of the tile patio upon the gentle breeze; time for being young and in love.

But time would not stand still, nor would events keep, as the afternoon of February the 8th was met by the unheralded arrival of sixteen of the most colorful-looking horsemen that Joe had ever seen. Up Portrero Street they came, raising both a cloud of dust and a crowd of curious spectators. Some of the riders sported frock coats and feather-crowned plug hats; others, simple homespuns, beaded buckskins and floppy felt hats. All were armed to the teeth. At the head of this peculiar parade rode a tall, wiry-looking old cuss, whose tangled, shoulder-length, flint-gray hair aptly matched the hue of his twinkling eyes. Eyes that were set back into a weathered, if rosy-complexioned, bone hollow face that looked somewhat grizzled, for want of a razor's edge. His presence did not go unnoticed for long.

"By gawd, it's Davy Crockett, or I'm a liar!" an observant volunteer hollered. And so it was. Davy Crockett, the living legend—there in San Antonio! The word spread fast until, before long, the plaza was filled with a throng of both citizen and soldier alike, all eager to catch a glimpse of the famous backwoodsman, bear hunter and ex-congressman from the illustrious state of Tennessee. Cries of "Speech, speech," resounded, somebody brought forth an old packing crate for Crockett to stand on and he didn't disappoint them. Removing his trademark coonskin cap, and pressing it to the center of his buckskin-jacketed chest, Crockett proceeded to speechify the multitudes in high form, concluding with:

"As my constituents have not seen fit to reelecting me to Congress, I have determined to remain here in San Antonio, fight for Texas liberty, and die in her defense, like the patriots of '76, if needs be!" There was a cheer of approval from the crowd when Crockett added: "No, I will not die! I shall grin down the walls of the Alamo and then lick up that pesky Spaniard, Santa Anna, like fine salt!" Another barrage of hearty cheering followed, whereupon Crockett stepped down to "mix it up with just the plain folks."

Travis, accompanied by Joe, personally escorted Crockett toward the cantina where the Tennessee Mounted Volunteers were already hard intent at whetting their whistles; apparently they'd heard Davy's speech before.

Before too long the cantina and its adjoining patio was teeming with people eager to get in on the celebration of Crockett's arrival. For others, any opportunity to party was enough of an excuse to gather, for this was a fandango sort of town.

As fandangos went, it was a humdinger! The transformation of the cantina from a lazy drinking establishment into a festive ballroom was a magical thing for Joe to behold. In no time, streamers, bunting, and colorful goody-filled pinatas decked rafters, cross beams, and tree limbs, while colored paper lanterns called luminarias, festooned the cantina patio like the grandest of dance floors.

Come dark and a bedazzling burst of fireworks lit up the night sky, to the accompaniment of the "oohs" and "ahs" of entranced onlookers. On top of all this, it was hard indeed for anyone with a romantic bone in his body to resist the cast of San Antonio's magical spell, when the air along the river hung full with an almost intoxicating fragrance of tropical foliage. Add a million stars encrusting the expanse of sky like a mass of diamond slivers flung upon sable, mix with the romantic strains of a Spanish guitar and the delirium was complete—so long as a fellow had a girl on his arm. *Why*, Joe gasped in surprise, *wasn't that Travis himself at the center of the dance floor with a pretty senorita in tow?*

"Looks like fun, Joe," Maizy's voice observed from over Joe's shoulder, momentarily breaking the spell. But when Joe turned around to see Silvie trailing Maizy from out of the darkness of the street, the spell resumed at full tilt and he had to gulp and look again. Silvie looked radiant. She was decked out like a regular Spanish lady, complete with off-the-shoulder blouse and close-fitting bodice and her hair was pulled back with a mantilla. The red shawl draped across her otherwise bare extended arm and the fan that she practiced waving completed the picture.

"Colonel Travis gave us a little spending money and we did a little shopping," Maizy explained with a look of triumph, gauging Joe's reaction.

"Spent well," Joe gagged appreciatively. "Spent well." Then he just stood there staring.

"Well," Maizy asked impatiently, "aren't you going to ask the lady to dance?" The question was accompanied by a shove that practically catapulted Joe into Silvie.

"Dance?" Joe blurted clumsily. "Would you...can you...may I...?" He stammered, clearly at a loss for words.

"Love to," Silvie bubbled, holding out her slender arm—the one without the fan—to her escort.

And this time, Joe knew what to do. There, in the shadows outside the patio, the young couple selected their own dance floor and made use of it. They danced and Joe swept the eager, graceful girl around the shadows with an intoxicating fervor, swirling, spinning, reversing; step, two three, step two, three; bow, curtsey and then repeat.

"My head is swimming; I am breathless, Joe," Silvie said, swaying giddily. "We must sit—a glass of punch, please."

"Sure thing, Silvie," Joe responded oh so willingly. "Set a bit on this low tiled wall here while I fetch us some."

But in truth, Silvie didn't want the punch that badly. "No need to rush, Joe," she said, gently tugging his arm to hold him back. "Just setting can be nice. Why," she pondered aloud, looking across the room with sudden interest, "would you look at Maizy, talking with Colonel Travis? I wonder what she's up to?"

Joe didn't see it. "What's unusual about that," he replied, puzzled. "Maizy and the Colonel do talk, you know."

"Pay attention," Silvie said impatiently. "Don't you see how they keep shooting glances over at us. Mama's up to something."

Finally, Joe's curiosity got piqued and he watched with interest as Maizy pointed and Travis looked sidelong, over to where he and Silvie were sitting. After a few moments, Travis nodded and Maizy took her leave with a half bow. Then Maizy walked over to the refreshment table, snagged two glasses of punch, and headed straightway for the wondering and worn dance couple by the low-tiled wall.

"Thought you could use some punch," Maizy beamed, giving Joe and Silvie a glass each. "I was speaking with Mr. Travis and—"

"We saw you were, Maizy," Joe cut in without invitation. "What was it all about?"

"Well, if you'll stop interrupting me and listen, I'll tell you. As I said, I was speaking with Mr. Travis and he allows how you and Silvie should take out the trap and give those poor horses a little exercise. Says that those poor beasts most especially dote over the moonlight on the river. Give those poor creatures a break," Maizy concluded in her most convincing tone of earnestness. "Won't you?"

"Horses?" Joe rejoined, stupefied. He still didn't get it. "Trap? We got no horses and trap, Maizy. What in tarnation are you talking . . . about?" But Joe saw and heard, before he even finished the sentence, as the anxious neigh of one of the horses betrayed the trap's presence in the shadows. How Maizy had conjured up the conveyance on such short notice only increased Joe's wonderment and respect for her. But, dumbfounded as he was, the smile on Joe's face said it all and expressed, he hoped, his undying thanks.

But it was Silvie who radiated the moment with an unabashed, toothy grin. *She really likes him*, she told her secret self. *She really does!*

"Run along now," Maizy reassured the two novice courters. "It's all right." They moved on her word.

Sensing Joe and Silvie's approach, the horses looked over inquisitively. But it was just another job for them after all, as Joe lifted Silvie onto the cushion of the trap then followed her up into the seat. Kicking the brake free, Joe started the horses forward with a commanding "Gee yaw" and a tug at the reins.

It was a beautiful night for a moonlight ride. As the trap rattled on, Joe followed the course of the winding San Antonio River for effect—and such effect! With the moon glistening across the face of the rippling waters and the steady cadence of insect song drumming in their brains, the young couple was soon soothed into a deep reverie.

"Joe," Silvie asked, breaking their silence at last. "Can we cross over to the other side of the river when we reach the La Villita ford? I'd dearly love to view the old Alamo by moonlight!"

They crossed over.

"All my life, I have dreamed of taking such a carriage ride," Silvie gushed. "But I never dreamed it would be as wonderful as this. Oh, I used to take haycart rides as a child, along with Maizy and the other children, back at the Sanders' place, but that is not the same thing; it cannot be compared. I," she paused with a sultry, sidelong glance, "I should have refused to go, you know. It's not considered a proper thing, the both of us taking off unchaperoned and in the dead of night! We are not married—no, not even spoken for! Maizy would've tanned my hide for sure over such a thing only a few months ago. I wonder what made her change her mind?"

"Maybe she knows something that we don't," Joe replied, sliding his free arm around Silvie's bare shoulders. "Or maybe it's just something that we've both been trying to avoid thinking on. War is coming to San Antonio and with its outcome being so uncertain, maybe Maizy thinks . . . maybe she feels that this may be our last chance to do such a thing—for a long, long time, I mean," Joe added, trying to sound less ominous.

Silvie pressed her head deep into Joe's shoulder. "Oh, Joe," she said, trembling. "Let's make the most of this night then. The very most."

"That we'll do," Joe avowed, holding Silvie even tighter and closer still. "But what would you say to a walk? I can brake the trap here and give the horses a feed. That'll give us some time to stroll the grounds of the mission. It looks especially grand at night, doesn't it?"

Silvie could not have agreed more. So Joe smiled, alighted from the trap and then lifted Silvie down, his strong hands fully encircling her waist. *This was so deliciously wicked*, Silvie thought to herself. *Unheard of! Unchaperoned—completely alone with a man! You shameless thing, Silvie*, she playfully scolded herself, chuckling inwardly all the while, for she was loving every second of it.

They began walking along a deeply rutted dirt road whose uneven surface was pocked with innumerable chuckholes that made footing especially dubious for all the night shadows. So it was that Silvie nearly turned her ankle in one of the invisible indentations. But Joe was there and he caught her up and drew her close and then they ambled on.

Just ahead of them, out of the darkness, the sun-bleached walls of the Alamo suddenly solidified, giving off a more definite outline for the couple to beat toward. Not that it would've mattered that much to either of them, though. For they could've been walking in circles and curly-queues, for all they cared. That they were walking together heart in heart and hand in hand was the main thing; on and on and on . . .

The Alamo looked kind of eerie under the soft moonlight. Why, it shone forth as a sort of pale blue, both milky and translucent.

A narrow bridge over an irrigation ditch led Joe and Silvie into a small yard in front of the cavernous looking Alamo church. They strode forward for a look.

"Why, it looks like a big cave in there," Silvie exclaimed, pointing through the building's arched portal. "Brings to mind an old bat cave we used to play in as children. We'd pitch stones up at the dark places and then run for dear life when the bats came a'flooding out. Let's try our luck," she said playfully. "Pick up a stone and follow me."

Joe scooped up a stone and then followed Silvie through the church's doorway. "There," Silvie pointed, indicating the crevices of some broken arches. "Cast your stone to the top and then see what happens!"

Joe cocked back and pitched his pebble. There was a re-echoing clatter, followed soon after by the fluttering sound of many wings. Some of the frightened and confused creatures reacted by swooping down low to the ground and one of them—white as marble—hit Silvie square on the side of the head.

"Sweet Jesus!" she screamed in terror, throwing both of her arms around Joe in a reflex motion. "Sweet Jesus! Ghost bats!"

Joe reacted by drawing Silvie even nearer still. "No ghosts, Honey," he chuckled softly, giving her a reassuring squeeze. "Only doves. As frightened as you, I expect!"

Seizing the moment, Silvie used her trembling to full advantage. "Hold me, Joe," she whimpered in instinctive exaggeration. "Don't let go!"

"Let you go? Silvie, I'll never let you go!"

Then he kissed her and she kissed him back, and the frightened doves returned to their nests and began to coo.

Ten

Parting Promise

The depths of a person's heart can sometimes be measured by the course of action he elects to follow, even though the following of that course might knowingly lead him to forsake the desires and feelings of that heart. When selfless disregard of one's own desires becomes an easy choice in considering the well being of another, that choice constitutes love of a very special pedigree. So it was that Joe found himself upon the threshold of his own true feelings for Silvie. The previous evening, there in the hollow of the Alamo church, they had freely and outwardly expressed their depth of feeling in the exchange of love's first kiss. Now, in the quiet of the early morning, Joe harbored serious thoughts of sending Silvie away.

    As far as his own well being was concerned, Joe could accept the idea of facing the coming war head-on, if push came to shove, but oh how he longed to spare Silvie of it. *If only she'd have stayed in San Felipe*, Joe thought, figuratively kicking himself. *But now that she was in San Antonio, how to get her away?* As sympathetic as Travis had been in the past, even he could bend only so much to Maizy's winning ways. Anyway, Joe reasoned, it wasn't Maizy's place to get things done for him. This was his fight and his problem. *How*, he pondered on, *How, how, how?*

    But, as mysteriously as it sometimes will do, fate stepped in to cast its own deciding vote. For as Joe sat pondering and deliberating over how he was going to manage to get Silvie to safety, the solution presented itself in the person of Colonel Neill.

Thunk, thunk, thunk, went the rap on the inn's door and Joe answered to find Neill standing there in both the dark and a suit of traveling clothes.

"Is Travis up?" Neill asked, without further greeting or display of formality.

"Travis is," William Barret replied, tucking his shirt into his trousers, and then stepping out from behind a partition. "What brings you here of such an early hour, Neill? We've no coffee to offer you, I'm afraid."

"No social call, Buck," Neill replied gravely. "Strictly military matters. To the point, if we don't get sufficient funds or provisions to sustain our men and soon, a lot of them will likely desert Bejar for more promising pastures. I myself have some influential friends in New Orleans who may be able to raise some money to pay our sullen and suffering soldiers. I'm off thither this very morning to achieve those ends and am leaving you in command of the garrison until such time as I should return. Hold the men together as best you can, in the meanwhile."

"What about Bowie?" Travis asked guardedly. "Such a move on your part will not set well with him, to say the least."

"At present, Jim Bowie is sick and indisposed," Neill sighed, not wishing to believe the weight of his own words, "else I may, I admit, have considered him over you. In his flower, Bowie's worth his weight in cold steel and then some, but, sick or well, you'd be better off having him as an ally than an adversary. Remember that. Now," Neill continued, shifting back to his original train of thought, "if you have any letters or dispatches to go out, let me have them. I mean to be off by daybreak."

Off by daybreak, Joe thought with an anxious chill. *Why, that was little over two hours away! He'd have to do some fast-talking if he hoped to convince Travis to send Silvie away.*

"Sir," Joe began, as Travis was buttoning up his tunic, "I need to ask you something important; something that won't keep. It's about Silvie."

"What about Silvie?" Travis asked in genuine interest. "Did she enjoy her ride in the trap last night? Did you?" Travis added with a knowing grin.

"Very much, sir. Thank you. But the thing is that I'd like for Silvie to be riding in a trap again. Today, now. Colonel Neill's heading east and I want Silvie to go along. There's going to be a war here for sure—you said so yourself—and I cannot bear the thought of Silvie getting caught up in it. I'd rest a whole lot easier just knowing that she was safely back in San Felipe. Excuse my familiarity, sir, but aren't you glad that Miss Rebecca's there, instead of here? Well, that's the way I feel about Silvie. I know that it's a lot to be asking of you, but then I never thought that an opportunity like this would happen by. And anyway," Joe swelled, drawing himself to full stature, "I'd do anything for Silvie, Colonel Travis. Anything!"

Taken aback by the forcefulness of Joe's speech, Travis could only smile. "What does Maizy have to say about all this?" Travis responded at last, placing a hand on Joe's shoulder, "or Silvie herself, for that matter?"

"Haven't spoke of it to them," Joe said, shaking his head.

"Well, then, you'd better," Travis returned, with a twinkle in his eye. "They'll need some time to get used to the idea—and for Silvie to pack."

"You mean . . . It's yes . . . she can go?" Joe chortled in relief.

"You're wasting time, Joe. Go to Silvie now. I'll work it out with Colonel Neill. Then," Travis paused for a beat, as though something had occurred to him, "there's something else I need to attend to."

Joe walked over to the other side of the porte-cochere and knocked upon Silvie and Maizy's door. Following a pause, and the sound of muffled footfalls, the door opened a crack to reveal Maizy, squinting to adjust her eyes to the dark.

"Joe? What are you doing here? It's the middle of the night!"

"Colonel Neill's leaving this morning and Silvie's to go with him," Joe informed Maizy straightforwardly. "She needs to pack lickity-split!"

On the sound of Joe's voice and her own name, Silvie stirred. "What do you mean, Joe?" she asked, both in shock and bewilderment. "Where am I going? And why?"

"Colonel Travis says that you are needed in San Felipe," Joe lied. "Young Miss Cummings is ill. Needs someone to look after her. Colonel Neill will be passing through San Felipe on his travels and will escort you there. You'd best hurry."

Silvie pouted. "I don't want to go," she implored. "I don't have to go, do I, Maizy?"

Maizy took a long, hard look at Silvie. Then she read the pleading in Joe's eyes and understood. In full knowledge that she was joining in on the deceit, Maizy took hold of Silvie by the shoulders and said, "You got to go, Honey. You got no choice."

With a moan of despair, Silvie looked at Joe one more time and then resigned herself to her fate. Turning slowly, she began a search of the dark corners of the room for her canvas travel bag.

Travis was soon along, and with him, William Garnett, a Baptist preacher. "It's all set then," Travis announced. "Colonel Neill's traveling in the company of Neddy and Violet Malone who are on their way to San Felipe, anyway. Silvie can travel in the comforts of their wagon. Meanwhile, Joe, I've taken the liberty . . ." Travis paused to indicate the preacher. "Bill Garnett's a man of the cloth and if you and Silvie have a mind to . . . well, it could be a long time before you'll be seeing each other again and I thought . . . well . . . "

"Thank you, Colonel," said Joe, relieving the, for once, tongue-tied Travis of his need to go on. Then Joe walked over to where the bewildered Silvie crouched, packing, and put his hand on her shoulder.

"This," Joe said hesitatingly, "was not my idea, Silvie, though I wished it was. Because I want with my whole heart to be thought of by you as a man that you would even consider taking to husband. I figured it was all too soon and too fast. But things have got so pushed together lately, that it makes the dragging of my feet seem pointless. I do love you and want you to be my wife. If not now, then someday. I . . . "

But Joe never got the chance to finish what he was trying to say, for Silvie silenced him, placing her finger across his lips. Then, in a voice that laid bare the depths of her emotions, Silvie replied, "My head's spinning in circles, Joe, and my feet are moving in a direction that I do not want to go. But my heart is fast with you. That is the only certainty in my life now. I love you, too, my Joe and, yes, I will marry you!"

The short ceremony was over in a few minutes. The vows said, the "I do's" done and the bride kissed, Joe helped Silvie finish her packing. And then, as they stood there in the porte-cochere, waiting for the Malone wagon to come along and spirit Silvie away, the young couple—husband and wife—embraced as though they were loathe to let go. Maizy kept her distance, all in tears.

"I'll be back for you, Silvie," Joe avowed tenderly. "When this is all over, I'll be back in San Felipe, horse Shannon and all, and we'll be together for good."

"And I'll be waiting for you," Silvie replied, her eyes a well of tears. There was nothing more to be said.

Bye and bye, the Malone wagon creaked up, followed closely thereafter by Colonel Neill on horseback. Upon seeing this, Maizy lost it. Unable to contain herself any longer, she rushed forward with outstretched arms, gathering both Joe and Silvie into a wide embrace. "God bless you, children," she sobbed throatily. "We'll all be together soon, I am sure. The Lord go with you, my little Silvie!"

"Mama!" Silvie wailed tearfully, hugging Maizy for dear life. "Mama . . ."

Mrs. Malone hated to interrupt the moment, but interrupt she did. "Joe, Silvie," she announced solemnly, "it's time."

Joe had to practically tear Silvie away from Maizy's embrace. But it was a far harder thing for Joe to break away from Silvie's own enfolding arms, as with a gentle boost, he assisted her into the back of the Malones' wagon. Their eyes locked; Joe's on Silvie, Silvie's upon Joe. They would remain in that attitude, gazing intently, until one or the other was clear out of sight.

Travis, meanwhile, had other things weighing on his mind—and a packet of letters for Colonel Neill's attention. But when Travis had said his own good-byes, the wagon and its passengers rolled out for far away San Felipe at last. And as they moved, the dawning sun, rising in the east, walked over the tops of the hills to greet them.

Eleven

A Decidedly Different Tune

Travis' assumption that Jim Bowie would react none too kindly upon hearing that Colonel Neill had left him, and not Bowie, in command of the garrison was right on the mark. Bowie flew off the handle, claiming that Neill had no authority to appoint anyone in his stead and that, by strict adherence to military protocol, he, Bowie, was senior in rank to the younger Lt. Colonel.

So an election was held to decide who would, in fact, be running things in Bejar and Bowie won, hands down. Most of the men who'd voted were volunteers and Bowie was very popular with them. Travis took the defeat with dignity, but seethed inside over it. His visions of glory seemed dashed.

Maizy did her best to try and cheer Travis up and to somehow soften the blow, but even she could not dispel the gloom that seemed to hang over her master's head like a pall.

Joe, meanwhile, felt a twinge of guilt for having sent Silvie away. His last image of her beautiful, if pain-creased, visage staring at him accusingly from the back of the Malone wagon burned in his brain like a searing brand and he could not dispel it. For she was gone—his wife—his very life's companion—gone. But to safety, Joe reminded himself and *temporary* safety at that—not forever. So, with that thought in mind, Joe breathed a sigh of relief, hoped for the best, and then went on with his daily duties with a lighter heart and firmer resolve.

It was early morning on the day after Bowie's election and the vendors in the mercado were just beginning to lay out their wares on display, when Maizy stepped forth from the cocina at the inn with a pot of coffee and a basketful of breakfast for Travis and Joe. She was nearly halfway through the porte-cochere, when a sudden commotion on the plaza rent the silent air. An approaching mob of apparently drunken men was singing—or at least that's what it sounded like they were trying to do, anyway. The tune that they were so spiritedly mangling reminded Maizy of a song that Davy Crockett had been fiddling away at during the fandango of the previous night; something to do with "The Hunters Of Kentucky."

> Oh Travis, he's a low down skunk,
> Jim Bowie is a bravo!
> The latter's game and full of spunk,
> The former's fit to grovel!
> He spends the day and half the night
> At his forsaken prattle,
> While Travis talks a mighty fight,
> Jim Bowie wins the battle!
> Oh Kentucky, Jim Bowie and Kentucky!

Such a sight, Maizy declared hushedly, shaking her head in disdain. Yet even if they could have heard her, Maizy's sober opinion would've held little sway with the drunken revelers anyhow. So taken were they with their idea of a song that the sots did not even give much care to where they were going. When half a dozen of them went down in a pile, the act only served to start those yet standing crowing with laughter. Two of the characters attempting to free themselves from the tangled pile of human debris were familiar to Maizy. One of them was Davy Crockett, while his companion, none other than Jim Bowie himself!

Suddenly, the door to Travis' room at the inn opened and out stepped the Colonel himself, barely awake and still tucking his shirttail into his trousers. When the mob beheld Travis, they were ready for him.

"Hurrah for Jim Bowie!" they roared. "Bowie and Texas!"

Then, as Travis and Maizy looked on, the mob staggered on down a side street, tossing aside empty tequila bottles and full epithets as they went.

Colonel Travis must have been so perturbed by the drunken irregularities of the mob that he didn't even sense the presence of Maizy. Bang went the door in her face, before she could even offer up a "Good morning, Colonel." So Maizy laid her basket and coffeepot down upon a low wooden bench outside and then gave the door a knock. It was Joe who opened it this time.

"Morning, Maizy," Joe greeted her. "Noisy enough for you?" he grinned.

"Hello, Joe," she returned. "Tell Colonel Travis that breakfast is here and to watch how he slams doors on folks." But Travis had heard her come in.

"Maizy. What a nice surprise, after such a rude awakening. Sorry about the door. But come; join us, if you will."

As he was speaking, Travis tore a page out of an ordinary child's copybook—his son, Charles', perhaps—folded it, and then handed it to Joe. "Before you set, Joe, take this note to Mr. Baugh on the double. We'll save you some choice morsels from Maizy's bountiful basket, I promise." Joe complied begrudgingly and left.

"I was just outside, Colonel," Maizy explained, pouring out a tin of coffee as she spoke, "and I could not help but notice the temper of the crowd. That song they were singing was cruel. I'm sure that Mr. Bowie does not approve of it."

"Approve of it!?" Travis snapped, clearly flabbergasted. "Do you realize what he's been up to? Baugh has briefed me how Bowie and his rabble of volunteers have been roaring drunk since last night. Not only have they been hurrahing the town, they've also broken into the jail, turning common criminals loose into the streets! It's anarchy, that's what it is; anarchy, plain and simple!"

"I'm sorry, Colonel," said Maizy with sympathy. "I will speak with Colonel Bowie. Perhaps he will listen to me."

"Talking to him will do none of us any good," Travis said

unbelievingly, shaking his head. "But you have my leave to try. That letter that Joe is taking to Baugh is for Governor Smith. Bowie and his men will be singing a decidedly different tune when Smith hears of the comings and goings of these past few days."

Maizy left Joe some corn bread and a hard-boiled egg to eat with his coffee. Then she gathered up her basket and retreated out of Travis' door in a beeline for the Verimendi Palace, where she hoped to find Jim Bowie. To her surprise, the double doors of the dwelling were standing wide open, and just inside, sprawled upon the floor, was Bowie himself, still clutching the neck of a half-empty rum bottle whose contents were gradually gurgling out onto the rich velvet carpet.

Sighing in disgust upon the sight, Maizy picked up a basin of water from the side table and unceremoniously doused the sagging head of the fallen man.

Bowie responded quickly with a "What in the hell?" Then he looked up with a stupid expression. "Oh, Maizy, it's you," he slurred. "Helluva way to pay your re-specks, Maizy, just a helluva way!"

"And this is a fine way for the commander of the Bejar Volunteers to be conducting himself," she retorted sharply. "Some of the local Mexicans allow that Santa Anna is on the march to this place and yet you men seem to be acting like you got no cares in the world. What, may I be so bold to ask, are you trying to do, sir?"

"Santa Anna is a fortnight's march from this place, if a day," Bowie replied nonchalantly. "I know that, my scouts know that. Matter of fact, Torribo, one of my best scouts, was thrown into the callaboose just last night for, some say, being drunk and disorderly. So we broke him outta there. Sure we did! Released him back into the tender arms of the military, where he belongs. For the good of the service, for the good of Bejar, and for the good of Texas, I might add!"

"Travis doesn't know that," Maizy pointed out. "All he sees is that he's lost his command and that you've lost control of your men. Travis is a fighter, Mr. Bowie, and he loves Texas, perhaps as much as you yourself do. Work with him—and let him work with you!"

Bowie hauled himself up onto a stool and then ran his fingers through his wetted hair. "You've given me something to think on, Maizy. I'm obliged. Truth is, I've been kicking around the notion of offering young Buck Travis co-commandancy of the garrison here—wet behind the ears, though he may be," Bowie added wryly, wiping behind his own ears with the sleeve of his shirt. "I'll pay him my re-specks as soon as . . . " There was a pause as Bowie attempted to rise, but failed, "as soon as I can stand up."

Twelve

A Choice in the Matter

Once again, Maizy's winning ways bore noble fruit; Bowie and Travis put their heads together, deciding at last that the quest for Texas freedom was a far worthier goal than was the mere drive of personal ambition. And, as Bowie and Travis' joint-commmandancy solidified, their abrasive clash of wills all but disintegrated.

The timing proved none too soon, for as the Texians were fandangoing the night away in honor of George Washington's birthday on the 22nd of February, Bowie's scout Blas Herrera came riding in with startling news. Santa Anna's advance units were encamped upon the Medina River, scarcely thirty-five miles from Bejar. And then, when on the following day, Travis' sentry in the bell tower of the San Fernando Church spotted those very units poking their way into Bejar itself, the siege of the Alamo officially joined in earnest.

Now, Joe was at the north wall of the Alamo on this Saturday evening, the 5th of March, helping to bolster up the glorified pile of dirt as best as he could. Laying aside his shovel for a well-deserved rest, Joe heaved a deep sigh of both melancholy and weariness. So dog-tired was he that he scarcely noticed the approaching clatter of the Louisiana Dockman's water bucket.

Although it was the Dockman's duty to haul around the weighty water bucket to the different battle positions to quench the throats of both thirsty men and cannon, he still insisted on shouldering his old musket, cumbersome as it was. The Dockman had fashioned a leather sling to the gun for that purpose and Joe thought that it made him look all the more soldierly, in spite of the bucket. Jean offered and Joe graciously accepted a big dipperful of water.

"So," the Dockman mused, as Joe drank, "this hill is considered a wall by Texian standards, yes? There is more dirt involved in her than stone. At least we shall not run out of dirt!"

"Don't I know it," Joe sighed, returning the dipper. "I eat about as much as I tote to the walls, then wear the rest of it to sleep at night—when I can sleep at night."

"Some of Captain Juan Seguin's local Mexicano volunteers could not so much sleep last night, Joseph. They considered it much more healthy upon the wide open prairie, than in the fort, I think, and took a little stroll, or so it seems."

"Deserters?!" Joe said in surprise. "How many?"

"Nine . . . ten," the Dockman shrugged, "what is the difference? Though Captain Seguin and his aide have galloped off on dispatch duty for Colonel Travis, I count some nine or ten of his followers still with us. Esparza, the one they call Brigido, a few others I know not. Poor devils will be in a bad way when Santa Anna's soldiers climb these walls. Fighting their own fellows, and all. But then, in the end, it matters not so much. We all die, just the same. But, forgive me, Joseph," Jean added hastily, "I know that you do not like so much, this talk."

"Forget it," Joe replied glumly. "Right now, I'm inclined to maybe just agree with you. Things aren't getting much better and even Colonel Travis is seeming to take notice. Ever since Captain Bonham rode in with the news that Fanning and his five hundred at La Bahia are not coming to our aid, Travis just keeps to his room, not wanting to be disturbed. Funny how quiet it is, isn't it?" Joe digressed.

It was indeed peculiar how the Mexican fire had tapered off, then ceased altogether. Grateful for the respite, some defenders decided to take advantage of the sudden lull by easing down at their posts upon the dank rooftops and earthen parapets. Others decided to get cookfires going while they still had the opportunity.

"Best go attend to Colonel Travis," Joe said, taking his leave of the Dockman. "I could use a little grub myself. Thanks for the water."

"But of course," Jean said, waving him on his way.

Joe set off across the plaza toward the cookstove before the headquarters room, but his mind was far from thoughts of food. He thought of Silvie and his promise of returning to her in San Felipe, after the war was over. But just the thought of returning to her as a bound slave galled Joe. *What sort of future could he possibly offer her? What sort of future, would they have together under such unacceptable circumstances, for that matter?* Back at the beginning of the Alamo siege, when hope had still sprung bright for reinforcements and eventual victory, Travis had promised that he would think on Joe's talk of freedom. Now, with hope fading and the prospect of reinforcements dim, Joe figured that the time had come for him to ask Travis straight out about freedom for Silvie, Maizy and himself—while he still had the chance. So, taking a deep breath, Joe stepped forward into the arbor covered area before the headquarters room and knocked upon Travis' door.

Travis opened the door upon Joe, squinting as he did. It was such a dark little room, that even the fading light of dusk hurt his eyes.

"Ah, Joe. Do come in. I was just sitting here thinking hard. And well, it looks as though we're all alone in this fight against Santa Anna. Fannin at Goliad, Houston away, God knows where, the scattered colonies . . . all have failed us. Oh, I had such high hopes, Joe," he reflected sadly, re-echoing Joe's own thoughts. "I had thought that our brethren would assist us in this time of Texas' most dire need. I was wrong to have had such blind faith in our countrymen and like those misguided countrymen, such disdain for the capabilities of the Mexican army. It is a formidable force we now face, Joe, and now, those brave men out there on the wall must suffer the bitter consequences of my own haughtiness. As I mentioned to you in our talk, oh so long ago, it now seems—I am willing to give up my own life for the cause of Texas freedom, plain and simple. But then, do I have the right to ask as much of the men—or even of you, Joe," he added pointedly, "for that matter? I may have no hope of rescuing this garrison, but I can make a difference in your life. I still command the power in that, even though it is only a paper power."

Turning to his writing table, Travis gathered up some documents, eyeballed them a bit, and offered them over to Joe. Joe noted that the Colonel must've spent quite some time penning the papers, for they all appeared to be filled on both sides with the Colonel's trademark hasty scrawl.

"These papers are for you, Silvie, and Maizy, Joe. Do you know what they are?"

"No, sir," Joe gulped, hoping that he knew, all the same.

"They're freedom papers, Joe; freedom for you, Silvie, and Maizy. Maizy already knows, but I asked her to remain silent on it until I had the opportunity to tell you myself. You're still going to have to try and survive this fight, Joe, but at least you'll now have something worth the fighting for; a free future for both you and Silvie. I'll rest easy now in my thoughts, knowing that I've struck a small blow for freedom in that. Here is my hand on it, Joe," Travis concluded with a weary smile.

To say that Joe was struck dumb over what just transpired would be putting it mildly. Why, he hadn't even had to put in a word of his own, edge or otherwise. Maizy's magic, Travis' generosity of spirit, Joe's own desire and perseverance, perhaps all of these factors had helped in bringing the moment to fruition. But for now, in the full realization of that moment, all Joe could do was to accept Travis' hand in friendship and then pump it with a grateful fervor. With his free hand, Joe stuffed the precious papers into his shirt.

"Thank you, sir," Joe's voice whooshed out, betraying the depth of his emotion. "And I shall do my level best to live up to my new station as a free man, believe you me. Both Silvie and Maizy are in good hands, that I vow. But meanwhile," Joe continued, temporarily putting his own plans and desires to the side, "what do you reckon to do about the rest of the men here? Can't rightly lay freedom papers on men who was born free."

Before responding, Travis stared at the wall for a good long moment. "I'll have to let them know how and where we stand, Joe. But just how to tell them is quite another thing. That's what's eating me now."

"Well," Joe said, looking Travis straight in the eye, "don't go selling the men short, Colonel. We're all of one mind in this place, though nobody cares to admit it. These boys is used to fighting for their rights and God-given liberties, just like your own self. I expect they likely knew the odds well enough long before Bonham rode in with the news about Fanning not coming. But," Joe noted, "you got the gift of words, sir. Look what your words did for me! Now, if you can go out there and make those boys feel half as proud of themselves as you made me feel just now, then I reckon you got no cause for worry. A man's pride means a lot to him, Colonel Travis. I know for a fact, it does."

"Thanks, Joe," Travis whispered with a smile of profound humility creasing his lips. "Perhaps pride is all I have left them with. But in the very least, I mean to let them know that I stand together with them, survive or perish, sink or swim. Meanwhile, Joe, please go and get Maizy. I want her to be there when I talk to the men. I think that she's in the sacristy room of the old church looking in on the other women and children who are sequestered there."

"Yes, sir," Joe saluted, surprised by the natural feeling of the wholly reflex act; for it was the act of a soldier saluting his officer. And Travis, in turn, not missing a beat, returned the salute with full flourish.

Joe took this as a sign to retreat from the room. But when he started to back out through the opened door in his best imitation of military decorum, he practically collided with Adjutant Baugh who was just on his way in. "Sorry, Joe," Baugh offered. "You sent for me, Buck, er, Colonel Travis?"

"I did, Baugh. Go and assemble the men. Sentries and those incapacitated excepted, of course."

As Baugh set forth to gather the garrison for assembly, Joe headed off to the church to gather Maizy.

Entering the very portal of the Alamo church that he and Silvie had passed through on that faraway day when they had practiced pitching pebbles at Silvie's "ghost bats," Joe gingerly picked his way across the dank, debris-strewn floor of the nave in search of the sacristy. But for a glow of light issuing from the room's low door, Joe might have lost his direction altogether. Well, that wasn't exactly true, for the merry laughter of children and the booming voice of Davy Crockett guided him a little.

When Joe ducked in through the low door into the vaulted chamber at last, he had to squint to adjust his eyes to the fresh dark. The sacristy was both stuffy and cramped and smelled of stale air, damp smoke and bad digestion, but at least the thick walled little chamber provided the non-combatants safety from artillery barrages.

Joe discovered Maizy sitting upon a small keg and holding one of the Esparza children upon her lap. Mrs. Esparza and two of her other children were there, as was Juana Alsbury, her young ones and her sister Gertrudis' brood. The Loysolas, the Guerreros, Mrs. Dickerson and her daughter, Angie, all sat, or stood, or paced the tiny enclosure, sharing the same foul air and limited scenery. And then, there was Crockett. The kindly bear hunter had often stopped by the church to cheer up the frightened children with a heaping helping of his colorful yarn spinning and tall tales; Joe had arrived just in time for a fresh sampling.

"Wal, young-ins, it's like this," Crockett began and the spellbound children gathered in even closer, "in Texas, you got yer longhorn cows an' yer prairie pups, yer jackrabbits, armadillys an' yer buffalos. An' these thing'll set well enough t' take th' smart out of an empty stomach in an emergency. But you ain't never set to any real eatin', lessen you had uh nice, juicy b'ar steak to sink yer choppers into! Now Tennessee's a b'ar state an' Davy Crockett's a b'ar hunter! Winter, summer, spring, er fall, I could smoke those critters out an' turn 'em into steaks afore you could say 'Rumpilstiltskin!'

"Now it so happened that one day when a sartin b'ar heared that ol' Davy was in his neck o' th' woods, he starts a'tappin' siginals on th' trees with his great claws, so as to warn his b'ar brethren to either skip out, or start sayin' their prayers. But did that fool ol' Davy?"

"Did it?" little Enrique Esparza piped in.

"No, sir, it did not! An' I'll tell ye why! It's cause ol' Davy knows b'ar tappin' siginals an' when he hears that b'ar a'tappin' out a warnin' he counter taps th 'all's clear' siginal, which so confuses all the other b'ars that they comes right out' o' their caves an' holler logs to investigate. An' such is their undoin' Pop, pop, pop! Bam, bam, bam! An' it's b'ar steaks for Tennessee young-ins an' their Mas an' Pappys too!"

Though the children clapped and begged for more, Joe had to interrupt Crockett, for he knew that this was not the time for further yarns or the tending of babies. "Excuse the interruption, Colonel Davy, sir, but Colonel Travis is calling for an assembly in the plaza. All hands that are able, that is."

"Right you are, Joe," Crockett replied. "Reckon those critter tales'll just have to keep for another day, Sprouts!" Crockett announced, turning once again to face his eager audience. "Sprouts, take notice! Ol' Davy's a'leavin' but it's a sartinty, he'll be back. So get t' hintin' in them corners of this yar cave an' don't quit! Davy Crockett's a right ornery cuss when he gets set with honger! So go ahead!" Then Crockett was gone, leaving behind his squealing passel of fledgling hunters.

Maizy stopped rocking the child upon her knee and looked

up at Joe, considerably hard. "You've talked with Colonel Travis," she said matter-of-factly. "Didn't have to tell me a thing," she said, grinning, "I could read it in your eyes. Oh, Joe! The future will be so different now—so different. Not that it won't be rough on us," she added, stanching the euphoria, if only slightly. "But, whether we fall on our faces, or soar to the heights, it's going to be of our own doing—not some boss man's, not his family's, kin's, friends or neighbors'—no! What we do with our lives from now on will be our choice. Our decisions from this point on will decide our future. Think on that, Joe! Think on it!"

"Have been, ever since the moment it became real, Maizy," Joe beamed. "It came on so sudden I'm still kind of lightheaded over it. But right now, Colonel Travis is about to lay a decision before the whole garrison, one that will affect us all. Says that he'd like for you to be there, so as to hear him out."

"Then we'd best get going and show Mr. Travis our support, Joe."

Joe and Maizy made their way across the plaza toward the headquarters room where a sizable crowd had already gathered, drawn up in a semi-circle before Travis' door. Haggard, bedraggled, unshaven, and unwashed as they were, the scarecrow force yet bore a sense of dignity, such as only a free man could notice, or understand. Joe saw and understood. Why that dignity was even evident in the gait and poise of the Louisiana Dockman.

"Hello to you, Joseph," Jean saluted, waving from the center of the file of men. "And to you, Maizy," he added, with a tip of the hat. "Come to join our little party, yes? Step forward, step forward," he induced them, gesturing toward a break in the line, directly beside him. "Colonel Travis, he is going to speak."

William Barrett Travis stepped out from beneath the headquarters arbor to face his men. Freshly groomed and shaven, his uniform brushed, and with his light dress saber dangling at his side, the Colonel looked the picture image of a commander. With his hands folded firmly behind his back, Travis gazed down the long line of men before him, searching their faces for perhaps a hint of what was on their minds. A slight commotion momentarily interrupted his thoughts as Davy Crockett and three of his Tennessee boys brought the pallet of Jim Bowie forward, then laid it down on the ground amidst Bowie's men.

Then Travis spoke: "Men," he began with a determination, "I shall not burden you with weighty garlands of flowery rhetoric. I have called you together because you deserve the plain, unvarnished truth. It's as simple as this: Jim Bonham has informed me that Fannin is not coming. There will be no help. When Santa Anna launches his all-out assault, its results should be painfully evident to you. We are outnumbered ten, perhaps twenty, to one. Notwithstanding, we have succeeded in holding back the fangs of the viper Santa Anna from the throat of our beloved Texas for twelve long days. And for that, you have my undying thanks and respect. But now, even as I speak, Mexican sappers are fitting together their scaling ladders in plain view and we have all, I am sure, witnessed the accelerated troop maneuvers around the mission. It seems more than probable that our time is very near at hand. But, few as they may be, there are still a number of options open to us. Shall we attempt a futile escape across the open prairie, through the enemy lines, only to fall victim to the cruel point of a cavalry lance? Shall we surrender at discretion to a butcher who flaunts a 'no quarter' banner in our faces? Or, shall we band together like brothers within these walls and fight it out to the final extremity in the hopes of blunting Santa Anna's edge so severely that he will be unable to march against our countrymen? Unable to march against them until they've had the time to raise an army of sufficient magnitude to ultimately expel him from Texas and thus ensure final victory? It's a bitter set of choices to digest, I admit, but choose, each and every one of us must. I, myself, have elected to remain within these walls and fight, so long as breath remains within my body. This I will do, even if you leave me alone. Those of you who wish, however, may attempt to escape under cover of darkness, or even surrender, should your heart dictate such a thing. This place is no prison—not yet. Bonham got in unscathed; some of you may withdraw in like manner. The choice is yours."

Then, as Joe looked on, his former master drew his saber and proceeded to scratch a long, wavy line in the dirt before the file of Alamo defenders. "Those of you," Travis challenged, "who are for sticking it out for God and Texas, home and family, cross this line. Who will be the first? March!"

As both the words and the sentiments of the Alamo commander's speech registered in Joe's brain, his heart went out to Travis; from that moment on, Joe felt a new sense of kinship binding him with his former master. Little did Joe realize in the emotion of the moment, however, just how drastically this feeling would come to affect the very wheels of his destiny—and Maizy's.

Joe glanced over at Maizy, then at the Louisiana Dockman. Strange, that at such a time as this, they should all be beaming smiles at each other, but such they did. Joe puffed with pride as the Louisiana Dockman shouldered his musket and Maizy stood erect between the two men, linking arms and wills with them. Then, after a simultaneous deep breath, the threesome crossed over the line in a body to stand alongside of Travis.

After a short pause to perhaps measure the consequences of their collective choice, the rest of the Alamo defenders started forward. First in twos and tens, next in clumps; finally as a single surge. All of them ultimately crossed over for a plunge into oblivion. All except Jim Bowie, that is.

Rising in his pallet to speak, Bowie addressed his buddies in a hoarse whisper. "Boys," his voice cracked, "I cannot make it over to you of my own power, but if some of you would be so kind as to drag my pallet over, I'd be much obliged."

With the assistance of Joe, the Dockman, Davy Crockett, and Adjutant Baugh, Bowie was soon on the same side of the line as his mates. A smattering of cheers went up for Colonel Jim in acknowledgment of his cool bravery. The die was cast.

Put to the test, the Alamo garrison had not come up wanting. It had remained intact and of one mind, but oh how mixed were the individual feelings of the defenders. While Joe, Maizy, and Jean had made their choice with a newfound sense of hope, none of the other defenders seemed too keen on the prospect of possibly dying. The young men Joe beheld were far too full of life to readily accept the notion of death, so long as there yet remained the slightest thread of hope. But now, with that wispy thread gone, eloquently yanked away by Travis, the youths were left to contend with brutal reality. As their woebegone expressions attested, they simply did not want to believe that this was actually happening. Not now, not to them.

"We're dead for sure," one middle-aged man remarked in almost bland resignation. "Best get to writing up your Last Will and Testament, gents."

"Travis killed us," moaned another, a shaken youth. "Kept us here with lies."

"Nobody killed no one, son," a weathered oldster replied sternly, but with a sense of mature calm. "That's just the way the stick floats, sometimes. Cutting stick and running wouldn't help Texas none, or your Ma, or Pa. You want your baby sister living one minute in a land without freedom? Well, not this child. Buck up, boy," the old man said in a comforting tone, though his own eyes glistened full.

Tears welled in more than one pair of eyes, and while a few souls sought comfort in the depths of prayer, a few others simply cursed under their breath. Some, so wholly and utterly struck dumb by the prospect of their imminent doom, merely stood there like statuary, listening with pricked up ears for what they took to be the none-too-distant tolling of their own death knell.

Travis spoke at length. "Thank you, men," he muttered, clearly moved by the moment and the response of his citizen-soldiers. "Whatever transpires from this point on, always remember: the Lord is on our side. Who are we to fear? Rest easy in the knowledge of that and try to get in a little shut-eye. May God bless and keep you all." He paused for a beat. "Dismiss!" he concluded at last, breaking up both the spell and the assembly.

As the men began to disperse, some of them made a curiously conscious effort to muffle the sounds of their clattering accouterments. It was as though their freshly heightened senses were wont to exaggerate even the slightest jostle or footfall into a resounding thunderclap.

Through the thinning crowd, Maizy saw Mrs. Dickerson start to totter, and then fall to her knees in tears, clearly overwrought. Maizy reacted, with a comforting arm around Suzannah's shoulders. With her free arm, Maizy gathered up baby Angie. "Be brave," Maizy whispered. "See how the men are behaving? I'm sure that some of them would cry out loud, too, if they could. But they cannot. It is for you to stand beside your husband now. Be brave!"

In all fairness, Suzannah did try. But with each rallying effort to speak, her voice failed her, dissolving instead into husky, heartrending sobs. "It's . . . it's like he's already dead!" she wailed, rocking her head from side to side as she spoke. "And how brave must I be then—and why? I—I won't break his heart, Maizy. I won't. It'll be all right. For Almaron's sake and for Angie's sake, it'll be all right. It must be."

Noticing Mrs. Dickerson in her distress, Travis walked up upon the two women. "Mrs. Dickerson, you are all right?" Travis voiced in concern.

"She's fine, Colonel," Maizy replied, sparing Suzannah the trouble. "She's tired, is all. Best be getting her and the baby back to the church room. Come on, Miss Sue," Maizy imparted with tenderness. "Let's tuck Angie in for the night. Goodnight to you, Colonel." Then the two women and infant girl were off, church bound.

Joe walked back across the plaza to the well to get himself a drink. The drawing of the line had left him especially dry mouthed. And as Joe sat sipping from a long-handled ladle, the

Louisiana Dockman ambled up to join him upon the low wooden bench.

"Nice speech, eh Joseph, but not so much one of surprise, no? Well, we get to fight for our liberty, after all, so it seems," Jean said with a laugh of irony. "These other men? They fight for land and family—and for liberty. But, you and I? I expect the only land we shall get is the little piece our fallen body, it occupies when this is all over. And, as for family? Ooh La! You have your Silvie to consider and that is a fine thing. But I? No woman have I that will mourn or miss me. And then and finally, this liberty thing. As you yourself once mentioned to me Joseph, death breaks all chains. But I think that it is the manner of one's death that speaks for him in the end. Travis said that I could go over the wall and perhaps escape and live, but in my mind that is not a choice at all. A man must fight for his freedom, I think—not skulk away like some frightened, yelping puppy. So you see, I made for myself, my own choice, and for it, I am happy. For you? Deepest sympathy and regrets have I for you, Joseph. You are here, facing your destiny, while your own, dear Silvie, she pines away for you as a slave woman, with no choice in the matter. Perhaps it is best in the end that no woman have I to mourn my passage, not if that mourning shall only lead her to feelings of hopelessness—and despair. Sacre Marie! It is a difficult thing, indeed!"

Joe grimaced, but for a time said nothing. How could he tell the Dockman about the freedom papers? It wouldn't do him any good, anyhow, the knowledge. So Joe, with the freedom papers tucked safely within his shirt, said instead, "There's always hope, Jean. As long as we're still walking and talking and breathing, there's hope. And who knows that but Silvie and I will come out of this all right: and you. You may not have a woman just yet, but you got true friends. Me, for one, Maizy for another and Silvie, when she gets to meet you, that is."

"You are kind, Joseph," replied the Dockman with a smile. "Perhaps, if we had met long ago, I could have shown you the river, yes? Once you are on the river, you do not want to leave her—ever. Perhaps she is my one, true love, after all. But enough, all this talk. We'd best be getting us some rest, yes?"

"Yes," Joe yawned, realizing at last how tired he actually was. "Goodnight to you, Jean."

"And goodnight to you, Joseph. Dream of the river for me, mon ami."

The Dockman made off for the far end of the Long Barrack, while Joe himself found his weary way back to the headquarters room arbor for a stab at precious repose.

Inside the dimly lit sacristy room in the church, meanwhile, the women with children were trying to put their young ones to bed upon some straw and blanket pallets. While most of the nodding youngsters harbored few qualms about surrendering to the sandman, baby Angelina Dickerson seemed more intent upon outlasting Mama Suzannah. Indeed, the exhausted mother seemed nearer to sleep than her fussing infant did.

"Let me rock her for a while, Miss Sue," Maizy said softly, cradling baby Angie into her arms as she spoke. "Get yourself some rest, else you'll be no good to the child at all."

"Thank you, Maizy," Suzannah replied, much relieved. "But as tired as I am, I just can't seem to sleep. If you don't mind, I'd like to pay a visit with my husband for a spell—only a very short one," she added almost apologetically.

"Take your time, Honey," Maizy reassured her. "Angie is in good hands."

Suzannah left the makeshift nursery at peace to seek out her husband, Almaron. And in spite of the several torches that pocklined the rising walls of the nave, Suzannah nevertheless found it prudent to carry a small stump of a candle to better aid her as she picked her way over the hard earthen floor. Scattered debris from the fallen roof and its tumbled supporting arches made her footing especially dubious, as did the slimy puddles that lingered in the darkness, courtesy of the recent rains. The defenders had implemented some of the debris into a sloping ramp that ran from about the center of the nave to a twelve-foot-high cannon platform in the rear, or apse of the building. It was to this battle station that Suzannah headed, for upon it her husband was stationed.

But all that Travis could see upon entering the church's front portal was the glow of Suzannah's candle as it rose closer to the top of the cannon platform with her every step. Travis' mind, however, was not so much focused upon the departing mother as it was with her resting child. Inside the sacristy, Travis found Maizy doing her best to calm baby Angie to sleep. The Alamo commander looked down upon the yet alert face of the child with a smile of genuine tenderness. Perhaps, at that moment, he was thinking of his own little child, Charles, and of the future they would never share together. For, as Maizy looked on, Travis reached out his little finger to Angie and delighted in her powerless, yet persistent grip. And oh, how Angie tugged! The object of her interest seemed to be a battered cat's-eye ring that graced the tip of Travis' little finger. The ring was a love token that Travis had acquired ages ago from his sweetheart, Rebecca; he'd promised never to remove it. But slip the ring from his little finger, Travis now did, as with a stray thread snagged from his tunic, he strung the ring like a sort of amulet.

"You keep it, Honey," he brightened, gently looping the love token around the delighted baby's neck. "I'll have no further use for it. And you," he addressed Maizy, "good heart and true friend that you are. Take care of yourself and your future. If you should manage to get back to San Felipe, give my best to the Cummingses and . . . tell Becky I love her. And Maizy, tell her to take care of my little boy."

"I will, thank you, sir," Maizy managed to utter through a veil of tears. "And may God bless you along every step of your way . . . Little Charles will be in good hands, I am sure." There was nothing more she could say. With a parting look, Travis was gone.

"What did Colonel Travis want?" Suzannah asked in curiosity, poking her head back into the sacristy door, candle stub and all.

"Almaron's asleep and I didn't have the heart to wake him."

Maizy showed Suzannah the cat's-eye ring Travis had looped around Angie's neck and what it implied. And though the young mother went all tingly with goose bumps on hearing, her eyes remained tearless. Moved though she was, Suzannah was all cried out.

Back at the headquarters room, Travis, accompanied by a gangly youth of about sixteen or so, nudged Joe awake. "A little late night business, I am afraid, Joe," Travis said, "and a favor to ask of you. I'm sending out young Jim Allen here with a dispatch and I want him to have the best edge possible, so tight have the Mexicans got us boxed in. I would like him to ride out upon Shannon, Joe. She's the best chance Allen has of getting out of here both safely and swiftly. I know how much you cherish that horse, but we need Shannon now. Could you . . . could you help her get used to Allen and the idea?"

Joe felt a twinge of anxiety, but suppressed it. With Shannon going out of the Alamo, at least she would not be falling into the hands of a complete stranger. And just perhaps, she could somehow make it back to Silvie in San Felipe. Perhaps, maybe. "Yes, Colonel, it's a good idea," Joe replied. "Come on, young Mr. Allen, and I'll introduce you to Shannon."

"Thanks, Joe," Travis said, relieved that Joe was being so cooperative. "I'm calling for personal letters and mementos to go out with the dispatch. This might very well be the last opportunity to get messages of any kind to the outside world. You and Allen meet me over by the northern postern in about a half an hour."

In the horse corral, behind the Long Barracks, Shannon whinnied upon Joe's approach. Whispering in an affectionate tone, Joe tenderly caressed Shannon beneath her muzzle. "Shan, this is Jimmy. Mr. Allen, this is Shannon. Scratch her under the muzzle, so she can get used to you. Now Shan, Mr. Allen is going to climb aboard you and you're going to let him, easy, easy now," Joe added, as Shannon began backing away nervously. "There's a great girl," Joe went on, as Allen nimbly swung up over the horse's bareback, by use of her halter. Shannon reacted with a controlling shudder, up and down her back, as though she were trying to dislodge her unfamiliar cargo. "It's all right, Shan," Joe said, steadying the horse with a firm grip upon her bridle. "You're going to get to go out on a ride, stretch your legs. You'll like that. Mr. Allen's gonna be gentle with you and he certainly don't have spurs. There's a great girl," Joe concluded, upon Shannon's bray of resignation. She understood, at last.

With Allen aboard, Joe walked Shannon across the plaza toward the northern postern where a number of defenders stood, fists full of precious paper scraps. Precious cargo, indeed, were these scraps, for with them went the hopes, dreams, and, perhaps, final wishes of the Alamo garrison.

With the collected bundle of letters secreted in his shirt, Allen was just on the point of exiting the gate, when Travis stopped him. "One more, Allen," he said, handing the eager youth a small packet of his own, along with the dispatch. "Something for my little boy," Travis mumbled, with a faraway look in his eyes. "I might've made for him a splendid fortune . . . Go with Godspeed, Allen."

"Nothin' to it," the youth beamed, gently nudging Shannon forward with his heels into her flanks. Soon, they were clattering off into the dark void of the night.

"Good-bye, Shannon darlin'," Joe whispered under his breath.

Watching the whole episode transpire from the parapet above the gate, Adjutant Baugh remarked down to those below, "From what I could see, Allen made it all right. There's one less egg for Santa Anna to fry, anyway."

"Saint Anna does not take the time to fry his eggs," Travis replied with chilling candor, "he steps on them."

"Well," Joe observed wryly, "he may just step on us and he may not, but one thing's for certain sure, he's gonna be getting one royal hotfoot for his trouble, if this egg's got anything to say about it!"

"Amen to that," Baugh laughed, and even Travis grinned.

"But, to business, Baugh," Travis said, breaking up the mood. "I'm especially concerned about the condition of the northern defenses," he said, pointing toward a jumble of adobe and limestone fragments, junk-lumber and packed earth. "Jameson's shored it up some, but another bombardment could bring it all down. Have Jameson resume work on it in the morning. I won't rest easy about it, until then."

With Jim Allen away, the compound grew unusually quiet. Why, even the town itself seemed deathly still to Joe, as he lay listening upon his pallet beneath the headquarters arbor. So silent was it, in fact, that Joe could denote the faint, monotonous sounds of men snoring around the compound. He could even distinguish the unhappy whinny of a horse from beyond the Long Barrack, displeased perhaps on its having been disturbed by the efforts of a defender, relieving himself in the commodes there. Then there was the steady, clomp, clomp, clomping of a sentry's shoes upon the wall above Joe, and the whooshing sound of wind passing through the trees in a peach orchard, just to the north.

Night sounds. Joe had become so accustomed to the steady booming of an artillery barrage that he almost forgot what simple pleasures the cover of night held. And now, in all the reigning silence, Joe found that he could not sleep.

In his unbidden wakefulness, Joe watched a pair of weary piquet guards stumble across the yard to relieve comrades who'd been standing watch outside the Alamo in the oozy ditches to the north and east of the mission. But the relief guards appeared to be no fresher to the duty than the sleepwalkers they were supposed to be replacing. Notwithstanding, the weight of their weariness seemed to work its contagion upon Joe. He pulled his blanket up over his head and then eased himself down in the prickly straw, as the barely audible whimper of a child from far across the yard, over in the sacristy room of the church, ushered Joe to the land of Nod.

* * *

Joe was dreaming of Silvie. But how could it be otherwise? Life had both treated and cheated Joe and Silvie, what with their whirlwind romance, their last-minute wedding, their swift and painful parting, and, finally, their newfound, then unfulfilled, passion.

Though Joe had experienced this very same dream countless times before, it had never meant so much to him then as now. For the fantasy of bygone lonely nights now bore the promise of a future reality—a reality only thwarted by the obstacle of time and space—the reality of Joe and Silvie, husband and wife, together at last.

In the dream, Joe was once more in the Cummingses' livery at Mill Creek, all in the dead of night. The rude straw beneath him pricked through his garments and itched like sin, but he had slept in worse. Meanwhile, within the inn itself, just across the yard and achingly close by, Silvie lay asleep beneath clean sheets and an eider down comforter. Even within the dream-state itself, Joe seemed able to remember the countless nights before when he had longed for Silvie, all in vain, and in a rush of fiery passion. But dreams, when we know that they are but dreams, can sometimes work to our advantage; we can manipulate them.

Joe did, conjuring up a scene that only his vivid imagination had theretofore played witness to . . . a sudden rustling of greenery was followed by the sound of soft, approaching footfalls. The clicking of the livery door latch preceded the creaking door itself, slowly fanning inward with a stream of moonlight that flooded in through its narrow aperture. And then and finally, came Silvie. Silhouetted in an aura of soft moon glow, Silvie's curvaceous figure shone plainly discernible through the sheer fabric of her blue gingham shift, to create an effect that was both eerie and phantomlike. Without a word, Silvie loosened the belt of the gingham, letting the garment float/slide gently to the ground. Joe gulped on the sight, as for a moment, for an all-too-brief instant, Silvie stood before him in all of her splendor. Then, as Joe sat gazing upon this glistening apparition, the girl, the livery, and the moment itself all exploded in a flash of brilliant color.

Thirteen

One Domingo Morning

Startled by the rocket's glare, Joe was upon his feet before he even knew that he was awake. Though his nerves had grown accustomed to the suddenness of Mexican night maneuvers and artillery barrages, there was something unsettlingly different about this. For, instead of the occasionally lobbed shell and annoying serenade of Santa Anna's massed bands, a crescendo of garbled shouts, cheers, and trumpet calls filled the night air, punctuated by the resounding echo of thousands of feet thudding across frozen earth.

If Joe still harbored any doubt as to what this was all about, the appearance of Adjutant Baugh, charging out of the darkness that was the north wall, swiftly squelched it. "Colonel Travis," the animated Adjutant bellowed, still on a run, "the Mexicans are coming!"

There was no need for Joe to alert Travis, for the Colonel he saw was already outside the headquarters door, buckling on his sword over his tunic.

"Grab your shotgun, Joe" Travis ordered. Then, with a loaded pistol stuffed into his belt and with his own shotgun in hand, Travis beckoned Joe to follow him to the cannon platform at the weakened center of the north wall.

They were halfway up the ramp way when Travis turned suddenly to face his freshly awakened, scrambling, shirttail men. "Come on, boys!" he rallied with a fiery roar. "The enemy are upon us and we will give them hell!"

Reaching the top of the parapet, Travis and Joe peered out in vain over the nearly three-foot-thick adobe wall into the nothingness of the inky dark night. But directly below them, thanks to the glare of expended rockets, they could distinguish a swelling mob of shouting and cursing Mexican soldados, pressing the wall's outer face in a jumble of confusion. In their overzealousness, the attackers had apparently reached the wall before the ladder bearers had and so it was moments before the first ladder uncertainly clattered against the fortress and whole bunches of men began their clamber to the top.

Travis could have merely toppled the ladder back down into the crowd, but it would've only been raised again. So, in an act of blazing dissuasion, Travis swung his shotgun down over the ladder's uppermost rung and let go both barrels. The succeeding screams of the mangled and the dying were swallowed up in a new din created by defenders already to their posts who sliced into the massed columns with a devastating hail of rifle, musket, and small arms fire.

Without embrasures in the walls to enable the gun crews to deflect their pieces, the big-mouthed cannon were all but useless at such close quarters; but the riflemen more than adequately picked up the slack. Experts at the trade could pop off a good three shots a minute and their prowess made the devastating fusillade seem almost continuous.

Joe emptied his shotgun over the wall, then took on the task of ramming fresh loads down the barrels of expended muskets, as marksmen handed them back to him. At times, the sickeningly sweet stench of burnt powder nearly caused the "Veteran Soldier" to retch, but Joe doused his offended nostrils with a wet rag, then fought on, all the same.

The fort was holding. The few ladders that the Mexicans had managed to plant along the broken northern parapet lay in a jumbled mess of men and equipment at the base of the wall; the ladder bearers themselves either shot, or else hunkering down. Then the Texians' long twelve-pounders on the top of the church opened up venting their rage in a belch of fiery debris that melded the staggering splash of approaching humanity into distorted blobs and shredded fragments of raw, quivering flesh. *Nothing could survive such punishment,* Joe observed to himself. *The whole column must've gone down.* But through breaks in the billowy cloud of smoke and to his amazement, Joe saw that he could not have been more wrong, for the undaunted Mexican troops merely dressed down their depleted column and came on.

Then the defenders started taking their own casualties, as lead stricken Texians lurched and tumbled backward down the incline of the narrow parapet. The dead lay ensprawled where they landed, while those yet living shrieked out in inhuman tones or else sat, clutching stupidly at spouting geysers of dark blood.

Litter bearers appeared from out of nowhere to tote the wounded to the hospital ward in the Long Barrack, but some of the sufferers concluded to proceed there under their own power. Joe witnessed little Galba Fuqua receive a speeding missle full in the face. Poor Galba! He had to hold his shattered jaws together with both of his hands. It was a painful way he made to the hospital, blubbering and spitting up blood.

And then here was Maizy with her homemade bandages and water bucket; Maizy, in the thick of battle! One look and Joe wanted her gone.

"This is no place for you!" he roared his concern. "Musket balls don't play no favorites! Get back to the church, Maizy, please!"

"I'll stay where I'm needed," Maizy shot back. "And right now, I'm needed here. Look after your own business, Joe; I'll look after mine!" And then, without another word, Maizy turned to lend succor to the growing number of the wounded and the dying.

Further on down the north wall to the east, Joe noticed the Louisiana Dockman merrily bapping away with his musket into the retiring column. The thwarted Mexicans peeling away from this stalemate of an assault needed no coaxing to propel them out of the range of the demonic inferno that seemed to play along the top of the jagged wall.

In the gathering light of dawn and a parting volley of flame from the fortress, Joe beheld a startling sight. The once-dim field below the north wall now took on the appearance of a cadaverous mound of crawling clusters of arms, legs, and hands that spasmodically thrashed the air in grotesque exaggeration. Pitiful remnants of shredded and blistered faces babbled and cried amidst the shattered piles of equipment and an entanglement of searing and scorched mesquite.

"Hurrah, my boys!" Travis cackled from a parched throat. "We've driven them from the field! Stand firm!"

In response to his own burning thirst, Joe scooped up a ladle of Maizy's water bucket and gurgled the cool, refreshing liquid between his own parched lips, heedless of the fact that the most of it ended up dribbling down his chin.

"You there, Joe!" hollered Adjutant Baugh. "Go sparingly. We're going to be needing plenty more of that water to cool down these guns and the men are swilling down more than we can afford to spare. Get to the well and fetch as much as you can carry, then get back here on the double."

Joe went.

At the well, Joe had to wait his turn, as other water-toters there in a queue filled their receptacles from an oversized bucket someone had fashioned from a flour barrel. Arriving back at the north wall, his buckets sloshing a splattery path in his wake, Joe noticed the Louisiana Dockman and a few others with picks and axes hard intent at wearing rude embrasures in the crumbling adobe wall.

"We are not loco, us, Joseph," Jean grinned, pausing to wipe the beaded sweat from his brow with his bare wrist. "We chop holes in wall so that cannon may shoot downward. Otherwise, they are but worthless scraps of iron when Mexican soldiers get under wall. Mon dieu! Would you listen to the sound they are making, those on the ground, poor fellows! Still," he considered reflectively, "better them, than me."

Even as the Dockman spoke, gun crews worked, manhandling their cannons in alignment with the freshly hewn embrasures, while yet others crouched, stirring up some white-hot coals in braziers that stood alongside each gun. The constantly lit braziers were necessary to ensure the searing reliability of slow matches called linstocks that would be used to touch off the readied prime of each cannon.

"Better see to your weapon," the Dockman cautioned Joe. "I am minding the roof in the corner there," he said, pointing toward the "L"-shaped building that formed the northeast corner of the plaza. "The wall is fell down some in front, and the roof is caving in, she. Big hole. My eyes maybe shall see you later on, Joseph, but I doubt much. Bon chance, my friend," he concluded, turning to pick his way back along the broken wall at last.

Unencumbering himself of the water buckets, Joe double-loaded his shotgun with nails and broken glass, then took his place alongside of Travis who was stirring up the brazier next to his cannon with a poker.

"God o' mercy!" quaked a jumpy defender, prematurely discharging his musket straight into the air. "Here they comes again!"

Joe could see it, a solid gray mass, steadily pressing forward across the cluttered field and toward the north wall. And as the Mexican columns advanced, the first frigid rays of the rising sun glinted along their converging hedge of bayonets.

"Hold steady, lads," Travis imparted, "Steady . . . "

Now, here and there, individual forms started becoming more discernible as the column surged forward within yards of the acequia that separated the open plain from the Alamo's field of fire. They were so close that Joe could actually pick out the facial features of individual soldiers in the advance columns. And those soldiers were hurling bundled sticks called fascines into the muck and mire of the acequia to help provide a firmer footing for their fellow troops in the rear. Behind the fascine hurlers, ladder bearers stepped. Now, they were at the acequia; then, they were over it, veering closer, closer . . .

Out of range to the north, the massed band of the dictator Santa Anna blared out their choicest repertoire of blood-curdling strains for the listening ears of the waiting Texians. This, along with the rattling bristle of advancing bayonets, served their purpose well in inducing heavy breathing tension along the walls of the Alamo. Upon the point of hyperventilating, a few of the defenders snapped under the pressure, as here and there, a musket cracked.

"Damn your eyes, hold your fire!" Travis himself snapped out of character, clearly betraying the limits of his own frayed nerves.

Now the Mexican columns were scarcely thirty yards away and even Joe found himself failing beneath the pressure. "Take 'em," the Alamo commander bellowed, at long last. Travis touched off the prime of his eight-pounder with a poker, then stepped back as the carriage lurched and a crinkle of flame slapped into the foremost of the attackers, mashing them to the earth like so many potatoes. Then the entire wall erupted in a billow of smoke, a billow streaked with persistent and darting tongues of flame that bloomed sometimes white and sometimes orange, as though it were contesting the very dawn itself.

It was irresistible. The columns shuddered at first, then collapsed altogether before the merciless hail, as the Texian defenders poured their leaden efforts into the very heart of the assault. But, as in the first wave, the Mexicans dressed down their diminished ranks and kept coming until the pummeled remnants ultimately reached the base of the wall. The ladder bearers had gone down in the first volley from the fort, but the Mexicans wrenched their charges from dead fingers and planted them along the outer surface of the wall. But just as swiftly as the ladders could be planted, Texian gun butts swept them away, sending ejected climbers crashing down upon the bayonet tips of their fellow troopers below.

Down the impalers and impalees thudded, only to be trampled underfoot of the advancing rear columns in their blind push forward.

The Mexicans soon found a way to meet the impasse, as ladders raised against the wall once more, and half a dozen or so sturdy troopers braced themselves against the base of each, making them all but immovable. Up the attackers scrambled to meet the fury of the waiting defenders upon the parapets; then the fighting took on a more personal nature.

The first troopers to make it to the top of the wall were the first to die, as rifle butts, pistols, hunting knives, and even an occasional ax throttled, shot slashed and hewed any head brash enough to appear over the crumbling adobe summit. Soon, corpses stacked like corkwood in the ground space around each of the ladders.

But the defenders did not come out of it totally unscathed. In their hurry to get off a better shot, some of them unwisely resorted to stand upon the exposed top of the narrow wall where they became easy targets for the troops in the rear. Joe observed one such unwise Texian get literally carried away into the plaza by a devastating volley from the Mexican ranks that shot the riddled body to the packed earth with a nasty thud. Flinching on the gruesome sight, Joe hastily discharged his weapon over the wall, then ducked backed down to reload empty muskets.

All the while, through the deafening roar, Travis continued to sing out orders and encouragement to his men. "Keep it up and don't surrender, boys!" he shouted. "No rendirse, muchachos!" he added, for the benefit of Juan Seguin's Tejano fighters.

Some of the attackers, meanwhile, exasperated by their lack of progress, began hurtling blindly over the shoulders of their comrades ascending the ladders to attain the unknown darkness of the fort's interior. Joe could only stare in disbelief at such daring shows of foolhardiness, for the Texians above hurled the bludgeoned, bloodied bodies of every one of those brave hearts lifeless from the ramparts. That was enough for the surviving troops below the wall. With their officers cursing at them to press forward the attack, they quailed, lost heart, and broke.

Some of the Mexican troopers, however, were too stunned or enraged to do even that. With platoons and squads dashing past them in full retreat, all they could do was throw down their weapons, shake their fists, and shriek "Diablos!" in their wild amazement at the "Texian Devils" and their incredible firepower.

As the sun continued its gradual ascent, its new light accentuated the throes of the fallen, until the undulating, carnage-glutted grounds outside of the mission appeared to take on a life of its own. The wailing, the crying, the moaning, the appeals for "agua, agua," were almost more than Joe could bear.

There was precious little time to pity the wounded, however, as the renewed discordant strains of the military bands drowned out all lamentations and beckoned the soldiers of Mexico back into the slaughter.

"It's the Deguello," remarked one of Juan Seguin's Tejanos. "It means 'no mercy—slit their throats.'"

"I didn't need to know that," Joe spoke aloud, yet to himself.

Hearing the blood-curdling strains, the defenders of the Alamo tightened their grips upon their weapons and awaited the inevitable.

It came. A wall of men, now discernable in the gathering light, was moving forward and this time the defenders could actually pick their targets. Although still out of range, it was the Mexicans this time who began firing and musket balls pocked into the lower extremities of the outer wall. Then a steadier, if thinner, fire erupted from the fort, taking down individual figures in the closing Mexican columns. And once those columns reached the acequia, Texian cannon, firing through their jagged embrasures, dumped soldiers into the ditch by the dozens. There would be small need for fascines this time around.

Joe, meanwhile, kept loading the muskets and handing them

around until there were no more takers. Then he fired off a few shots of his own, before ducking back behind the parapet when he saw Maizy and Carlos Espalier drag a stricken Tejano out of the field of fire.

When it looked as though the Mexican columns would once more waver, their officers spurred them on with the flats of their swords. In this way, ladders raised once more against the north wall. And once more, the troops began scrambling up.

Travis was ready for them. With his gun crew either dead, or out of action, the Alamo commander abandoned the cannon in favor of his shotgun and blasted the mounting assailants out of their shoes. Then he lifted the brazier of flaming hot coals with a section of canvas and dumped it over the wall upon the heads of the troops just below. Chilling screams and the odor of searing flesh filled the air, the ears, the nostrils.

Then, as Joe looked on in horror, a returning volley from without caught Travis square in the head and bowled him down the ramp like a sack of grain. Joe rushed to Travis' side and crouched over his prostrate form, hoping to render whatever assistance he could. But one look at the splintered, purple hole at the bridge of Travis' nose told Joe that the Alamo commander was well beyond hope or earthly care. Travis was dead and the blunt finality of it hit Joe like a ton of bricks. That the rush of battle swiftly stirred him back to his senses was a blessing in disguise for Joe, for he would have to get to cover and fast. Still, Joe just couldn't bring himself to leave Travis in such sad estate over which the enemy could gloat. He owed his former master at least that much courtesy. So Joe raised the lifeless burden from under its armpits and dragged Travis to the side, propping him up against an upright timber by the side of the cannon ramp where he would be comparatively out of the way.

"Dear Lord!" cried Maizy, appearing at Joe's side, "Is he . . . is he . . . ?"

"He's gone, Maizy," Joe replied helplessly. "Nothing we can

do. Now go back to the church room, before . . . "

But Joe never got the chance to finish his sentence. A stray bullet from who knows where dug into Maizy's chest with cruel velocity, slamming her into the wheel of a cannon.

"Maizy!" Joe shuddered in rising horror, cradling the stricken woman's head with his one free arm, while the cannon's wheel supported the rest of her convulsing body. "No! No! Why'd you have to come out here? Why?"

"No time for nonsense talk, Joe—no time," she gasped. "You got to get yourself safe now and get back to Silvie with those freedom papers. Think of Silvie and not so much about yourself. Aaah!" she winced in pain, trying all the while to retain her faculties. "Promise me quick you will! Promise me . . . "

"I promise," Joe replied, sobbing openly.

"And Joe," Maizy continued, her voice reduced to a harsh whisper now, "tell that little girl I love her . . . tell her not to be mourning me too much . . . because I'm dying free, Joe. Tell her that."

"Yes," was all that Joe could choke back in reply, though Maizy never heard him. Her head sank back, her body shuddered and then, she was still.

Joe wept. With a battle raging around him, the "Veteran Soldier" pressed his face into Maizy's chest and vented his grief. Then he remembered her final words. He would have to survive this conflict if he were ever to fulfil Maizy's dying wish. Joe's sole remaining thought then was to reach the refuge of the Long Barrack and from where he now stood its thick walls seemed miles away.

With a parting glance at Maizy, Joe turned to make his move, then halted, as a Mexican officer clambered over the wall and into the fort. When the officer noticed Travis' body at the slope of the ramp, he descended upon it with a gleaming upraised saber. But Joe would not abide the officer's intended mutilation. Returning to the lifeless Alamo commander's side, Joe wrenched the loaded pistol from Travis' belt and cocked it with one motion. When the officer attempted to make a swipe at Joe with his saber, he caught his foot in an entanglement of pulley rope instead and struck wide. Seizing the moment, Joe pressed the barrel of the pistol into his assailant's face and felt a jolt, as the discharge reduced the officer's features to a fine hash. Like a marionette with cut strings, the officer tumbled back over an empty water bucket to rise no more.

Momentarily blinded by the dowsing of splattered blood, Joe used the sleeve of his free arm to clear his eyes. What he saw upon clearing them of the foul mess was an unsettling sight: squad upon squad of Mexican soldiers, already inside the fort and coming over the walls unchecked. The few Texians on the northwest corner were quickly overcome, the northern postern was thrown open from within and there were soon more assault troops in the Alamo than living defenders. Flanked, the north wall survivors began dropping from the parapet of their own accord to seek shelter. It was a far better choice than remaining, only to drop under the deadly crossfire of the troops already on the plaza floor.

Adjutant Baugh assumed control of this remnant of resistance. "Make for the Long Barrack," he rallied. "No panic, boys! Don't show 'em your backs!"

Joe started to move, then stopped dead in his tracks. For there, upon the northeast corner of the plaza upon the roof of the "L"-shaped building, the Louisiana Dockman fought, alone. With an ax in hand, Jean stood tall, flailing for dear life at a passel of blue-shakoed troopers. For some reason, Joe took in the brief scene as one spellbound. For even as Jean smashed away at the bayonet-tipped barrels of the probing soldiers' muskets, he regaled the startled men with a jolly song.

> Jolie had a sister,
> And good she was to me.
> A femme libre de couleur,
> C'est vrais! That girl was free!
> I took her to the river,

> But she stranded me at sea—Oui!
> Now, have I what but left, but my own Jolie!

Strange how, only hours before, this same Louisiana Dockman had spoken of his desire to follow his beloved river to the end of his days. Why, he had even scoffed at the idea of being a soldier! Now, as Joe looked on in admiration, the weight of the pressing soldiery upon the sagging roof ended both Jean's dream and his life, crashing him and the whole crowd of surprised Mexicans down into the darkness of the room below.

But this was no time for Joe to be mourning yet another loss. With troops tumbling over the west wall, hot on his heels, Joe made for a room on the northern end of the Long Barrack and then bolted himself in.

Within the windowless Long Barrack room, Joe had to squint to adjust his eyes to the fresh dark. But by beams of light issuing in through some crudely bored musketholes in the wall, Joe was able to discern that he was not alone in the chamber. There were dark figures crouching along the far wall; some of them were moaning. The discovery made Joe step back a little too suddenly, and when he did, he sent a unseen stand of muskets clattering down upon the hard, earthen floor. When one of the upset muskets discharged, its resounding boom panicked one of the room's resident wounded.

"No more shooting, water, please!" languished the faceless voice from the shadows. "Lordy God, I'm on fire!"

"We all need water. There's three of us here," another voice intoned. "Charlie Zanco there's gut shot. Water won't do him much good."

"Shut up with yer goddam opinion," a third voice spat back. "If I could only stand I'd fire one of those bloody muskets out them loopholes myself!"

Joe cut short the verbal exchange. "Got no water, sorry. But I can still shoot."

Joe peeked out of the loophole and saw a high-shakoed

trooper charging on the door, bayonet leveled. So Joe poked a musket out of the hole and let the fellow have it. Propelled forward by the force of his momentum, the trooper involuntarily rammed his bayonet into the ground, then tripped over the upright stock of his musket. The force of his body snapped the bayonet at the hilt, as both trooper and musket struck the earth with a jerk and were still.

Unable to see anything further through the clouds of smoke that choked the plaza, Joe kept at it, banging blindly away with his stack of muskets. But he needn't have worried about hitting a living Texian by mistake, for the only living souls now out of doors were wearing the blue uniforms of the army of Mexico.

Bap and toss, Joe's muskets clattered upon the hard earthen floor until, all too soon, the very last of them was expended and Joe was left standing with an empty, smoking gun. Then, all he could do was wait, like the unfortunate wounded men in the chamber. Trapped.

Outside, a growing number of soldiers started ramming against the thick wooden door with the butts of their muskets, as though they were trying its consistency. Then, to Joe's amazement, they stopped and pulled back. *Could they have given up on the room*, he thought. Hardly likely. Something was up and Joe got the sudden urge to find a corner—any corner.

Kabam! went the earsplitting roar, choking the room with smoke and flame, whereupon the door and section of limestone wall were no more. They had blasted their way in with a cannon! With the door gone, Mexican musket barrels clogged the jagged new opening, blasting an eardrum shattering broadside that sent 69-caliber leaden balls ricocheting around the limestone walls. Then the troopers advanced into the dense smoke to finish the job with cold steel.

When Joe heard the death screams of his wounded comrades, he made himself small against the surface of the far wall to await the inevitable thrust of dull steel. It did not arrive. Instead, two officers appeared and cleared out all of the troopers from the room with flaming oaths. Then one of the officers, holding a lantern, moved into the cell for a look, while the other remained silhouetted in the shattered doorway.

"Are there any Negroes here?" asked the officer at the door with caution, as the lantern bearer made straight for Joe.

"Si, hay una," replied Lantern Bearer.

"Come out," he reassured Joe in perfect English. "No one will harm you, I assure."

Under the circumstances, Joe had no other choice but to comply with the officer's command. So, shielding his eyes from the lantern's light, Joe rose up cautiously and moved forward. Luckily for him, the officer did not see the yet hot barreled musket still standing where the "Veteran Soldier" had discharged it only minutes before.

"I am Colonel Almonte," doffed the lantern bearer politely, "and this is General Castrillion. We do not make it a practice of waging war on slaves—only filibusters and land pirates. These three," Almonte said, gesturing at the mutilated remains of the unfortunate and lately wounded, "'Diablos Tejanos' the men called them—'Texian Devils.' They shot down seven of our men. It took a cannon to dislodge them! You yourself were indeed fortunate to have survived."

As Almonte continued, it was all Joe could do to keep from involuntarily choking back a nervous gulp.

"It appears as though the remainder of these buildings must be carried in like manner," Almonte sighed, shaking his head sadly. "Pirates they may be, but cowards they are not. I fear there shall be no survivors. The men have all gone mad with the scent of blood . . . but come. I shall guide you to a place of relative safety."

"I am thankful to you," Joe said, following the Colonel back into the plaza.

Once outside the door, Joe had to blink, as the diffused rays of morn, filtering down through a wall of sulfurous black smoke, stung into the depths of his reddened sockets. Looking around, Joe was taken aback by an unsettling sight. It was Adjutant Baugh, pinioned against one of the shuttered windows to the right of the door by a brightly decked lance. The long shaft of wood must've been thrust through the Adjutant's belly with such fierce velocity that its owner had been unable to dislodge it. The corpse's gaping mouth revealed a distended tongue, while its eyes bulged wide with a look of both horror and disbelief.

With his own look of both horror and revulsion, Joe turned away, trying to avert his eyes from the skewered Baugh, but the slaughter he saw in the plaza looked far worse. A mosaic of mangled and contorted human remains glutted the yard from end to end like a demon's coverlet. Then there was the smell—an inconceivably foul stench of shredded, exposed human entrails intermingling in a broth-like film of warm, fresh blood, urine, excrement, and vomit that sizzled and churned in this makeshift oven which was the Alamo.

One look induced Joe to bring up the contents of his own guts. The involuntary reflex act may well have saved Joe's life, for an overzealous trooper fired directly at Joe and would've hit him, had he not doubled up to retch. As it was, the musket ball creased Joe's thigh, taking off a good quantity of skin, but not much meat.

The soldier's action seemed to infuriate a gallant young officer who was standing nearby, for he not only twitched the gun from Joe's attacker, but also drove the butt end of it into the fellow's groin in retribution. "There is no controlling this trash!" Castrillion raged, coaxing the yet stunned and newly bloodied Joe to his feet with a mild prodding. "Captain Barragan," Castrillion continued, addressing the officer who had intervened in Joe's behalf, "see to your men!"

"Come," Almonte said. "We are gathering such other noncombatants behind that high mound of earth in the center of the plaza."

Joe felt his way across the grisly obstacle course and it was all that he could do to keep his footing in the oozy slime.

Up on the high mound, a Mexican gun crew was busily blasting away with two captured cannonades against the armory doors, to the east. Kaboom! A double salvo ripped into the splintering framework, driving shafts of jagged door bits and hot shrapnel into the depths of the building and its occupants. Through the thick smoke, Joe saw a throng of soldiers sardine their way into the building, wasting anything that moved. From the sounds of the firing and cheering, Joe guessed that they were fighting their way up the stairs to the hospital ward on the second story. A few returning shots suggested that even some of the perishing sick were resisting to the end. Joe could only imagine the pathetic scene: dozens of muskets, banging their loads into the helpless sick, with gun butts and bayonets finishing the rest.

Though the shrieks of the expiring patients were almost more than Joe could bear, there was more to come. For, as Joe stood watching in horror, the naked and bloodied bodies of the dead Texians were pressured out of the second story windows to flop to the ground below like soiled rag dolls. Then, with that sad chore accomplished, some of the troopers contented to poke their heads out of the windows, waving, cheering, and holding up their grisly, blood-spattered spoils of war. Save those, not another sound issued from the building. The Long Barrack had fallen.

Joe turned his face from the gruesome scene, inclining his gaze instead upon the small, palisaded area in front of the church where Crockett and his men did battle. Joe's heart sank on the sight, for the only figures now filling the yard were those of the shakoed invaders. The old Tennessean was nowhere to be seen.

Shoulder pressed to shoulder, troopers continued to vault the four-foot high wall that separated Crockett's yard from the plaza. Some of them, Joe saw, were pausing a moment to lance at something at their feet with their spear bayonets, before moving on to the church. Joe felt that it was just as well for him that he could not see the object of their collective labor.

Meanwhile up on the thick church façade, a few Texian snipers perched, firing their last rounds of lead into the milling mass of soldiery below them. And there was movement yet upon the high platform in the apse of the building, where Bonham, Dickerson, and a small gun crew labored over a single cannon in a desperate attempt to train it upon the inner precincts of the fort itself. With musket balls buzzing all around them, the cannoneers finally managed the proper deflection of the piece and blasted a heap of iron trash straight through the chapel's arched portal and into the troops still clogging Crockett's yard.

Though there were other "non-combatants" gathered there with him behind the high mound in the center of the plaza, Joe found himself only aware of the little huddle of defenders now cornered in the upper reaches of the Alamo church. For those few stalwart souls represented the last pocket of Texian resistance—perhaps a dozen men against the thousands!

Joe watched as expert Mexican gunners dragged the eighteen-pounder down from its platform on the southwest corner of the plaza and trained it against the stout church defenses. Kaboom! The big gun thundered at last, slamming into the timbers of the high platform of the apse to squash a few of the remaining Texian gunners there. Baroom went another round into the very mouth of the building, while, off to the side, anxious Mexican soldiers stood, waiting for their cue to rush its door-less aperture. Theirs was not a long wait. With the nave cleared of defenders, the attackers swarmed into the church, cheering and firing as they went. Varoom went the final discharge of the Texian's last manned cannon, laying a swathe through the incoming troops like a knife through butter.

Momentarily stunned, the Mexican soldiers pushed on, gingerly picking their way across the gooey flooring of flesh and bone debris and through a bilious, black fog. Now, only the thud, thud, thudding of muskets re-echoing in the vaulted places could tell the tale, so Joe strained his ears to their limits and silently prayed.

For fifteen minutes and more, the firing continued, yet Joe suspected that the troops were probably just shooting at each other in the blind chaos. He had little doubt that all of the defenders must've perished.

Still the firing went on. Some of the troopers, those who'd entered the Alamo after the main fighting ceased, now had nothing to shoot at. So they took out their fevered vengeance upon the stilled corpses of their vanquished adversaries, firing until their shot supply was exhausted and their tunics soaked red with spattered blood. So intent were some soldiers in their efforts of target practice and general mutilation that a trumpeteer, sent in to sound recall, was all but ignored. To curtail the mayhem, Santa Anna's military band was rushed to the scene to stage an impromptu rendition of recall in full complement. It turned the trick.

Firing from within the dark chambers of the barracks and church gradually died down, then petered out altogether. In the silence, dazed troopers started filing out of the building to regroup their depleted units and to gawk upon their fallen comrades-at-arms who lay scattered in heaps about the large open yard.

Then there was a clatter of horse hooves resounding through the main gate, as a splendidly bedecked horse and rider came thundering into the yard accompanied by a slew of lancers. With the Alamo cleared of those who would wish to smite him, the bold Santa Anna was making his grand entrance. As though he were unwilling to incline his gaze upon the shattered remains of his army, El Presidente held his head aloft. Suddenly, as he was turning to jabber something at one of his lieutenants, a few scattered shots rang out from somewhere upon the church façade. The lieutenant by his side pitched backward from the saddle—and landed on his back, stone dead. That was enough for Santa Anna. Waving decorum, he turned his horse and beat an undignified retreat, clattering back through the main gate of the Alamo and toward the town, cordon of lancers trailing far behind.

The hero of all Mexico, Joe mused incredulously, shifting his eyes from the departing form of Santa Anna toward the jagged chapel façade. *So there were still a few defenders "playing possum,"* Joe thought with a thrill.

But the Mexican soldiers were quick to meet the challenge; dozens of musketeers began blazing away at the summit of the church façade. Unfazed by the continued hostilities, Colonel Almonte started walking toward the building to check out the story that there were other non-combatants still secreted in the sacristy room. One of the women who'd been rescued from the ruins of a room along the west wall had mentioned the possibility to the colonel and through her demonstrative gesticulations, Joe was able to interpret the gist and purpose of Almonte's present actions.

Moments after Almonte had disappeared into the church, a resounding shot from the interior of the building had Joe actually fearing for the kindly Colonel's life. But thankfully, Joe's fears were proved unfounded, as shortly thereafter, Almonte reemerged from the church, leading out a sullen procession of bedraggled women and children into the sunlight. Amongst the rescued, Joe recognized Sue Dickerson, walking with a decided limp. From the ugly, telltale stain upon the calf of her skirt, Joe guessed that, like him, the young mother must have been shot. Suzannah hobbled on nevertheless, bundling little Angelina to her breast in the folds of her slain husband's Masonic apron in the hope of shielding the child from the prevalent horror.

Almonte did his best to comfort both mother and child. Finally, he released them into the care of Gertrudis Alsbury and her sister Juana, whose acquaintances Suzannah had made back in those younger days of peaceful coexistence in Bejar.

Nearly half an hour passed before the disposition of the noncombatants was determined: determined by the reappearance of Santa Anna. As the dictator of all Mexico rode in through the main gate of the Alamo, the troops crowding the plaza clambered to attention, while the massed bands struck up a martial air.

Once dismounted, Santa Anna stood with folded arms, staring off across the plaza, while his boisterous staff of bootlickers huddled all around, hurrahing El Presidente's name to the skies over the noble victory.

"Noble victory," Almonte sneered disdainfully, though under his breath. "Another such 'noble victory' will ruin us. If not our fighting spirit, at least our honor and good reputation."

Though the fanfare continued, it subsided somewhat when General Castrillion brought forth five badly wounded Texians who had been found hiding under some moldy mattresses in the Low Barrack. The venerable old officer looked his granite-faced commander-in-chief straight in the eye, speaking and gesticulating, as though he were trying to plead for the lives of the helpless prisoners.

But Santa Anna was immovable. Unimpressed. A snap of his fingers, a few mumbled commands later, and the women and children were ushered from the scene, out the main gate and toward town.

Then it was Castrillion's turn, as the dictator turned his vinegar upon the unflinching old soldier in a language that Joe could only interpret as both demeaning and spiteful. Castrillion's face seemed to flush with horror on Santa Anna's words, as Joe witnessed all too soon the chilling reason why there were to be no women and children on hand.

With Castrillion still protesting, Santa Anna muttered something and then turned his back as a file of soldiers swiftly surrounded the prostrate prisoners. "Listo," an officer barked and muskets cocked in unison. "Fuego," the officer commanded, whereupon the readied muskets banged their loads point blank into the non-resisting sick men whose bodies, in turn, jerked and thrashed about spasmodically in response to the force of the invasive lead. A yelp of terror from one of the living prompted anxious bayonets to finish the job with squashy thrusts.

Other troopers shot and skewered an unfortunate stray cat

they'd found cringing in the guardhouse, simply because it was thought to have belonged to one of those terrible Texians.

Would there be no end to it? thought Joe. Apparently there would not, for some soldiers found yet another living defender secreted in the Long Barrack and dragged him out, kicking and screaming, before Santa Anna. But this particular fellow's protestations, Joe noted in some surprise, were all in Spanish. Then Joe recognized the captured man as old "One-Eyed Brigido" Guerrero, one of Juan Seguin's local volunteers. And oh, how that Guerrero could grovel. Down on the ground he slithered, practically licking the dictator's silver-laden boots in his wholehearted plea for mercy. Though Santa Anna gazed down upon Guerrero with a look of utter contempt, he nonetheless, and to the surprise of all, waved off the obnoxious old hoodwinker and then ordered his release.

Joe gulped—and with good reason, too! For now the throng of unsympathetic eyes were cast solely upon him. The soldiers had expressed few qualms about the release of Guerrero. At least he had been blood of their blood and a fellow countryman. Joe, on the other hand, was just another "Norte Americano" to them and as such, liable to face the stern judgment of El Presidente.

Harsh hands secured Joe's arms and as two soldiers led him on, two others prodded him from behind with the points of their spear bayonets. When Joe turned to protest their treatment of him, one of the soldiers jabbed him so hard that the bayonet tip gouged into Joe's thigh about half an inch, drawing both blood and the ire of Colonel Almonte. Ordering the soldiers back, Almonte drew a small knife to sever Joe's bonds. "I am sorry for this treatment," Almonte said with sincerity. "The soldiers are very tense at the moment. We all are," the Colonel added. "Allay your fears. I will speak in your behalf to El Presidente."

When they halted before Santa Anna at last, Joe found himself averting his eyes to the president of Mexico's splendid boots. It was all Joe could do to distance himself from the dismal reality of the moment; a moment that seemed like hours.

After Almonte and the dictator had exchanged words, Almonte translated for Joe's benefit. "El Presidente asserts that, should you consent to identify the cadavers of Bowie, Travis, and the one called Cocket, he shall find it in his good grace to spare your life. In your best interests, I strongly recommend that you do this thing."

Without any real choice in the matter, Joe could only shake his head in grim compliance and then motion the passel of officers on across the plaza and through the break in the low wall that led into the palisaded area in front of the church.

The party, with Joe in the van, walked on and as it did, some of the officers paused to examine the faces of the fallen along the way for those of family, friends, and comrades-at-arms. But to their horror and dismay, the little court only presented them with an indistinguishable jumble of broken bodies, some of them still clutched in the death struggle.

From the looks of things, Crockett and his Tennessee boys had fallen fast, but furious. They looked so horribly mutilated, in fact, that Joe had his doubts that he would even be able to recognize, let alone identify, Crockett's remains in this nightmare of mortal mincemeat. Yet there he was. Backed into an angle of wall where the palisade joined with the eastern end of the Low Barrack, the once fun-loving frontiersman lay in exanimate repose. A look of pain contorted Crockett's once jesting lips, while blood soaked up his buckskin shirted torso. An ugly saber cut had evidently laid open Davy's forehead, for great clots of crusty black scab matter splashed across his weathered features. His capless lanks of graying hair tossed in unruly knots in the morning breeze. The coonskin cap itself, strangely unfazed in the furor, lay in an orderly fashion at his side, as though unseen hands had made an attempt at posing the demised in a more tasteful fashion.

Crockett's hands, once so skillful at fiddle-playing in all those spirit-raising musical duels with bagpiper John MacGregor during the course of the siege, now clutched thin air in the death grip. And then, Joe saw something that sent goose bumps shivering up his spine. For there, wedged in between two upright cedar posts of the palisade, was Crockett's very fiddle. Then some soldier saw it too and snatched it up for a prize.

'Oh Kentucky! The Hunters of Kentucky!'

Further on across the yard, meanwhile, some other soldiers were entertaining themselves by striking and stabbing at some object at their feet, just out of Joe's line of vision. But Joe didn't need to actually see the object to know what it was, for he still had two good ears. The screeching sound it made, not unlike the squeal of a stuck pig, could have come from nothing less than John MacGregor's bagpipes. Apparently none of the soldiers had ever seen such an instrument, for they all seemed to regard it as though it were an almost living thing, thrusting their bayonets into it, then jumping aside as the pipes responded in wheezy discord. Finally, with its plaid workmanship in shreds and tatters, the pipes parted, drawn asunder by the victors as trophies of war.

Looking on, Colonel Almonte could only shake his head sadly on the sight. "The oldster Cocket should have left the fighting to the younger men. He deserved far better than to have died at the hands of these unscrupulous primitives. The prime troops were left to the mopping up duties. Had they been in the fore, I am certain that much bloodshed might've been prevented. But," Almonte concluded, "no sense remaining upon this scene. Lead on to Colonel Bowie, that your duties may be fulfilled to the letter."

Joe pointed, mumbled, and the procession tramped on.

The weather and battle-scarred façade of the church gazed down sorrowfully upon the party as they passed in single file through its now jagged aperture. Ornamented blocks of limestone, once framing the portal with a hint of the stone carver's glory, now lay shattered inward by artillery blasts, like teeth irreverently broken by an iron fist.

The party moved into the nave.

Only the previous dusk, Crockett and a few of his men had moved Bowie from his quarters in the Low Barrack to a room in the church, just to the left of the sloping ramp and next to the sacristy room where the women and children had taken refuge. With its stout walls, the church had at least seemed a safe sanctuary then. Now, Joe saw that that sense of sanctuary was but a cruel illusion and nothing more. For just outside of the room's door, wallowing in its own gore, lay the remains of the Alamo's knife-fighting co-commander. Bowie had been horribly mutilated.

"Savages," raged Almonte upon the sight of the grisly handiwork. "They conscript brute savages to do a soldier's duty! I saw them with my own eyes! They made sport of tossing Bowie's body into the air and then catching it upon their bayonets! I stopped them when it was already too late! And yet they would call the vile scum soldiers! Mexican soldiers! It is an indelible stain upon the honor of the nation!"

Breathing a heavy sigh, Almonte collected himself. "But come, to the task," he said.

As the party began processing out of the cavernous tomb that was the chapel, Joe thought that he actually saw Santa Anna soften on the sight of Bowie's desecrated remains. But the stern jawed Commander-in-Chief also collected himself and moved on.

Slowly the officers with Joe in the lead inched their way across the scene of wanton destruction and toward the north wall . . . past the high mound in the center of the plaza where the muted cannon yet trained upon the doors of the armory, to the east . . . beyond the face of the Long Barrack where swathes of Mexican dead lay ensprawled from their struggle to carry the building . . . past the very door of the room itself where Joe had emerged after having piled up how many bodies? Seven, Almonte had said. Total strangers who had wished Joe dead, yet men nevertheless whom, under different circumstances, might've even been his friends.

But Joe could not afford to think of such things at the

moment. He had to remain focused. He had fought his own good fight with a clear conscience. *Why hadn't he stuck beside Travis to the bitter end?* Indeed, he had. *And hadn't he made Travis' cause of freedom his own? Hadn't Maizy?* Yes and yes! But now, with both Travis and Maizy dead, the focus of Joe's loyalties suddenly took on a more personal nature. For loyalty now meant fighting for both his and Silvie's concerns exclusively. And to achieve those ends, he would say and do most anything. *Anything!*

So there could be no remorse; he would not take sides. For all Joe cared, the Mexicans could have the Alamo; have it and welcome. Look at the price they had paid for it. Joe would live to fight another day and fight, he would! But first, as Almonte stated, to the task at hand.

When Joe and the party of officers mounted the cannon platform at the center of the north wall, they arrived just in time to see stretcher-bearers lugging down a body upon a litter. From the pasty, crimson rag, thrown over its face in perhaps a show of respect, Joe recognized the corpse as the officer who had sought to desecrate Travis' body.

"Holy Mother," Castrillion exclaimed, as he too recognized the man. "Poor Mora, he was my friend."

Then Joe tensed up; almost cringed upon the thought of having to see poor Maizy's lifeless form. But poor Maizy was not there! Look, though he did, Joe could find no trace of her. A panic began to well up in Joe. "Maizy," he demanded pleadingly. "Where's Maizy?"

"There *was* a woman here," a voice said and Joe turned to look upon General Castrillion. "I have seen to it that she will have a good Christian burial, along with military honors. She was your friend? I am sorry," Castrillion concluded with a look of compassion.

The bluntness of Castrillion's words hit Joe like a ton of bricks; he felt an emptiness gnawing him at the pit of his stomach. Without knowing exactly why, Joe felt that he would've actually felt less anguish in looking upon Maizy's lifeless body, than in having to accept the fact that she was gone—forever. Nevermore to be looked upon, conversed with, or touched by for the rest of his natural born days on earth.

Though deep in the well of denial, Joe shook off the thought, as swiftly as Almonte cleared his throat. "Please, if you would," Almonte asked, motioning, "is *this* Colonel Travis?"

It most certainly was. Although somewhat slumped to the side, Travis lay just where Joe had placed him, by an upright timber support. The feet were bare; the Colonel's saber was gone. The looters and scavengers, in plying their trade upon the dead, had not even exempted the fort's commander.

With folded arms, Santa Anna stood over Travis' corpse, considering it while drumming upon his silver-laden epaulets. Finally he turned to Almonte, muttered something, and then strode back down the ramp to remount his horse. Off he spurred at last through the main gate with a cordon of lancers trailing close behind.

"We must return to the Plaza del Las Yslas to arrange for your disposition and comforts," Almonte told Joe. "Let us be off, as it is best to be prudent in all things concerning El Presidente."

Back across the plaza of the Alamo Joe and Almonte trudged, while funeral and hospital parties toiled all around them separating the dead from the wounded, the Texian corpses from those Mexican. And before them all went the looters, scavenging and despoiling the Texian dead of anything and everything worth saving.

Seeing the look of disgust on Joe's face, Almonte said in way of an explanation, "Many brave soldiers have fallen today. Hundreds more lay wounded. Their surviving comrades must be granted *some* recompense for all they've endured and *your* companions did not leave many spoils to choose from, at that. You will notice that the shoes go first. Some of the men have never owned real ones. Only sandals, or bare feet, have they known. El Presidente provided them with sandals for the assault, but even those have to be returned to the commissary, or else bartered for with sufficient loot. Boots are a real prize, constituting perhaps a year's wages. Best look out for your *own* feet," Almonte concluded, half in jest.

Joe retraced his shoes' steps across the plaza, committing to memory the smoking ruins which had, in their last gasping billows, infused in him a newfound resolve to survive toward his own purpose.

Under the arched portal of the main gate at last, Joe gave a parting glance to the battered façade of the Alamo church. It looked to be staring at him. Joe shuddered on the thought and while the church in turn gasped a heavy sigh in smoke, Joe passed beyond its range of vision.

Moving on toward the footbridge at the bend of the river, Joe noticed how the tall grass had been tromped down in shaky aisle by the surge of assault troops. Here and there, casualties began revealing themselves in the fluffy beds of greenery and Joe practically tripped over the stiffened, upraised arms of one such body. It was Texian. Joe recognized the unfortunate as Quartermaster Milton. In an apparent run for his life, Milton had only managed to get this far, before being overtaken and then skewered by lancers. *Who,* Joe thought, *would inform the poor man's family?*

Everything in sight looked different to Joe since the battle. Judging from its well-worn condition, the footbridge must have seen considerable traffic during the thirteen days since he had last crossed it. Why, even Portrero Street itself had taken on the appearance of a battlefield, with not so much as an inch of its surface left unmarred by foot, horse, or caisson. Soldiers seemed to be everywhere, crowding the narrow causeway; most of them were bearing litters of the wounded and the dead.

Standing along the wayside, the few citizens of Bejar who turned out to pay tribute to the victorious troops, could only cheer halfheartedly at best. Even the bells of San Fernando church seemed to sense the nature of the atmosphere, as their hollow tones imparted not cheery chords of conquest, but rather dismal dirges for the dead.

Now Joe and Almonte were walking upon all too familiar ground. They'd reached the Musquoz house where the Dickersons had stayed prior to the siege. Just across the way stood the inn where Joe, Travis, Maizy, and Silvie had abided those oh so many days before. What a sight it looked now, with the litter bearers leaving their splattered trails of blood along the way to and then through each and every door of the inn, as hospital space began running out.

On Almonte's approach, the sentries at the door of the Musquoz' house snapped to attention, whereupon, the Colonel and Joe shuffled through the opened door and into the main room of the dwelling. Other survivors, Joe saw, had preceded them there. Nervous women, frightened children, but not a *single* adult male.

Amidst the mild clamor, upon a straight back wooden chair, Sue Dickerson sat, trying her best to soothe baby Angie to sleep. An officer paced the room, keeping his eye upon two privates who were distributing woolen blankets to the ladies. With each distributed blanket, the officer would add a few coins from a small pouch, counting them out to each woman. Thusly blanketed and with some monetary means of sustenance, the women were rushed out of the room with their children tagging noisily behind. Only Suzannah, baby Angie, Gertrudis Albury, and Joe remained.

"Your Mrs. Dickerson has already had conference with El Presidente," Almonte briefed Joe. "Her unfortunate wound has been bound up and she is being well-attended to, as you can see. I will have your own wounds seen to, just as soon as El Presidente allows your departure. I have alerted the sentry to make your presence known—Ah, it is done," Almonte concluded, as the sentry bid them enter.

Joe gulped, looked both ways, then started forward through the opened door.

El Presidente was sitting cross-legged upon a cushioned red velvet stool in the center of the room. He was a tallish fellow by the standards of the day, but must've appeared even taller, due to his lean, almost gaunt frame. His grayish, almost ashen, complexion suggested a bout of dysentery. Dressed as he was in a plain, black suit with long tailcoat and a flat, low-crowned hat, Joe reckoned that Santa Anna looked more like a Methodist preacher than he did a victorious general.

Santa Anna surveyed Joe from head to foot with cold, calculating eyes. His demeanor soon brightened however, as with a thinlipped smile he bid Joe be seated. As the dictator's command of the English language was decidedly limited, Almonte served as interpreter.

"His Excellency states that your Colonel Travis was a brave man, but a foolish one, bearing arms against a government of which he had sworn to uphold. He has met with the fate of a brigand, as have his misguided followers! His Excellency adds that it is not his intention to wage war upon slaves, but to free them. You may remain with the army, or wander at your will, as soon as the situation eases down. With feelings running as they are, some of the men may, understandably, try to harm you. His Excellency therefore suggests that you remain within this dwelling under guard—solely for your protection, of course—until such time it is deemed prudent for your departure. El Presidente further enjoins that you make clear to the remnant of these so called 'Texian' rebels that resistance is utterly hopeless—that the fate of all taken under arms shall be that of the garrison here at Bejar. Any further actions waged against the Supreme Government shall precipitate total decimation. Meanwhile," Almonte concluded on a somewhat softer note, "El Presidente bids you rest and refresh yourself."

Left once more without much choice in the matter, Joe's only response was a somewhat awkward bow that backed him into one of the sentries at the door. Somehow, Joe made it out of the room alive.

El Presidente would be favoring him to a grand review of the troops in the Plaza del Las Yslas, Almonte informed Joe, as Gertrudis Alsbury knelt, binding up the "Veteran Soldier's" wounds with rude strips of cotton rag. Sue Dickerson would also be granted the opportunity to witness the most impressive of spectacles. They must hurry, for the military bands on the plaza were even now announcing that the event was close at hand.

Bound up and somewhat refreshed by a jug of water and wash cloth, Joe stepped outside in wide-eyed astonishment. The Main Plaza was fairly teeming with long files of fresh troops who not only ranged the court from end to end, but overlapped it, spilling out onto Military Plaza as well. Judging from the condition of their uniforms, most of these men looked as though they had not even participated in the storming of the Alamo. Oh they looked a bit mud spattered and dusty, but these were only telltale signs of the trail and not of battle.

It looked to Joe like a force of at least eight thousand men stood facing him. Eight thousand and they had not even been needed to carry the fort! Joe felt like kicking himself for having once believed that the Alamo stood even the slightest chance of holding out—maybe even conquering! There in the Plaza del Las Yslas, Joe felt like crawling into a hole and covering himself up.

Fourteen

Shaking Off the Dust

Santa Anna was more than willing to accommodate the "Veteran Soldier." For no sooner had Joe finished witnessing the grand review of the troops than he was led to a dingy storeroom just off the rear of the Musquoz house and bolted in.

There he was, locked once more inside a dark and musty room, with but a jug of water and a small ration of hardtack to sustain him for who knew *how* long. *If this were Santa Anna's idea of freedom,* Joe figured, *then he would just as soon take his chances at the hands of the Texians. At least they had not tried to shoot him on sight.*

In spite of his frayed emotions and the chain of seesawing events that had brought him to this shuttered place, Joe found that he was unusually hungry. But when he tried his palate upon the hardtack, the coarse, moisture-less biscuit gagged in his throat and refused to go down without something of a fight and a pull at the jug. *If there was any truth in the phrase that "an army travels on its stomach," then the collective stomach of the Mexican army must be a cast iron one,* Joe mused.

As the minutes wore on into hours and the air in the storeroom grew stale, Joe began to feel that the walls were closing in on him. Up above him, a solitary sunbeam issued through the roof and by its sparse light, Joe noticed that the ceiling itself looked jagged and uneven, as though someone had deliberately punched a hole in it. Then Joe remembered hearing how Ben Milam and his boys had captured Bejar by boring holes in the walls and roof of the buildings. The poor efforts of someone else to repair the damaged roof had left the room insubstantial shelter against the elements; the puddle of water on the clammy floor below Joe's feet attested as much, anyway.

The boards covering the hole appeared loose. If Joe could somehow reach the ceiling, he could wrench the flimsy planks aside, then make his escape across the flat rooftops of Bejar; but how to get up there? There were certainly enough barrels and crates in the room for him to stack up, but all the same, Joe figured that any such attempt would probably come off a whole lot better under the cover of darkness.

Outside the Musquoz house, but still within earshot, Joe could hear the Mexican hospital crews at their weary chore of hauling the wounded back into town and into some sort of shelter. Soon the monotonous, creaky droning of their wagons and handcarts lulled Joe toward much needed slumber. So he leaned against a crate in the only house in town not disturbed by the pitiful moans of shattered men and took in a few snatches of welcome sleep. Evening would find him at a much more spirited activity.

It was the creaking of the door that stirred Joe from his slumber, as a lantern-bearing sentry entered the storeroom to replenish the prisoner's water supply and to serve him up something of a supper.

How long had he been asleep? Joe wondered. Light no longer shone down through the hole in the ceiling, so it must be nighttime, he figured. There was light shining in from the outer chamber however, and that, along with the in-rush of cool air through the open kitchen window provided a welcome respite from the stale atmosphere of the room.

Joe swiftly calculated the position of the hole in the roof with his eyes, even as the sentry banged the door shut, consigning him to the darkness once more. Joe finished his meager meal of beans and corn tortillas, then washed it all down with a long draught of water from the jug. It was time to make his move.

Outside, a heavy pallor of death hung over the gloomy town and it seemed to invade the very senses of the populace, reaching out with a cold, clammy hand. It horrified the eye, it wailed upon the ear, it assaulted the nose and it tasted of hell. Yet it was a *sixth* sense—the pervading fear of the unknown—that hastened the superstitious Bejarians behind closed and bolted doors, ere the sun went down. For it was then they believed that ghosts of the recently departed would be on the prowl in search of their war-ravaged bodies. Spirits of those who died a violent death were supposedly doomed to wander the earth in incessant toil to wail and gnash their teeth with little hope, or relief. It was a good thing that Joe did not put much store in such childish tales—well, not much, anyway.

Silently, Joe began his tower of boxes and crates, commencing with a heavy oaken barrel for a base. Reaching as high as he could, Joe finally placed the last of the boxes in place, then stood, surveying the results of his efforts as well as he could in the near-pitch-darkness of the room. Satisfied, Joe paused a moment, listened for precaution's sake, then started up.

Mounting the barrel was easy, for it sat fairly stationary. The dubiously balanced crates and boxes on the other hand, were another thing altogether. To keep them from falling, Joe had to shift his entire weight against both crates *and* the wall as he was ascending. After quite an effort, Joe finally reached the top of his teetering tower. From there, it would either be one good leap to freedom, or a treacherous tumble to discovery.

With a deep breath, Joe launched himself roofward. He tottered but an instant before his palms thrust firmly against the ceiling, clacking the uncertain boxes flush beneath his feet. He'd reached the hole in the roof.

When he tried the planking for looseness with a free hand, Joe discovered that the boards were neither weighted, nor nailed down. So he slid them aside with comparative ease and then felt the blustery night air come rushing in. Now if only the crates beneath his feet would stay put, he could be up and out of here.

Were the crates to fall, however, their crashing would doubtless alert the sentries and leave Joe the object of countless soldiers' guns. Glad guns; happy guns; more than willing to accommodate guns.

But there was no turning back now, so Joe grasped the jagged edges of the hole and hoisted himself up and over the ledge and onto the outer surface of the roof. Then he paused with his heart in his throat, listening and waiting.

Prone against the roof, Joe surveyed his new surroundings. The rooftop was sparsely furnished with careworn and scattered wooden furniture and a few sun-bleached clay pots. Then there was a sort of trap door with the upper rungs of a ladder visible. Joe remembered once hearing how the Bejarians had a custom of taking their evening meals aloft during the sweltering days of summer. Some would even deign to lay their pallets right out upon the flat roof and then sleep beneath a shimmering sheet of stars. But luckily for Joe, the weather of late was bitter cold and the roofs deserted.

Slithering to the edge of the roof to make himself less conspicuous, Joe peered down into the streets below where not a soul was stirring. The stillness of it all gave Joe the creeps, for the clarity of silence was so heightened that even the slightest movement of a creaky gate became amplified and registered like rolling thunder.

Self-consciously checking the sound of his own breathing, Joe looked across the way toward the familiar outline of the inn. How strange it felt to be viewing it like this—like a criminal.

Suddenly, one of the inn's doors banged open and a pair of soldiers appeared from beneath the porte-cochere dragging a sagging bundle between them. Into a waiting cart, the pair unceremoniously flopped down their bundle, for the bundle was a body and they were taking it to the Campo Santo, Bejar's cemetery. Joe waited until the lumbering, makeshift hearse was out of sight.

There was a bougainvillea-laden trellis that extended all the way up beyond the roofline and Joe decided that it would make a good ladder. First, he tried his weight upon a crosspiece of latticework, then started his descent. It proved rough going, for the woody vine snatched at his clothes all the way down until they were a tattered and ragged mess and he himself was covered with scratches. But he had reached terra firma.

Though scarcely a month had passed since he and Silvie had sat beneath this very trellis and under the same beams of moonlight, it felt to Joe like a lifetime had come and gone. How tranquil those times were—and how fleeting.

After a swift reality check, Joe made himself small against an angle of wall to see if he'd been seen. Apparently he hadn't, but where to go from here? Portrero Street, with its meandering burial details, seemed a bad bet, so Joe opted to skirt the Musquoz wall instead. Cutting across the far corner of the yard, he hurdled over the low barrier of sloping wall at that point. Then, upon all fours, Joe inched his way to the end of the wall and then backtracked his way to Main Plaza.

Just across the plaza to Joe's left there squatted a low, well-lit dwelling surrounded by a platoon of shakoed troopers and Joe suspected it to be Santa Anna's headquarters. So, deciding that it would be more prudent to make his escape in the opposite direction, he headed south across the plaza and right past Nat Lewis' old store. By ducking down a side alley that ran east, Joe ended up on the west bank of the San Antonio River.

Now where to go? The river itself seemed a logical course to follow and so Joe took it down to the La Villita ford, praying all the while that he would go undetected. He clung to the shrub-ingrown bank, quickening his pace as the desire of flight and a mounting fear of apprehension got the better of him.

The river, however, sludged on by in its own good time, carrying debris and snarls of driftwood along in its lazy wake. There was something downright peculiar about one of these logjams, Joe suspected, for it was throwing off glints and reflections of something suggestively metallic. Upon closer examination, he saw that the shining things were row upon row of brass buttons and silver buckles—buckles that held together a twisted mass of once-white cross belts. This was no logjam such as Joe had ever seen; these were dead soldiers.

Rather than carting them off to the cemetery, the sickened and weary burial details seemed to have dumped some of their cadavers into the water, hoping that the coursing waters would carry away all such damning evidence of their neglect. But disturbingly, such was not the case. For the river's choked current only swirled by in circling pools, while the bloated, buoyant corpses bobbed in place, flapping their stiffened fingers, as if in reproach.

Joe shuddered and moved on. With the burial details possibly still in the area, this was no safe place to be anyhow.

Stumbling into an abandoned hut of La Villita at last, Joe assumed, from its smashed doors and the deep wheel ruts running within, that a battery must've seen action there.

And then Joe saw it. Water. Damned water. Getting in his way, keeping him from Silvie. Wasn't that just like water? Joe had to get to the other side of the river, and without a bridge, he'd just have to make do on foot, hoping for a low point to strike for, someplace that wasn't so deep, or treacherous. Bloody damned water!

The river was running so low at the La Villita ford that a small island had risen up in midstream. It looked like a promising enough landmark to aim for, so Joe did, wading into the water without so much as pausing to roll up his pants legs. This was a mistake. The mucky slime comprising the river floor sucked him down until he was buried up to his knees in the mess. Moving at all became a mammoth effort and a slow-going one at that, for with each successive step, the mud would pucker and smack its objections until it was a much-fatigued Joe who reached the bump of an island at last.

But there could be no rest stop for him there, for the solidity of the island proved to be but an illusion. So rather than staying to be sucked down by the near quicksand of the spot, Joe descended once more into the silent, watery ooze of the river and somehow managed to reach the further shore.

This was the Alamo side of the river, Joe thought, as he sat regaining his breath under the shadow of some burned-out huts. Espalier and Brown had done their work all too well in razing those huts in those early days of the siege and now Joe poked though the jetsam and ash, searching for anything serviceable. All he got for his efforts were the charred remains of a musket with a fairly decent bayonet attached. Joe wrenched the bayonet free and stuck it in his belt. Then he moved on.

Joe *had* hoped for one last glimpse of the mission fort, but for the distance and the night, the Alamo appeared as but a wrinkle on the otherwise flat horizon that stretched back to the hills. But Joe found that he could still follow the landmark aisle of tall pecan trees that flanked the Gonzales Road, so he felt his way toward them, moving eastward over the dark and broken ground.

At one point, Joe had to broad leap a section of the dammed Alamo acequia and very nearly didn't make it. And when he'd finally passed over a plank footbridge that spanned a broader branch of the mission ditch, the swaying outline of the pecans materialized before him.

Pausing a moment near the pecan trees on the south side of the Gonzales road for one final look at the silent town, Joe saw no sign of approaching torch lights to suggest that his escape had been detected. But when he looked toward the peach orchard to the north of the mission, Joe thought that he could see some flickering embers of light, blinking from the trees with the randomness of fireflies. *Who, or what could it be?* he wondered. Certainly no superstitious citizen of Bejar would dare abide *those* grounds at this ungodly hour of night.

Joe felt an intense fear welling up in him as he struck off upon the east road for Gonzales in heightening strides. And as he continued on, he imagined that he could feel an icy breath playing upon the back of his neck, as though someone, or something were bidding him turn to behold the specters yet flashing from amidst the peach trees. But Joe would not look back.

From where their broken and bled physical bodies had been dragged forth beyond the mission premises and then burned by their conquerors, the Texians in the timber blinked out a final farewell to Joe as he passed beyond the realm of their astral claim. Then the Texians themselves, released of composition and all fetters of earthly indignity, joined anew once more, as their ashes, blown from the funeral pyres, picked up, then sailed heavenward upon the dispersing winds.

Fifteen

Red Vengeance—Yellow Accord

Foot by foot, step by weary step, Joe's legs carried him on along the lonely road from Bejar, while the hushing winds, passing through the swaying aisle of stately pecan trees, skipped their own way over the sluggish waters of the insect-humming San Antonio River.

But for all of his feelings of loneliness, Joe was not alone, for emboldened packs of coyotes and red wolves thronged the isolated prairies beyond the town, drawn there as they were by the growing stench of death and decay. With their blood-curdling howls splitting the night air, the dark figures of the animals darted and scurried alongside of the trail so close to Joe, that he could actually smell and feel their foul, heated breath as they passed. Joe tightened his grip upon his newfound bayonet, but its meager means of defense offered him little solace. Right then, he would've even settled for the "worthless" musket of the Louisiana Dockman.

He kept moving. Keeping to the center of the road as best he could, Joe steered well clear of the low thickets and dipping gullies that now seemed to make up the better part of the landscape. For Joe had an imagination vivid enough to fill each dark patch of foliage and crevice fair crawling with rattlesnakes, scorpions, tarantulas, centipedes, yet more red wolves and coyotes, panthers, bobtail cats and, of course, a war party of screeching Comanches. He got an especially awful start when a squirrel scurrying by snapped a few twigs in its flight. it was then that Joe finally began to realize what a mighty toll the siege had played upon his nerves.

When he'd been walking for what seemed like hours, Joe's feet began to drag like leaden weights and he felt that he could proceed no further without a rest. But to rest, he would first need shelter and a place of concealment. So he searched. What he found was a small ravine, several yards off the trail, and almost hidden in the shadows of a massive oak tree whose gnarled branches overreached the circumference of the pit like a natural canopy. Chaparral choking the roadside completed the camouflage.

Exhausted beyond caring, Joe did not even take the precaution to reconnoiter the area for wild bugs or beasties before descending to the bottom of the woody hole. All the same, he tried the tangled roots and musty leaves for unwanted occupants and, upon discovering none, curled his tired body up in line with the angular attitude of the roots themselves to sleep and sleep deep.

Awakened by jabbing rays of sunlight seeping in through the narrowing upper branches of the oak, Joe found that he was not alone. A monstrous centipede with row upon row of clinging legs and a wicked looking pair of clicking pincers was making its way up his shin with an eye full of business. Not waiting an instant to find out what sort of business that might be, Joe swept aside the insidious insect with a stick, then shook his leg for good measure. Then he surveyed his surroundings more carefully in the gaining light.

When compared with the doleful, discordant days of the Alamo siege, this was a new and altogether different sort of day for Joe. For in place of booming cannons and trumpet blasts, squirrels chattered in the overhead branches, while numerous birds burst forth in song, warbling their little hearts out in harmonious intonations. Joe, in turn, could only take it all in with great relish, thankful that life went on in the world around him and that he was part of it.

But life was only granted to those who would seek to prolong it, so back up the incline toward the road above Joe climbed, squinting as the fully risen sun and a gentle breeze hit him full in the face.

By the looks of the deeply rutted surface of the road, quite a few wagons and carts had passed this way, more than likely carrying departing townsfolk who'd fled Bejar to escape Santa Anna. The knowledge gained in this disclosure made Joe feel that he would never be completely safe until he'd completely shaken off the dust of Bejar and the Bejarians from his garments. So, drawing down the visor of his shiny, patent-leather cap, Joe moved on.

Trodding on under the broiling sun, Joe felt the need for water very soon. Too bad that he hadn't found a canteen or at least an old goatskin water bag on his way out of town. His reliance on the river for liquid relief, he quickly discovered, was a dry, parched mistake. He'd half a mind to find another ravine where the moisture from its damp, rotting leaves would at least relieve his cracked lips a tad.

As it transpired, he didn't have to fall back on that resort after all for, as if in answer to his prayers, a gurgling artesian well appeared from out of nowhere beside the trail, blurping its flowing manna into a dense rise of prairie grass beyond. Upon Joe's approach, a family of rabbits who'd been patronizing the spring bound off toward the safety of the tall grass. With the spring to himself, Joe knelt down and with his cupped hands, splashed globular rivulets of water into his face. Then in a "to hell with it" motion, Joe dunked his entire head into the clear, bubbling pool.

When he'd drunk and wallowed in his fill, Joe lay down upon a thick cushion of tall prairie grass to rest his weary bones. Under such pleasant conditions, it was easy for him to imagine that he was upon a Mississippi riverbank, somewhere near Natchez, or possibly New Orleans, somewhere, at any rate, a million miles from this place and all his present cares.

Mounted bareback upon a painted pony, the Comanche had been observing Joe at his antics for quite some time, before

Joe finally took notice of *him*. It was the excited whinny and bray of the impatient animal that betrayed the Indian's presence and shook the "Veteran Soldier" back to the dangers of his present reality.

Under the quizzical stare of this scarlet warrior of the plains, Joe's initial reaction was to forsake the protection of the bayonet at his belt and instead, make a run for the questionable shelter of a thicket. Bad choice for taking flight, a mesquite thicket. For though Joe made a headlong dash into the entanglement with upraised hand to shield his eyes from the cruel thorns, he got gored to pieces and was soon trapped.

What would the end be like? he thought. *Would it come from the tock of an arrow thudding into the full of his back, or perhaps from the blunt edge of a tomahawk, burying itself deep within his skull? Maybe the throbbing entry of a musket ball tearing into his groin would complete the most unwelcome deed.* None of these things happened.

Scratched, bleeding, and out of breath; hopelessly entrapped in the mass of mesquite thorns, Joe could only stare in resignation upon the bloody red devil yet sitting astride the painted pony by the spring. While the pony drank its fill, its warmongering master dipped a deerskin bag into the pool to replenish his own dwindling water supply. *What sort of laziness,* Joe wondered, *would compel an Indian to draw water in such a fashion without dismounting?*

And then Joe saw it. It was a very old and haggard brave—hardly the warmongering spectacle of Joe's imagination. The Indian's incredibly weathered face bore the deep creases and pocks from the elements of hunting parties long since past. A faded calico blanket that was drawn almost haphazardly about them covered his almost skeletal frame and hollowed shoulders. As for the pony, its amazing swaybackedness and protrusion of ribs and mange sores made it a none-too-imposing mount, to say the least. As a matter of fact, calling it a pony at all would've been an act of considerable kindness and generosity.

Joe felt abashed and foolish for having taken cover from the apparently harmless oldster. Still, a savage was a savage, he reasoned; no sense in taking unnecessary chances unnecessarily. So Joe just stood there within his entanglement of brush while the painted plainsman calmly concluded his task at the waterhole.

Joe could see plainly that the Indian was considering him, too, and what a pitiable sight he must have presented; one to evoke even the most common of sympathies from one example of perishing humanity to another.

At long last, the ancient tied off his replenished water bag swung it wearily across his shoulders, then fished into a deerskin pouch with his gnarled fingers. The sight made Joe flinch, then clutch frantically for the bayonet at his side. But he was hopelessly entangled in thorns. He was helpless and this was the end. *The irony of it,* Joe thought, *to have survived the Alamo, only to die like this.*

Joe squeezed his eyes shut to await the inevitable. It came with the sound of a rattling plop, followed by the light clopping of unshod hooves. Minutes, hours . . . days seemed to pass, but still nothing happened. No death blow, no wild war whoop . . . nothing.

After agonizing moments of tugging and goring himself even more, Joe finally broke free of the thicket and approached the spring. The Indian was gone. So with moistened strips from his tattered shirt, Joe bound up the more painful of his wounds, then drank his fill anew of the sweet pool, as though he'd been deprived of water for a week or more. That done, Joe sank down upon the grass to regain his composure.

In fluffing up the tall grass to make himself a more comfortable bed, Joe discovered something that the Indian must've left behind; a little sack fashioned from deerskin with a looped drawstring securing its opening. Loosening the thong in growing curiosity, Joe spilled out a portion of the sack's contents into the hollow of his opened hand. The revelation of what they were and why they'd been left there filled Joe with a mixed feeling of shame, melancholy—and gratitude. For the coarse, yellow kernels of parched corn would see Joe through the next few days, if he were careful.

Sixteen

Can't Be Too Careful These-A-Days

Joe, in fact, managed to sustain himself for three days upon the parched corn and by supplementing that meager ration with the bitter wild nuts from pecan trees growing alongside the trail.

It threatened rain on the fourth day, but luckily, Joe found shelter from the deluge in a small clump of woods.

The rains came. Like great pigs of lead, the spluttering droplets poured down upon the treetops, seeping their way in through the leafless entanglement of twigs above to pelt Joe almost in glee, it would seem. All he could do to gain warmth and shield himself from the persistent damp was to draw himself up in a ball and hug his knees, while the plop, plop, plopping droplets searched out the back of Joe's exposed neck with a deliberation that he almost took as personal.

So long as he suppressed the urge to move, or shift position, the cushion of leaves beneath Joe remained warm and dry enough. He actually managed to fall asleep in that attitude, stiff as a board, and dreaming only of things dry.

It was yet dark when Joe arose from his snatch of slumber, but at least the rains had abated a bit. And once the obstinate screen of clouds had passed beyond the face of the moon, Joe decided to take advantage of the situation and get in a few extra miles by moon-bright.

Morning dawned and with it a clear sky. How breathtaking was the sight that spread out before Joe as he struck off eastward into the ascending sun! The broad prairie bathed in the after-throes of the spent storm, sparkled, and glistened like a never-ending sheet of shimmering crystal. Joe had never seen the like of it before and odds were that he never would again either, for such was but one of life's rewards to the early sojourner.

In spite of the glorious, bone-warming, clothes-drying bright morning, Joe's shoes still sluiced and sloshed mushy waterspouts over their tops with every step he took. But Joe remained optimistic. Should worse ever come to worse, he reasoned, he could always drink his soggy shoes.

On the "Veteran Soldier" trudged along the flooded roadway until he came upon what had *once* been the lazy little Salado Creek ford. Now the waters of the creek churned by in a frothy brown torrent, dashing all of Joe's thoughts and hopes of making a crossing at this point. And anyway, he certainly wasn't about to *swim* across. That old, pervading fear of water had Joe trapped once again. He figured that he had two options: wait there on the spot for the waters to subside or else move on down the creek in the hopes of finding either some sort of natural bridge, or a more crossable ford.

In the end, Joe opted to locate a more crossable fording place. Though it would mean abandoning the more reassuring road for the traceless underbrush, it could not be helped. With his food supply exhausted, he'd have to replenish it and fast and that's not something a person can do by sitting in one place. Food usually does not just come up and fall into your mouth.

Joe's decision was further bolstered by the spirited activity of the creek's indigenous insect life. Stirred up by the storm, the buggies lashed out at him with their singular modes of torment. So Joe pressed on, shielding his eyes with one hand, vainly slapping and waving the creatures off with the other. And as he continued his exploration of the creek's overlapping banks, the eager insects seemed to follow him down every step of the way.

When the desire for rest got the better of him, Joe made day camp in a patch of tall grass not far from the creek, mashing it down into a comfortable bed. While he could count on the foliage to conceal him from human scrutiny, there was no fooling the hellish, whirring bugs.

Joe took a drink of the cool, if muddied, creek water, but when he tried his hand at eating the thick bladed prairie grass, he found it rather bitter and unappealing. So he laid down upon his make-do mattress there in the minimal comfort of the tall grass to rest away the early afternoon, dreaming of food.

Joe awakened with a start to the distinct clip clopping of approaching horses, then went taut with tension, listening with pricked up ears for some sign that the riders were either friend or foe.

Soon there were voices, and familiar ones at that. Not in the Comanche dialect, nor of the Mexican. This was distinctly, unmistakably *American*. Joe felt his heart leap in his throat as he recognized one of the voices—a woman's—to be none other than Suzannah Dickerson's!

Out of the tall grass Joe came in bounds, casting all sense of caution to the icy blue northers. "Miss Suzannah!" he halloed, stepping forth upon the exposed banks of the creek to greet the newcomers.

Taken aback by Joe's sudden reappearance, it was some time before Suzannah could compose herself. "So the Mexes let you go, Joe," she said at last. "Thought maybe they'd shot you for being Travis' and all. They got Ben here," she went on, gesturing toward her swarthy companion, "to guide us back to Gone-zales and our people . . ."

Suzannah paused for a moment with a faraway look in her eye, then her voice rose to a near hysterical pitch. "Did you see 'em?" she asked, to no one in particular. "All in gold and silver . . . and the colors! Uniforms—everywhere! Ten thousand men and more, marching and marching to that terrible band! Our boys didn't stand a chance! All of 'em are dead. Dead! My Almaron, Señor Esparza, Davy Crockett, poor Jim Bowie—all dead. How," she continued, calming down at last, "how did *you* escape, Joe? Thought maybe they'd shot you. Mighty glad they didn't, though," she added.

"Got taken prisoner," Joe explained. "Made to point out the bodies of Travis, Bowie, and Crockett. Santa Anna said that I could go free afterwards, but then he locked me up in a storeroom. I broke out as soon as I could and skedaddled. Mighty glad to be seeing *you*, too, Miss Sue," Joe concluded.

Suzannah's companion rider listened intently to Joe's whole sorry Alamo story, before breaking his own silence. His name was Ben, he explained. Late of the steamer *Charleston*, but more recently, of the employ of Colonel Almonte, for whom he'd served as a cook. Like Joe, Ben was black, but unlike Joe, a freeborn man who'd wandered the most of his adult life at his own will.

"*Charleston's* a steam packet," Ben continued, dismounting to assist Suzannah and baby Angie from the saddle. "Going to change the course of shipping in a big way! Such power and no need depending on the wind . . . We'll light right here, Miss Suzannah," he said, gesturing to the weary young woman. "Seeing as it looks we can all use the rest, anyhow. How's the baby?"

"Thank you, Ben," Mrs. Dickerson replied, relieved. "She's as well as possible, under the conditions. She weren't exactly reared for a life of luxury and she hasn't seen one. Still," she sighed, "to have it all back . . . "

Joe unsaddled and hobbled the horses, while Ben continued at his gab. "Might as well stir up something of a meal," he said, scattering his kit upon the ground. "Mexican Commissary only gave us a little corn meal mush, but I managed a little sugar and salt, compliments of Colonel Almonte—although he don't know it," Ben added with a sly grin. "Get that pigsticker out of your belt," he said, pointing at Joe's bayonet, "and we can fashion some pone on it. Cook it right over the open fire. We can also heat up some of the mush in my kit tin for the baby. Nothing fancy, but leastwise, it'll be hot, if I can get a fire going."

Ben gathered a few twigs and dead branches together, then struck his flint. "Hope this lights all right," he said with concern. "Too much smoke draws too much attention and we can't be too careful, these-a-days."

But the wood did not smoke so much after all and soon a lively and welcome little blaze was going under sizzling cornpone and bubbling hot mush. Ben took a taste of the mush, but was not much impressed with the results of his efforts. "I'll have to cook you up some of my famous peas porridge," he promised Joe, "that is, when we get near anything that even half resembles a pea. Steward on board ship's how I got the knack of cooking. Gotta be halfways good to please a seaboard lot, though they ain't got much choice in the matter! Anyway, we sails from New England, rounding the Florida Keys for New Orleans! Such a town, New Orleans! Mouth of the Mississippi and gateway to the interiors! Bye the bye," Ben digressed, doling out the hot mush into tins and handing Suzannah the first, "was there a man name of DeSaque in the Alamo with you? Heard he'd been in San Antone. Didn't know him, mind you, but knew his man, Jean, a cargo loader. Used to jaw with him when we put in to dock. He surely was one for jawing!"

Joe grimaced on this. Since the Alamo and with everything that had transpired in between, he'd all but put the Louisiana Dockman out of his mind. Now, the none-too-distant memory came flooding back. "DeSaque wasn't in the battle," Joe explained, hearing the sound of his own voice forming words. "He skedaddled before that, going messages for Travis. Jean, he stayed put and fought! I saw him die!"

Ben knitted his brow. "Too bad to hear that," he said gravely. "Much too bad. Good man was Jean—the old Frenchie! Such a jolly sort of fellow—always with the jokes. What was he fighting for, anyways? Don't seem right. No, it just don't seem right at all. But in respect for you, Miss Suzannah," Ben veered tactfully, "I'll close my mouth on this grub. He sure was the one for jawing, though . . ."

Save for the restless cooing of baby Angie in her sleep, the rest of the meal was partaken of in silence. Afterwards, Joe helped Ben clear away the utensils and washed them in the muddy creek. Then they both fed some more fuel to the fire and sat huddling around the rising flames as the early evening drew on.

"Don't have any spare shirts to give you," Ben said, almost apologetically, as the camp was preparing to bed down for the night, "but we each got an extra blanket, complements of His Excellency. You can just cut a hole right here," he gestured, "and wear it like a sere-rappie coat. Nothing fancy, but it's sure keep you warm in a pinch, least-a-ways."

With the aid of the hot grub and his new "sere-rappie" coat, Joe began to feel a bit more human again. He and Ben remained upon watch by the cook fire, while the much-fatigued Mrs. Dickerson turned in early, joining her daughter in a less-than-fitful repose.

"Suppose you're wondering," Ben began, stirring up the ember of the cook fire with a stick, "how I got tied up with the likes of old Santa Anna? Sailed right into it, I did, so to speak. Ship laid over in Vera Cruz and I got shanghaied there by the authorities for loitering, or some other such grievous infraction. Anyhow, when they gets wind that I'm a steward and as luck may smile upon me, I ends up with Colonel Almonte as his personal article. He pays me fair enough—better than soldiers' wages—and I be decent enough clothed and messed."

"Texas campaign's a godalmighty horror," Ben continued, feeding some more twigs to the fire, then slapping away an entire squadron of flying bugs attracted to its light. "Mexes travel funny. When they go to war, the whole family goes to war, kit and keboodle! Women folk, sprouts, distant relations—*everybody!* Marching hundreds of miles across desert and ice, rain and snow, over mountains, through valleys—and all in the dead of winter! Soldiers ain't been provided with foodstuffs and other such necessaries—no such thing! They has to pay for them from the commissary wagons out of their own wages. That don't beat all, huh? Families has got to feed on the same wages as the soldier, and the soldier, he don't make enough to hardly feed himself! It were a sadly effecting sight. If you reckon that you seen death and destruction at the Alamo, that ain't hardly nothing compared to what I seen along the trails and gorges. Soldiers dying by the dozens of the retches. Dropping like flies and no one so much as lifts a finger to help 'em. Just heaves 'em to the side of the road, or else runs clean over them with wagons and caissons, as thought they weren't worth much more than used up goods. Them that didn't take down with the stomach disorder froze to death in the snowstorms, or else catched pne-monie in the rains. But the worst sight of all was of the womenfolk and sprouts. They didn't stand half a chance and died by the hundreds. All along the trail of march they drops and, if it ain't time to be pitching camp, then there they lies to rot, or freeze, and the soldiers got nothing to say about it. When we *did* pitch camp, there was them that took down and died in the nighttime and the men would attempt to bury 'em in the frozen ground, chopping away at it with their bayonets. It were hard to sleep at all, with the moaning and crying going on forever, it seemed. I was more fortunate and had a fine shirt to my back and officer's grub to eat, but in the face of all that suffering, I lost my appetite considerable. When we reached San Antone, there were scarcely a quarter of the families left alive of them that started the march! Those that *did* make it did so on their hands and knees. Looked about as well as overused scarecrows, and the soldiers not much spryer. They really wanted the blood of the Alamo men in payment for all those lonely deaths and the loss of their wives and sprouts. Can't say as I hardly blame 'em, but then who's to say who's right, or wrong? Young Mr. Travis felt that he was right and now he's dead. Mexes thought that they was right, but they died too. And being right ain't hardly going to see them home to Mexico again. I don't rightly want to kill anybody, but then I got no stake in this frucus. Does that make *me* right?" Ben concluded.

Joe scrinched up his face thoughtfully. "So many things've been happening lately, that I don't rightly know what's right," he replied. "It seems I've seen Santa Anna's idea of right and the Texian's idea. Right now, I'm just plain kerplumexed about finding my *own* idea—if I live that long. So you were born a free man, Ben, but freeborn or not, it appears that you are sitting in the same boat that *I* am, right now. What's in it for you, when this war's over—if you live that long?"

"I lay no claim to reading the future," Ben retorted, "but I hope to maybe get back to the sea, if it be written in the stars. Least-a-ways, there I has to be accepted, else somebody goes hungry. But then, it's a different sort of breed of men that takes to the sea. Everybody's equal, 'cause everybody's been through the grind and knows the score, from the officers on down. Oh, there's some bad eggs, as everywhere, but most is all right. It's not as liken we puts out to sea where the captain is akin to the Almighty. We makes port every few days—never more than a fortnight, the most of stretches in between—'cause of the need to refuel and all. So we sees a lot of towns and a lot of people, whilst still feeling the freedom of the open wave. Yes," Ben concluded, rolling up in his minimal bedroll with his back to Joe, "that's what I'd do."

He spoke no more and Joe took it as a sign of turning in for the evening. So, after heaping a bundle of twigs and gnarled branches upon the fire to dissuade the beasts of the night, Joe arranged his own bedroll, then curled up beside the blaze. He faded to slumber to the hissing and crackling of the dry leaves, as both the flame and the night consumed them.

Seventeen

Inferno Revisited

Inexplicable as it seemed, Joe was back in the Alamo again. At least it looked like the flat roof of the Low Barracks that he was standing upon, anyway. Instinctively, Joe raised, and then fired his musket into the direction of where he only supposed the enemy should be. "Supposed" was the right word, for the shapes pressing the fort before him were enshrouded in such a heavy gray mist that they appeared indistinct, almost wraithlike. The wavering wisps and vacant swirls of phantom foe appeared to roll forward more like an ocean wave than a human one. Indeed, the traces of Joe's discharged musket balls only seemed to get sucked up into the peculiar fog without making any lasting or measurable impression upon it.

Joe's companions on the wall, when he took the time to consider them at last, were themselves wraiths. Silhouetted against a flaming orange horizon, these mere shadows of men seemed to float, rather than walk and when they spoke at all, their voices came out both hollow and distant. But what struck Joe as an even more peculiar characteristic of his fellows was that the repercussion of their firearms was neither audible nor visible. In fact, the flashes of their discharges seemed instead to be sucking up pinlines of the red screen down their cylindrical barrels, as though these efforts were part of a sort of vacuum attempt at obliterating the whole sorry scene.

Then ladders began to raise noiselessly against the outer barrier of wall as whatever it was that was once outside, was now trying to come up, over and in. Joe turned in determination to meet the challenge, but found to his surprise, that he could make little headway. With everything around him seemingly lunging ahead at full tilt, Joe felt himself moving in exasperatingly slow motion. Then, as bad went to worse, a powerful, paralyzing force dragged Joe down, prostrating him flat against the rooftop. Uncontested, the wave of mist along with its wraithlike foe rolled over the summit of the wall, sweeping away the few remaining wraith/defenders in one belching billow. Finally, the shades of nothingness had only Joe left to contend with.

One of the wraithlike foes gradually began to take on a more definite shape as, with saber in hand, it moved across the flat rooftop toward a crippled and helpless wraith/defender that lay writhing upon the brink of the wall. Like a captive audience, Joe could only watch in tense frustration as the standing figure converged upon the fallen one, its saber gleaming like a blazing shaft of pure light. In less than a heart's beat—and Joe could measure each thundering palpitation in his suspended state—a companion of his would be smited to death by this adversary, if not for his immediate intervention.

So, with a willful effort, Joe stretched his arms free and then grabbed a musket that was floating by in midair. Joe didn't even take the time to question the gun's strange origin, as he pressed the butt into his shoulder and fired. In turn, the dull, hollow sound of the musket's billowy discharge wholly engulfed the charging saber-bearer, tumbling him back upon the rooftop planking in slow motion and without a sound.

But, oh what unimaginable horror Joe now faced as he knelt down to draw aside the topcoat of the fallen wraith/defender whose life he had just saved! That face before and below him! That oh so familiar face: Colonel Almonte!

Joe drew back with a start upon the discovery. But oh how much more slowly did he turn to examine the body of his victim/adversary, the saber-bearer. For although its parted lips yet gurgled their final release of life's breath, the splintered, purple hole at the bridge of the saber-bearer's nose told Joe all too well that Travis was quite dead. Colonel Almonte, the wraith/defender whose grace, benevolence, and cool courage had saved Joe's life on more than one occasion, would survive for the time being, the debt repaid to the hilt.

"So, what you think of that, Soldier?" taunted a familiar voice from out of nowhere, yet everywhere, as Joe recognized the unmistakable laughter of the Louisiana Dockman. "So, you like this soldiering business, yes? Rid yourself of your enemies, plenty quick, this one," he exploded gleefully, pointing at Travis' crumpled body, while his own spectral form seemed to fade from solid to shadow and then back again, at no fixed momentum, or pattern. "This Almonte, plenty nice fellow, he. Think of you as a man, Joseph! Now what you doing, running off to Gonzales for? They think of you as but niggaire there, you bet. Run, Joseph, run! Run back to slavery!"

"Not so, Jean," Joe insisted, shouting vigorously to make himself heard. "Not so! Colonel Travis freed me! I should've told you that!" *I should've told him,* Joe whispered to himself, before continuing aloud. "Almonte's a fine gentleman and no mistake Jean, but Travis is—was—too. Neither of them deserved to die, do you hear me? *Neither!* And neither did you, Jean," he added in a softer, more melancholic, almost reverent tone.

But the Dockman only responded with regales of mocking laughter that seemed to not only intensify the flaming orange hue of the horizon, but drain the Dockman, in turn, of any given substance, or form. Soon, only the arms clutching fast to the "worthless" musket were discernible in the dominant field of orange, while the gun itself appeared to float of its own accord, as though it were supporting the hovering arms, instead of the contrary.

Suddenly, without warning, the hovering arms thrust the musket into Joe's grip. "Have this weapon to defend yourself from your friends, Joseph," cackled the disembodied voice of the Dockman, before giving over to uncontrollable laughter, as the musket itself burst into a shaft of searing flame.

Try as he did, none of Joe's frantic efforts could shake, or dash, the almost molten musket free. His hand had become melded with the infernal thing and he was burning, burning, burning!

Suddenly, Joe was awake, or at least he *thought* he was, for it was moon-bright, the middle of the night, and he was upon the open prairie, sitting painfully close to the campfire with a scorched shirtsleeve and painfully blistered wrist. His nocturnal thrashing must've upset the smoldering embers of the dying fire; so it had all been but a bad dream and nothing more! Still, Joe could only be half-thankful in that revelation, for at least two elements of the nightmare had a foot in reality: the fire and the pain in his wrist.

Joe bound up his blistered wrist with a poultice he'd made from a strip of his ruined shirtsleeve soaked in creek water. Then he fed some more fuel to the fire. There were still wild beasts of the night to contend with—that, and the fear of total darkness in unfamiliar surroundings. Joe decided to keep vigil until first light.

In spite of his unpleasant encounter with its little brothers in the embers, Joe huddled close to the rekindled fire, grateful for its warming effect in the chilly hours of night. Transfixed by the licking tongues of golden flame, Joe stared deep into their core, marveling whenever the coughed up clusters of airy sparks would first corkscrew skyward, then rain down like shooting stars high above the camp.

While some of the airborne embers came darn close to touching down upon the bramble and high grass of the mesquite thicket, most would ultimately blink out. One pair of sparkling embers in the mesquite, however, refused to blink out. *Curious*, Joe thought, *how they aligned instead in a stationary fixture from within the growth of tangled foliage.*

A low growl, followed by the whinny of frightened, hobbled horses, shattered Joe's puzzlement soon enough. A panther or some other sort of wild cat had its eye on the camp and fresh meat. And while the encircling cat dared not draw near to the tended blaze, the horses, hobbled as they were some distance from the camp, were there for the taking.

Without a moment to spare and only a bayonet with which to ward off the beast, Joe seized a flaming fagot of wood from the fire and sought the panther out. He bounded at the cat with his flaming stick at the same moment the cat chose to pounce upon its prey.

Joe's "Hi-yaiing" at the top of his lungs only caused the startled cat to spin around and hiss in defiant displeasure. Its displeasure swiftly dissolved into an instinctive "Rrrrrrow" of terror, however, when it sighted its most dreaded enemy, fire.

Ben was up; Suzannah was up; baby Angie was wah-wahing; Joe's pulse was racing.

Imprudent Joe; perhaps it was the heat of the moment that made him react without first measuring the consequences of his actions, but react Joe did, hurling his torch at the panther to disperse it. Snarling, the big cat sprang back into the far reaches of the thicket and the night. But the yellow flame of the torch remained, exploding the cured mesquite into an instantaneous inferno. In moments, the camp, then the entire prairie would be engulfed in a wall of flame.

"The horses! Get the horses!" Ben thundered above the frightened whinny of the animals themselves. "Get the baby across the creek," he shouted to Suzannah and the young mother lost no time, sloshing both baby and blanket across the wade toward the safety of the opposite bank. Upon firm ground once more, Suzannah gave a reassuring wave to the two men yet upon the opposite shore, but preoccupied Ben and Joe scarcely noticed her.

Suzannah was more fortunate than even she might've believed, for with only the light of the rapidly spreading fire itself to guide her, it was a wonder that she hadn't snagged her feet in the debris and potholes that snarled the creek bottom. In all the confusion, smoke, and darkness she might not even have been missed until it was too late.

Amidst all the bucking, rearing, and animal screaming, Joe and Ben somehow managed to unhobble both horses and lead them to the water's edge. Once there, the mounts bounded into the creek, very nearly dragging their rescuers in with them.

With his hands firmly dug into his horse's mane, Joe finally made it to the opposite bank, whereupon he reined the beast to a halt to curtail its inclination to bolt. Ben, however, was not so fortunate as Joe for his own mount continued to rear and thrash in dissention, unseating him at last with a terrific jolt. Then, with its legs flailing wildly, the horse slashed the unfortunate steward with its razor-sharp hooves, before bolting off for good into the night.

Joe did his best to calm down the remaining horse by shielding it eyes with a blanket, while Suzannah tended to the stricken Ben. The flown horse had dealt the steward a long, stinging slice down his left calf. Fortunately, the wound was not very deep or worrisome, so the young woman bandaged it with ease with torn strips from her already tattered petticoat.

It was time to be moving again. So, with wracked throats and eyes weeping sooty tears courtesy of the raging conflagration, the little party gathered itself for the continuing journey. Holding little Angelina in the folds of her shawl, Suzannah sat astride the bared back of the lone horse, while Ben limped behind as best he could. With the horse's reins firmly within his grip, Joe led the pilgrim eastward toward Gonzales and well out of the path of the prairie fire. And fortune traveled with them.

For the wind shifted suddenly, pushing the fire back onto the already-consumed prairie to where it would eventually peter out due to lack of combustibles. As the pilgrims moved into the wind and the wavering darkness of early morning, animals taking flight from the fire skittered on by them. *How nice it would be,* Joe thought hungrily, *should one, or two, plump rabbits just happen to die of fright.* Well, it was a nice *notion* to feast upon, anyway, for it was still a long way from this waning hell to breakfast for the weary foursome, plus horse.

The first rays of dawn disclosed that, by the sheerest luck, or the hand of Providence, they had wandered back onto the east road. The realization of that raised most everybody's spirits; Angelina whimpered.

It was decided that they should pitch camp beside a trickling tributary of the Salado to rest, breakfast on the remaining soggy corn meal, and take stock of the situation. They had come through the adventure with their lives and little more; one horse, two blankets, three and a half people. But even in this, they were grateful.

"I remember this place," Suzannah remarked, nestling the little girl in her lap as she spoke. "The brook was most dry then, but we carried our own water. Reckon we're about two-thirds home," she sighed, scanning vacantly eastward. "Home . . ." she whispered, trailing off to the premises of her memory.

Eighteen
Nettlenuts and Cornbread

They rested the morning away there beside the little brook, basking in the golden sunshine, until all were dry enough to consider traveling. Even the lone horse, whinnying nervously, pawed that it was high time for them to be on their way.

So with a blanketful of bull nettlenuts that Joe had gathered to supplement the meager staple of cornpone, and with gourds of water that Suzannah finished filling at the creek, the party proceeded on.

They'd been trodding on for nearly three hours with the sun at their backs, when suddenly they beheld specks moving on the horizon. The specks, they could see, were definitely advancing toward them from some distance up the road and raising anxious clouds of dust in their wake.

"What do you think they are?" Joe asked, not really wanting to hear the answer. "Tumbleweeds in a twister?" He guessed. "Wild cattle?"

"Riders," Ben replied without elaboration, as the dust begetting specks drew even nearer, then nearer still. "*Two* riders, for a fact."

Joe knitted his brow, while his voice betrayed his growing concern. "Could be Comanches. I had a run-in with one clear on back the trail. Best take to the high grass for cover."

"Comanches wouldn't be using the main road, Joe," Suzannah responded in exasperating nonchalance.

"Then it could be Mexican soldiers, Miss Suzannah! I've had

my fill of them and don't want to pleasure any more of their acquaintance than absolutely necessary. Please, Miss Sue!"

"Joe's right, Miss Sue." Ben interjected skittishly. "We'd best get."

But Suzannah just sat there, staring up the road. "I'm tired and tried beyond caring," she said resignedly. "And this is a bald prairie. Mexes, Comanches, or old Lucifer himself! Let 'em come! "

They came; galloping in fresh determination upon this strange little party that seemed rooted to the center of the road, the not-so-distant riders sped. And as they closed in, identifying characteristics became more distinguishable. Joe saw that they were clearly not Comanches, but then neither were they Mexicans, for they sported wide, flat-brimmed hats and rode harnessed horses, whose martingales seemed clearly of Yankee manufacture. And if that wasn't enough of a dead giveaway, both riders looked to be wearing greasy, fringed, beaded, darned, typical, average, run-of-the-mill Texian buckskins.

"They're white men, Miss Sue! " Joe announced assuredly.

And so they were. Gnarly and grizzled Erastus Smith, the old Indian scout, and his youthful companion, Hank Karnes, soon reined up and identified themselves. Houston, Smith stated, had dispatched the two of them to San Antonio to apprise him of the situation of the garrison there. The main Texian army, such as there was of it, was rallying at Gonzales to press to the relief of the Alamo.

"No relief . . . no comfort," choked Suzannah throatily. "No nothin', ever again!" Then, in sentences torn by sobs, she relived the little band in the Alamo's final hours, sparing no detail of the horrific butchery she'd played witness to in the fortress' last minutes.

Of the fate of young Jake Walker from Nacodoches, who'd worked the cannons upon the high ramp in the back of the church, along with her husband, Almaron. Almaron! It was so hard for Suzannah to spit out the words, for their harsh reality caught in her throat, so she snapped them off through gnashing teeth, while the kindly Smith could only stand by, gripping her hand in support.

"He . . . they . . . " she attempted. "So much noise! Little Walker ran into the room—wanted to hide. Then the Mexes came in. 'Don't shoot,' he says. 'Wounded . . . no gun.' But they did. Oh, yes, they did, anyway! Lifted him up on their bayonets and then tossed him around like farmers' pitching fodder. I couldn't look no more! Then Almaron ran in to say that all is lost. He held me and I held him so close. Then he pulled away, ran out and I never seen him again. No one again."

There was an emotional pause.

"Gone . . . " she finally relinquished. "All gone."

Putting duty first, Smith inclined his attentions on Karnes. "You high tail it t'Gen'l Sam n' let 'im know th' worse has fallen. I'll stay wit' these people an' lead 'em in as soon as is posserble. Vamoos, sprout!"

And Hank Karnes was off in a clatter, beating back toward Gonzales and Houston's camp.

"Folks in town uz mite concerned, as you kin reckin," Smith explained, while gently lifting little Angelina into his own saddle to allow her overwrought mother a brief moment to collect herself. "All kilt, yuh say?" he continued under his breath. "Don't seem posserble."

As Smith and Suzannah were talking, their horses trotted along at a slow gait that suited the dismounted Joe and Ben just fine. For their blistered feet and empty stomachs would only have to endure a little more, before Gonzales would see them to fresh food and perhaps, clothing.

By nightfall the companions had reached the edge of a well-tended orchard. Just beyond the trees, a small, yet steady, light flickered through an oilcloth-covered cabin's window.

"S' here I leaves yuh," said Smith, pointing toward the welcome sight. "Brunos'll tek care o' yuh 'til yer fit t' make town. Olny a few shakes more up th' road. I gots t' report yer news t' Gen'l Sam in details. Til we meets again, adieu," he saluted with a wave of his hat and a dig of his spurs into his horse's flanks.

The commotion raised by Smith's hurried departure alerted the occupants of the cabin to action. In moments, the creaky door banged open to reveal a lone figure bearing a lantern suspended from his wrist, along with a readied musket. "Who goes there?" the figure challenged in a gruff male voice. "Speak up, er *this* will," he concluded, sweeping the musket back and forth menacingly.

Upon sight of the musket, and the tone of the challenge, both Joe and Ben thought it prudent to take to the cover of the orchard once more. But Suzannah did not budge. Her daughter needed food and care, so she did not budge an inch.

"Hallo the house," she shouted. "It's Sue Dickinson, recently of Gone-zales—wife of Almaron Dickinson, a former smithy there. Late of the Alamo and Be'ar. Alamo's lost. My husband—the defenders—all butchered by Santa Anna. Please! My baby needs attentions!"

"Land sakes, Jack, let the poor woman in," sang out a voice from within the cabin and its owner soon followed the remark outside to reveal the woman of the house. "Can't you see what the poor dear's been through? Let me have the baby, child," she offered, bundling little Angelina into the house, while the sentinel from the stoop assisted Suzannah from the saddle.

"Stable that horse," Mrs. Bruno resumed, "then get in here and stir up the fire again, Jack. Folks has got to eat an' thaw out! "

"Yes, Sarah, anything you say, Sarah," the gun-toter replied resignedly, escorting Suzannah to the fireside seat.

Outside again, Jack Bruno finished stabling the horse, then clomped back across the yard to clear the mud from his boots upon the porch scrape. Then, with a final, backward glance, Bruno slammed the cabin door shut against the cold and the night.

"So why'd we take to the trees, instead of the house?" Ben bemoaned, as he sat shivering at the base of a stately pecan tree. "That's what I get for following *you*, instead of falling back on my own good judgment! What now, Cap'n Joseph? I awaits orders, sir!"

Joe got defensive. "How's I to know *what* to think?" he shot back, his feelings clearly bruised. "He may just as shot us and then asked questions later! Maybe we could sack down in the stables—won't be the first time for me—leastwise, it'll be warm."

"Not me," the steward declined promptly, waving Joe off. "I'm inclined to just wait it out here until first bells. Mayhap, things'll have cooled down by then. All Missus Dickinson'll be thinking about *now* is her baby, her own self, and dead Al in the Alamo. Be a while before she recollects us, if she does at all. Meanwhile, what's two black men in the dark good for to a jumpy white man with a gun? Shooting, that's what! No sir," he concluded, "here I stay!"

This was too much for Joe. "Then what are you blaming *me* for?" he retorted sullenly. "I didn't bring on the present situation!"

"Gotta blame *some*body," Ben returned apologetically. "And I can't rightly blame the night for being cold! Best just try and get some sleep."

Aside from the icicles that Joe imagined were forming upon his eyebrows, the last thing that the "Veteran Soldier" remembered as he lay shivering upon the hard, frozen ground was the blinking out of the house light. That and the welcome, if useless, sight of the billowy white clouds of smoke that puffed out from the chimney top and into the frosty atmosphere.

When morning dawned at last, it was to the rattling and chattering of three mischievous squirrels that were rummaging through Joe's stash of bull nettlenuts. How bitterly they fought over the prize, until Joe's raised voice sent them scattering frantically up a tree.

"Get, you varmints!" he shooed. "Ain't hardly enough for us alone, such as there is!"

In retaining both the field and the booty Joe decided to taste the fruits of his victory by cracking open one of the poddy shells with his teeth. But, like the squirrels' fight for possession of the stash, the nuts themselves proved bitter and far from edible.

"Lordy, it's cold," Ben remarked shivering, having been stirred into wakefulness by Joe's campaign against the squirrels. Now the steward sat upon his haunches, hugging and shaking himself to get the blood flowing into his numbed extremities once more. "They up at the house yet?" he asked.

"Seems like," Joe returned, glancing cabinward. "Leastwise, the little girl is up, for all the hollering she's commencing. And if she's up, then all are likely up."

Ben and Joe waited in their hideaway of brush, braving the blustery, nipping non-sunrise when a moment could pass for an hour. Finally, the door of the cabin creaked open wide and Sue Dickerson stepped forth, laden with a heavy wooden tray. For a moment, she paused there, looking this way and that, as though she was searching the yard for her two missing traveling companions.

"Ben! Joe! Hello, you two!" she beckoned them. "Come out an' have something to eat! Corn bread an' honey an' some hot coffee!"

"Over here, Miss Sue," they acknowledged at last, stepping forth from their hiding place in the orchard.

"There's only one cup," Suzannah said, pouring the steaming elixir from the kettle, "so you'll have to share. Sorry you had to spend the night out in th' cold," she went on, while Ben and Joe thawed out their insides with the coffee. "Thought you was in th' barn! Ends up that th' Brunos never even knew you was with me 'til this morning! They gone an' packed us some extra food, casen there's none to be had when we reaches town. Also, here's some work shirts Sadie Bruno managed to dig up—an' some fresh woolen socks, as well. Nothin' fancy, but warm."

Slowly, painfully, Joe hiked off his loosened shoes to reveal swollen feet that resembled pork barrels; his socks, meanwhile, seemed appended like a second layer of skin. After he'd peeled them away from his aggrieved toes, Joe took the time to wriggle those toes in the coolness of the morning air. Then came the fresh socks.

Re-shirted, shod, and properly grubbed, Joe felt ready for practically any fresh adventure that lay ahead of them, while Ben, with his leg properly bound at last, was of the same mind.

The party prepared to move out. Jack Bruno refitted the horse with a precious saddle and then led the beast out into the yard. With Suzannah and baby Angie mounted upon its back the horse, led by Joe and followed by a yet-limping Ben, clip-clopped upon its merry way, whereupon the travelers bid farewell to their generous hosts and made for Gonzales.

Even little Angelina was all smiles for once, as her mother's voice issued forth in steamy utterances. "Brunos is nice people. Best there is. Likely, they'll have to pull up stakes with all they can carry an' flee for their lives, lessen Houston's army is anything compared to what we seen in Be'ar. I much doubt it, though," she added in disgust. "If they was worth their spit, they'd of saved our boys in th' Alamo! I've a feeling that our journey's end in Gonezales'll just be th' stepping off place for another. Whole town'll skedaddle when they gets th' word. Still," she concluded, trying to find something positive in the horrible chain of events, "we'll be amongst our own people."

Will we though? Joe pondered to himself, trodding on in bewilderment.

Nineteen

The Handy Way to Houston

The scenery before them passed pretty much the same, with the usual high prairie grass, mesquite thickets, and an occasional tree to break the monotony of the expanse of flat prairie. But when Joe and his companions drew nearer to Gonzales, the lay of the land gradually became more verdant and welcome to the eye.

To the south of the trail, a tiny lake stretched with glistening ripples sheeting its surface, complements of a tardy sun. The lakes lush banks seemed to spring up like an oasis in stark contrast to the surrounding region, for it was here that the slithery, winding, Guadalupe River emptied its coursing channel of life.

The river flowed into the lake on its eastern end where the pancake flat land along its banks deemed it an ideal location for a village site. Beyond a looping bend of the Guadalupe to the north, stood the town of Gonzales itself. Dwarfed by the surrounding expanse of nothingness, Gonzales stood out much like a beacon in the night might, were it indeed the night.

But it was nigh on noon before the travelers finally reached the outskirts of town, and even from that distance, they could see that the place was already in an uproar over the news relayed by Smith and Karnes. Frantic citizens were hurrying belongings and remnants of families out from the clapboard dwellings and shops and into the narrow, wagon, and oxen-jammed lane that passed as "Main Street" in this predominantly Texian settlement.

Above the confusion of crying children, complaining animals, and cursing men rose the wailing voices of dreadfully distraught women whose husbands had all perished in the Alamo. Though Joe attempted to shield Mrs. Dickerson from the sight and reach of these new widows, his efforts proved of little avail. For upon recognizing Suzannah, the pressing throng practically crushed her with a battery of painful questions.

But the responses they received from Suzannah were always the same. "Wash Cottle?" "Gone." "My Johnny Gatson?" "Gone." "Not my Dolph Floyd!" "Yes, gone."

That did it. Suzannah's blunt responses dissolved the wailing widows and all within earshot into a hysterical mob, as the sharpness of their heartrending shrieks rudely severed away Gonzales' already unraveling last threads of hope.

Joe was led to the town's livery stable where he was subjected to his own grilling of sorts. But at least *his* interrogators were soldiers and less inclined toward hysteria. Still, the telling of his unembellished account did little for the morale of the listeners. Some of the soldiers squatting in the hay began debating as to whether they should stay or leave. Newcomers to the forming army, they had trickled into town with high expectations of savoring the conqueror's sweet taste of glory. But this fresh news of the Alamo disaster, rolling around in their collective mouth, was a bitter herb to chew. Now they had to make the choice of either joining up with Houston's army, encamped just east of town, or of skedaddling for the settlements.

Skedaddling? No, that was not the proper word for it. These men were not cowards. They had come to Gonzales, they said, with the intent of sending Santa Anna home to Mexico like a whipped cur. But they hadn't come to be massacred. They had families and property to consider and if the Army of the Republic was incapable of standing and fighting for its citizens, then these citizen volunteers should at least be granted the duty of looking after their own. Such seemed the general consensus, from what Joe could gather.

That independence had been declared came as news to Joe. But declared it had been on March the 2nd, back when the men of the Alamo were still fighting for their lives. The delegates—59 of them—had met in Washington-on-the-Brazos in a ramshackle, windowless little structure dubiously dubbed the "Constitutional Convention Hall" for it was, in fact, little better suited to the task than the stable where these volunteers now squatted in their own debate. But a government had been wrangled and a new nation born: The Republic of Texas. Now, with the life of that new country hanging in the balance, these volunteers had to make a tough decision.

The interior of the airless livery in which Joe sat fairly reeked with the stench of tobacco smoke, spent chaws, manure, damp hay, and unwashed bodies. There was a partition separating this section of room from the rest of the building and beyond that stood a blackened forge adjoining an incendiary. This was the smithy shack of the settlement where, in quieter times, horses were shod and damaged plows repaired. Business of late, however, seemed of a more malevolent nature, for all the junk iron in Gonzales now lay stacked up beside the incendiary to be molded into bullets and cannon balls. In a very real sense, the good citizens were preparing to beat their ploughshares back into swords.

This smithy, Joe reckoned, might well have been the very shop where Almaron Dickerson had plied his trade, prior to his family's fateful sojourn to the Alamo. *Poor Suzannah*, Joe grimaced. *Would the townspeople ever leave off and give her a bit of rest?*

As Joe sat thinking and trying not to breathe, the door of the smithy opened and in walked a dandified, butternut-haired youth. Sporting two great horse pistols thrust into his belt with their handles protruding from between the parted folds of his maroon frock coat, the newcomer eyed the colorful assortment of men in the livery until his gaze rested upon Joe.

"I take you to be Travis' Joe from the Alamo," the newcomer said in pleasant resonance; Joe nodded in affirmation. "I am Eden Handy, Colonel in Houston's scouts. I, along with Deaf Smith and young Henry Karnes, was dispatched by himself to gather news of the situation at Be'ar. Looks like Deaf's gathered in the whole pot, with you survivors. At any rate, Houston wants to see you, so to Houston you shall go. Let's be off," Handy concluded with a gesture of his hand.

Handy led Joe outside of the livery and into the fading twilight of the street where Mrs. Dickerson and Angelina already stood, under guard.

"Colonel Bob," the scruffy guard blurted, "this 'ere's th' Dic'son party." There was a pause as the fellow took the opportunity to discharge his juicy wad of tobacco goodmannerdly to the side. He continued. "Deaf says t' tell ye Gen'l Sam I'nt t' his biv'wac, but is recky-noy-trin south o' camp an' t' j'in with 'im thar 'bouts."

"Thanks, Mase," said Colonel Handy. "I'll take it from here. See if you can assist the evacuees in any manner."

"Right char," spat the soldier; then he was off.

"This way, if you please, Mrs. Dickson," Handy said, gesturing the Alamo party toward the outskirts of the Texian camp.

Even the carefree disarray of the bivouac of rude tents and smoky cookfires could not diminish the presence of Sam Houston. He was standing in conversation with a young recruit, examining a rifle with a broken lock. Though he'd pared down his once full beard to enormous mutton chop side-whiskers and had foregone his greatcoat for a smithy's apron, Houston still commanded the air of one of authority.

"Leave the rifle with me, Sonny," Houston was saying. "I'll see that she gets back in good order."

"Thank you, General," the youth beside him stammered in reply, clearly embarrassed. "Thought you was the gunsmith."

"I am that, Sonny," Houston returned with a smile. "I'll fix both your gun *and* this sorry excuse for an army. How's that?"

"Fine, sir," the youth said, grinning in relief at the general's candid attitude.

Then, as the youth was walking away, Eden Handy walked

Mrs. Dickerson into the fire's light and introduced her. Houston offered Suzannah the services of a stump, while he himself chose to recline upon the ground cross-legged, in Indian fashion. Somewhat awkwardly, Joe and Handy joined the general upon the ground for the powwow.

"Hockley," Houston thundered to his aide who was standing nearby. "Get all of this down on paper. I shall want to read and reread it."

Hockley joined the party, cross-legged upon the ground, pencil at the ready. Suzannah spoke, letting out her emotion-rent discourse to its bitter finish, while the Texian Commander-in-Chief listened with tears welling in his eyes. In a surprising display of tenderness, Houston leaned in toward Suzannah, gripping and patting her hand in genuine empathy.

Looking on, Joe couldn't help but wonder what manner of leader this "Raven" was that he would exhibit such apparent frailty in the presence of his troops. Well, they would find out soon enough, both friend and foe.

When Suzannah had finished speaking at last, Houston shot off a few questions of his own for her, concluding with, "What of Jim Bowie, Ma'm?" he asked of his old friend. "Was he valiant? Did he die splendidly?"

"Colonel Bowie was sick and helpless on his couch," Suzannah replied. "They cut him to pieces. To pieces!"

The veins in the general's temple began to bulge spasmodically upon hearing this. "On my honor and by the Eternal," Houston vowed with vehemence, "I shall not allow this atrocity—this abomination to go unanswered! On my honor and by the Eternal, Madam!"

Then, just as suddenly as they had begun, Houston's outward manifestations of tenderness and passion dissolved and he was the general once more.

Then Joe gave *his* statement. As Houston listened, soaking it in, his bushy brow raised and knitted reflectively. "Your master was a brave man," Houston said at last, unknowingly re-echoing the sentiments of his gaining nemesis, Santa Anna. "But Houston needs living men to smash Saint Anna! The graveyards are glutted with the broken bodies of the brave. There must be no more Alamos! We must curtail the shutting up of our troops in forts—Leonidas and his three-hundred Spartans at Thermopylae, be damned!"

For moments after that heartfelt vow, Houston's steely eyes shot off into night space. Then he turned and spoke to Suzannah once more. "It appears that you shall be gracing the company of the Brunos once more, dear lady. Mr. Bruno and his good wife both arrived in camp not an hour ago and said that they would be more than pleased in accommodating both your daughter and self in the comforts of their wagon. Is that suitable to you?"

Suzannah said that it was, Handy escorted her away and Joe was left under the frosty glare of the general.

"There's a place for you as well, Joe," Houston told him, as they were striding back to the center of camp. "Almonte's chef, Ben's taken on as my cook—hopefully to my benefit," he added with a twinkle in his eye. "You can assist him in whatever manner of duties he may present you with. There shall be no sluggards in *this* man's army!"

As they stepped into the light of a lively cookfire, Joe and Houston found Ben, squatting down upon his haunches over a pot of *real* coffee. "Ah, here we are," Houston said, eyeing and sniffing the aromatic brew with interest. "Ben, Joe here says that he should be more than pleased in helping you however he may, good soldier that he is, ay Joe?"

"Yes, sir," Joe sighed, resigning himself once more to the drudgery of servant status and camp life.

"Sentry," Houston snapped, causing a drowsy sentinel nearby to snap to attention in turn. "I shall be in conference in Major Hockley's tent and do not wish to be disturbed!"

"Suh," returned the sentry somewhat in exaggeration, as

Houston threw open Hockley's tent flap and ducked inside the shelter's dimly lit interior.

"Well, so here *I* am cooking and there *you* are fetching, just like before," Ben intoned wryly, pouring up a tin of the boiling brew. "Same duties, different army. Here," he offered handing the coffee to Joe, "you might as well have some of this hot java as anyone. Gen'l won't touch it. Won't touch most anything. A fine thing," the steward quipped, "standing mess for somebody that don't eat! But then he got an army to worry himself over, so don't *you* go looking so down in the mouth over *your* lot. I mean what'd you expect? A medal?"

"No medal," Joe rebutted, pricked by the sudden barb. "Not even honorary mention. Just a chance to prove myself and sort things out. Weren't much sense in wandering the prairie alone! I figure I'm no better off than I was before, but then I ain't no worse, neither."

"Don't speak too soon, Mister Philosopher," Ben cautioned. "Army's moving out tonight as fast as *can* be. No pleasure trip, like we took from Bejar. Rough, roving bumpy miles and no pause! Drink up, whilst you still can and enjoy it!"

Joe drank. It had been so long since coffee had passed his lips that it took a few hard sips just to reacquaint his taste buds to it. After yet another sip, Joe looked over to Hockley's tent. By the aid of the flickering lantern within, both Hockley's and Houston's silhouettes vacillated against the canvas wall in response to a sudden change in the wind. Elsewhere around the camp, soldiers and volunteers were slapdashing hither and yon, gathering their belongings and bedrolls, or else checking their weapons. Others seemed to merely mill about in small groups of four or five to await orders. Clearly, the camp was breaking up.

"Get ready to heave to and strut," warned the sea cook, as Houston and Hockley reemerged from the tent.

Clearly put off by the utter lack of proper military decorum ensuing all around him, Houston grabbed the scruff of a young officer who was spurting by and bellowed, "What in Hades do you think you are doing, sir?"

"Gettin' ready to march, Gen'l," came the startled reply.

"Name of God, man!" Houston remonstrated. "Do not show hastiness. Wait until we are well ready, then proceed in good order!"

Then, when the officer had staggered off in the best order that he could muster, Houston turned his attentions upon Ben. "Stow most of your gear, but keep the coffee boiling—if there's any left to be had," he added, catching Joe in mid-sip. "It's going to be a long night. It will be a succession of long nights."

Then Houston stomped off across the camp toward a gathering of his officers, leaving the displaced steward and the "Veteran Soldier" to their duties.

Twenty

Retreat to Lilliput

The eastward retreat from Gonzales of Houston's ragtag force commenced upon a strange and eerie note. For, even as the soldiers—ranked four-deep in a long, ragged line—were answering the call to move forward, the last of the camp's lights extinguished and the pending procession was given over to the night.

And was it dark! In an exercise of blind faith, Joe hung onto the pack mule's mane for guidance, while Ben procured the animal's other flank. The idea was that if anything afoul should happen, then it would happen to the mule first. Other Texians, meanwhile, in an elaborated version of the children's games of "blind man's bluff" and "crack the whip" grasped the pack of the marcher directly in front of them to prevent *anyone* from stumbling off into the inky darkness.

Silence reigned. There was not even the irritating grating of cart or wagon wheel to be heard, as Houston had requisitioned the most of those conveyances to aid in the evacuation of the civilian refugees.

When the column of troops had been marching on for several hours, Joe suddenly sensed that something was clearly amiss. For, although they'd been moving eastward and into the eventual rays of dawn's early light, an orange glow was blossoming in a rage across the night sky to the rear of the column. Other soldiers began to take notice of the oddity, too. The glow was coming from the direction of the town that they'd just quit and it was not long before the knowledge became general that Gonzales was in flames.

Houston noticed it, too. *Not* the glow in the sky, but rather that his army had come to an almost complete standstill. Casting caution to the wind, Houston galloped on back down the line of troops to get them moving again and would've nearly trampled Joe, if not for an abrupt tug at the reins.

"Move along here! Goddamn you, move along!" Houston roared in exasperation. "It's only a fire! Haven't you ever seen a fire before?"

"Mexes burnin' the town!" yelped a young recruit, throwing down his gun and dropping to his knees in despair. "We'll all be killed!"

"Pick up that gun!" bellowed the General, waxing crimson. "Pick up that gun, won't you? Somebody pick up that gun and knock his head in with it! Better still," Houston threatened, pretending to dismount, "I will do the act myself!"

That was enough for the frightened recruit. Jumping to his feet in fresh terror, he swiftly shouldered his musket and got back into line.

Then Houston resumed his saddle and his poise. "It's not the Mexican army by a long shot, son. Don't you go worrying about *that*. That's Houston's job, to worry. No, most likely, it's just some tom-fool of a civilian exercising his notions of soldier-boy tactics, to leave the enemy with neither shelter, nor sustenance. Posh! The cretin little considers that we shall eventually have to reclaim and retain what little remnant of that village he has so spiritedly consumed by flame! And by the Eternal, we *shall* reclaim it, lads! All in good time. In the meanwhile, back into ranks with you that we may move forward to our business. March!"

Mollified if only slightly by Houston's explanation, the army moved forward and Joe moved with it. The orange hue of the flaming town gradually passed beyond their visibility, but oh, how it burned in their brains!

The true dawn arrived and a brief halt was called to pick up stragglers and to water down the pack train. The army had no time to spare for striking up the breakfast cookfires, but some of the men did have some jerked beef to gnaw upon and parched corn to choke down.

Joe's foraging through the general's baggage netted him a few ears of the parched corn, some coffee beans, and a sizable quantity of chewing tobacco.

Then a twig cracked and Joe turned with a start to behold Houston himself, still asaddle, but with his nose buried deep within the leaves of a book. The volume's colorful cover particularly struck Joe, for it displayed a prostrate giant with all manners of little people scampering over him in an apparent effort to tie him down. Some of the tiny folk had the giant well-entangled with rope, while others, Joe observed, were securing that rope to the ground with wooden mallets driven into sturdy pegs. As far as Joe could see the giant's name was G-U-L-L-I-V-E-R T-R—something, or other. For the rest of the fancy gilt lettering was concealed behind the general's great paws.

Houston craned his face around the book's cover to see what Joe was doing and beamed on the sight of the tobacco.

"Ah! Backy! The very thing! Toss us a few plugs, ay Joe? You read my very thoughts!"

When Joe fumblingly complied, the general bit off a sizable chaw, thrusting it into his cheek with his tongue. "We move in five minutes," he warned juicily. "Look lively!"

And then, when he'd nudged his horse forward with the toe of his boot, the face of the Texian Commander-in-Chief immersed itself once more between the parted covers of the strange little volume as though he were quite oblivious to the fact that an army was on the march with an enemy in hot pursuit.

* * *

Here was camp life again, but with an exasperating twist for Joe. Whereas serving Travis had been dangerous, exciting work, what with the Colonel's guerrilla raids and such, serving Houston now limited Joe's movement to an almost methodical tedium. Packing, unpacking the mule. Making coffee. Marching. Unpacking the mule. Sleeping. Marching again.

And while the army kept on the move, steadily clomp, clomp, clomping its way ever eastward, its Commander-in-Chief seemed to act like anything but. Without giving ear to any of his officers in a conference, or discussing a single battle plan, Houston was instead reading about giants.

Officers fumed; men deserted. First in small peelings-off, but gradually, as the days wore on, by the tens and the dozens. And though recruits did continue to drift in from the east, their addition by no means set off the imbalance caused by the continuing tide of deserters.

A week of this monotony made Joe almost wish that he were back in the Alamo. There, the soldiers had at least acted with a purpose and a zeal. Here, in Houston's rapidly diminishing, retreating column, the malcontents and the disillusioned stumbled blindly forward toward who knew where. They remained a testy lot, indeed.

Houston, for his part, continued to ride up and down the ragged line, raging and cursing the men not to break step. He seemed to have, at long last, abandoned his book.

There were times, though, when Joe would wonder why the army didn't just up and skedaddle in a bunch. But each time, upon reconsidering, he would come to the understanding as to why they did not. These men had salt, all right, but they wanted to fight. Four hundred odd of them, by gawd, and they wanted to turn and fight an army!

Perhaps, just perhaps, Houston's display of caution and patience would pay off after all. For word had it that Fannin was on the march from Goliad with his own four hundred troops and a baggage of artillery, to boot. With such a reinforcement, even Houston might be coerced to turn and fight. But then again, Joe had his own misgivings about Fannin. Fannin had made promises to the Alamo, too.

"When we going to fight?" Joe snapped in earshot of Ben who was traipsing alongside the opposite flank of the mule. "Fanning, or no Fanning, we got to do something soon, else there'll be no army at all left to do the fighting when the time finally comes."

"What Houston's doing, only Houston knows," Ben returned with a shrug. "What *we's* doing is following. And from the looks of that river there," he said, gesturing, "we'll be camping down presently."

And so they were. Orders were hollered and the exhausted little army fell out without coaxing.

Joe grabbed a bucket to draw some water for the coffee, but when he dipped it into the rapidly flowing water, the liquid had an unhealthy, clay tint to it. It looked hardly drinkable.

"Colo-raido," Ben explained, in answer to Joe's quizzical expression. " 'Red River' and rightly handled, as you can see. Most likely tastes like pizzen, but we can bile it down good and proper, so the mud'll settle."

When Joe and Ben returned to camp, they set their buckets of fresh drawn water down along side of Houston's baggage. Saddlebags and saddle and that was the sum total of the general's accoutrements. Commander of an army and yet Houston could not even lay claim to a simple tent, or a common horse blanket. When the general slept at all, it was out under the stars and with the bulk of his shivering troops.

Twenty-one
Over the Walls Like Sheep

Colonel Eden Handy strode up upon a reclined Joe and nudged him back to conscientiousness with the toe of his grimy boot. Glancing up from his bedroll, the "Veteran Soldier" rubbed the crusty sleep from his eyes and then tried to focus them in the dim light of the pre-dawning day. "We ride for Washington," Handy said in a whisper.

So, while the rest of the camp lay sleeping, Joe followed the silent scout beyond its perimeter toward a piquet post concealed somewhere within a small thicket. Upon reaching the post, Joe and Handy were challenged in the dark by one of the vigilant guards.

"Halt, friend. How's it been?"

"It's *Ben* Milam," Handy responded correctly.

Satisfied, the sentry stepped forth from his place of concealment, leading a pair of saddled paints into the humble light of the watchfire. "Horses is ready," he said.

Mounting up, Joe and Handy trotted their beasts beyond the earshot of the camp, whereupon Handy indicated a livelier gait. Soon, the two riders were loping a northeasterly course and into the rising sun.

Handy spoke. "Convention wants to review your account of the doings at the Alamo. Keep your speech short, but answer as many questions as you can, concerning the heroism of the brave defenders. Play up on the glorious end of Colonel Travis and dare not omit the gallantry of the much-beloved Crockett. The wavering patriotic sympathies of the delegates must be rekindled and you're just the man who can do it. General Houston and Texas herself are relying upon the simple honesty of your oratory to prevail."

"I'll do my best," Joe replied with gravity, wishing that, at least for that moment, he could just forget the whole thing and reassume the undemanding servile duties of a manservant. Just for the moment, mind you.

It was in the early morning of March the 20th when Joe and Handy trotted up upon a rude collection of clapboard huts and shanties, some of which were still under their final stages of construction. This was Washington-on-the-Brazos and a truer example of a town carved out of the wilderness there never was. Stumps of trees, long since hewn for building purposes, yet marred the cityscape, while dense woods menacingly encompassed the whole sorry sight. Main Street proved itself to be nothing more than a mere trace that had been hacked through the goring entanglement of the Brazos bottom.

Joe and Handy reined up upon a squatting circle of bummers who were roasting *some*thing over an open fire. Handy hailed them. "Where," he asked, "are the delegates rallying?"

"They *were* talking up a mighty storm in that formidable structure yonder," choked a tattered vagabond who sat, waving off the greasy swirls of smoke from his eyes with a wide-brimmed hat. Joe took the "formidable structure" to be nothing more than a livery. "But," Tattered continued, "they's reconvened 'cross the river at Groces'. Leave your mounts here. Raftsman'll float yuh across. Just kick him and he'll get to it smartly."

Thanking the man, Eden Handy tied off the horses outside the makeshift capitol building, then struck off with Joe on foot for the water's edge. The raftsman *was* asleep and Handy *did* have to nudge him a bit, but the fellow oblidged them swiftly enough and the raft was soon making its way toward the river's opposite bank.

When Joe and Handy stepped ashore upon the Groces' side of the river, they found the landscape to be a deal more pleasant to behold than that of the Washington side. For small, but neatly situated houses gave Groces' a sense of symmetry and order. Why, there were even rolling lawns stretching down to the waterline and a gravel path before the principal structure.

"Jared Groce is a planter of long standing in this region," Handy explained to Joe, as they were approaching the building's main entrance. "His plantation stretches clear on up the river and he stands to lose a'plenty, should the revolution against Santa Anna fail to succeed. Small wonder then, Groce is offering the delegates his highest courtesies."

Arriving at the door, Joe and Handy were challenged by the bayonet-tipped musket of a sentry. "Who goes there? State your business."

"Colonel Eden Handy of Houston's scouts and Travis' Joe, late of the Alamo massacre. We *are* expected," Handy concluded with an air of authority.

Inside, the building was fairly abuzz with tension and newspaper reporters. The delegates themselves sat milling around a long, wooden plank table positioned in the center of the "parlor," if such the room could be dignified. For, unlike most of the other local dwellings that were one-room buildings, Groces' home stood out unique in that it was partitioned off into two sections. While the rear chamber was reserved for sleeping quarters, the front room was set aside for all other daily social duties and functions.

Mid-table of the delegates, Handy approached a stocky gentleman, whose shock of wavy, red hair could only be matched by the fiery hue of his overfull chin whiskers. The two men shook hands.

"Mr. President," Handy saluted, nudging Joe forward, "I have been enjoined by General Houston to present to you none other than Travis' man Joe here, who survived the Alamo assault. With the Cabinet's permission, he shall relate the particulars, even up to the final moments of the ordeal. Gentlemen?"

Using the butt end of a horse pistol in lieu of a gavel, President Burnet got both order and the attentions of all presently gained.

"Gentlemen," he admonished, "the floor is surrendered to Travis' man Joe, late of the Alamo. He shall present his statement and in the course of its utterance, questions may be fielded. The Honorable attorney, Mr. William Fairfax Gray, will set down the deposition on paper. You may proceed," Burnet concluded, flashing the "Veteran Soldier" a stiff glance.

Standing alone before the wave of faces as though they were a hanging jury, Joe gulped, arrested his jittery knees, and then began.

"Well sir, it was still dark that morning. Colonel Travis was still asleep in his room, as I was, outside the door. All of a sudden, the whole sky went bang and I woke up with a start. The adjutant, Mr. Baugh, came running across the yard, yelling, 'Colonel Travis, the Mexicans are coming.' Out the door came Colonel Travis shouting, 'Come on, boys! The Mexicans are upon us and we will give them hell!' He headed for his cannon on the north wall and hollered for me to follow, which I did. We both had our shotguns and fired them off at the same time. The firing and noise was fierceful loud, and the Mexican army was pressing us from all sides. Our boys beat them back twice, but on they came a third time and Colonel Travis got shot in the head. He fell down the ramp, but sat up anyway with his sword pulled, just as the Mexican soldiers commenced coming in with their ladders. An officer coming over the wall—I recollect his name was Mora—tried to finish off the Colonel, but Travis ran him through and then they both died. A nurse . . . " Joe paused a beat in reverence, for Maizy's sake, "a black nurse named Maizy who came to help the Colonel was killed by a stray bullet. She fell in between the two cannons there, by the north wall. Suddenly, there seemed to be no Texians left standing and the Mexicans poured over the walls—like sheep over a stile. Adjutant Mr. Baugh took command after that and ordered everybody indoors. I took cover in the Long Barrack, myself."

"How was Colonel Bowie killed?" a delegate asked and Joe was ready for him.

"Colonel Bowie was found most sick and to his couch, but

when they busted down his door, he shot two with his pistols. Other soldiers were afraid to go in, so one of them shot poor Mr. Jim from the doorway. But when the soldier ran in to finish the job, Colonel Bowie stabbed the killer with his big knife. Then other soldiers rushed into the room and carried out Mr. Jim on their bayonets."

"It seems almost unbelievable that none were spared, Joe," someone said and Joe recognized both the voice and the face of Dr. John Sutherland. "Were *none* of the wounded granted their lives?"

"None, Doc Sutherland. They were all shot, or stabbed. Five were found hiding under some mattresses in the hospital room after the battle was over and some kindly officers asked Santa Anna to let them be. But Santa Anna only got mad and had them all shot, or bayoneted."

Appalled murmurs of disbelief fanned the room.

"What of Davy Crockett?" questioned a reporter, beating all others to the punch.

"Colonel Davy was the last to die," Joe responded. "He swung his Betsey long rifle round and round like a club, knocking soldiers down like tenpins, 'til he's shot down. Then he used his hunting knife with deadly effect, even as they came swarming over him with their bayonets slashing."

That was enough to get the entire room caught up in the fervor. "Which Alamo defender slew the most enemy soldiers?" a delegate shouted.

"Colonel Crockett had the biggest pile," Joe replied, scarcely noticing the smile creasing Eden Handy's face. "Colonel Almonte's cook, Ben, told me that there were twenty-four dead Mexicans lying around Davy and two of his boys, though I didn't cipher 'em myself."

"How did you effect your escape, Joe?" Dr. Sutherland asked.

"Like I said," Joe continued, "I fell back to the Long Barracks room and stayed there until nearly the end when two officers came in and asked 'Are there any negroes here?' 'Yes,' I replied and they led me outside. Straight away two soldiers tried to kill me by shooting and sticking, but the ball only slighty wounded me, while the bayonet did not go in that far. A kindly officer named Barragan stopped the soldiers and saved my life. I'll always be thankful to him for that. Anyway, after that, I was led into town where a huge parade of soldiers was lining up in the plaza. Though all the men in the Alamo were dead, there were still so many Mexican soldiers left."

"How large a force are you talking about?" President Burnet demanded.

"Couldn't rightly cipher 'em at the moment," Joe responded, "but I could swear for a fact that there must have been at least eight thousand men grouped up there."

That was enough to set the assembly abuzz once more. So, to avert a possible panic, Burnet tactfully cut the interview short.

"I believe that we have heard quite enough, thank you Mr. Handy. (He ignored Joe.) You both may proceed back to Houston with godspeed, whilst the cabinet decides upon a course of action. Good-bye," Burnet thundered with finality.

So Handy and Joe left the assembly all atwitter.

And someone else followed them outside. He had large, almost doe-like eyes and his wavy brown hair was swept back casually from his broad brow. Slight in stature and rather frail-looking—from illness, Joe thought—the fellow was smartly dressed in a high-collared waistcoat, with cravat.

"Mr. Austin," Handy saluted, when Stephen Fuller Austin, the "Father of Texas" hailed them.

So this was Steve Austin, Joe thought. Austin's father, Moses, had started the whole ball rolling back in the early twenties when he'd wrangled a land grant for a colony of 300 American families from the newly formed Mexican government. Upon his father's death, Stephen Fuller *had* tried to make a good go of it, adamantly stressing to his colonists to follow all the laws of Mexico as loyal citizens. For a time, the colony flourished. Then Santa Anna gained power, set up a centralist government, and all bets were off. When Austin traveled to Mexico City to present a petition to Santa Anna concerning separate statehood for Texas, Santa Anna's response was to have the kindly, unassuming Austin imprisoned. Upon his release and with the last gasp of his father's dream still ringing in his ears, it was with an understandably deep sadness that Austin declared war.

"Colonel Handy," Austin said, returning the scout's salute. "I'd like to speak to Joe here in private, if you do not mind. There are a few items I'd like to free my mind of."

"Certainly, sir," Handy acquiesced though a little surprised. "I'll just go and nudge that raftsman awake. Meet you at the ferry, Joe."

"That was quite a powerful talk you gave in there, Joe," Stephen Fuller began. "Perhaps it was enough to turn the energy of all those stuffed shirts away from their own personal petty bickerings and *toward* the salvation of Texas, for once. So many good men fell in the Alamo. So many dreams left unrealized. It now remains for us, the living, to keep those dreams alive. You have certainly proven yourself a loyal Texian, Joe, though I must say, I'd never been able to like your late master. Travis was a hothead and we were often at odds. In the end, though, he gave his all for Texas and I could certainly ask no more of anyone. What I want to know from you is what do you make of Santa Anna, Joe? Is he really the cold-blooded brute propaganda would have us believe and does he *really* intend to wipe every North American off the face of Texas? While I myself have certainly suffered at his hands, he did not kill *me*. What of the loyal colonists—those who have not taken up arms against him? What is his intention concerning them?"

"Santa Anna made it clear that he wants no American left in Texas, Mr. Austin, sir. He was even bragging that when he had kicked out all the Yankees that he would march clear on up to Washinton and plant his flag in the Capitol. No American is safe, sir. One thing, though, he did say—and so did Colonel Almonte—

was that they did not make war on slaves, but freed them. If Texas is truly to be a free country then how can it still have slaves living under its flag? My friend Maizy once told me that it don't ring true and now I'm beginning to see what she meant."

With a sad smile spreading over his face, Austin responded. "Some things don't change right away, Joe. In America, the idea of slavery is accepted in some quarters and rejected in others. Time may tell. America's a young country—but Texas is barely a newborn babe, in comparison. The government's got to be a viable entity first, before anyone can go calling for 'change, change.' Meanwhile, while I can't promise you anything, I do hold some influence with that government. Come and see me when the war is over and I will do what I can in your behalf. While I may be powerless to shift public opinion, I *can* assist you as an individual. For you certainly do have a friend in Stephen Fuller Austin, fellow Texian."

"Thank you, sir," Joe responded, a little lighter of spirit. "I will come and see you. Right now, I've got to get back to Colonel Handy. Raftsman's ready."

So Joe crossed back over the Brazos River with Eden Handy. And as they were riding back to Houston's camp at last, Handy's curiosity got the better of him.

"So, what did 'The Father of Our Country' have to talk about that was so secretive?"

"Freedom," Joe replied and let it go at that.

Twenty-two

The Great Skedaddle

Things in general had been fairly humdrum in camp during his absence, Ben clued the saddle-weary Joe. In fact, the army seemed to have practically taken up residence upon the Colorado; six hundred testy men all spoiling for the prospects of an honest fight.

The muggy afternoon of March the 21st saw one brewing for them when Mexican cavalry suddenly appeared on the opposite side of the river and began aligning themselves in full formation and plain sight.

"So much for our worthy scouts," Ben quipped sarcastically, as both he and Joe watched the magnificent mounted men going through their maneuvers. "If not for the river blocking them, that horse could've ridden right over us without so much as a shot offered up in return. Talk is, it's Santa Anna himself, but some of the Tejanos allow that it's but Ram-A-Rez E. Sesma. Sesma was at the Alamo, as were most of his boys. They showed no quarter then and likely have no intention of showing it *now*. Nuff of 'em, aren't there?"

Enough for target practice, at any rate, or so thought some of the raw Texian recruits. A few harmless, scattered shots later saw the cavalry casually "retreating" upriver at an even gait, their reconnoitering done. But, as the cheering recruits could only see it as a glorious repulse, so it was that the "Battle of the River Red" was won.

The greater part of the army, however, was not so readily appeased, or bamboozled while milled in tension. They geared themselves up for the true fight they were certain was yet to come. They waited for five days.

In the pre-dawn hours of the sixth day, Houston called one of his rarely convened staff officers meetings and there was serious talk of a surprise attack upon the Mexican camp, while it was yet dark. But the bottom dropped out of the notion and all enthusiasms paled, as a courier thundered into camp with devastating news. And he was hardly the tower of discretion.

"Fanning's lost! Whole force captured and butchered by Urrea, near Coleto Creek! Shot, after surrendering on terms! Over three hundred dead—no survivors—not *one* spared!"

Houston finally succeeded in silencing the fellow, but the damage had already been done. There would be no attack; the army would continue its eastward retreat.

By the time they had reached the outskirts of San Felipe de Austin upon the Brazos River, Joe estimated that the army had been whittled down by a third, due to desertions and disillusionment.

San Felipe! To many of the footweary Texians, that town only signified a more comfortable place to bivouac upon their "Great Skedaddle" of a retreat. But to Joe, the humble hamlet signaled journey's end, for it was there that Silvie waited for him. Or, at least he hoped so. Maybe she had fled Mill Creek along with Rebecca and John Cummings, or perhaps she was in the hands of Travis' executor, J.R. Jones, the town's postmaster. At any rate, it was to Postmaster Jones that Joe eventually hoped to head, freedom papers, old Uncle Tom Cobbly and all. In the merest of hours and footfalls away, Joe and Silvie would be free to wander at their will and only the army's exasperating snail's pace prevented it all from happening. Small wonder then that the night of the 28th of March was a restless one for the "Veteran Soldier."

The column entered San Felipe just past dawn—and how silent it was! Debris, fluttering paper, and criss-crossing wagon ruts told the story of a hurried departure, as did a few stragglers left behind as a rear guard. Seems that the townsfolk had all fled eastward in a panic, the stragglers explained. The remaining town officials—Postmaster Jones included—had all proceeded upriver to join the cabinet at Washington-on-the-Brazos. As a matter of fact, Jones had been the very last to leave.

Irony of ironies! So Silvie had been in Washington-on-the-Brazos, perhaps at the same time that Joe had been! If only they'd seen each other there! Jones would have the freedom papers and Joe and Silvie would be together—for good. As it now stood, though, Joe was caught up in this godforsaken caravan and heading in an altogether different direction. Then Joe remembered Silvie's words from that day when he had sent her away from Bejar—how her feet were carrying her in a direction that she did not want to go. Joe now knew firsthand how Silvie must've felt and he ached for her all the more.

But then fate stepped in and in Joe's behalf when Houston called an officer's meeting. While both Ben and Joe stood by eavesdropping, it was Ben that got the gist of it.

"Cap'n Baker and Martin argue to push downwater toward Old Fort with their crews and Gen'l Houston allows that they may go to blazes, Old Fort, or wherever they like. That'll cut us down by about two hundred men, but the Gen'l's set on upriver, so upriver we goes, so it seems."

Hearing this, Joe could only breathe a sigh of relief, for Silvie was still within his reach, after all.

Twenty-three

Hot As Hades and Twiced As Damnable

Crouching upon his haunches in a vigilant stance near Sam Houston's cookfire, Joe watched the General's ragged, un-uniformed soldiers parade by in two columns and as many directions. While one column appeared to be heading north for the Brazos bottom, the other was clearly heading back downstream for San Felipe.

The camp was breaking up. Houston had already ridden off to head the northbound column and Joe was only waiting for the reappearance of Ben, before rejoining the General there. The steward had gone scrounging for foodstuffs in the hopes of supplementing Houston's dwindling stores and he had taken the mule.

"Wal! Ain't this a purty sight?" a voice from overhead commented. Joe reared back to see who it was and found himself staring up into the face of a burly, bearded, grub of a man.

"Es verdad," the Grub's mustachioed, serape-clad companion observed. "There *is* something familiar about him, mi amigo."

"There is at that," Grub agreed, adding, "cut the Mex lingo and talk American!"

The Grub squinted long and hard upon Joe, trying to place him; then his eyes lit up in absolute recognition.

"Sure, it's the horse-minder! Howdy do, horse-minder! How's the head?"

Horse-minder? Joe thought in surprise. And then he remembered. So these two miscreants before him were the thieves who had jumped him back in Travis' camp at Burham's crossing on the Colorado! *Of all the folk to be running into,* Joe grimaced to himself, for his outward expression was one of utmost defiance.

"Cookin' some chow, ay?" the Grub spat, twirling the ends of an incredibly matted beard between his pudgy fingers as he spoke. "Wal, that yaller livered sunnuva polecat Houston don't rightly deserve service o' *one* cook, let alonest two! We's fightin' men an' Cap'n Baker's gwinter skewer ol' Santy Anner like fun an' swallow him whole. You kin cook vittles fer Cap'n Baker an' march in a *real* army! Git along in line," the Grub threatened, further emphasizing his point with a razor-sharp skinning knife.

Under the circumstances and the glint of the upraised knife, Joe had little choice but to comply with the Grub's order, however begrudgingly. But in the awful realization that he would be placing painful distance between himself, Houston, Washington-on-the-Brazos *and* Silvie, Joe cast a longing, backward glance upon the diminishing rear guard of the main Texian army, until Grub urged him forward once more with a swift kick in the shins.

"Git along," Grub snarled. "Cap'n Baker's waitin' an' he ain't as kindhearted a soul as I are!"

"Thank the Lord for small favors," Joe sighed under his breath.

When Baker's company reentered San Felipe at last, they found a deathly silence hanging over the little town. Why, there was not even a stray dog to be seen, or eaten. Houston's main force had done a good job in stripping the place bare of anything and everything worth the salvaging, but that did not dissuade Baker's bunch from kicking in the boarded-up doors all the same in their search for hidden plunders. In no time at all, the personal mementos left behind by the rapidly departing citizenry joined the garbage in the streets. The men cursed on finding nothing, then cursed all the more when a search of the local tavern produced no whiskey at all.

As it turned out, it wasn't too long before some semblance of order was restored in San Felipe, as Mosley Baker rode up, looked over his pillaging force, and then cursed them back into ranks.

"We'll be needing lumber and sand bags to fort up along the eastern shore of the river—not gold, not whiskey; certainly *not* grandmother's shawl," he bellowed, noticing a soldier wearing a purloined quilt about his shoulders. "We've got to build barricades and dig some trenchworks. Boats that cannot be adequately concealed should be stove in and added to the defense work. Word is, Sesma's got fifteen hundred men. When they arrive, they'll find us ready, by gawd!"

But ready for what? Joe shuddered, on eyeing the all-too-familiar earth and timber palisades. With Wyley Martin and his hundred gone south to defend Old Fort, that left an equal number of willing amateurs here in these trenches to face off Sesma's formidable force of trained professionals. To the "Veteran Soldier," once again assigned to tote sandbags to bolster up the rude earthworks, it seemed another Alamo in the making.

Grub gave Joe a shove for pausing to daydream and then cursed him for a sluggard. "Get t' stackin' them sacks tight an' hurry yer lazy, good-for-nothin' bum along! Hain't no vittle to be had in town t' serve t' Cap'n Baker, but then that don't let you off, or give you head, nosir! You'll *earn* yer priv'lege t' serve in th' true Texican cause an' you'll have *me* to answer to, if'n ye don't!"

There was an ugly pleasure in Grub's tone and an evil smirk upon the man's face as he stomped off along the embankment to view the progress of laborers yet toiling over other lengths of entrenchment. But, as far as Joe could see, Grub offered up no visible effort of his own.

Hefting another sandbag into place, Joe measured his ill-fortune on having been placed under the beck and call of such a man as Grub. At this juncture, Silvie and Washington-on-the-Brazos seemed a lifetime away.

The jaybird roosting upon the makeshift battlements of Mosley Baker's fort took winged flight, as violent repercussions rent the early morning air. Already awake, but startled nonetheless,

Joe shifted his glance from the feathered creature itself to the town across the sheeted, marble sheen of the river's rolling surface. Flame and smoke, he saw, were billowing skyward from the nearly unrecognizable structures, from whose doorways, tiny, torch-bearing figures scurried like mad to escape the harvest of their own handiwork.

San Felipe was dying; put to the torch, on Mosley Baker's own orders. Now, from behind the safety of their fresh defense works, the Texians could only watch spellbound as the dreams of the town's citizens, as well as all evidence of the army's own plundering and pillaging, went up in great billows of soot and smoke.

The Grub's remark that there was no food to be had in San Felipe proved to be no understatement. The hungry men began butchering burro for sustenance, arguing how the lack of provisions had ended the burros' usefulness as beasts of burden, anyhow. "They's *beef* of burden now," some wiseacre quipped, and although his attempt at humor was in questionable taste, at least the burro meat was not half bad, after all. Hell! Anything was better than parched corn, day in and day out. Joe decided not to mention the merits of bull nettlenuts.

Come morning, there was little time for thoughts of food, after a Texian sentinel who'd been stationed in the charred ruins of the town across the river fired off his pistol midstream from a rowboat he'd been quick to put out in. The sentinel could have saved his powder, though. For even as he was turning to paddle for dear life toward the Texian trenches on the further shore, a volley of musket reports exploded from the direction of San Felipe followed soon after by leaden balls that splurched up little geysers of water in the tiny craft's wake. Somehow the lookout managed to reach the beach below Baker's position unscathed. Then, as shots continued to pock the mudbank all around him, he unceremoniously beached the boat and dove over a low point in the defense works.

Shaken, out of breath, and rattled as he was, the lookout nevertheless made his report, as ordered. "Greasers, by gum!" he wheezed. "Hundreds of 'em! They move fast—fannin' out ever'where. Nearly kotched me! Tell Cap'n Baker—they got cannon!"

Even as the lookout lay gasping out his report, Mexican lancers appeared, then divided, half going upriver, half going down. Next, infantry troops arrived. Taking up position in the wreckage of the consumed buildings, the musketeers waited and watched as their gun crews began unlimbering two tiny cannon. On witnessing the coordinated troop movements, some of the Texians began grumbling how the Mexican lancers were probably going to ford the river just out of sight, then roll up Baker's exposed flanks. Hastily, they began to dig in, burrowing little foxholes in the soft earth. But what good would such feeble defenses be against mounted lancers, anyhow?

Although a full city block of desolation lay in between the position of the enemy infantry and the water's edge, to Joe the distance appeared to be only about half as far. San Felipe, in its blackened, skeletal state, now seemed somehow less imposing than it had in its former, intact glory. Perhaps razing it had not been such a bad idea, after all. For, with no place to take cover, the Mexicans were having a hot time of it, as Baker's boys blasted a steady fusillade into the char and ash, until clouds of dust and soot, kicked up by the impacting leaden balls, choked the unfortunate troops deploying there.

Yet when Sesma's two small cannon were at last unlimbered, their gun crews set about opening up with their own brand of iron mischief against Baker's feeble breastworks. Out of range of even the Texians long rifles, the Mexican artillerymen literally had a field day. Cursing and exasperated, Baker's men could only hug the mud for dear life, or else leap for safety, as cannon discharges plowed up whole sections of barricade into smithereens.

"Who'd o' thought they'd uh brought up cannon?" a dazed defender shouted above the roar.

"Who'd o' thought they *wou'nt*?" came the disgusted reply.

With the sensation of screaming voices, trembling earth, billowing smoke, roaring thunder, and the flash and hail of the Texians own sporadic fire blending into the tumult of the Mexican bombardment, the overall effect was blinding, choking, deafening.

"Get thet water comin'!" bawled Grub, as Joe lay bearhugging a sandbag in numb determination. "Hot as Hades an' twiced as damnable! Get lively, else I'll waste ye m'self!"

Joe moved. With bucket in hand, he leapt over the barrier of earth at a point where a cannon shot had chomped away a big bite. Tumbling down the some six or seven yards to the mudbank along the waterline, Joe hugged mud, looking this way and that for some sort of cover; *any* cover.

Then Joe saw it; the lookout's abandoned rowboat. Puckering in the thick mud and only paces to his right, the craft had, so far, come through all the flying lead and iron curiously unscathed. So Joe made for it, inching his way through the slime like a mud turtle. With the side of the rowboat as a shield, Joe filled the bucket with the mucky, brown water.

But now, Joe was in a tighter position than even before, for Mexican skirmishers were moving forward to get into a better position and, once they'd accomplished that, Joe would be their first sitting duck.

On Sesma's infantry came, emboldened, perhaps by the lack of response from the Texian defense works. *What was Baker up to?* Joe wondered. *Had the Texians retreated?*

Well, whether the Texians intended to start firing or not, Joe had to make his move and quick. So he went, swinging the bucket forward to give him some momentum. And as *he* went, *it* came. First the explosion and a roaring sheet of flame, then a smothering wall of smoke that came fanning from the Texian breastworks, as thought someone had drawn a mantle of cotton across the sky.

This was the sort of cover fire Joe had been praying for, so he took advantage of it, hunching over to make himself small. With the handle of the bucket firmly within his grip, Joe barreled up the steep incline and over the breastwork at his initial point of descent, even as returning enemy fire ripped into the compacted soil.

But Joe's daring move and his narrow escape with death, he soon found, had all been for nothing. For musket balls had splintered the side of the bucket to such an extent that he did not even have a cupful of precious water to offer up, for all his expended efforts.

Grub came upon the scene to berate Joe for his failure. "No water t'all!" he blasted from beneath a savage scowl. "Git over that 'ith a new bucket an' may ye be split if ye returns empty handed! Git go-aah . . . "

The loud smack of a musket ball making contact with Grub's skull cut him off in mid-sentence and hurtled the stricken man back several feet to land spread eagle with a heavy thud.

"Madre de Dios!" Grub's companero gasped. "Surely he is dead!" But as he bent over the prostrate Grub to get a better look, the companero changed his prognosis. "No, he yet breathes. The ball merely grazed his head. He will have a terrific headache when he awakens, but no more. Venir aqui," he beckoned Joe. "Help me get him out of the way."

Joe helped. And when the two of them had lugged the Grub to a place of comparative safety, Grub's companero said, "I will take care of him, amigo. You take care of yourself."

So Joe left them there and made it back to the barricade, crouching low against stray musket balls as he did.

Crazy thoughts started racing through Joe's mind. His tormentor, the Grub, was out of action for the time being, meaning that he, Joe, was a free man. He could make his own decisions.

It would be drawing dark soon, Joe considered. Mexican fire would likely start to taper off with the setting of the sun, while the Texian camp, grabbing whatever sleep it could, would be dead to the world. It would be a time of escape. But to effect his escape in the lookout's small rowboat, to navigate the unknown river under cover of darkness? *Madness,* Joe thought.

But then he relented. For even if he were to make good his escape on foot, Houston's army still had a two day's march head start advantage on him. Navigating the small boat on the river would be the only way that Joe could possibly hope to catch up. So to hell with his fear of the damned water—if he were destined to die by drowning, then so be it. For he'd had his fill of death and found that there were far worse things in life to experience than crossing over that particular bridge. Anyway, the Brazos River was a far cry from the River Styx for, unlike that fabled river of death, *this* river would only carry him along toward life and hope—and to Silvie.

So, with his course set and his freedom papers secreted within his shirt, Joe felt a strange peacefulness welling up inside, as he stepped off to resign himself to the shackles of a free man.

Twenty-four

A Dip in the Brazos

Darkness at long last fell over the ragged battle line, as the last of the Mexican rockets burst, then fizzled harmlessly overhead. Apparently the enemy's supply of these aerial mischief-makers was limited, or else they would've surely granted the Texians a more zealous display of pyrotechnics.

The sudden darkness suited Joe just fine, for the low flicker of the smoky campfires would provide him with all the light he'd need.

Joe took one last look at the camp, before starting off. However disagreeable his brief stay had been there, the camp had at least provided him with the sense of safety in numbers. But safety was no longer Joe's main objective, he knew. He would leave that behind. For he was going. Going . . .

Joe clung close to the recess of the trench to make himself less conspicuous to some of the yet vigilant Texian sentries, as the new moon vanished behind a cloudbank, swallowing up all telltale shadows.

Stealthily slinking along in the blackness, Joe could hear some yet vigilant men whispering to each other in hushed tones, so as to not disturb, or awaken, their slumbering comrades. They needn't have bothered, though, for most of the weary lay sagging against the cold walls of the embankment, like dead men awaiting interment.

On Joe struggled, letting his spongy steps retrace their way back to the familiar cleft in the earthen wall where he'd made his death-defying reentry into the defense works on his ill-fated raid for water. 'Good-bye, camp,' Joe whispered to himself, giving the place one last looking over. Then he slithered through that impromptu embrasure without a sound, pausing only once to ensure that he was not being followed. But the only audible sounds carrying upon the heavy air were of rifle barrels clinking clumsily in the night, men snoring nasally and the raspy grating of a knife blade against a whetting stone. That, and the hushing gurgle of the water moving by.

Satisfied, Joe slid down the gradual declivity upon his backside, until he reached the slime of the mudbank along the river's edge where the beached little boat wallowed in stark black silhouette against the inky blue of the water's surface. From there, Joe could see the none-too-distant flickers of the Mexican campfires just across the river.

Holding his breath, muffling his grunts, Joe threw all of his weight against the boat's prow in an effort to dislodge it. But for all of his best efforts, both the boat and the mud seemed unyielding. Again he tried; again he failed. Finally, after an exaggerated pucker and smack that sounded not unlike the fulfillment of an untrained kiss, the craft relented and slid adrift. Joe clambered in.

It was a rough go, for he had to paddle against the current, upstream all the way. And though his arms ached in rebellion at each pull of the oar, Joe could not afford to slacken his pace for even a moment. For if he did, the current would only carry him back several feet to square one, from where he would be obliged to regain all of his hard won distance.

Joe moved in nearer toward the shoreline where the current was at its weakest but when sandbars and overgrown foliage clogging the channel proved that course a bad bet, he pulled out into midstream once more.

As he rowed on, Joe began to hear movement over on the Mexican's side of the river; axes felling trees, wood clattering against wood. From what he could gather, engineers were fitting together rude rafts—rafts designed to carry the waiting troops across the deep, if narrow, river and over to the Texian position. And if his own untrained ears could surmise as much, what would Baker's skilled woodsmen make of it?

It wasn't long before Joe received his answer in the form of a peppering rain of leaden balls that came screaming from the Texian defenses, as Baker's boys began to rake the beach. Briefly, upon each discharge, the Texians would stand out in silhouette against the darkness beyond them. But then, in the blink of an eye and a flash in the pan, the silenced shooters would be reclaimed by the nearly impenetrable veil of the night.

Over on the Mexicans' side of the river, however, only excited shouts and screams could tell the tale. Troops caught upon the exposed beach began to fall at an alarming rate and it wasn't too long before the confused remnant saw the wisdom of beating a stumbling beeline for cover.

But this was no time for Joe to be taking in the sights, what with musket balls plinking the water all around him. So he hunched over his oars even lower still in the hope of making himself a lesser target. But when the roar of a Mexican cannon and a cluster of grapeshot arcing by caught him off guard, Joe involuntarily shot up in his seat, lost his balance and tumbled into the dark and churning water.

Down Joe sank, all in a panic, blindly grabbing at anything that might draw him back up to the water's surface. On his third try, Joe caught the side of the boat itself and hauled himself back into it with such little care that it was a wonder he did not capsize.

For a while, Joe lay in the bottom of the boat, breathing heavily. Then he took stock. He was alive, the boat was still afloat, and he had one good oar left. The other had gone over into the water with him and, with a battle raging overhead, he wasn't about to go looking for it now.

So he continued on up the river as best as he could with the single oar, while a Mexican cavalry unit patrolling the shore cautiously pawed its way through the darkness. Suddenly, all was confusion, as an overzealous rider approaching the patrol from the opposite direction, thundered into it to a salvo of inaudible oaths and curses. Whatever tidings the messenger managed to relate in between his tongue-lashing was enough to send the cavalry unit plunging back toward its main encampment, until at length, the re-echoing clatter of horse hooves faded into the distance and the shoreline became silent once more.

By morning, Joe had paddled to the mouth of a trickling tributary of the Brazos that looked oddly familiar. The trees, the banks—why even the smell of the place—started conjuring up memories of sweet, if fleeting, moments passed there and Joe knew, before even laying sight on the Cummings' Inn, that he was back at Mill Creek once more.

How he longed to revisit the inn for information on Silvie. A hidden note, perhaps, a bauble, something that she might have left behind: *any*thing. But he could not afford to take the risk. For, were the inn still standing, the Mexicans might be using the snug and welcome structure as a headquarters. If, on the other hand, Baker's boys had burned the inn to the ground, the knowledge would only serve to drive a shard of misery into his heart. Sometimes it's best to just let memories be.

So, placing the memories, his weariness, and distance behind him, Joe resisted the magnetic pull of the waters of Mill Creek and rowed on.

As the miles continued to lapse by, Joe found that he could allow himself brief snatches of rest at different intervals by anchoring his oar into the thick mud of the shallows, then securing it to the boat with his looped belt. In such an attitude, the little craft would drift and bob in lazy circles until that motion and the welcome rays of the sun beckoned Joe to much needed sleep.

How tranquil it all seemed, this drifting along upon the river's sluggish current in the twilight-state of half slumber. Life and death, war and peace, love and hate—all these, plus a myriad more of mankind's body and mind straining paradoxes that had goaded Joe on to an uncertain destiny, now seemed a million miles away and themselves but dreams.

Why, even some bushy-tailed squirrels scampering along the shoreline for a dip in the Brazos seemed to sense the unusual calm, for the inquisitive little creatures paid little heed to Joe's rowboat, taking it for a beached log. All along the rim of the boat's frame they tiptoed, until the distant booming of an artillery piece sent them chattering and scattering for cover and dear life.

Then the "Veteran Soldier," roused from his brief snatch of sleep, remembered the gist and purpose of his present sojourn and rowed on.

Twenty-five
A Hard-Enough Decision

Paddling his little rowboat up the Brazos was both hungry and thirsty work for Joe. How long *had* it been since he'd last eaten, anyway? Properly, or otherwise, five days had elapsed since he'd quit Mosley Baker's camp at San Felipe provisioned with a scant supply of jerked beef and parched corn. Well, that hadn't lasted him for long. Now Joe's stomach was twisting him in knots; its demanding growling was even keeping him awake at night. On the positive side, at least the river would not leave him wanting for drinking water, he mused.

But the river, Joe soon found, had both a mind and ideas of its own, as his boat came to a sudden jerking halt upon a mudbank. Ravages of a recent storm had so drastically altered the river's course that its original main channel was now nothing more than a mucky array of circling stagnant pools. The new channel, Joe saw, went sluicing off through a dense grove of trees, just to his left. One look at the treacherous maze with its low, overhanging, snatching branches and hidden snarl of submerged roots made Joe realize that his journey by water had come to its end.

The muscle-wrenching voyage up the Brazos had gained Joe perhaps a day upon the trail of Houston's army. The little boat had served him well, so Joe saw to it that it was well-covered beneath a rude camouflage of brush and reeds. Then he proceeded on, striking off across the mushy landscape in search of firmer ground.

As Houston would no doubt be marching his force toward Washington-on-the-Brazos as the crow flies, Joe reckoned that it would better serve his own interests to try and avoid the General, if he at all could. For Houston would be ambling along at his own good pace, at a time when both time and speed were of the essence to Joe in his search for Silvie. By crossing over this low point of water toward the eastern bank, Joe reasoned that he could circumvent the Houston horde altogether and then perhaps even arrive in Washington-on-the-Brazos unheralded, with the edge of surprise on his side, if precious little else.

So, bearing this new resolve, Joe struck off across—and then down into—the slimy ooze of the riverbed, just as the ashen skies burst, sheeting rain down in pelting torrents upon the exposed prairie and Joe's patent leather cap. With bowed head and hunched shoulders, Joe pushed into the face of the driving rain to seek out the shelter of the boggy woods.

Once among the trees, Joe pressed himself to the knees of a towering cypress in the hopes of weathering the storm beneath its gnarled and knobby boughs. But the idea, he soon found, was not an original one, nor was he alone. For wringing wet squirrels, damp, droopy jackrabbits, and several other saturated little brothers of the plain had likewise scampered thither to seek refuge.

Before long, the storm had transformed the once sluggish trickle of the main watercourse that Joe had just abandoned into a frothing and churning rage, as the Brazos set about reclaiming its former passage. Once again, water had decided Joe's course of action; there could be no turning back.

Suddenly, through the crash and the din of the momentous drowning, Joe heard something that bolted him to his feet. It was the whinny of distressed horses and it was approaching. Peering through a parting of the droopy branches of the cypress Joe saw it to be a lone rider hunched low in the saddle against the elements, the halter of a riderless horse tied to his own horse's pommel. There could be no doubt about it; the mounted man was making straight for the shelter of the wood.

What could Joe do? However he chose to look at it, his

prospects did not seem at all bright. For, if the rider were a Mexican scout, then Joe might be forced into fighting it out with the fellow, like it or not. On the other hand, should the rider prove to be Texian, he might have it in his mind to take Joe prisoner as a runaway slave with a possible bounty on his head, or, even worse, shoot Joe down like a dog.

Should have kept that paddle for a weapon, Joe thought, also adding that he wished that he still had his old Alamo bayonet.

Unarmed, tortured by anxiety, Joe could only watch from his temporary place of seclusion, as the rider reined up beneath the brooding boughs of the cypress and dismounted. The stranger's butternut-colored hair, Joe saw, was plastered fast against his forehead and he'd drawn up the collar of his maroon frock coat for extra measure, to make up for the difference for his missing hat. So reappeared Colonel Eden Handy of Houston's scouts.

Glancing from side to side in a suspicious manner, as though sensing he were not alone in the riverside retreat, Handy tugged out one of the great horse pistols from his belt and cocked it menacingly. This motion so alarmed Joe, that he found himself shouting "Texas! Texas!" in a desperate effort to keep from being shot.

It worked. Handy lowered his weapon, then squinted upon Joe until he recognized him at last.

"Travis' Joe?" Handy asked, making no effort to hide his amazement. "We were told that Baker's people spirited you off to San Flippy. Houston had had other plans for you. But how, pray tell, did you get *here*? You're a wonder at escapement, I'll be bound!"

Through the bone-chilling furor of the storm, Joe did his best to fill Handy in with the details of what had transpired since their last meeting.

"Just as well you got away from Baker when you did," Handy remarked, when Joe'd finished talking. "Sesma's force is too big for Baker and Martin to beat. At least they're keeping Sesma's cavalry off of Houston's neck, for the time being. A fellow scout and I were tracking Sesma's activity and ran into a couple of his own scouts along the way. *They* have not to report again, but my poor companion, Bob, is likewise disposed. His mount is at your service—*and* Houston's! We ride for Washington-on-the-Brazos storm, or no storm!"

A horse at his disposal, Joe thought, *but more importantly, a fellow rider to share the rigors of the trail with that was also going in the same direction that he was! It was almost too good to be true,* Joe mused, as both he and Handy pushed out into the face of the pressing rain.

They made good time; and as the miles ate themselves up to the kerplopity rhythm of mud-encrusted horses' hooves, Joe could sense the distance that lay between Silvie and himself melting away, despite the fact that the indiscriminate sweep of winter's frosty wrath lay yet upon the land.

The storm had just about exhausted itself, when the two similarly spent riders drew up at a distance below Groce's landing and the Houston camp.

"Well, Joe," Handy said with a weary sigh, "we've made our return stint unscathed, if not, howsoever, unsaturated. But a few more paces and it's a warm fire and hot grub for us, ay?"

But upon Handy's solely casual observation, Joe began to feel a sick, tingly sensation welling in the pit of his stomach. For he realized that the time was nigh for him to either speak up as a free man, or else forever hold his peace as a camp cook and servant—without his beloved Silvie.

So it was, with his courage screwed up taught, that Joe responded, "In all respect, Colonel Handy, I can't go with you."

Somewhat taken aback by Joe's unexpected announcement, Eden Handy bug-eyedly replied with an, "Indeed? And pray tell, why not?"

"Well, sir," Joe answered with conviction, "my woman Silvie's in Washingtown under the care of Colonel Travis' will holder, the Postmaster Jones. Colonel Travis gave Silvie and me our freedom papers back at the Alamo," Joe gestured, patting his shirt, "and I need to get to her as quickly as possible with them. They're right here," Joe offered, withdrawing the folded documents from deep within his shirt.

Handy took the proffered packet from Joe and delicately attempted to unfold it. But the flimsy copybook paper had the consistency of a pulpy mush. And though Handy succeeded in peeling one sheet away from the other, the ink upon the disintegrating page had run off into splotchy, indistinguishable characters.

"This is unreadable, Joe," Handy said with compassion. "I can't even make out the handwriting. No one's going to accept these documents as the writings of Colonel Travis, let alone freedom papers. I'm truly sorry."

Joe's eyes went wide with disbelief when the hard truth of Handy's words hit him. Then he took the papers from the Colonel and just held them, not knowing what in the world to do. "I fell in the water, a-ways back," he said finally, thinking to himself that water had once again been the cause of his grief.

"It's not fair," Joe went on with mounting anger in his voice. "I mean, aren't things hard enough—haven't they been hellish enough? Why," he languished in despair. "Oh my God, why?"

Handy spoke solemnly. "I have little idea what this means to you, Joe, so I won't even pretend to understand. All I do know is that the loss of freedom at any level can be and *is* devastating. The question *now* is, what do you intend to do about it? If you go back to this Jones without your freedom papers, you'll be a bound slave once more. Nothing can change that. On the other hand, if you proceed with me to Houston's camp, you may just be able to fade into the woodwork, so to speak. So, I leave it to you, Joe. It's a hard-enough decision for you to be making, without my two bits thrown in to muddle things, but make it you must. So," Handy challenged with finality, "what's it to be?"

Though Joe *had* been listening to Eden Handy's speech, his

mind was off wandering, a million miles away. The bottom had just dropped out of Joe's life and here was Handy, asking Joe what he intended to do about it.

Joe gritted his teeth and then clenched his fists. For, as far as he was concerned, there *was* really no choice in the matter, none at all.

"Well, sir," Joe replied, "I rightly *could* join up with the army, I expect, so as to keep out of Mr. Jones' sight. But Colonel Handy, my Silvie's with the postmaster and my place is with her, come what may. So, it's the both of us, or neither, the way I see it. I reckon that I *owe* Silvie that much. Anyway," he added, "freedom without Silvie would be just another sort of link o' chain around me—a sort whose weight I couldn't rightly bear."

Eden Handy knit his brow and then just stood there, shaking his head from side to side, as though he were struggling for a decision. At length, he spoke.

"It is against all reason and my better judgment, but insomuch, I *shall* allow you to follow the biddings of your own heart. Do not, howsoever, imagine that you are being let off lightly. I cannot, for the life of me, envision a man of sound mind—and him a recently liberated slave, at that—rushing back headlong into the clutches of damnable bondage, save for the delivering love of a good woman. If you *do* manage to reach her and this Jones, then your trial will only be commencing."

Joe could feel a new sense of hope swelling in his bosom, as Colonel Handy continued.

"Take poor Bob's horse and his good coat," Handy offered. "He will have no further use for them. There's flint and steel in the saddlebags and a bit of jerked venison to sustain you."

Fully at a loss for words, the "Veteran Soldier" could only choke back, "I can't begin to thank you, sir, I . . . "

But Handy cut him off. "Let it go. You've a journey and then some ahead of you and I must to Houston report. I do not expect our paths shall be crossing in the future, so good luck and godspeed, for what it's worth to you, Joe."

"Thankee, sir," Joe said, swelling with both pride and gratitude.

Then, as Eden Handy was just about to canter off toward the Houston camp, he turned his horse suddenly upon Joe and said with a caution in his voice: "It'll be dark presently. Wait. Skirt that bunch of timber, toward your left, and you'll elude the pickets."

The wave of a hand, the clatter of hooves; he was gone.

Twenty-six

Sisters in Sorrow

Joe...

Silvie's journey back to San Felipe from San Antonio in Neddy and Violet Malone's wagon had been a long, lonely, empty, and helpless one. All along its bumpy, bone-rattling way, Silvie had thought of Joe, while the rolling expanse of miles carried her further and further away from him. And to think that Joe himself had engineered the whole thing! With Travis' help, Joe had sent her away—sent her away for safety's sake alone—she later learned. For, when the Malone wagon finally rolled up to the Cummings Mill on that bleak day in mid-February, it was in much surprise that Becky Cummings greeted the servant girl.

"Silvie!" Becky exclaimed in wide-eyed surprise and anticipation. "I didn't expect to be seeing you again so soon. Is Buck—is Mr. Travis with you?"

"No, Miss Becky," Silvie replied haltingly, sensing the disappointment in Rebecca's eyes *and* that something wasn't quite right. "He sent me back alone to tend to *you*. How are you feeling?"

"I'm feeling fit and fine, Silvie. Whatever gave you the idea that I was doing poorly?"

Not wishing to betray what she already believed to be true—that Travis had sent her back, out of harm's way—Silvie replied, "Must've been some kind of misunderstanding. But Colonel Travis wanted me here, so here I am."

Once they were inside the confines of the inn with a pot of tea on the hob, Rebecca wanted to know everything. "Sit, Silvie," she offered, pointing toward a rocking chair by the fire. "So how *are* things in San Antonio? Is Mr. Travis in command there?"

"Colonel Bowie and Travis *share* command," Silvie explained between tea sips. "Although there's hardly a force of men there to speak of; a hundred and forty, at most. Some of the townspeople allowed that Santa Anna was on his way. Some of them were packing up and leaving town. But Travis and Bowie—neither of them seemed too inclined on going anywhere. They've been forting up in an old wreck of a mission called the Alamo, just across the river from town. I . . . I do believe that they sent me away to be safe. Maizy and Joe . . . "

"Yes," Becky interjected with a gay laugh. "I can see *Maizy's* hand in this, at least. Well, don't you go pouting over it; you're here, you're safe and likely, that's all they wanted. I do declare, though, be there danger, or not, I'd just as soon be with my Buck right now, instead of having to endure any more of this waiting and wondering. It's . . . it's good to have you back, Silvie. We can get your own bed set up in no time. You must be tuckered—and sore," she added with a wry smile, seeing Silvie involuntarily rub her tailbone.

Time moved on; frigid February faded into a mid-March thaw. As the days passed, Silvie filled the dragging moments laboring over her chores at the inn, waiting for news on Joe and the Alamo. And then, in the waning hours of the 21st, it came.

Silvie had been sweeping the wooden steps in front of the Cummings' Inn when a trap rattled up, drawn by an unruly bay horse.

"Down, curse you," snarled the man on the box, in response to the horse's erratic pawing and back-stepping. "And curse me for rigging up a strange horse." The man on the box turned out to be Postmaster Jones, while the horse . . . Silvie recognized her immediately; Joe's bay mare, Shannon. Joe never would have let her out of his sight. *Never;* unless . . .

Silvie felt icy chills racing up her spine as she imagined the worst. Down the broom clattered from her hands as she ran up to steady the nervous Shannon. "That's Joe's horse, Shannon," Silvie said with trepidation. "How did you come by her, Mr. Jones?"

"Shannon!" the Postmaster returned, clearly miffed. "Travis' gambling trophy? I might've known! Nobody could break that filly. Small wonder that it took three stable hands to harness her. I am the bearer of ill news, I am afraid," Jones said, changing tone and stepping down from the trap at last.

"*What* sort of news, Jones?" a voice asked and Jack Cummings stepped up.

"It's hard," Jones fumbled. "Your sister, Jack, you'll have to prepare her . . . "

"My God, man, just say it," Cummings said tersely.

"Travis is dead. As a matter of solemn fact, *all* the men in the Alamo are no more. Santa Anna attacked the Alamo and killed them to the last man. It was a bloody shambles, by all accounts. The only reason that this horse got out of the fort is that Travis' last messenger rode out upon her. There's not much more I can say," Jones concluded, averting his eyes to the ground.

But there was no need for Jones to speak any further, for, standing in the open doorway of the inn, Becky Cummings had heard it all. And even her hand pressed solidly against her mouth could not suppress her heartrending scream.

Becky staggered and very nearly swooned, but Silvie's quick thinking and reflex actions caught the distressed Miss Cummings up before she could hit the hard wooden planking. Then, cradled there in Silvie's arms, Becky Cummings, moaning piteously, let out her grief.

"Buck, oh my Buck," she wailed. "Oh he *can't* be gone! Brother John!" she implored, searching the face of the yet standing and still stunned Mr. Cummings. But John Cummings only remained there, steadfast and unable to speak, while his eyes glistened with tears.

So Silvie held Rebecca and tried to comfort her with soothing tones and gentle caresses, but Becky Cummings was not one to be consoled so easily. For her well of overflowing hot tears ran deep and would have continued to course down her cheeks unabated, had her eyes not met up with Silvie's. Only then, by wading into the secret shallows of their liquid depths, was Becky able to measure the extent of the servant girl's own loss.

"Oh, Silvie," Becky moaned, as self-pity dissolved into empathy. "Oh, Silvie, I am so sorry. But how *could* I be forgetting about your Joe?"

And how could Silvie? Joe, gone? It was as inconceivable as it was irreconcilable. Ever since their parting, Silvie had, on numerous occasions, wrestled with the possibility of such a calamity befalling Joe. But each and every time, she had shaken off the vision for one of Joe, walking through the door of the inn once more to remain with her forever. Forever! How brutal was the finality that the utterance of that solitary word implied, for now "forever" meant a lifetime without Joe.

That thought crumpled Silvie and she began, for the first time, to give vent to the depths of her own grief. Embracing Rebecca even tighter still, Silvie wailed her heart's loss, while Rebecca, offering up some comfort of her own, reciprocated the embrace. Black and white, servant and mistress, in that moment, they were sisters in sorrow.

Postmaster Jones and John Cummings, meanwhile, just stood there looking helplessly upon the two distraught young women, until Jones pricked the awkwardness of the moment with a deep throated, "Harumph."

"An unhappy task, Jack, a decidedly unhappy task have I," Jones went on. "As executor of the late Colonel Travis' estate, I am compelled to settle up as hastily as possible, times being what they are. San Felipe is in a panic—you should see how those people are packing it in, lock, stock and barrel. If you've any business to attend to *yourselves*, you'd best not drag your feet. There's been some pillaging in the shops there. I was lucky enough to have reached Travis' law office before the true panic set in. Now I am left to take care of some of the last petty details and reams of legal parchment. And," he added with a sidelong look of embarrassment, "I am afraid that this concerns Silvie here. As Travis' property, she will have to accompany me until the whole of the matter has been finalized."

Becky Cummings turned to look upon her brother with an expression of both despair and protest. "Now, John! Say that Silvie can stay with us! I need her—she needs *me*! Say that she can stay!"

John Cummings could only answer his sister with a look of sadness and pity. His words were, of themselves, no comfort though. "I'm sorry, Becky, Silvie. But it's the lawful thing to do. With the whole of Texas collapsing around us, it is left to us to try and maintain *some* sense of order."

"Brother!" Becky pleaded, holding Silvie even closer still.

But John Cummings was immovable; for the first time, his voice rang gruff and stern. "Sister! There is no time for arguing. Silvie must go with Mr. Jones. *We* must set to packing and join up with the other refugees. *I've* got to board this place up."

Rebecca stepped back into the parlor from one of the back rooms where she'd been digging up some extra blankets and clothing for Silvie. Upon seeing Silvie, slouching forward upon a bench with her elbows upon her knees and her face buried into the hollow of her cupped hands, Becky gathered Silvie into her embrace and said, "I am sure that everything will work out for the best in God's good time. Grieve, we must, but move, we also must. I am sure that we will all be seeing each other again quite soon, indeed. Mr. Jones?" she sallied, shooting an icy glance of reproach over at the now more-than-ever embarrassed postmaster.

"Of course, of course," Jones repaired, stuttering. "We shall all be seeing each other very soon, indeed—in Washingtown. That is where the other town officials are bound, at any rate."

Silvie's only response was a deep-throated sigh. *These days, these days,* she thought. Arriving in hope and anticipation—leaving in grief and despair. Would this parting only serve to propel her further on down the bitter, unknown road of despair without her offering up at least *some* kind of a fight? *Was there no rebellion left in her?* she wondered. *Should she further object—stand her ground and for once, not give in?* She'd given in when Joe and Maizy had sent her away from San Antonio. Now, Joe was gone—and Maizy? No, she mustn't think of such things: not now. She must keep her wits and bury her grief. And though an unknown future lay ahead of her, for the time being, Silvie would deal with the reality of the present. So, in her self-imposed numbness of spirit, Silvie prepared herself to face . . . to face . . . to face packing her travel bag, climbing aboard the cushion of the trap, and *going.*

Before the trap and standing alongside the bay mare, Shannon, Silvie stroked the horse gently beneath the muzzle, just as she had seen Joe do, so many times before. And as Silvie spoke, Shannon, in turn, seemed to calm down in recognition. "Poor Shannon, be easy. I guess that you've been through a lot, too. But you've got to help us now, Sha'. We need you now."

"God bless you on your way, Silvie," Rebecca shouted emotionally as the trap, pulled by Shannon and carrying both Silvie and Jones, rattled back off down the road for San Felipe once more. Looking back, Silvie waved and waved until Becky was clear out of sight, never suspecting for a moment that she would never be seeing her friend or this place ever again.

Twenty-seven

How a Town Dissolves

San Felipe was all but deserted when Jones and Silvie arrived there. Discarded property and trash were strewn about the muddy, deep-rutted streets. Why, even the courthouse lacked its usual brace of sentries at the front door. So it was that Jones and Silvie were able to enter the building unhindered.

"Curse me for not having come here first!" Jones fumed. "Paperwork's a bloody shambles. That cabinet there," he said, indicating a heavy oak file in the very corner of the room. "See if there's a portmanteau in the bottom drawer. Zounds, a lot of these papers should've been burned, if not carried away!"

Approaching the cabinet as bidden, Silvie had to stoop over double to reach the bottom of the file. But though she tugged at it with all of her might, the clearly overstuffed drawer would not yield.

"Something's stuck," Silvie said with a throaty grunt. "Won't budge."

Hearing Silvie, Jones looked up from what he was doing. "Do you need any . . . help?" he started to say. But the sight of Silvie shifting this way and that in a manner that he considered provocative silenced the postmaster abruptly. In moments and without warning, his hands were all over her hips.

"No! Don't you!" Silvie screamed, wheeling around in a defensive stance that caused Jones to loose his grip upon her. "So help me, if you so much as touch me again, I'll run, Mr. Jones! Maybe not now, maybe not tomorrow, but run, I will!"

Jones stepped back, startled as he was by Silvie's unseemly show of defiance. "Do . . . do you know what you are saying?" he asked, practically flabbergasted. "Running's a felony offense. They could have the dogs after you and there would be nothing I could do about it! *I* didn't make the law!"

"No, you didn't for a fact," Silvie replied with vinegar, "but you certain sure follow it to the letter! Well, sir, *I* follow the law of my own nature. Treat me well and I will give you no call to worry. But touch a hair of my head, and so help me, I'm gone!"

"All right, all right," the postmaster stammered back in his attempt to let Silvie's steam out. "I'm bound, you *are* the testy one! I didn't mean any harm, Lord knows! It's just that I'm a man alone and you are a woman alone and I thought that you could use . . . "

But Jones could not so much as finish his sentence; Silvie cut him off.

"Thought that *I* could use?" she slammed back at him. "Thought that I could *be* used, is more on the mark! And don't you be bringing the Lord's name in on your villainous attempts!"

"Fine, fine," Jones replied, a little testy himself. "But just you fetch that portmanteau and help me get all this stuff squared away into the trap, that we may be on our way—to Washingtown. All right?"

Once loaded, the trap rattled off up the main street of San Felipe, while the lonely moan of the wind whooshed loose bits of debris and paper against the backs of Silvie and Jones, as though it were urging them on their way from the ghostly, silent town.

Clouds began gathering as the trap rolled over a rise, leaving San Felipe in its wake and beyond sight. But the trap's two passengers were not looking back, anyhow. Silvie was still lost in her own thoughts, while the Postmaster waxed solemn.

"How a town dissolves!" he voiced aloud. "All the orderliness that one tries to instill into a community. A sense of pride and high hopes for a prosperous future for all—all of it, gone! Oh, the citizens *may* return eventually, should Texas succeed—some of them, anyway. But it will never be the same. Those of us who saw the town grow from a patch of mesquite thicket into a thriving place will no doubt have other things to occupy our minds after this war is over. We'll be so busy wresting a government into order and protecting our borders from interlopers that it will be left to the newcomers to get the towns going again. Then, *we* will be the strangers!"

Silvie sat listening to Jones' observations as though they were something she was hearing inside of her own head. Nevertheless, she responded aloud.

"People've got to move ahead with the times, else be left behind in the past, Mr. Jones. The past is gone. Much as we would like to cling to the good memories of people and things we have loved and known, we've got to be prepared to let go of them . . . no matter how much it hurts," she added with a twinge. "*Your* dreams died in San Felipe—mine, in the Alamo. But, just think of what all those people were trying to do! They had high hopes and dreams too and now we can't just let them up and die. I ache, I grieve; I hurt, and feel empty. But then I reckon that I am not alone in this. *Got* to move forward. Makes it a whole lot easier when you don't have much choice in the matter, like me. You? Why you could high tail it back to the U.S., if you've a mind to—start over fresh there. But me, I gotta go where I'm told—where I'm ordered. It's the *law*, you know," she added, throwing Jones' own words back into his face.

"I'm a government official," Jones shot back in self-defense. "I've *got* to follow the laws, such as they are. Someday, they may change, but until that time arrives, I will uphold my office—such was the reason I was appointed and sworn in, honor bound. I truly am sorry for you, but inasmuch, I cannot see you running. I won't have it. It is for your own protection, as well as mine, that I say this. Lord, how the wind is picking up," Jones suddenly digressed, noticing the darkening skies. "We'd best be putting the top up and that means gathering some of our luggage into our laps."

They'd gotten the top up none too soon. The rains came; sheeting down at first then driven horizontal by the flogging winds that thundered against the back of the trap like a drum roll of hammers.

Shielded only minimally by the presence of the trap, the bay mare, Shannon, barely inched forward, her head bowed in dejection. Up ahead, through a haze of persistent precipitation, a small stand of mesquite thicket appeared.

"We can't keep up like this," Jones shouted above the din of the rainburst. "Best make for that thicket—for the horse's sake *and* our own!"

They went. And the bay Shannon, somehow sensing that shelter was to be had, clip-clopped forward toward the thicket at a livelier gait, giving little heed to the snarl of mesquite thorns and bramble that were clawing at the canvass top and sides of the trap.

"Whoa, curse you!" Jones roared, giving Shannon an abrupt tug at the reins that made her head jerk back. Whinnying in protest, Shannon fought back, sashaying from side to side in an attempt to twist herself free from the strangling harness.

Thinking quickly, Silvie jumped down from the cushion to try and steady the nervous bay, while Jones fought with the hand brake. For a moment, it looked as though Silvie's efforts were paying off, as Shannon came down on all fours and started pawing through the low mess of mesquite for a firmer footing. Finding none, though, only seemed to agitate the bay all the more, for she reared back one more time and then came down upon the unsuspecting Silvie with a glancing blow to the head.

Though the entire action transpired in a fleeting instant, the scene curiously registered in the stricken young woman's mind as though in slow motion. The horse rearing, its flailing legs descending, the contact of the razor-sharp hoof against the crown of Silvie's head . . . the sensation of falling.

Silvie never even felt herself hit the ground. Though the rain continued to sheet down upon her and Postmaster Jones stood bending over her prostrate form, all Silvie could recall seeing was the face of Joe, beaming and a little embarrassed. "If there's anything I can do," he was saying, as Silvie fainted dead away.

Twenty-eight
On the Wings of the Wind

She was drifting, drifting, drifting on a cloud. It was just a dream, Silvie thought, only a dream. Or was it? For it felt terribly real, this floating high above the trap, with the bay Shannon, Postmaster Jones, and the tangle of mesquite thicket, all dizzyingly below. Now she knew it had to be a dream, for she could very clearly see that Jones was lifting up a limp bundle of a body and placing it with care upon the cushion of the trap—and the limp body was *Silvie herself!*

Was she dead, she thought. *Is this what dying was like?* Silvie had little time to linger upon the fearful probability, for she was drifting again. Back across the trail that had led her away from San Antonio she floated, while mesquite thickets, creeks, and the broad prairie land appeared, then disappeared through little breaks in the clouds. Soon she was far beyond the storm, for its mighty throes were now but hushed echoes in her ears and the fluffy white clouds below her reflected naught but the golden moonlight like a candle through gauze.

Back across Washington-on-the-Brazos she floated, where flashes of light from both sides of the river served to indicate that a battle of some kind was going on, with soldiers and cannons and rafts. Beyond them she passed, past Burham's crossing on the Colorado River where she and Joe and Travis' company had made camp, oh so long ago. Next, prairie land and gullies spread on before her, followed soon after by hills and trees with enough lushness to make one's head spin.

Skirting the rise of a hill, Silvie guessed that she was within reach of civilization, as small clusters of flickering lights twinkled away like tiny stars across the dark landscape, silhouetting the approaching outline of a collection of buildings that seemed strangely familiar to Silvie. For she was back in San Antonio, at last, and this was the Alamo.

Now she was above the Alamo compound itself where soldiers lined the walls, or else sat around campfires, having supper. But the thing that made Silvie's heart catch in her throat was the sight of Travis and Joe, walking across the plaza toward the headquarters room in the soft blue moonlight!

It was a dream she reassured herself—it *had* to be! For Travis and Joe were both dead and if she was able to see them then she must be either dreaming, or dead herself. But the wings of the wind, or whatever she was drifting upon, did not allow her to long linger, before she was drifting again.

Below her, the running San Antonio River glistened and arced itself like a snake. Over in the town, troops filed through the streets in good order, while around the Alamo, the glow of the Mexican Army's campfires completely encircled the battened-down old mission like an illuminated Christmas wreath.

Nearing the town, Silvie imagined that she could hear music. Not military music, but rather a party—a raucous, spirited fandango—and a *Texian* fandango, judging from the exclamations of the crowd. *But how can this be so,* Silvie puzzled, *with all of the Texians over in the Alamo? Was she not only dead, but crazy, to boot?*

Silvie was still puzzling over this, when suddenly a profusion of light, one that practically blinded her, stabbed off into the sky toward her and Silvie felt that she was being sucked down into its hollow shaft. Down Silvie spiraled, until at long last her feet touched softly upon what appeared to be a tiled patio floor. Once there, the blinding fog before her eyes lifted gradually until a scene familiar, yet not quite so, spread out before her. For though the revelers here appeared no less animated than the ones at the last fandango she'd attended with Joe, it was an altogether different patio and occasion.

"Hurrah for George Washington! Hurrah for his birthday!" an enthusiastic Texian toasted. "Colonel Crockett, John MacGregor! Give us a tune!"

Three cheers from the crowd followed this thrown gauntlet, whereupon Davy Crockett himself stepped forward, fiddle and bow in hand. "I've acquiesced to sorrier requests, whilst in Congress," Crockett began, "but a middling comparison does not come to mind, at present. Ah me," he concluded, half-humouredly, rosining up his bow, "there's no accounting for taste."

Not to be outdone, the Scotsman, John MacGregor, all in plaid, stepped forward to the challenge, pipes at the ready. "Nut Brown Maiden," the piper announced. Then the two musicians set off at a roar, though hardly in unison, as the discordant notes issuing from each instrument painfully attested. The idea, Silvie guessed, seemed to be to try and see who could make the most noise. No matter, the crowd of revelers seemed to eat it all up with relish, dancing about in wild postures, quite oblivious to the world around them. MacGregor aired his lungs:

> Horo, my nut brown maiden,
> Hiri my nut brown maiden,
> Horo, my nut brown maiden,
> For she's the one for me!

Then Silvie turned and there was Joe, alive, whole, and dressed in his best shirt. Strange how Silvie did not seemed shocked or amazed on his appearance, but then, as she'd had enough shock and amazement over the past few days to last her a lifetime, seeing Joe standing before her with a slightly embarrassed grin on his face now seemed almost natural, in comparison. So Silvie accepted it, as well as his stammering offer for a dance.

"Could you . . . would you?" Joe mumbled.

"Love to," she heard herself reply.

Beneath the glow of the strung luminarias, at the center of the dance floor, Silvie and Joe, arms encircling one another, danced and spun around the patio to a music that seemed of their own origin, for it stemmed from their joined hearts and souls. Round and round and round the floor they went, until the lights, the scattering of faces, and all the surroundings dissolved into a soft blur.

Suddenly, it was dark and the haze before Joe and Silvie, a billowing gray. But this too lifted, as, gradually, the soft, blue glow of moonlight drew their eyes back into focus to reveal the shadowy façade of the Alamo church.

"Why, it looks just like an old bat cave . . . " Silvie heard herself say. "Pitch a pebble inside, Joe, and then watch for all the bats to come flooding out."

So Joe reached down and pitched his pebble into the cavernous mouth that was the church's door. But instead of the expected resounding clack of the thrown pebble and the fluttering of many wings, Silvie heard an earsplitting roar, as an explosion shattered the building's aperture in a cloud of dense smoke. Turning around to face the source of the explosion, Joe and Silvie beheld a passel of shakoed troopers tumbling over the low wall and into the little courtyard, their wave of glistening bayonets driving forward toward the startled young couple.

"What are you doing here, Silvie?" Joe's voice shouted in both anger and panic. "Didn't I send you away to be safe? You don't belong here!"

Then, as a shocked Silvie looked on, Joe dove in front of her to shield her from the descending hedge of bristling cold steel. But it did no good, for the soldiers skewered Joe, then drove right on, passing through Silvie, as though she really weren't there, after all.

Though she never opened her mouth, Silvie heard herself scream.

*   *   *

What was it... a face? So blurry, so cloudy... Silvie was doing her best to focus her now-opened eyes upon her surroundings to familiarize herself with them and to get her bearings. But when she attempted to raise her head up from the depths of a goose feather down pillow for a better look, a terrible throbbing sensation coaxed her back down again.

The face above her, for face indeed it was, gradually began to take on more definite lines, until the kindly features of a young Mexican girl with eager, deep brown eyes and a turned-up mouth that seemed to burst into a smile, materialized.

"Mama, she is awake," the girl chirped excitedly. "Don't be afraid, Tia," she comforted Silvie, "you had a bad dream, that's all."

The girl's mother soon appeared. Not yet quite middle-age, the bloom was still upon this rose, for Rosalia, in fact, was her name. *Mother and daughter were one and the same,* Silvie mused. While the daughter was a reflection of what the mother must've looked like at the age of twelve, or so, the mother herself seemed the very vision of how the daughter would appear, once she'd achieved the mature beauty of her prime years.

"Shhssh!" the mother mildly scolded her child. "Give her some time. Buenos tardes, Señorita," Rosalia said. "How are you feeling? You have been asleep for such a long time!"

Silvie turned her bandaged head slightly to the side and felt another throbbing sensation in reward of her effort. "My head feels like sin. Where am I? Who are you?"

"One question at a time, Señorita. My name is Rosalia Escalante and this excitable young thing, my daughter, Alma. You are in an inn in Washington-on-the-Brazos. Señor Jones brought you here after the accident with the horse. Do you not remember?"

Silvie remembered all right and she cringed on the memory. She was lucky to be alive. "How long have I been here?" she wondered aloud.

"Two days," Rosalia replied. "You and Señor Jones arrived at the very moment that most of the other politicians were leaving.

There was such a big gathering of them! There was talk of the Alamo, I hear. It made a lot of the people here want to leave. But Señor Jones? He seemed angry and disappointed that he had missed it all. Said that he would be leaving also, once *you* have recovered from your injury. Alma and I? We work here at the inn. But we will probably be leaving, along with all the other running people."

Alma left the room for a brief period, but then reentered it suddenly and without warning. "Mama. Señor Jones is here. I have brought him!"

And Jones entered.

"Silvie," he began with a smile, removing his hat as he spoke, "How are you? Feared that we'd nearly lost you there, for a while. You were in quite the delirium."

"I'll live. But what's all this talk about leaving again, when we just got here? Is there no safe haven in all of Texas?"

"Folks here are reacting to the Alamo again," Jones replied wearily. "They fear that Santa Anna is right outside their door, like some kind of bogeyman. Convention's gone to reconvene at Harrisburg. We can do no more service to the nation in joining up with them there, though. When you're feeling tolerable well, we can join the caravan of folks heading east. But don't worry about that right now. Rest some more."

"And after that," Alma added cheerfully, "I will bring you a big bowl of cocido! Mama makes the best soup."

"Thank you all," Silvie responded. "You are kind. I *will* rest now. I ache too much to be worrying about much else."

"That's right," Rosalia mothered, "but if there's anything else I can do for you . . . "

But Silvie barely heard her. Her eyes closed, the pain slipped away, and then she slept deeply.

Twenty-nine

Eastward with the Wayward Geese

Compared to all of the bustle and clamor that he'd witnessed during his last visit to the town, Washington-on-the-Brazos seemed deathly deserted to Joe, as he reined up his horse upon its outskirts in this chilly graying morn. Not a single bird chirped or twittered. This made Joe stiffen with anxiety, for the hollow quiet only seemed to scream out to him in mute intonations that he was already too late.

Riding up the narrow path that led to the Groce's manor house, Joe tried to shake off the feeling. But the roaring silence he encountered there didn't help much. The place was a wreck. The manor's ornate doors and windows, once the pride of all Washington, were now boarded over roughshod, while the passage of numerous shod horses' hooves gave its once immaculate broad lawns the look of freshly furrowed fields.

At the ferry landing, Joe encountered the lone raftsman and questioned him. Yes, the raftsman reassured Joe, there *were* still a few of the delegates yet in town, Jones amongst them. The rest, the raftsman allowed, had all fled eastward in a panic, along with the remainder of the townspeople. Why you couldn't even so much as get a room at the inn, lessen you wanted to serve yourself. Of course, there wasn't any *food* to be had. No, not even any clean sheets. Raftsman had looked his very own self and so knew. Oh yes, Jones? Why the postmaster was likely still at the livery—er, the Capitol House, attending to some business.

Raftsman ferried Joe across the river to the Capitol side and got some jerked venison in payment. But as Joe was walking his horse toward the Capitol, whom did he run into, but the very same bunch of bummers that he and Eden Handy had encountered on Joe's last visit. The bummers were upon their haunches around a smoky cookfire and they were roasting a dog.

"Holt on y'ere," one of the bummers challenged, making a move on the horse's halter. "Whussa cotton picker doin' 'ith uh fine hoss liken that? Like as most, yuh stealt 'em, ay?"

"No such thing, sir," Joe stammered, "I'm riding dispatch for General Houston," he lied. "I have to see Postmaster Jones, if you please, sir."

"I *don't* please," Bummer One threatened, brandishing a massive Bowie knife that yet dripped of dog grease. "What yuh got s'worth anythin' in them saddle packs?"

"Jerked deer meat," Joe offered, throwing open the flap to view. "You're welcome to it and kindly, but I got to see Mr. Jones, for a fact!"

Bummer One was all smiles as he purloined the dried deer meat with a jab of his wicked blade. But when his eager companions started scrambling toward him for their expected shares, Bummer One exploded, "Holt on thar, you no count sunzabitches! This are mine, fa'r and squar'! *You* wanted dog meat an' so you kilt *my* dog! An' now b'gawd, youse gwinter eat 'im! You," he snapped ugily at Joe, "git on t' Pose-massa Jones, afore these polecats set their de-signs on hoss meat!"

Swiftly obliging Bummer One, Joe left the testy stragglers to their cookfire and continued upon his way for the Capitol House. Once there, Joe tied off his horse and then approached the livery entrance with caution. Rap, rap, rap, went his fist upon the rude plank door.

Moments passed before the door creaked open a few inches and the bore of a monstrous horse pistol poked out.

"Who is it and what do you want?" challenged the voice beyond the door. "Speak up, or else receive the harvest of Plenty's horn here!"

"It's Joe," the "Veteran Soldier" replied. "Travis' Joe. I came from General Houston to join up with you, just as Master Travis told me to."

The door creaked open and Joe was admitted. Once inside, Joe rehashed the Alamo tale for Jones. As he sat listening, Jones eased his vigilance, brought the pistol barrel down, and then uncocked the piece.

"You did the right thing, Joe," Jones assured. "Truly, you are as good and faithful a servant as Travis painted you, God rest him. As for myself, I'm gathering up a few important papers and then, it's off eastward with the rest of the wayward geese. You *have* a horse, I perceive?"

Joe nodded in affirmation.

"Splendid! I've a trap with but one beast to the duty. The addition of yours should assist the three of us admirably. You," he paused in suspicion, "you didn't *steal* him, did you?"

Joe let Jones' "the *three* of us" sink in, before offering up his reply. "No, sir, Mr. Jones. Got him fair and square from Colonel Handy of Houston's scouts."

"Good and well," Jones responded with a sigh of relief, though Joe never heard him. For Jones' words were only a distraction that Joe pushed to the back of his mind. "Things already set hard enough against us," Jones went on, all the same, "that I shadn't be needing the likes of some hotheaded hooligan attempting to blow my brains out for horse thievery. Get lively now and help Silvie load up the trap."

What happened next seemed almost like a dream to Joe. After all he'd been through—all he'd endured—he was finally going to see Silvie again. She was alive and he was alive and they were but steps apart. It was almost unbelievable to him, but believe Joe did. So, out the door of the livery he stepped toward the trap and to where he knew that Silvie would be waiting.

Silvie was standing with her back to Joe as he strode up. Though she was bundled up in a coarse blue shawl and a dowdy gingham skirt, the all-too-familiar figure concealed beneath the unflattering garments was, nonetheless, Silvie's.

Minutes, hours, days seemed to pass as Joe just stood there staring at the vision of the love of his life. Then Silvie turned with a start and the spell was broken.

"Oh, my God!" Silvie blurted in wide-eyed disbelief. "Oh, my God, Joe!" Then she rushed to him and he to her and they embraced as though they were loathe to let go.

"I thought for certain sure that you were dead," Silvie sobbed, covering Joe's face with wet kisses of joy and relief. "I ached so bad, Joe . . . so bad. You can't imagine . . . "

"I can imagine," he responded. "When I thought that I might never see you again, I felt like I *did* die. I can imagine . . . "

"What," she asked at last, "what happened to you at the Alamo?"

"I was taken prisoner by Santa Anna. I escaped San Antonio and I've been trying to reach you ever since. Maizy . . . " he began, then his voice trailed off to a halt; but the pain Silvie read in Joe's eyes told her the rest.

"Maizy's gone?" she asked, not really wanting to hear the answer. "Joe?"

"Yes," Joe replied in a whisper, as though not saying it out loud would have made it any less true. "It was an accident. She was helping the wounded during the battle . . . a stray bullet took her away. Maizy and I were both with Colonel Travis when he died. She was helping *him,* when it happened."

Silvie let go of her grief in an uncontrollable burst. "Oh, Mama," she blubbered in anguish, embracing Joe tighter than even *she* thought possible. "My only Maizy."

"Sorry," Joe whispered back consolingly. "I'm so sorry, Silvie. Maizy said . . . she told me to tell you not to be mourning her too much, 'cause she died a free woman. She wanted you to know that. She wanted you to know."

"Thank you for telling me that, Joe," Silvie whooshed throatedly, though she could no longer see Joe. Silvie's eyes were blinded over by wells of stinging hot tears.

Then Silvie shrunk back and looked at Joe hard. "You've been wounded!" she responded with compassion, upon feeling Joe's battle scars through the tattered remnants of Jack Bruno's old shirt. "It must've been horrible in the Alamo. We only got scattered bits of news, here and there—especially about Travis. It's hard to imagine that *he's* gone, too. Travis was the only white man who ever treated us half-ways decent. And then, for him to have suffered so!"

"He didn't suffer," Joe reassured her, gently stroking the top of her head. "Like I said, Maizy and I were at his side when he went. One bullet and he was gone."

"Ow!" Silvie exclaimed, involuntarily pulling back when Joe's "gentle stroking" caused her to wince in pain. "What's wrong?" he said.

Drawing back her shawl, Joe saw: Silvie's head, all swathed in bandages.

"You're hurt, too," Joe said with concern. "What happened?"

"It's nothing," Silvie pooh-poohed, trying to make small of the incident. "Your horse Shannon, got excited and accidentally kicked me. I'll be all right."

"*Shannon* kicked you?" Joe asked, a little amazed. "You're sure that you are all right?"

"Quite sure. Shannon's a good girl. The storm just frightened her so. She missed you, too," Silvie added. "Come see her."

Shannon recognized Joe right away and brayed a warm hello. Joe stroked her back and mane. It was a joyous reacquaintance, all around.

"We can hitch up the other horse to the trap and give poor Sha' a rest," Joe said. "Other horse is bigger and stronger than

Shannon, anyway. So young Jimmy Allen made it out of the Alamo all right? That's good. And I'm glad that Sha' got back with you, too, Silvie. Wasn't expecting no accidents, though."

"A lot of things happen that we don't expect," Silvie replied reflectively.

"Yes," Joe agreed, a little more solemnly. "They do. But there's something that you've got to know Silvie. Something happened back in the Alamo that affected us—and Maizy, too."

Silvie looked puzzled. "What do you mean, Joe? What . . . "

But Joe cut her off. "No, let me finish first. When I told you that Maizy said not to mourn her because she was a *free* woman, I was speaking the truth. Because, Silvie, Colonel Travis freed us: all three of us. Gave me the freedom papers his own self."

A look of sublime joy started to spread upon Silvie's face, but just as suddenly Joe wiped it away.

"Travis gave me the papers," Joe reiterated, "entrusted me with them. And I ruined them. Fell in the water and soaked them to pulp. I lost your freedom, Silvie. I lost everything. I'm sorry. Sorry," he trailed off.

Silvie looked at Joe in amazement. But instead of voicing her disappointment, Silvie stood for a moment with her heart in her throat. For here was a man. And she was his.

"You mean you came back anyway, when you knew for certain sure that you'd be caught and kept a slave. You came back . . . for *me*?"

"I came back for *us*, Silvie," Joe reaffirmed with a passion. "Do you think that I could ever really feel free without you? *Be* without you? You're part of me now."

"And you're part of me, Joe," Silvie responded tenderly, reaffirming their love.

Joe looked deep into Silvie's eyes and clear into her heart. "Well," he said, "as long as we remember that, we'll be all right. Freedom will come, even if we have to run. But when the time comes, we'll make our move—*together.*"

There was nothing more that needed saying. So Silvie and Joe embraced for the longest time until, remembering what they were supposed to be doing, they loaded up the trap for the departure from Washington-on-the-Brazos.

* * *

A spring calm had taken the land, leaving winter's fury to abide, if only temporarily, in check. Muggy mornings followed blue norther nights as the laden trap and horses rattled both master and slaves across the vast, spreading spaces of East Texas. The tiny shoots of new grass that Travis had long hence mentioned would herald the arrival of Santa Anna, were now proud, waving blades, rising and lapping in the gentle winds of the prairie sea. It was mid-April and the little party was athrong in the great "Runaway Scrape" of Texian citizenry.

They rattled on.

The temporary capitol at Harrisburg offered the three refugees little solace, or sanctuary, for the dictator's dragoons had already sacked the place, nearly bagging Burnett and his cabinet in the bargain. Now, with the descending forces of both factions zigzagging their way across the countryside, there seemed to be no place to hide along the general exodus route leading to the Sabine River and the Louisiana border.

Now and again, Joe and Co. would happen upon the day camp of other eastward bound travelers and stop for a chat, over a humble bowl of beans or stew. But as the days progressed and the exodus of weary pilgrims dissolved into a mad, hurry-scurry flight to safety, it became an "every man for himself" sort of go. So Joe and Co. learned to keep a safe distance after that. For it wasn't out of pure meanness or even selfishness that people turned their thoughts inward; it was survival. Folks with a clutch of hungry young-in's to feed simply could not afford to share the pittling remnant of their foodstuffs with two slaves and one damned, almighty government official.

So Joe, Silvie, and Postmaster Jones did the best that they could with their scant provisions. And though the food they partook of was usually of the cold staple, there was always enough hot coffee to go around to cut the bite of the evening chill.

The "evening chill" being especially up on this particular day's end, warm blankets and a hot fire seemed just the ticket to the three tuckered travelers. But while the campfire crackled in the descending veil of eventide, and Postmaster Jones snored in his bedroll nearby, Joe and Silvie sat up, talking, stargazing, and making the most of the fleeting, precious hours. And though they knew that dawn would doubtless find them begrudgingly awake and to their duties, for the moment they would trod the very firmament itself in a state of suspended reverie.

Basking in the radiance of Joe's newfound zeal, attitude, and sense of purpose, Silvie sensed their love for each other growing stronger every day. For it was a love that had been nurtured daily in the strength of shared trials, unflagging trust, a willingness to both communicate and compromise and a ripening, mutual respect. Anyhow, however you chose to slice it, spending twenty-four hours a day with someone for weeks on end and at close quarters was some kind of love, indeed.

Thirty
Rivers of Return

Although its native populace had fled, the muddied lanes of Trinity, on the Guadalupe River, were far from deserted, as the trap, with Joe at the reins, rolled into town and reined up. Refugees from West Texas, Postmaster Jones explained, were still flocking to the settlement, as though it was some kind of great jumping off place from where they could rest and get their bearings, before moving along on the final leg to the Louisiana border.

It proved slow going, for Trinity lay on the opposite side of the river and there was but one small raft employed at the ferry. Anyone in the throng multitude of pilgrims who wished to cross over would have to have either a hefty bribe for the lone ferryman, or else the patience of Job.

The first sights to greet the eye of disembarking ferry passengers on the Trinity side were no more heartening. Hand and oxcarts, buggies, and wagons, horses and mules, women and children, old men, goats and chickens, impromptu packs of yapping dogs—all jammed the narrow causeways in a jumble of confusion. While some parties brashly overlapped their encampment onto private property, others contended to merely strike up cookfires in the middle of the street. Ransacking abounded, as a door here, or a table there, ended up as fuel for cooking.

Joe didn't like the look of it one bit and so figured to circumvent the crunch of nomads, then pitch camp on the far side of town where they would still be in close proximity to the water's edge, but near fewer people. While Postmaster Jones was too exhausted to care *where* they set up camp, Silvie pitched in as cheerfully as she could, until, in no time at all, the three pilgrims had staked their space in the curious community of wayfaring strangers.

It was the postmaster's idea to tarry there in Trinity, until the bulk of the caravan had passed beyond the river. As a representative of the infant republic, Jones considered it part of his civic duty to await the possible appearance of couriers bearing war news. It was Joe and Silvie's duty to remain with Jones—for the time being.

The days passed, just as surely as the river ran ever by. Then, in the early evening of April the 23rd, as Joe sat adding broken fuel to the fire and Silvie engaged herself in laying out the bedrolls, sudden explosions—unmistakably gunfire—rent the dusky skies over Trinity.

The scattered encampment of nervous refugees responded in a mad clamor. "The Mexicans is on us!" wailed one panic-stricken woman and the terror in her cry transmitted to both man and beast alike. Roosters crowed, chickens cackled, goats bleated, horses whinnied, dogs barked, cats meowed, cattle lowed nervously, babies wah-wahed, while above it all, grown men cursed and shouted in an attempt to disguise the degree of their own alarm.

Horror and despair, however, soon gave over to cries of utter disbelief and triumph, as a fagged-out rider came thundering into camp upon a lathered horse. "Hurrah for Texas," he shouted, waving his hat aloft in mighty sweeps. "Houston's whipped ol' Santa Anna on the banks of the San Ja-cinto River! Eight hundred of our boys against twiced that number! Caught 'em napping and nabbed the dictator hisself! It's the Santanistas turn to skedaddle this time! War's over and it's victory, boys! Liberty and independence forever!" Then, with a parting whoop, the rider galloped off into the night, screaming himself hoarse, that all might hear and so comprehend the significance of his marvelous tidings of joy.

As word of the victory spread throughout the town, hallalujahs and whoops became genereal, while men with firearms blammed their loads up into the sky, seemingly oblivious to the fact that lead balls going up must eventually come down. But although the Texas skies ran high in mixed, glorious choruses, the only sound to issue from the lips of the "Veteran Soldier" was a curious sigh of relief and resignation.

Somewhere in the darkness, Joe's hand found Silvie's and he responded to its delicate clasp with a reassuring squeeze. For their course, at long last, was set.

Thirty-one
That Which Must Be Done

The spring of 1837 came late that year to Bailey's Prairie in the environs of Columbia, Texas, where Joe and Silvie abided in the keep of their new master, J.R. Jones. But before the primrose and blue bonnet could even inch their delicate shoots through the rich soil to majestically blanket the yawning Texas landscape in a blaze of color, a killer frost blew in and nipped them in the bud. Unable to withstand the chill, Postmaster Jones' own planting of corn and pumpkin had perished. But it wasn't merely the crops alone, for along with their failure went Jones' high hopes for a prosperous fresh start in the new republic.

Tightening his belt and cutting his losses, Jones was left with no other recourse but to let go Ubaldo, his faithful groundskeeper. Though he hated to do it, the postmaster simply could not afford to keep on the extra help.

Ubaldo's sacking could not have come at a more inopportune moment for Joe, for it occurred at a time when he was trying to work out some sort of escape plan for Silvie and himself. The last thing Joe needed was to assume additional duties and—even worse—to find himself catapulted into the spotlight at a time when both secrecy and stealth would be crucial. But such was the run of Joe's luck.

The victory at San Jacinto was already a year in the past, during which time Joe had grown so much in esteem with his new master that Jones had put him in charge of the livery. While he'd enjoyed grooming the horses, especially the bay mare, Shannon, working in the livery had also allowed Joe more opportunity to rendezvous there with Silvie for a few quiet moments in the long working day. And Silvie, having resumed her former lot as a chambermaid, had effected all the outward signs of resignation to the situation. But all outward signs notwithstanding, Joe and Silvie had never lost their resolve to someday escape. For no state of bondage, however soft, or undemanding, could ever again appeal to this determined couple.

So it was, in the deep of the mid-April night, while the rest of the plantation slept, that Joe beckoned Silvie to the livery for a clandestine meeting. Stealthily, Silvie arose from her room in the plantation's big house and made for the livery, barely guided there by a dim lantern that shone through the cracks in the structure's door far across the dark yard. Silvie gave the door a tap.

Joe admitted her. And as he was closing the door gently to muffle its sound and block out the lantern light, out of the shadows stepped Ubaldo, the sacked groundskeeper. Though apparently only of middle-age, the deep creases of adversity marred the fellow's face.

"It's high time for us to be on our way, Silvie," Joe said matter-of-factly. "Ubaldo here is going to help us. We've got it all planned out. First off, though, I don't like the idea of you being chased across the width and breadth of Texas by dogs and guns and such, so—"

"I'm willing to take my chances, same as you," Silvie interjected firmly.

"First hear me out, Silvie. We hatched an idea to put the slave hunters off of *your* scent, leastwise. What with the weather being hard and all, wolves have been prowling in close to the fields; snatched a young calf, just the other day. Now, if you was to get Ubie here one of your old house dresses, we could tatter it up some, sprinkle it with chicken blood, and then make like you was carried off by the pack. Won't anybody be looking for you, after that. Meanwhile, Ubie can hide you out in a lean-to he built in the high reeds along the river. You'll have to stay there a few days, but Ubie will bring you food until we come back for you with horses. That's the way of it, Silvie."

Silvie frowned. "By the river? What's to keep the wolves away from me *there*? Prayer?"

"Prayer and a sharp machete, Señora Silvie," Ubaldo responded patting the blade in his belt. "I will sleep during the day and keep watch over you by night."

Silvie looked upon the former groundskeeper with a hint of suspicion. "Why are you doing this, Ubie?" she inquired. "What'd we ever do for *you*?"

The reply of the sacked groundskeeper took on the lines of a soliloquy. "This country, mine once," he began, staring right through Silvie, as though transfixed. "Own farm, own casa. Then the war comes and the Texian army, they take *every*thing. For the glory of the revolutionary cause, they say! Then, they run away. Santanna is not far behind them and *he* takes the rest. While I am away to get food for my family, Santanna returns and takes my wife and the ninos along on the retreat to Mejico. I am left alone. Señor Jones gives me work in the fields, that I may stay alive. Working for *him* on *my* own land! But," he signed in bitter irony, "a man must do that which must be done to stay alive."

Then Ubaldo's impassioned voice rose with a fervor. "I work long and hard for Señor Jones, and what is my reward? To be driven from even the small relief of honest work! Joe has been good to me, Señora. I will help both him *and* you run—to Mejico! This is no place for ones of your color, or mine, to live, *if* we intend to live like men! Rest easy Señora Silvie," Ubaldo reassured, "Joe and I will come for you when the time is ripe."

The "Wolves have carried Silvie away" plan worked. Jones bought it. After a half-hearted search, volunteer riders turned up Silvie's bloody and tattered dress several miles away in a ravine; they even bagged two wolves in the area, to boot; an area nowhere near to where Silvie actually lay, concealed.

Jones was uncommonly sorry for Joe; he had come to care for Silvie, too. As a matter of fact, the extent of Jones' compassion for Joe almost made the "Veteran Soldier" feel guilty about the necessary deceit. But he kept up the façade and the charade and tried to look as much like a man in mourning as possible.

As for Silvie, alone in her little shelter hidden in the high reeds by the riverbank, the hours passed in daydreaming on the things of promise that were yet to come, far away from this dismal swamp hut. But in spite of Ubaldo's constant state of vigilance nearby, Silvie took care to maintain hers. For all of their sake, Joe's, Ubaldo's, and her own, she could not afford to be discovered, or taken by surprise.

* * *

They would be taking the service of the bay mare, Shannon, without question. She was as much Joe's as any horse ever belonged to anybody, at any rate. Shannon had carried both Joe and Silvie upon many a journey, but none so important as the one that they were about to embark upon. Even Shannon seemed to sense this, for as Joe was cinching up her saddle, she began to whinny in nervous anticipation.

Ubaldo arrived at the livery door the very soul of caution and stealth and Joe admitted him through the barely opened aperture to an inrush of icy midnight air.

"Was you seen?" Joe asked.

"I was as the shadows themselves," Ubaldo replied. "The sorrel is for me. It was of my land anyhow and it is therefore," he reasoned, "no sin to reclaim that which is my own."

They walked their horses beyond earshot of the big house, but once they were safely away, they mounted up and then trotted forward toward the river at an almost casual gait. Arriving at the thicket along the bank, they had to dismount, tie their horses off, and then continue on foot into the dark, dense entanglement. A dim pin-light from a lantern that Joe had instructed Silvie to light in the swamp hut was all the beacon that he and Ubaldo had to steer themselves through the foot-catching confusion of dark foliage by the invisible water's edge. At length, they reached the hut and ducked inside to find Silvie, crouched and waiting.

"It's time, Silvie," was all that Joe had to say.

It was early morning, the 22nd of April, 1837—a year and a day since Houston's victory at San Jacinto. With any luck, the three mounted runaways would have seven, perhaps eight, hours of precious head start, before their lack of presence was felt.

Thirty-two

The Passage of Hope

Into the waning night, Joe, Silvie, and Ubaldo rode, clinging close to the river and its shield of dense foliage. Upon approaching Columbia, however, they called a halt to discuss their best and safest route of flight. Joe reckoned that, come morning, Postmaster Jones would be hard upon their trail with a posse of slave hunters and dogs. And he'd probably begin his scour in the territory between Bailey's Prairie and Brazoria, reckoning that that town would be the logical point of descent upon the Brazos for a scantily provisioned company of travelers in search of temporary asylum and succor.

"So, as nice as Brazoria sounds," Joe said, "we'd be fools to go there. Jones would nab us right away, truss us up, and maybe even hang us as horse thieves. We've still got a few hours until daylight and I want to make the most of them. Ubie, you stay here with Silvie and the horses. I'm going into Columbia to see a man."

"Into Columbia?" Ubaldo returned, astonished. "You want to get caught right away? That is the place to go. As you said, a few hours, we have till daylight. We need to ride west, cross the San Bernard River. There's Indians there and those who will be following will wish to avoid them. It is our best bet. But we need to go *now*."

"Give me an hour, is all I ask," Joe said determinedly. "Mr. Austin is in Columbia. He told me once, did I ever need any help, to come and see him. I believe that it is a chance worth taking, but if I am not back in an hour, don't wait for me. Take Silvie and the horses to wherever you think it's safe."

Silvie's visage descended into a frown. Angry and upset that *her* opinion had not even been considered, she put in her own two bits. "Now hold on here, Joe. I said I'd stick by you, come what may. But that means staying *together,* Joe. You can't just go running off and leave me like this, you just can't."

"I'm *not* running off on you," Joe reassured. "I'll be back, Silvie, honest I will."

"Time presses," Ubaldo reminded the both of them. "We will wait the hour. If by then you are not here, we will go this way," he gestured, pointing westward, "and wait for you for a time along the San Bernard. From there, we will steer southwest toward the coastal town of Matagorda, on the bay. I have friends there who will help us."

It was decided. So, after embracing Silvie, Joe advanced toward the faint lights of Columbia upon foot. In spite of the darkness, it proved to be only a ten-minute walk, or so, to the edge of town.

It was just as well for Joe that few souls were stirring as he skulked in and out of the shadows down what looked to be the main street of the place. But as he was slipping down behind what appeared to be an inn of some sort, someone coming out the back door startled Joe. Slop went the contents of a commode. Joe stepped prudently back.

Now it was the holder of the slop bucket's turn to be startled. "Who's there?" the fellow challenged, shooting glances all around.

Joe looked at the man and, in spite of the shadows, recognized him straight off. It was Ben. Sea-cook Ben. Ben of Colonel Almonte's service and later, of Houston's own. Ben, the slop-bucket man?

"It's Joe, Ben," the "Veteran Soldier" confirmed, stepping out of the shadows. "Didn't rightly expect to be seeing you slopping out the dung jars, though. That's a far cry from cheffing for the military, ain't it, Ben?"

"Alamo Joe?" Ben returned, squinting. "What you doing here? I heard tell you was working over at the Jones' place. Didn't run off, did you?"

"I'm running. But came by town on the happen chance that I might see Mr. Steve Austin. He told me once he'd help me, if he could, and I surely could use some help now. Know where he's staying, Ben?"

Ben's face dropped. "Don't you get *any* news on Bailey's Prairie? Mr. Austin's dead."

"Dead?" Joe said in sad surprise. "When? What happened?"

"Just around Christmas," Ben replied. "Had the consumption, or something. Over in that little shack there," he went on, gesturing toward a *barely* one-room clapboard structure with boarded up windows. "Died quite alone, as I understand. Him there gasping out his last and not a soul to so much as hold his hand, or offer up any words of comfort. 'Father of his country,' some called him," Ben considered sadly, shaking his head. "To be treated like that. *Forgotten.*"

Joe felt a tugging at his heart. But it wasn't just in sadness for his not getting any help from Austin. No, it was for the man himself. For if someone like Austin could be forgotten so easily, what amount of sympathy could Joe possibly hope to engender for his own paltry participation in the revolt? Joe began to realize in the brutal finality of the moment that freedom rested solely upon his own shoulders. So there wasn't much reason to linger any longer in Columbia. He would be off.

"Well, that settles it," Joe said. "Me and Silvie and a friend are running off to Mexico, Ben. Come with us. Isn't freedom worth more to you than cleaning someone else's slop?"

"I do some *cooking* here, as well," Ben returned in his own defense. "Even mind the stockroom. Got my *own* room, too. No," he said with an awkward grin, "running ain't in the cards for me, just now. Once I save enough money, I'll likely return to the sea one day. Get my own boat and then work for no one else but *me.* I *am* a free man, Joe, but just like you, I gotta work at it all the time. You got a hard road ahead of you, so you'd best be on it."

"Good-bye, Ben," Joe said. But as he was turning to move away, Ben stopped him. "Here," Ben offered, handing Joe a folding knife. "This might come in handy. Also this bill of sale for dry goods," he added, producing a folded piece of crisp paper from his jacket. "It's printed all legal like and might fool some slave impressers, can they not read. Might let you slip by, might not. Don't have much else to offer, but my best wishes."

"Thanks, Ben," Joe returned with gratitude. "Best wishes is a heap more than we've got going for us right now."

Back in the brush along the Brazos, Joe rallied Silvie and Ubaldo. "Best move on," he said.

"Did you see Mr. Austin?" Silvie began hopefully. But as her eyes met Joe's the hope went right out of them before she could even finish the sentence.

"Mr. Austin's dead," Joe said flatly. "You're right, Ubie. We gotta be looking after ourselves from now on."

It was still dark when they set off—westward, toward the San Bernard.

Thirty-three
As Far from This Place As Possible

The journey did not pass without incident. Three days out of Columbia, well beyond the waterfowl rich marshes of the San Bernard, it happened.

It happened around sunset, when the party was just starting to pitch camp within an island of timbers on the vast prairie sea. Silvie had just gotten the fire going and Joe was still hobbling the horses, when Ubaldo, standing guard with his machete, saw something that made his heart race. There, not two miles back along the ground they'd just covered, the light of a campfire glowed.

"Put her out," Ubaldo shouted in warning. "The fire—she is noticed—we are found!"

In a hairsbreadth, Silvie flung dirt into the tiny fire pit, while Joe finished off any remaining stalwart embers beneath the thick soles of his shoes. In almost the same instant, the mystery fire also blinked out, giving the vast prairie over to complete and utter darkness.

"Who could it be, Joe?" Silvie whispered nervously. "Mr. Jones?"

"We'd be lucky if it *was* only Mr. Jones," Joe replied with gravity. "Leastwise, it's not Indians—not with a fire like that. Hunters, maybe?"

"Maybe, maybe," Ubaldo replied without much conviction. "Someone, it was who had no fear in being themselves seen, yet who became cautious, upon spying *our* campfire. It is a possibility that they are surprised as we. No chances should we take, though.

It is best that we move as far from this place as possible, before morning finds us trapped in the open, or the nighttime brings us death by the knife."

And so promptness broke the camp. Horses were saddled quietly and led away at a walk. Then the party proceeded on foot for what seemed like hours, guiding their mounts through the prairie blind in cautious footfalls, lest the four-legged creatures so much as dash their hooves against a stone.

All too soon, though, dawn came streaking across the broad horizon at their backs and with it, the realization that even the false sense of security provided by the cloak of night was no longer theirs.

Pausing, Joe looked back, craning his head around for a sign of their pursuers. "Should we take to saddle, Ubie?" he asked. "Try to outrun 'em?"

But Ubaldo only shook his head to the contrary. "There are two of you to one horse. How far would you get? And where is there to run? One mile of prairie is as the next. No, we must continue on as though we are but fellow travelers upon the trail. Any sudden movement will say to them as much, that we are not."

So Joe and Co. proceeded on to meet the inevitable; it came in the form of two riders, ambling out of a thicket toward them. Although the distance made clear identification impossible, one thing was evident—both of the approaching horsemen were heavily armed.

"Joooe . . . " Silvie said, filtering her tension through clenched teeth, while the "Veteran Soldier's" own heart pounded on the sight of the steadily advancing strangers.

It was then that Ubaldo suggested that they halt and face off their antagonists. "If we cannot talk ourselves free," he said soberly, "then we are as the dead already."

For their floppy brimmed hats and "Mex-cut" round jackets, the two riders looked very much like wandering vaqueros—maybe friendly ones, even. Ubaldo seemed to hope as much anyhow, for as the riders were drawing their mounts to a halt before the runaway party, Ubaldo decided to greet them in the "Christian Language." This was a mistake.

"Cut the Mex lingo an' talk American!" snapped the lead stranger, clearly no Mexican.

"Quieta la boca! Let him speak!" returned the second stranger, a companero.

Then Joe recognized them. *Damn!* he exclaimed inwardly. *It's the Grub and his Mexican friend from San Felipe—again. Maybe…maybe they won't recognize me,* Joe hoped. He was banking on the fact that he had drastically altered his appearance since their last encounter by shaving off his side whiskers, getting his hair close cropped, and growing a rather substantial mustache. At any rate and just to be on the safe side, he would let Ubaldo do all the talking.

"I am a traveler on the road, as you," Ubaldo began. "Mi companeros and I have arrived upon hard times and have lost a caballo. We are in much need of food supply, as ours is all but gone. Have you fared much in this manner?" he concluded in a hopeful tone.

"Kotched squirrels some," drawled the Grub in reply. "Rabbit in a snare. Some fish. Not much fer brag. Exter keerful not t' go shootin' off our cannons, lessen we's pre-voked. Draws Injuns thicker 'n hornets. These your'n," he inquired mockingly, tossing his head in the direction of Joe and Silvie.

"We're freeborn," Joe lied. "Got papers to prove it's so," he added, producing Ben's dry goods bill for Grub's perusal.

Grub took the paper in his two hands and then stared down at it for a good long while, as though he was giving it special scrutiny. "Yassir, yassir," he said at last, "mighty fine paper ye got chere. Tarnal shame I cain't read," he snorted self-consciously.

Joe heaved a sigh of relief on hearing this and then mouthed an almost silent "Thank you, Ben."

"We's bound for Be'ar," the Grub continued, "but we be a bit side-tracked, huntin' up vittles, liken your own selfs. Been keepin' an eye on ye in hopes that ye'd be obligin' us a mite o' yer fare. Got anythin' fer barter?"

"Beans and corn meal mush," Joe responded in distaste. "Mush is most thick to make you gag and the beans never do boil down to much less than the consistency of musket balls."

"Little rabbit grease'll tame 'em down to buckshot," the Grub mused askance. "What say we jin ye for vittles an' see what we kin knock together?"

So it was decided. While Silvie did her best to boil the beans down with chunks of the Grub's greasy rabbit, the Mexican stranger worked at forming thick tortillas from the coarse corn meal. A searing hot flat rock resting in the center of the firepit serviced the cook as a skillet of sorts and in no time at all, he was flipping sizzling hot tortillas with the flat of his machete.

The Grub was not much interested in helping with the cooking, howsoever; he had his eyes playing over Silvie's every move. And though his attentions were focussed upon Silvie, it was Joe that he addressed.

"S'what two free nigras doin' struttin' th' gran' Republic o' Tex-us? T'aint no ab'lish'nists 'ithin two thousand miles t' pamper ye, an' no *real* sunna Tex-us is gwinter hire ye? S'what's yer wampum? *Horse* thievin'?"

The cat was itching its way out of the bag. Joe hesitated, but before he could articulate a reply, Silvie did. Jumping to Joe's defense, she fairly and irreparably sent puss howling.

"We aren't thieves!" Silvie blurted. "The horse was Master Travis', good and legal! We—" she halted abruptly. But her error was realized; the damage was done.

"*Masta* Travis?" the Grub exclaimed, snatching up his long gun. "From the Alermo? We hear'd thet Jones from Columbia's bin ferritin' th' country fer uh runaway slave! I know'd there was somethin' a'spicious, the moment I laid eyes on ye, Horse Minder! Nito!" the Grub rallied he of the Christian tongue.

But "Christian Tongue" never got the chance to reach his

firearm, for Ubaldo snatched the now abandoned tortilla-laden machete from the fire and sent the sizzling saucers full into the face of the startled Grub. The would-be slave catcher reacted by dropping his rifle and slapping both of his hands to his affronted face in a howl of pain, mixed with rage.

"I'se fried, I be fa'r kilt!" wailed the Grub in defeat, as Joe snatched up the fallen long gun.

"Easy, my friend," Ubaldo cautioned he of the Christian tongue, leveling the greasy machete tip maliciously at the fellow's throat.

But it was pity alone that stirred Silvie's actions, for, as Joe looked on, she wetted a small kerchief from Ubaldo's goatskin waterbag and then handed it to the Grub to soothe his blistered countenance.

Then Joe mouthed a mechanical, "What can we do with 'em, Ubie?" knowing all too well the scant options that were left open to them.

"If we were they, we would shoot them down like dogs," Ubaldo considered aloud, causing both the Grub and Christian Tongue to pale several shades. "But we are *not* they," he continued, "else they would have as much claim to the right of killing *us*."

So Joe and Co. left the two would-be slave catchers afoot, with flint and steel for firemaking, and a little food (fresh tortillas) and water. Joe even let Christian Tongue have Ben's folding knife strictly for utility purposes.

While Silvie would be taking charge of the Grub's mount, Joe promised to hobble the remaining horse several hours ride distant. Weaponless and straddling one horse, Joe reasoned that the pair of slave catchers would prove little threat to the now well-armed mounted and provisioned runaway party.

"Reckin' I should be grateful t' ye," the Grub drawled sourly, shaking his head in a hangdog attitude, as Joe Silvie and Ubaldo were trotting away. "But m'heart ain't in it. If it be anyone elsen *me*, I'd liken our chances of survivin' worth lessen spit!" And then, though he'd fallen well behind the riders, he continued to bellow, "E'en so, do we survive, I'll nary live this down, does news reach th' settlemen's! Us half-horse, half-alligator boyses got our pride, too!"

By then, the riders had skirted a low swell of waving prairie grass, well out of sight of their regaler. "I'll see ye in hell, mark me!" Joe heard. Then the Grub was out of earshot.

The miles ate themselves up without much of note, as the "Veteran Soldier" urged the horses forward in mounting, restless anticipation. Bye and bye the frosty whip of a gulf breeze met the party full in the face and Joe noticed how Silvie was letting the wind play upon her extended tongue. In curiosity, Joe tried a morsel of the element himself. It was both salty and strong and it nipped icily, but no matter. For it tasted of freedom.

Thirty-four
Freedom by Water

It began as crimson and amber rising—a pale glow upon the inky translucence of the water's surface. Then the glow increased in its luminous intensity, fanning out in shimmering sheets, layer upon rolling, undulating layer, until at length, it sliced a gradually more distinct horizon out of the opaque nothingness of sea and sky. Then, out of that raging horizon, flaming jets erupted, slashing out the full, if inconstant, spectrum in kaleidoscopic, mad streaks. Break of day over Matagorda Bay, such as it had ever ascended.

"Glory be, now that's a sight to behold," Joe said in wonder, looking upon the spectacle from where he, Silvie, and Ubaldo had drawn up their horses upon the high ground, just above the town.

"And I thought that prairie sunrises were beautiful," Silvie gushed. "I've never seen the sea before, but I do believe that I could fall in love with it in a minute. It's got a certain draw . . . "

"Some men will love the sea like she is a mother," Ubaldo concurred, "others, as a wife. Myself, I love the feel of rich soil under my fingernails and the smell of the land after a rain. Anyway," he grinned, "I get seasick. Then, my only connection with the ocean is her color: green."

They had practically a birds-eye view of the town, as below them a series of docks stood, clustered along the arcing shoreline of the broad and sheltering harbor. Matagorda itself lay gracing the mouth of the murky Colorado River, along whose own lush banks smaller docks jutted forth like outreaching fingers. It must have been quite an undertaking indeed for the town's founders to have hauled all the lumber necessary toward construction, for the nearest decent stand of trees was a Mexican league's distance from the place. The houses of Matagorda, while of the usual clapboard design, were whitewashed smartly and stood out in stark contrast to the flat, unornamented planks of the boardwalk.

The decided absence of boats bobbing along the docks suggested that the fishing fleet had already taken to sea. So, feeling all the less conspicuous for it, the three riders trotted/walked their horses down from their observation point and toward the deserted boardwalk along the waterfront. But the place, they soon found, wasn't so deserted, after all.

"Bleeding idjits!" blasted a testy dockworker whose fiery brogue and shock of red hair seemed decidedly Scottish. "Dinner now ye say the sin?" he raged all the further pointing at a sign that was posted in bold, red lettering. "Wick yair hairse, ere ye be fained!"

Getting the gist of the jibe, Joe, Silvie, and Ubaldo dismounted and led their horses past the dockworker. They were nearly out of earshot, when the fellow spat in spiteful farewell, "Cairse they kin't raid, felthy haythens all! *I* be the bluidy idjit!"

Moving on along the riverwalk, the three dismounted runaways halted at last before a rude shack where a scruff of a lad sat dawdling on its doorstep, shaving away wood chips from a stick with a small knife. Upon seeing Ubaldo, however, the tousle-haired youth beamed a toothy grin of recognition and arose from his playmaking.

"Miejo," Ubaldo commanded, but with affection, "see to the care of the animals. Your Uncle Danilo, I would think. I see your mother. Quickly!"

"Si, Tio Baldo," the youth replied. "Tio Danilo!" he shouted, shooting off like an undercharged shot, until the thudding of his bare feet upon the planking became lost in the exaggerated clip-clopping of shod horses' hooves.

Ubaldo's tapping upon the shanty's entrance roused the

woman of the house, who, after taking pause to wipe her hands of maize flour upon her coarse apron, threw wide the creaky door. She was gaunt and middle-aged and her weatherworn visage and gray-shot hair betrayed her far beyond her years. But the smile she beamed, upon recognizing her visitor, took about ten or twelve of those years off of her—at least.

"Baldo," she said cheerfully, "a surprise this is to me! Come inside and be fed and rested. You are not alone," she shifted thought, seeing Joe and Silvie upon the stoop.

"It is so," Ubaldo replied, edging his companions forward into the flickering light of the shadowy cocina, or kitchen. "These are my dear friends, Joe and Silvie," he said warmly. "We have traveled much and far together. And this vision, Joe and Silvie, is Emelia, wife of mi companero, Luis, who catches fish like no other." The fisherman's wife giggled coyly upon the half humor of this touch; Ubaldo continued. "We are in need of shelter for a time. We cannot and will not stay overlong, but I could think of no other place to go, but to the bosom of mis amigos. May we remain?"

"But of course!" Emelia replied, pooh poohing his even having mentioned it. "That is understood." Then Emelia's intuition kicked in and her tone of voice sank. "You are in trouble. How bad is it?"

"It is all a question of property," Ubaldo answered plainly. "We claimed only that which was ours in the first place, though our former boss, he is in disagreement. It is certain that we are followed."

Emelia knit her brow pensively, on hearing this; at length, she spoke. "Something will be worked out. But we must await Luis' return from . . . " she hesitated, "his daily catch. He will know what to do. Meanwhile," she brightened, gesturing toward some low stools beside the stove, "make yourselves comfortable. My house is as your own to you who are the friends of *my* friend, Ubaldo."

*   *   *

The fishing boats had returned to dock. The late afternoon sun was already on the wane as the net-laden fishermen came scrambling ashore to get their catches squared away, hang their nets, and then set off for home, each to his own direction.

Then, as the sun commenced its final plunge into the fathomless depths of the sea, flickering lantern lights began to blink on around the tired little village like so many fireflies. But as Joe, Silvie, and Ubaldo sat resting in the shanty in the glow of a lantern's light and Emelia warmed them up with a steamy bowl of piping hot sea chowder each, Luis had still not returned.

It was, in fact, several hours past dark before Luis' feet were, at long last, heard upon the planking outside the shanty door. Once inside, Luis embraced his wife, but then, somehow sensing that the two of them were not alone, he turned with a start. It was not until Ubaldo came stepping in from out of the shadows and into the lantern's glow that Luis dropped his guard.

"Such a surprise, Baldo," Luis beamed with a sigh of relief, embracing his friend with the gnarled hands of a seafarer. In fact, Luis was the very picture of a seaman—pigtail cue and all. He was wiry and weatherworn and his leathery, hollow face, clean-shaven as a baby's behind. He continued speaking: "But what passes to bring you here?"

Ubaldo told him. The two companeros conversed for a time in Spanish; then Ubaldo translated his friend's intentions in English.

"Luis says that we can stay here for a time, but not, I fear, a long one. If we are as yet followed, then our being here may be harmful to all in this house. Luis *does*, however, have a friend who may be useful to us." Ubaldo hesitated before continuing in a lower tone of voice: "Very plainly, they are smugglers of goods. Luis has just returned from such a venture up the bay, stowing cargo aboard a ship outward bound for Mejico. He might be persuasive in getting us all a passage on such a vessel. There is risk involved, true, but then we are no strangers to her, I think. We get ourselves smuggled to Mejico, come Domingo—Sunday morning—if all goes well."

Holding Silvie's hand, Joe drank in the proposal like a bitter tonic. Then he barked a short, nervous laugh. For irony was once again showing her hand and they would be getting their freedom by Joe's old nemesis—water.

Thirty-five

From the Reaches of the Cow and King

Though explorer Rene-Robert Cavelier De La Salle had staked his high hopes and good reputation on the notion that he had reached the mouth of the Mississippi River, a series of mishaps eventually proved him wrong. As a matter of fact, it was only after his sole remaining ship, the *Belle* had ventured up the river's shallow channel that he'd come to realize the error of his assumption. For the once-broad channel abruptly tapered down to a narrow flow whose banks were met—not by overshadowing woods, as he'd anticipated—but rather by vast reaches of rolling prairie land inhabited by a myriad of shaggy buffalo.

La Salle had christened the unostentatious little river "La Vaca" in honor of those beasts, and then constructed a blockhouse at its mouth on the bay, dubbing it "Fort Saint Louis" in deference to the then-reigning king of France.

Indians, plague, and treachery eventually erased the settlement of "The Cow" and "The King" from both map and memory. But the bay itself and its immediate environs nonetheless looked pretty much the same in the May of 1837 as they did on that February day in 1685 when La Salle had first chanced upon them.

Toward the southeast lay the bay itself, with flower flung meadows extending clear on down to the waterline. The harbor entrance, however, was a narrow affair, plagued by innumerable reefs and sandbars that seemed to defy passage. La Salle's own ship, the *Amiable*, had foundered in the breakers there.

Toward the center of the bay crouched a bump of land inhabited by pelicans and the very presence of these natural fishers was assurance enough of the good fishing—whether salt, or fresh water—to be had. Oysters and crustaceans abounded on the tidal flats, while stout ducks and geese kept to the marshes near the river. There were alligators.

Thus was the lay of Joe, Silvie, and Ubaldo's destination: the smuggler's anchorage!

Aboard Luis' skiff at last, the runaways began to feel the exhilaration of a dream nearly realized. For, with fair winds prevailing, the pilot would steer them up the coastline and through the narrow channel in mere hours, making port on the La Vaca while the sun was yet high in the sky.

Standing upon the sloping deck, Joe, Silvie, and Ubaldo watched the shoreline gradually shrink away in the wake of the skiff, while over to starboard, Luis arranged passage for the fugitives with the skipper of the smuggling vessel. With luck and continuing fair winds, the coming of night would see them outward bound for the bustling port of Tampico, Mexico.

Surprisingly, Joe's aversion to water excluded a propensity toward seasickness, for the rising and falling of the deck did not seem to faze him at all. Silvie, on the other hand, more than made up the difference and retched for both of them. By the time that the skiff arrived on the La Vaca at last and all three runaways were safely ashore upon the sandy beach, Silvie gave voice to her pitiable condition.

"Don't reckon I can take another trip like that on a boat, Joe," she moaned feebly, hand over mouth and all. "The voyage to Mexico will probably be at least *twice* as long! Best leave me behind to die here."

"That's just the sickness talking for you, Silvie," Joe replied in a soothing tone, gently cradling Silvie's sagging head in his arms as he spoke. "The next boat will be a heap bigger and so the deck won't rock so much. You'll see! Meanwhile, you just lay down and rest. Won't be much longer now."

They waited. Afternoon soon gave way to evening, and with the evening came the winds. Waves churned and crashed in foamy breakers upon the shore, while a bank of billowy, black clouds rolled in to obliterate any hint of starshine in the overhead skies.

Though Ubaldo tried his best to build a bonfire as a beacon for the expected smuggling ship, it proved a futile attempt. For, before he could even get the flame to hold and catch decently, the gathering breeze swept the pile of fuel away in an avalanche of scattering soot and embers. Yet it *had* been observed; the Grub had seen it.

The runaways' riding off and leaving Christian Tongue and himself afoot had humiliated the Grub so badly that he wanted nothing less than sweet and swift revenge. So he followed the mounted party and stayed upon their trail, even up to the hobbled horse that that soft-hearted Joe had left behind. Well, Grub didn't have a soft bone in his body, be it for enemy *or* friend. For when he and Christian Tongue got into an argument over the wisdom of either proceeding on to Bejar, or of pursuing the runaways, an unhappy compromise was reached, one that left Grub in possession of the lone horse and Christian Tongue with the broken blade of sea cook Ben's folding knife protruding from his chest.

Reaching Matagorda a day upon the heels of Joe and Co., the Grub wasted no time in rounding up a passel of miscreants, all bearing the common desire of acquiring some tainted money fast. The rum-pickled tongues of the lowlifes in Matagorda were loose enough to begin with, so it only cost the Grub a few rounds at the grog house to learn all that he needed to know—of smugglers and sailing ships and a little river called the La Vaca.

"Och! So they be bluidy ruawahs!" slurred the Boardwalk Dockworker, after Grub had plied him with a noggin of rum. "Yea, I seen them as planly as th' naws on yer fess!"

Two blacks—one of them a woman and one a Mexican,

Dockworker clued Grub. Yes, they all three of them had horses. Dockworker had even seen a little boy leading three horses to the stable. The child often dawdled there. Must know someone who works there, or something.

So Grub and Dockworker went to the stables to wait. Bye and bye, the little boy appeared and, without his knowledge, led the two bounty hunters to the house of Luis where Emelia sat waiting for news—alone. It took a lot of abuse to get Emelia to talk, but talk she did, even unto her last breath. The little boy himself never even knew what had hit him.

From there, with five picked men to the task, all heavily armed and mounted on horseback, the Grub galloped up the coast, arriving upon La Vaca well before the skiff. Grub chose a campsite within an island of timbers about a league or so from the shore. It was a good choice. For it not only provided his men with a good vantage point, but a safe haven as well, from where they could wait and watch the beach, without themselves being detected.

So it was that the slave hunters finally spied Luis' sail on the approach and readied themselves for the pending jolly medley. Ubaldo's failed attempt at a bonfire had made things easier for the cutthroats, for they now knew exactly where to strike—and when. For a squall had blown up and the Grub reckoned that the ship's captain would hesitate to launch a boat to pick up the runaways in the fear of being dashed to pieces on the rocks. Too, without reinforcements from the ship, the runaways would be at a numerical disadvantage: three unsuspecting men and one woman, against six determined, greedy slave hunters. The Grub liked those odds— liked them a lot. It was time for he and the boys to make their move. So, sheltering their muskets against the storm, the slave hunters skulked their way down the declivity of bluffs toward Luis' camp near the water's edge.

Down along the shoreline, meanwhile, Luis seemed little deterred by the sudden turn of the weather, nor was he one to be caught at his unawares, in the event of such an emergency. With a dark lantern in hand, he blinked out a signal to the expected ship at the expected hour, even as the swelling waves tumbled and surged over the rocks and sand all around him.

Seaward, a faint pinpoint of light blinked in reply, heralding the ship's arrival. Cutting through the gale, the ship's lantern signaled that anchorage was an impossibility under such adverse weather conditions, but, yes, they would launch a long boat to pick up the refugees. The boat would attempt its approach by way of the landward side of the island of pelicans where a sheltering inlet would help prevent it from being dashed to pieces in the tide, or else run up on a reef.

Luis frowned on the prospect, for such a gamble could well mean the lives of all involved in the attempt. So, instead of responding right away, he merely acknowledged the signal and then left the decision to Joe and Co.

Joe didn't like it one bit. "We could get drowned," he noted matter-of-factly. "Anyway," he continued self-consciously, "I can't swim, for the life of me. Can't they at least wait until the storm tuckers itself out, Luis?"

"They cannot hold the ship long, else she will break up in the storm," Luis replied, cupping his hands like a trumpet to be heard above the din of the storm. "If we do not go now, she will surely sail away."

Joe hesitated in a moment's indecision—but only for a moment. Silvie's moist lips, pressed against his ear, bid on his wavering resolve. "If you say 'go' Joe, then I'll go. And if you say 'stay,' I'll stay. But, one way, or the other, we've got to do *something*!"

Crack!

No time for a reply.

Crack again!

Joe turned just in time to see Ubaldo crumple to the ground on the report. With both of his hands pressed to his side in marked pain, Ubaldo uttered the dismal truth. "Shot, shot..." he moaned.

What happened next, happened through the half-darkness and the tumult of force winds.

Upon the second musket report, Joe dragged Silvie down behind him, assumed a low crouch, and then retrieved Ubaldo's abandoned carbine, all in what seemed like the same instant. Then a bulky figure came hurtling forward from out of the darkness. Joe raised his weapon, squeezed the trigger, but got no response; the gale force winds had caused his weapon to misfire. Reacting, more than thinking, Joe clubbed the carbine anyway and raked it across the fellow's kneecaps, splintering both of them in one foul sweep. Down the would-be attacker went, howling in pain. The only way that Joe knew of to silence the stricken man's lamentations was to dash him senseless with the butt end of the carbine.

Luis, prepared for any turn of events, demolished two more attackers with a sawed-off shotgun. Then, throwing the yet smoking weapon aside, he drew his cutlass and waded into the fray.

The musket-ball-ridden Ubaldo was all but helpless upon the sand, trying to pull himself up upon his elbows in a desperate effort to edge back out of harm's way. Suddenly, the Grub's savage-looking Bowie knife came arcing in from out of the darkness. With one fatal pass of the heavy blade, Grub splintered the vertebrae in Ubaldo's throat in a geyser of thick blood. Poor Ubaldo sagged back down to the ground without a moan and remained still.

Retribution for the murder was swift, if hollow. For, in a vain attempt to aid his stricken comrade, Ubaldo, Luis drove his cutlass through the underbelly of the surprised Grub, then heard the blade snap off at the hilt under the deadweight of the pending corpse. "Haarg...uuh," the Grub moaned, dropping his Bowie to grasp with both hands at the long sliver of naked metal protruding from his abdomen. His body shivered, his hands slapped upward, as though someone was jerking at them... and the Grub was gone.

The rest of the slave hunters—those yet upon their feet—lost heart and fled the field of action, giving up their dead. A knife in the dark at the throat of the unsuspecting was one thing, but they had hardly counted on such stiff resistance.

Five bodies now lay prone upon the gale swept shore. And, as Joe stood, shuddering upon the sight, the very winds themselves seemed to moan out a mournful dirge for the freshly fallen. Four of those slain were unknowns whose passing to the netherworld would go, more or less, unlamented. But one of the fallen was Ubaldo, a true friend whose lack of presence upon the planet would be deeply felt, indeed.

Joe found Silvie crouched over Ubaldo's body, her hands smeared in blood. She had thought to help. She had tried. Seeing Joe, Silvie turned, looked up, then upraised the cupped palms of her crimson covered hands almost imploringly.

Joe guided Silvie back to her feet with his right hand; his left hand wiped away the red smears from Silvie's own with a handkerchief.

Then, throwing the soiled rag aside, Joe wrapped his arms around the still trembling young woman. "You all right?" he asked tenderly. Squeezing Joe even tighter than the grip that he held her in, Silvie merely nodded the affirmative into his shoulder.

"Ubie's dead," she said, letting the fact register in her own mind.

"I know," Joe replied thickly. "All else have pulled through all right, it seems. I worried for *you* mostly."

"And me, for you," Silvie returned, burying her face back into the folds of Joe's coat to blot up her hot tears. "Who were they, Joe?"

"Slave hunters. One of them, that damned Grub," Joe added bitterly. "Ubie and me spared his life back on the trail and now he's gone and killed Ubie! Killed him for protecting *our* freedom. That's it, Silvie," Joe added with an assured finality in his tone. "That's the final straw!"

Though the fires in the crucible of Joe's spirit had been building up for a long time, it was the blazing fury of the day's events that finally and irrevocably steeled him in his resolve to either gain freedom, or else perish. And when the brittle shell of self-doubt, hesitation, and indecision dropped away from his tested spirit at last, what it revealed was a Joe reborn. He really *was* the Veteran Soldier, now.

Joe's eyes stabbed out to sea with a determined fix. "We got to try and make it to the boat, Silvie," he said. "We may not make it, but we got to try, all the same. It was an important enough of a thing for Ubie to risk everything on and I reckon that it was important enough to Colonel Travis to go and do the very same thing at the Alamo. And it's for certain sure that Maizy wouldn't have had it any other way! Right now, we're standing between life and death, but I ain't about to just lay down and die without a fight, when living's worth as much to me and you as anyone that ever lived. Let's do 'er!" Joe exclaimed, drawing Silvie even nearer still. "For life and for love, Silvie, let's do 'er!"

Though the waves continued to crash all around them and the gale force winds threatened to carry the young couple away, Silvie suddenly felt steadfast in the power of Joe's love, newfound strength, and conviction. Hope had brought them upon the threshold of their once-distant dream and it now stood a very good chance of becoming a tangible reality. *So let the winds throttle them,* she thought, *and the sea waves bury them beneath their frothy surge, if they inevitably must.* For now, in this hairsbreadth of a moment, she and Joe were truly free—and they were *together*!

Unusual things sometimes occur at equally unusual moments, and this was one of them. It was almost as though the willfulness of the Veteran Soldier and his mate had tapped the energy from the very soul of the storm. For, as the fiery passions of the two lovers rose with a fervor, the winds abated and the rains surceased. Then it was quiet—and such a quiet, as an eerie lull fell upon the once temperamental bay.

Luis' voice shattered the temporary calm. There was a discernible thickness in his tone. "The storm, she is let up for a time. Baldo would have wanted you to go on, even without him. If it is your wish, then I will signal the ship to meet you beyond the island of pelicans. Your enemies may yet return in greater force, so it is of much necessity that you make your decision quickly."

Looking Silvie straight in the eyes, Joe read her answer in their warm, reassuring glow. "We're game, Luis," he himself voiced aloud, through the lump in his throat.

"But what . . . " he hesitated, "what about . . . Ubie?"

Luis seemed wholly touched by Joe's display of genuine concern. "I myself," Luis said, "shall perform the last act of kindness for our rudely used friend who is no more. There is no time for you to attend, or assist. Baldo would understand. My men shall row you out in the skiff to my boat and then deliver you to the rendezvous point where the smuggling ship will be waiting." Luis paused to fish a scrap of paper out of his pocket. "Here," he said, producing the document. "This is the arrangement drawn out for the Capitan. He is one who is in debt to me for many favors rendered. But wait . . . "

With the stub of a pencil, Luis dashed off a few extra lines of his own upon the outer leaf of the folded page. "Here," he continued, handing it to Joe. "This should see you safely to Mejico. I twice regret the loss of your companero and mine, but rest assured that the Capitan shall see that you are well-received upon your arrival in Tampico and not as mere strangers in a strange land. Go quickly now and go with God!"

Joe was more than ready to go, but he had one more thought on his mind. "I never even had the chance to say goodbye to my horse, Shannon," he said regretfully. "After all we been through. Luis, you take Shannon. She's a good horse and, well, it's the least I can do. Give our thanks to your wife, Emelia, when you see her and to your little boy—what was his name?"

"Jose." Luis replied with a smile. "Just like you. He has a great love of horses. Maybe one day, Jose will ride your Shannon back to you in Mejico."

Poor Luis! If he only knew . . .

When the skiff from Luis' little coasting vessel slid into shore near Joe and Silvie, the three seafarers aboard splashed knee deep into the frothy water. Only when Silvie was safely deposited aboard, did the crew scoot the little rowboat back into the shallows. Then, when it was fairly seabound, they tumbled back in themselves with Joe following in his own fashion. Thus laden, the little craft bobbed erratically into the converging swells and it was all that the fore oarsman could do, turning the bow into the worst of them, to keep from capsizing.

Yet Joe and Silvie *did* manage to make it to Luis' coaster and, once that vessel was drawn up along side the smuggler's ship, they were hauled aboard.

With the ship's deck firmly beneath their feet, the two runaways breathed a little easier. And as the vessel eased its way through the narrow mouth of the bay and unto the open sea, it put Matagorda, Texas and all their trials and tribulations in its wake. But, standing upon this little section of deck, Joe could only ponder upon the course of his future together with Silvie. And that was enough. So there would be no looking back; there could be no regrets.

As for Silvie herself, she clung close to Joe, as though he were a towering oak tree protecting her from the storm. "Ubie may've helped us get started in Mexico, Joe," she mused aloud over the misty crash and roll of the parting waves. "Do you think that we'll have a fair chance there *alone*?"

"We'll make it, Silvie," he reassured her. "Long as we got feet to walk with and hands to work with and free air to breathe. Anyway," he mildly scolded, "what's all this talk about being *alone*, already? We're together, like you said your very own self once, and that's half the battle won right there. We'll make it!"

She believed him and they embraced, even as the frothy arms

of the sea embraced the smuggler's prow. Then Silvie, having at long last gained the capacity to look ahead in a communal spirit with her chosen life's mate, voiced aloud her own projections for a safe passage to journey's end—and a whole new beginning!

"So," she playfully teased, putting emphasis upon her uttered "we's." "What's the first thing *we'll* do when *we* get to Mexico, Joe?"

"That's looking too far ahead," Joe cautioned, "after all the things we've been through. But," he added with a twinkle in his eye, "I reckon that I know what *I'll* do first. I'll likely kiss the ground," he said.

Afterword

On May the 26th, 1837, the *Telegraph and Texas Register* ran the following advertisement:

Fifty Dollars

Will be given for delivering to me on Bailey's Prairie, seven miles from Columbia, a Negro man named Joe, belonging to the succession of the late Wm. Travis who took off with him a Mexican and two horses, saddles and bridles. This Negro was in the Alamo with his master when it was taken; and was the only man from the colonies not put to death; he is about twenty-five years of age, five feet ten, or eleven inches high, very black and good countenance; had on when he left, on the night of the 21st of April ult. a dark mixed sattinet round jacket and new white cotton pantaloons. One of the horses taken is a bay, about 14-1/2 hands high, very heavy built, with a blaze in its face, a bushy main and tail and a sore back; also the property of the said succession, the other horse is a chestnut sorrel, about 16 hands high. The saddles are of the Spanish form, but of American manufacture, and one of them covered with blue cloth. Forty Dollars will be given for Joe and the small bay horse (Shannon) and ten dollars for the Mexican, other horse and saddle and bridles.

If the runaways are taken more than a hundred miles from my residence, I will pay all reasonable travelling expenses, in addition to the above reward.

John R. Jones, Ex'r of W.B Travis
Bailey's Prairie. May 21st, 1837

Beyond this documented evidence of Joe's escape, little is known of the Alamo hero's whereabouts thereafter.

The Travis family legend has it that, upon escaping, Joe made his way back to Conecuh County, Alabama to give a firsthand account of William Barret's demise to his surviving kinfolk there.

Miss Mary Sutherland, granddaughter of physician and Alamo messenger, Dr. John Sutherland, on the other hand, recalled that "there was Joe, the servant of Colonel Travis. Grandfather had some words of praise for this Negro boy... In after years, Joe ran away from his new master, to Mexico, it is thought."

And finally, on April 7th, 1877 (when Joe would have been about 65 years old), Editor John Cardwell of the *Austin Daily Statesman* published the following item for consideration:

"There are several old soldiers of the Texas revolution in Austin and in adjacent towns and counties and these should meet on the twenty-first instant—San Jacinto Day. Two years ago, the colored body servant of Col. Travis was in this city and his home was not far away. The only white survivor of the Alamo is here (Suzannah Dickinson Hannig) and we do not see why the veterans should not be feted by the city government or by the citizens of the capitol."

Sadly, the suggestion seems to have gone unheeded, for the event passed without much fanfare, and Joe from the pages of written history. More's the pity, for it would have been a fitting thing if the Veteran Soldier had indeed, and at long last, come home to be feted by Texas—the land for which he had fought so well.